CAUGHT IN THE ACT

The smoke spread, then appeared to freeze in place, a golden glaze coating the surface of the scrying dish. Michael slid his chair to the side, curious to watch, but she shook her head. "Stay opposite me or I won't continue."

"See anything?" he asked after what felt like an hour.

"Shh. I'm concentrating." She narrowed her eyes. Slowly, she tilted her head to the side. "Oh. Oh my goodness." Her hand flew to her throat. Her cheeks turned scarlet.

So she could see his future after all. Michael was out of his chair and around the table in an instant. He leaned in beside her, searching the mirrored surface, desperate to know what would happen when they arrived in Wales.

What he saw stunned him. Naked, he lay tangled with an equally naked woman in a very imaginative position. Despite his somber mood, heat flared in his belly. The woman in the mirror threw back her head and moaned, the sound from the image filling Cordelia's small room. She dragged a hand through her hair, lifting the strands off her face. For a disbelieving moment Michael stared, then he whispered, "Sweet bejesus, Cordelia. That's you."

THE
PHOENIX
CHARM

HELEN SCOTT TAYLOR

LOVE SPELL NEW YORK CITY

To Bill and Diana Crann.

LOVE SPELL®

January 2010

Published by

Dorchester Publishing Co., Inc.
200 Madison Avenue
New York, NY 10016

ISBN 10: 0-505-52828-2
ISBN 13: 978-0-505-52828-5
E-ISBN: 978-1-4285-0792-0

Visit us online at www.dorchesterpub.com.

ACKNOWLEDGMENTS

With thanks to my son Peter for his off-the-wall imagination and creative ideas, and to my daughter Katherine for her Photoshop work and creative visuals. Special thanks to Joan Leacott and Mona Risk my wonderful critique partners.

THE PHOENIX CHARM

Chapter One

The sun sank into the Atlantic, painting the water molten gold and casting a warm glow over the granite manor house set atop the rocky cliffs of Cornwall. After years of neglect, Trevelion Manor, ancestral home of the Cornish pisky troop, now thrived under the care of the new pisky king and queen. Sun sparkled off the tiny diamond panes of glass in the windows. Tumbling creepers dotted with purple and yellow flowers clothed the walls, while granite tubs on the terrace overflowed with scarlet, pink, and white geraniums.

Seated on a Windsor chair at the table in the library, pisky wise woman Cordelia Tink paused at her work and glanced out the open window, inhaling the floral-scented air. She ran her hand down the crease of the huge leather-bound book laid on the table before her and took a moment to reread the last few paragraphs she'd written. With a sigh, she set aside her pen and rubbed her eyes.

The task of recording the history of the pisky troop fell to her, but she would have gladly handed the job to another of the piskies. Two years ago, Niall and Rose O'Connor, the new pisky king and queen, had rescued the troop from thirty years of imprisonment in the shadowy nothingness between life and death called *in-between*. Today, Cordelia had finally summoned the strength to relive her failure to protect her people from that horror and enter an account in the pisky annals.

Lazing in the last few rays of sunlight on the desk at

Cordelia's side, her gray cat Tamsy opened one eye. She peered at Cordelia critically and flicked her tail. "You're right, poppet." Cordelia nodded to her cat. "Enough doom and gloom for one day." Cordelia closed the book with a thud and pushed it away.

She stroked the soft fur on Tamsy's belly and smiled at the rumbling purr of response. What she needed was something to take her mind off the past—something pleasurable. Just the word "pleasure" summoned the image of Michael O'Connor's seductive smile in her mind. A quiver of awareness ran across her skin, light and tickly as the brush of a feather. She'd once seen him do that—trail a feather across a woman's naked body . . .

Cordelia screwed her eyes closed, trying to rid herself of the image she'd seen while foretelling his future. Instead, the memory became clearer, his long naked body spread languorously on the sheets while he brushed the feather over the woman's breasts.

Cordelia stood and swiped her hands down the front of her dress to rid herself of the tingling sensation tightening her skin.

Although the pisky king Niall O'Connor was not Cornish, but half noble Irish Tuatha Dé Danaan and half leprechaun, he was a strong, caring leader they could depend on. How the womanizing rascal Michael could be related to Niall, let alone be his twin brother, baffled her.

She pressed her hand to her bodice where the hot thud of Michael's psychic presence beat in her chest like a second heart. She was powerful enough that fairy glamour didn't affect her, with one darned annoying exception—Michael O'Connor.

Unwillingly, her eyes rose to the silver divination dish she used to foretell the future. The skin on her scalp prickled and her cheeks warmed as she tried to pretend she wasn't thinking of doing what she *was* thinking of doing.

"Not again. I promised myself I'd abstain." Despite the

firmness of her tone, her feet were already moving toward the door. She pulled it open just enough to poke her head out and check that the hall was empty. The ancient oak creaked as if trying to alert someone to her wicked intent. She drew back quickly and turned the long iron key, grimacing at the thunk of the lock.

Pressing her back to the door, she rubbed her temples. In anticipation of what she was about to see, the sensual water nymph allure she'd inherited from her mother churned within the confines of the restrictive magical wards painted on her skin.

She drew a slow, deep breath and stared through the dust motes dancing in a shaft of sunlight at her divining dish. Were the gods themselves tempting her to indulge? Surely everyone was allowed one illicit pleasure—even she.

Tamsy sat up and watched with enigmatic gray eyes as Cordelia gave a defiant huff and marched back to her seat. She lit the three fat white candles floating in the silver, water-filled dish. Within seconds, wide ribbons of smoke rose before her.

Raising a hand, she sketched a magical symbol in the air. The smoke stilled and glazed over into a mirror. Her insides trembled expectantly while she concentrated on Michael's psychic signature and waited for an image of his future to appear in the shiny surface.

She pressed her fingers to her lips as the picture became clearer. When she peeped into Michael's future, half the time she saw him performing routine activities at the pub he owned in a nearby village, the other half . . .

Her breath caught. She stared, too entranced to blink as an image of Michael's naked shoulders and lean back filled her scrying surface. Muscles rippled beneath smooth skin when he moved. His biceps clenched as he lifted a hand and flicked back a handful of dark wavy hair from his face.

A woman appeared before him, an indistinct form clothed in muted colors. When Cordelia watched Michael, she chose to ignore the identity of his numerous human lovers. All her attention focused on him.

Cordelia's heart thudded as he prowled forward, faded jeans riding low on his hips. Slowly, sensuously, he ran his hand down his ribs, over his abdomen, flicked open the buttons on his fly one by one with a little flourish of his hand like a magician performing a trick. Although it was no white rabbit he was about to pull out. As the last button popped and the jeans slid lower, a small needy sound escaped Cordelia's lips.

Heat flashed across her flesh, gathered and swirled, a hot whirlpool in her belly. Her sensual water nymph allure flowed closer to her skin, preparing to draw in and capture the man she desired. When the energies met the barrier of the magical Celtic symbols painted on her skin, her temperature shot up as though she were trapped in a pressure cooker.

She flapped a hand in front of her face, fanning herself. If she kept watching Michael, she would expire from lust.

Although she was burning up, a breath of chill through the window raised goose bumps on her arms. She caught a whiff of something rotten on the breeze and reluctantly dragged her eyes from Michael to glance out at the twilight sky.

When she looked back to the divination mirror, darkness oozed across the gilded smoke like oil on water, obscuring Michael and his faceless woman. Cordelia blinked in surprise and leaned closer to get a better view. A howl issued from the murky surface, a mournful wail that slashed fear through her. Her cat shot to its feet, fur on end, puffed up to twice her normal size. Hidden within the mirror's shadowy image, other creatures joined the lament until the eerie clamor of baying filled the room.

Tamsy scooted off the table and crouched beneath a chair in front of the huge stone fireplace, but Cordelia had no time to comfort her. She stared at her divination mirror, searching the gloom for any clue to the meaning of the augury. Was this still Michael's foretelling? Had another possible future for him intruded? The hair on her neck prickled when pairs of small red dots appeared. They looked like animals' eyes glowing evilly in the darkness.

Her fists curled against the table as the memory of being imprisoned in-between crawled back to haunt her. Then, on the edge of perception, a whispered name snapped her to attention, trapped the breath in her lungs.

Gwyn ap Nudd.

The King of the Underworld.

Her concentration shattered. The murky image dissolved with a pop, scattering wisps of smoke. Her eyes watered, and she waved a hand to clear the air. The thought of the red-eyed creatures unsettled her, but more worrying was the fact that the whispered words had *not* come from the mirror. Someone nearby in Cornwall had actually spoken the name Gwyn ap Nudd.

She thrust out her awareness, tried to identify who'd called the King of the Underworld. Behind the deep pulse of Michael's psychic signature, the members of the Cornish pisky troop filled her senses with the white noise of their presence. Cordelia focused on the lingering chill of the dreadful name.

She was sure the call had not originated from inside the manor. She puffed a misty sigh of relief in the cold air, wishing the granite fireplace held a roaring fire instead of a stoneware pot full of dahlias.

What would happen if the Welsh King of the Under-world answered the summons and came to Cornwall? Niall and Rose had left for two weeks to search for displaced piskies in America, leaving her in charge. Why on earth did this have to happen now? Cordelia glanced at the Queen Anne clock on the oak mantelpiece. They'd already be in the air over the Atlantic. The earliest she could call them for advice would be the following day.

She traced her finger across a lacy layer of ice that had formed on the water in her divination dish, and shivered. When the pisky troop had been trapped thirty years ago, she should have foreseen the danger, but she'd been so distracted by the old king's death, she had let her duties slide. This time she wouldn't let the piskies down.

She glanced at the rows of massive leather-bound tomes holding records of pisky life going back centuries. She must find out quickly if the piskies had any history of conflict with Gwyn ap Nudd or the Welsh fairies in his domain.

Tamsy slunk out from beneath the chair and jumped on the desk. She padded closer, mewed softly, and butted her forehead on Cordelia's chin.

Cordelia laid her cheek against Tamsy's shoulder and considered what to do. She couldn't check through a whole shelf of books in one night on her own.

She winced. "Oh, rats' tails!" If she needed help, the logical choice was Michael. Not only was he the pisky king's brother, but while the king and queen were away, he was responsible for their twin boys. He had a right to know immediately if the children might be in danger.

With luck, she might catch him upstairs putting the babies to bed before he went down to the great hall below the manor house for the night's entertainment. In Ireland, he'd been Seanchai, the official storyteller in the Irish fairy court. Now that he lived in Cornwall with the piskies, he'd fallen into the routine of telling a tall tale to the assembled troop most evenings.

Cordelia stood and peered at her rosy cheeks in a small mirror near the door and thanked the gods that Michael would never guess the reason she was flushed. She fastened the three small buttons on the front of her dress, closing the garment to her throat.

When she reached the nursery, she found Michael's leprechaun half sister Ana dozing in a chair beside the cot, keeping watch over the babies. But no sign of Michael.

She huffed as she closed the door. Tamsy wound between her legs and looked up at her with inscrutable gray eyes. "All right, I know. I'll have to look for him in the great hall."

After she descended the stairs, she strode purposefully along the moth-eaten carpet runner covering the passage. She'd rather stick pins in her eyes than walk into the packed hall and interrupt Michael when he was telling a story, but if she wanted his help, she had no choice.

When she reached the top of the narrow staircase that led beneath the house, she paused for Tamsy to catch up, and grabbed a fortifying breath. Then she descended to the rooms carved from the granite underneath the manor grounds. At the bottom, she grasped the doorknob for a couple of heartbeats before she pushed the door open.

The jaunty beat of Irish music assailed her.

She slipped in and pressed her back to the wall, hugging the shadows. Rising on tiptoe, she peered between the tall brown-haired piskies. Most of them worked the land, turned wood or forged metal, and lived in cottages around the estate. Many were still dressed casually in work clothes, but a few had donned brightly colored jackets and hats in anticipation of the rowdy evening that always ensued when Michael told one of his bawdy tales.

A lump formed in her throat when she glimpsed Michael O'Connor on the far side of the room putting a mug down on the bar. His shaggy dark hair shone in the low light. The divine masculine shape of his wide shoulders and narrow hips silhouetted against the lamplight sent a hot shiver through her. How she hoped she could get the image of him naked out of her mind before she talked to him.

Michael grabbed the hand of an older pisky woman. She grinned up at Michael like a teenager on her first date and giggled as he spun her into a dance. The piskies clapped to the beat. Cordelia plucked at the neck of her dress, the collar tight on her clammy skin. Despite its size, the confounded hall was always stuffy in the evenings.

Tamsy pressed her silky body against Cordelia's legs. Relieved at the distraction, Cordelia scooped the cat into her arms. She rested her cheek on Tamsy's head and watched the laughing crowd of piskies.

Mewing, Tamsy turned a speculative eye on Cordelia. "I know." She buffed the top of the cat's head with her fingers. "No need to bully me. I'm about to ask him."

Michael had escorted his partner to her seat and was now weaving between the tables toward his storytelling stool. As usual, the spiky auburn hair of her ward, Thorn, marked his presence a few steps behind Michael. She wished Thorn had chosen a more suitable male role model: Niall for instance. But at least Michael had generously taken the young man under his wing. She couldn't fault him for that.

Cordelia threaded her way through the crowd. When people noticed her, they stepped aside with deferential nods. She pasted on her serene wise woman mask and held her head high.

When she entered the brighter circle of light near the bar, Michael looked toward her. He caught his bottom lip between his teeth and flicked up his eyebrows in question. Cordelia nodded in answer to his unspoken query. He grinned the wide seductive smile that had women falling at his feet.

Streamers of heat unfurled inside her, rippled beneath her skin. Her heart raced and she gritted her teeth. She could hardly think straight when she got close to Michael. But she'd eat worms before she admitted as much. The reprobate was already far too cocky.

He held out his arms and shimmied sideways between the tables, heading in her direction. The disreputable faded jeans he wore were the ones she'd just watched him unbutton. Cordelia swallowed. She wanted to look away; she really did. But his fairy glamour entranced her so much, she couldn't fight the compulsion to stare.

Since St. Patrick's Day, he'd insisted on wearing a green

trilby with shamrocks embroidered on the band. He turned to face her, tilted the hat at a rakish angle on his mop of dark wavy hair, and captured her with his sinful blue gaze.

"You be wanting me, darlin'?"

Cordelia opened her mouth to answer, but there didn't seem to be any air in her lungs. She sucked in an embarrassing gasp that made Michael's lips twitch. "I need to speak to you on troop business."

Michael reached out and rubbed a finger underneath Tamsy's chin. The cat tipped back her head and purred, vibrating against Cordelia's chest.

"Here's me hoping you might be wanting me for something a tad more interesting." As his finger lazily caressed Tamsy's fur, he glanced up at Cordelia from beneath his lashes. A hot spurt of desire shot through her body, making her legs tremble.

This is ridiculous.

Fantasizing about him in private was one thing, being seduced by his glamour like a gullible human was another. After the effort her grandmother and father had put into hiding her uncontrollable sensual allure, she couldn't let them down and shame herself—again. The price she'd paid the one time she defied them still haunted her night and day. Cordelia tightened her arms around Tamsy, shielding herself. The poor creature squeaked and Cordelia hastily loosened her grip.

"This is no time for joking. It's a matter of urgency." Someone chose that moment to reduce the volume of the music. Her final word came out rather louder than she intended. A few anxious glances shot her way.

She smiled reassuringly. The last thing she wanted was panic.

With a nod toward the exit she said, "Come upstairs where we can talk in private." She ignored the wicked sparkle in Michael's eyes.

"Your wish is my command, darlin'."

In the two years since she'd met Michael, Cordelia could count on one hand the times they'd exchanged more than a polite greeting. Yet the way he called her darling with that deep Irish lilt to his voice was exactly the way he spoke to the women she watched him take to bed. She reached the door and ascended the first few steps, then paused and looked back at him. "I'd rather you didn't call me . . . darling. I don't feel the name's appropriate." And if he kept speaking to her in that tone of voice, she was likely to muddle fantasy with reality.

He grinned up at her, mischief twinkling in his eyes.

With a sigh of exasperation, mostly at her own ludicrous reaction to him, she hurried up the stairs, promising herself she was strong enough to ignore his glamour.

He grinned as he stopped in the doorway at the top and rested his shoulder against the frame. "Maybe I should call you sugarplum? You have the sweet ripe fullness of fruit ready to be—"

"Michael!"

In the silence that followed her explosive retort, all she could think was *ready to be what?* A small part of her wished she hadn't interrupted him.

And she hated that she fell for his suggestive banter.

Anger bubbled up, giving her words a harsh edge. "Just call me *Cordelia* in a normal tone of voice like everyone else."

He flicked up his eyebrows, unabashed.

"Enough nonsense." Cordelia smoothed her skirt, reluctant to admit she needed his help. "While I was foretelling in the library, darkness invaded my divination mirror. I also heard someone whisper the given name of the Welsh King of the Underworld."

The mischievous half smile that always hovered on Michael's lips dropped away. He pushed off the door frame and straightened, his expression serious.

"When did this happen, lass?"

"About fifteen minutes ago."

He rubbed the back of his neck, turned, and glanced up the stairs. "Ruddy Badba," he cursed. "I hope the babies are safe."

Before she could reassure him that she'd just visited the nursery and the boys were fine, he took off, running up the stairs two at a time. She stared up at the landing while he put his head in the nursery door.

Thirty seconds later, he closed the door quietly and descended more slowly, a look of relief on his face.

"The babies are still there. When we tried to put them to bed, I half expected them to disappear and reappear somewhere else." At Cordelia's raised eyebrows he continued. "The rascals have just discovered they can walk unseen like me father."

Cordelia shook her head in disbelief. Rose had told her the children took after their air elemental grandfather. But it had never occurred to her the children would exhibit the rare air elemental gift of walking unseen: disappearing and reappearing in another place.

"What sort of threat do you think Gwyn ap Nudd could be?" Michael asked.

"We've had no dealings with him during my life, but it's possible he holds an ancient grudge against the piskies. You know what long memories these immortals have."

He nodded and something dark passed behind his eyes. "Aye, I know."

When Michael and Niall had lived in the Irish fairy court, Niall had apparently had problems dealing with the self-obsessed Irish fairy queen. Perhaps life had been just as difficult for Michael.

"I want to check through the pisky troop records for references to Gwyn, but there are at least fifty volumes in the library. I need another set of eyes to help me."

Michael took off his trilby and ran his hand through his hair, lifting the luxuriant chestnut waves off his face, then letting them tumble back. All thought deserted her as she watched the silky strands settle against his skin.

"'Tis not a problem, lass. I'll gladly offer you me eyes. I read fast, so we'll be through the books in no time."

Cordelia blinked, pulled her attention back to the conversation. Michael O'Connor might be a master storyteller, but the possibility of his speed-reading seemed as unlikely as his sprouting wings. "Great. Thank you," she uttered, feeling a touch guilty for doubting his word when he'd offered to help. "I'd rather not involve anyone else until we know if the danger is real."

Michael nodded and popped his green hat squarely on his head. "We don't want to go causing alarm, to be sure."

He extended an arm graciously in the direction of the library and smiled, a hint of mischief creeping back into his expression. "Lead on, sugarplum."

For a moment, Cordelia debated whether to argue over her name. With a sigh, she decided she must choose her battles, and this wasn't important. She marched off toward the library, acutely aware of him striding behind her, probably ogling her bottom.

Michael enjoyed the view as he paced along the hall to the library. Cordelia Tink might be uptight, but she had a damn fine arse. Although she'd covered herself from head to foot in a nondescript gray dress, it hugged every curve—and she had plenty of curves to hug. Her waist nipped in neat and small, accentuating the sweet roundness of one of the sexiest rumps he'd ever seen.

Realizing she'd halted, he raised his eyes to find her peering at him over her shoulder with a frown.

Oops.

He did the same thing he always did when he was caught out—grinned, infusing the expression with glamour.

She rolled her eyes and pointed at the massive green leather-bound books that filled the bottom two shelves of the wall facing the fireplace. "We need to start from . . . here," she said, resting a hand on a book.

Michael dragged out five volumes and hefted them onto the desk where she'd cleared a space. "A bit dusty." He wiped his hands on his jeans and then drew in a deep breath.

Her hand shot up. "Don't you dare."

Confused, he let the air go.

"You'll spread dust everywhere if you blow it." She marched to her desk, pulled a duster from the drawer, and arched an eyebrow at him.

He stepped away, leaned an elbow on a chair back, and watched while she dusted each book, shaking the cloth out the window at regular intervals. Niall was always full of praise for Cordelia's prophetic skills and thoughtful advice. But on the one occasion Michael had approached her because he thought having his future read would be fun, she'd nearly bitten his head off. According to her, she wasn't a carnival sideshow for his entertainment.

Her gaze flicked up to him, then darted back to her book. She was attractive in a repressed way, as though she didn't want anyone to notice. But whatever she wore, she couldn't hide the fact she had a damn fine body, and incredible hair. Up close, he could distinguish pale gold strands mingled with the dark, and her braid was as thick as his wrist. He imagined her naked, her loose hair draping her shoulders like a cloak. He pressed his lips together to keep from smiling. She'd be all covered up, but he'd bet her nipples would poke through.

"Michael."

He jumped guiltily.

"Are you going to help me or not?" She held out a dusted volume.

Book in hand, he settled in one of the wing chairs before the fireplace. He'd tried not to worry about Gwyn ap Nudd, but the possibility his nephews were in danger flipped his stomach with a sick lurch. He pictured the sleepy little lads snuggled together in the cot they shared. The mantle of responsibility hung awkwardly on his shoulders, but he would do whatever was necessary to protect them. He loved the boys. Besides, Niall would string him up if he let anything happen to them.

Taking a steady breath, he focused his concentration on the key words to search for, then scanned the first page, flipped it over, scanned the next page, flipped, read, flipped, read—

"Michael! If you're not going to take this seriously, I'll find someone else to help."

He blinked, adjusting his gaze. "Crikey O'Reilly, lass, I can't go any faster."

Confusion swept the annoyance from her face. She set down her book and swiveled in her chair to face him. "You're reading the pages?"

"Aye." He grinned. "I'm thinking you didn't believe me when I said I could read fast?"

She opened her mouth—closed it again without making a sound, her gray eyes huge and soft. Beautiful eyes. Not like the normal pisky earth elemental brown or hazel. Somewhere in her lineage, she must have an ancestor who was not a Cornish pisky.

Cordelia swallowed audibly. "You're sure you know what's on each page?"

"Aye." He gave her a moment to absorb the truth.

She stared at him as though he'd suddenly grown an extra head, but in a good way, as though the extra head impressed her more than the original. The possibility that reading fast would impress females had never occurred to him. Actually, he didn't need any help attracting women. His local fame for telling tall tales meant there were always eager human women crowding his bar on the lookout for fun. Using his fairy glamour it was oh so easy to send them home with lovely memories but no recollection of his face or name.

Cordelia cleared her throat and turned back to her page.

Michael settled again and did the same. When he finished the book, he placed it back on the shelf, and selected another from the pile. He forbore to comment that Cordelia was only on the tenth page of her first book. Ms. Starchy Pants would not appreciate the comparison.

As he prepared to start his second book, the library door cracked open. His friend Nightshade, the vampiric fairy, poked in his head. The lamplight cast a sheen on his ebony skin, and his silver eyes glinted with predatory satisfaction. Michael suppressed a sigh. Since he'd allowed the nightstalker to bite him and forge a blood bond between them two years ago, Nightshade hardly let him out of his sight. The way the vampire watched his every move was worse than being handfasted to a jealous woman.

Nightshade sauntered in, bare-chested, his wings folded tight to his back. He tilted his head and with one hand swept his long black hair off his face "I wondered what had become of you, bard. They're asking for you in the great hall."

Michael smacked his forehead. "I can't believe I've gone and forgot about tonight's tale. You'll have to tell one."

The vampiric fairy gave Michael an incredulous look.

"Erm, you're right. 'Tis a bad idea." Although Nightshade's mother had been a pisky, and his nightstalker father had left before his birth, Nightshade had confided that he'd always felt like an outsider. Thirty years ago, he'd betrayed the piskies and conspired with an evil druid to trap them in between life and death. He'd later repented and helped Niall and Rose free the troop, but the piskies had never forgiven him.

"Could Thorn tell a story? He's listened to you often enough." As Nightshade spoke, Thorn's cheeky grin appeared around the door.

"I've been down to the hall and told them you're busy tonight and won't be back." Thorn's green eyes sparkled with mischief. "They assumed I meant busy with the babies."

Thorn dogged Michael's heels, but the lad was full of fun.

He'd just turned twenty and needed some mates to have a laugh with. Michael had no idea what had happened to the young man's parents. Cordelia seemed to be his surrogate mother.

Thorn grinned. "Hello, Dee. What you doing?" Without waiting for her to answer, he hurried to Michael's side and stared eagerly at the book on his lap. "Can I help?"

Cordelia released a resigned sigh, nodded, and placed a hand on the pile of books. "Grab one each and make yourselves comfortable. We're looking for any reference to Gwyn ap Nudd, Welsh King of the Underworld."

Thorn lifted a book and took the chair across from Cordelia. Nightshade remained standing, hands on hips. "Why?"

Cordelia rubbed her temples. When her eyes met Nightshade's, the tension in the room thrummed. "Someone nearby called his name this evening. I need to know if he has any reason to threaten the piskies."

Nightshade remained rooted to the spot. Cordelia stared at him, her soft gray eyes now hard as flint, her lips pinched. The antipathy rolled off her in waves, far stronger than the other piskies' dislike. Michael's curiosity pricked to know what had happened between them to cause such hostility.

When Nightshade continued to glare at Cordelia, Michael decided that as he was blood-bonded to the vampire, he might as well make use of the connection. "You going to be helping us or not, boyo?" he asked softly.

The tension snapped when the nightstalker turned to him, his gaze softening. "Whatever you want, bard." He gave Michael's shoulder an affectionate squeeze, then hefted two volumes off the table before claiming the seat beside Michael.

Michael purposely avoided Cordelia's questioning gaze. He did not want to explain his relationship with Nightshade. Ms. Prim and Proper would disapprove of the fact that he'd enjoyed the illicit pleasure of a vampire's bite.

He resumed flipping pages. He knew little about the

Welsh fairy king, but as Cordelia had observed, these immortals could be difficult. Growing up in the Irish fairy court, Michael had learned to survive the whims, wiles, and spiteful temper of the Irish fairy queen. If Gwyn were at all like the Queen of Nightmares, he did not want to meet him anytime soon.

Chapter Two

Nightshade stared blankly at a page of pisky history. How could he read a word when Michael sat in a chair beside him? The sweet blood surging beneath his skin was pure temptation.

He craved him.

He craved the touch of his fingers, the musky fragrance of his skin, the musical Irish lilt of his voice.

Nightshade's gaze rose inexorably to Michael's face. The ceaseless twist of pain and anger in his gut eased when he saw the characteristic half smile curving Michael's lips. Nightshade even managed a smile himself as he watched the gentle slide of Michael's fingers caressing the book's pages with the finesse of a lover's hand.

Love—an impossible concept to fathom. This burning desire for Michael that defined Nightshade's life, ruled his actions, his thoughts, was surely no more than an addiction: an obsession with the heady burst of energy he felt after he took Michael's blood.

An obsession with someone he could not control.

The blood bond Nightshade had forged when he first bit Michael two years ago should have held Michael in thrall. Yet inexplicably, Michael remained in command, dictated when and where he'd submit, kept Nightshade trailing after him like a dog on a leash, forever hungry.

After adjusting his position to flex his wings, he read a few lines, reread them, closed his eyes.

The burn of a gaze made him raise his head. Cordelia stared at him through narrowed eyes. If he were not Rose and Niall's friend, she'd throw him out of the troop. She'd always hated him.

Maybe he had earned the piskies' animosity for being misguided enough to help imprison them, but even when he was a child, they had not accepted him as one of their own. He yearned to belong, even if just to one person.

Cordelia tried to focus on her book, she really did. But concentrating was impossible with a nightstalker in the room. The sweet scent of the almond oil he rubbed on his wings nearly made her gag. The scars on her neck tingled, and she made a conscious effort to relax her tense hands.

After a few minutes of fighting the urge to look at him, she gave in and raised her eyes. There he sat, legs slung over the arm of the chair, wings twitching like a huge bat. He glanced at Michael with a soft smile as though butter wouldn't melt in his mouth. In reality, he was just like his father Dragon—a predator likely to fall into a blood lust and strike when they least expected. She wanted him gone, banished. Until then, she'd never feel safe.

She dragged her eyes away and gave her attention to the book.

Once she settled, Michael looked up. "I'm sensing something odd."

Cordelia concentrated on the plethora of psychic feelings bombarding her senses, checking for unusual energies. "I don't think there's anything out of the ordinary." As if to make a liar of her, Tamsy leaped onto the desk and puffed herself up like a brush. She hissed, the sibilant sound lowering to a growl in her throat.

"Wretched cat. That's all we need," Nightshade complained.

"Shh." Cordelia flapped a quieting hand. Foreboding

prickled across her skin. She blended her mind with Tamsy's, jolted in shock at her cat's spiky fear. Cordelia examined the corners of the room and the shadows for movement.

"Shit. I feel something too now." Nightshade leaped to his feet, assuming a combative posture.

They all froze in place, the air vibrating with tension while everyone watched for intruders.

A spark caught the edge of Cordelia's vision. Three points of light appeared in the center of the room, grew brighter, then morphed into shining orbs floating at head height.

"*Tylwyth Teg*," Michael whispered.

Servants of the Welsh King of the Underworld. An icicle of fear pierced Cordelia's solar plexus. Without taking her eyes from the shining spheres, she stood and gathered Tamsy safely in her arms, ignoring the prick of claws.

The orbs burst into millions of points of light that coalesced into three Tylwyth Teg, two males and one female. With ash-blond hair, they were whip thin and renowned to be just as nasty.

Standing in the center of the room, the Welsh fairies took only an instant to gather their senses before they focused their pale blue eyes on Nightshade, obviously discounting the rest of them as a threat.

They were taller than Cordelia had imagined, the males over six feet, the female not far behind. All three wore black leather; the dark clothes intensified the impact of their pale skin and hair. They looked eerily like ghosts made flesh.

She held Tamsy tight, steadied herself. "What do you want?"

Instead of answering, the male with dark runes tattooed on his cheekbones stepped toward Nightshade and brandished fingers tipped with wicked silver spikes. "*You* are not required, nightstalker." He nodded at the door. "Leave us . . . slowly."

The stalker faced them down, wings slightly extended for

balance, the tense muscles in his chest and belly gleaming and hard as armor.

Cordelia's breath locked in her throat. She thrust a warning look at Thorn, indicating he should stay safely behind the table.

Although Cordelia distrusted Nightshade, if a fight ensued, he could probably take all three Teg. She stepped forward. "Nobody leaves," she said, managing to keep a surprisingly steady voice.

None of the Teg responded.

Nightshade rattled his thumbnail across his teeth in a derisive gesture. "You leave us, Teg. *You* are *not required*."

Hostility vibrated through the air, escalating with each tripping heartbeat.

With slow, smooth movements, Michael closed his book, placed it on the floor at his side, and stood. His usual half smile on his lips, he doffed his green trilby and bowed. "Grand as it is to welcome our friends from the valleys, 'tis normal for guests to come knocking at the front door."

Looking bemused, all three of the intruders relaxed. The tension drained out of Cordelia's neck and back; a subtle sense of well-being flooded through her. Storytellers often possessed a silver tongue, all the better to manipulate the emotions of their audience. She wasn't surprised Michael displayed the gift. But she'd never before been on the receiving end of such an effective use of mood control.

The tallest male marked with the black runes recovered first. He swung around to face Michael and inclined his head. "I bring greetings from the Welsh fairy king."

"I return them in the spirit in which they're given," Michael replied.

Cordelia stifled an impatient breath. Yes, we all hate each other, but gods forbid we forget the ritual greetings.

"Am I addressing the pisky king?"

Michael gave a genuinely amused if slightly incredulous chuckle. "Who is it wanting to know?"

Head high, the leader slapped a hand on his chest. "I am Arian of the Tylwyth Teg, here on the orders of our king, Gwyn ap Nudd. We three are gatekeepers to the Underworld. This is Dai, and this Olwyn." He indicated the other male, then the female.

For long seconds nobody moved or spoke. Cordelia found her voice first and asked the question they must all be thinking. "Why has he sent you?"

Irritation blended with frustration inside her when all three Teg ignored her and continued to stare at Michael. "Are you the pisky king?" Arian asked again.

Michael shook his head.

Arian glanced from face to face, eyes narrowed suspiciously. He flexed his fingers, the silver spikes rattling together like bones. "Where is the pisky king?"

Cordelia glanced at the clock on the mantelpiece. "Flying over Iceland, I should think." She raised her eyebrows. "I'm the pisky wise woman. I've been left in charge. Either you deal with me, or you come back in two weeks when the king gets home."

He flicked her an impatient look as though he thought she was joking. When she remained quiet, he compressed his lips and turned back to Michael.

She straightened her shoulders, tense again now that the effect of Michael's verbal tranquilizer had worn off.

Arian thought he could treat her with disdain, did he? "What business do you have in Cornwall?" she demanded, her voice sharp.

Once again, he ignored her question and concentrated on Michael, a frown creasing his brow. "Who are you?"

Michael gave the Teg an enigmatic look, laden with enough glamour to entrance a football team. Nightshade gave a small needy grunt. Cordelia clutched the table as tendrils of desire snaked through her. Thorn appeared unaffected, and the Teg remained unmoved.

Cordelia gritted her teeth. Losing her temper would not help anyone. "He's the king's brother," she said.

Surprise flashed across Arian's face. "Why then are you not leader in his stead?"

Michael scratched his head, tilting his hat off center, and summoned a crooked grin. "Now that's a good question, boyo. Me brother and I have never quite seen eye to eye on subjects like responsibility and work—"

"Enough!" Arian squinted at Michael, obviously trying to decide if he were purposely making a fool of him. Then he turned to Cordelia, his face set in resignation. "Gwyn ap Nudd sends greetings to the pisky king. Or in this case"—he flicked his silver-tipped fingers at her—"his . . . representative. A few hours past, someone opened an unauthorized gateway to the Underworld."

The blood drained out of Cordelia's head, leaving her ears humming.

She clutched her cat like a lifeline as an image filled her mind of dark, hideous creatures pouring out of the Underworld into Cornwall. She'd be powerless to protect the piskies—again. The breath stalled in her lungs. Then steadying strength flowed into her from Tamsy.

This was worse than she'd imagined. A million times worse.

While she struggled to breathe, Michael fixed his gaze on the three intruders and spoke. "Tell me exactly how this happened." Gone was the playful tone. His demand cut through the silence sharp as a honed blade. The compulsion of his silver tongue dragged at her mouth to answer, making her mumble nonsense.

All three Teg started talking at once until Michael pointed at Arian. "You speak."

But all he told them was that Gwyn sensed the gate open and dispatched the gatekeepers to close the breach.

Suddenly the female hissed, an eerie sound that set the

hairs prickling all over Cordelia's body. "Shield yourselves," she whispered to her companions. "He spins silver shackles with his words."

All three Teg glowed, their skin luminous as though they were about to change back into orbs of light, but didn't complete the transmutation. The leader pointed at Cordelia accusingly. "You piskies must have opened the gate."

She shook her head; her stomach knotted at the loathing in his eyes. "Would we be sitting here reading if we knew monsters from the Underworld could be skulking around outside?"

He grunted. "The pisky king is liable because this happened in his domain. Protocol demands you accompany us when we attempt to close the gate."

"No." Michael stepped in front of her. "I'll be coming with you."

Cordelia tensed as Michael tried to take over. Then she realized Michael O'Connor was protecting her. She stared at the dark T-shirt stretched across his muscular shoulders. Why would he volunteer to take her place? She'd expect Niall to do such a noble thing, but Michael? She raised a hand, hesitated, then did what she'd dreamed of doing—touched him. Warmth flowed into her hand, zinged up her arm and through her body, defying the restrictive wards painted on her skin.

He was dangerous to her equilibrium. So dangerous, she shouldn't have anything to do with him.

"Michael." His name fell from her lips as a reverential whisper. He turned, so close his arm brushed her dress. She placed her tingling hand back on Tamsy. "I accepted responsibility for the troop. I'll accompany the Teg. You have other duties."

"The babies," he whispered, his gaze clouding.

As if thinking of the children could summon them, Michael's nephew Finian materialized on the carpet in the middle of the room.

In a flash, Cordelia recalled Michael's comment about the babies taking after his father and being able to walk unseen, disappearing from one place and appearing in another. What a terrible moment for Niall's son to practice his new power.

Michael lunged toward the baby, but Olwyn was closer. She snatched Fin up beneath the arms and held him while he twisted and kicked, reaching his chubby arms out to Michael, and crying.

Michael halted, still as a statue, palms spread in a calming gesture. "Don't you go hurting the lad. Give him to me."

Arian stood between Michael and Olwyn and flexed his spiked fingers. "The child is of the pisky king's blood?"

Fear blossomed in Cordelia's chest. Why did the gatekeeper want to know Fin's bloodline?

Michael's strained breaths filled the silence.

Arian jerked a single nod, obviously satisfied he was right. "The child comes too."

"No," Michael and Cordelia answered in unison.

The Teg leader appeared to grow in stature. Cordelia realized he'd floated a couple of inches off the ground. He pointed toward the door. "You both come with the child, or we take the child alone."

"Only if you give him back to me now." Compulsion laced Michael's voice, but all three Teg glowed, protecting themselves from the effect of his silver tongue.

Fin wailed and wriggled in Olwyn's arms. Arian glanced over his shoulder at her and nodded. She stepped forward and held out the child.

Michael clutched Fin tightly to his chest, his large hand cradling the boy's golden head against his shoulder. "All right, lad. 'Tis all right, you are."

He looked down at Cordelia. "If there's an open gate to the Underworld in Cornwall, it must be closed," he whispered. "I'm thinking we should go with them. Not risk a fight. Especially now Fin's involved."

She nodded, thoughts and emotions tangled so she couldn't separate the threads.

Michael headed for the door, giving the Teg his back to shield the baby as he passed them. Cordelia followed. "You stay here," she threw over her shoulder when she heard Thorn's footsteps behind her. He groaned in answer but the footfalls ceased. She had enough to worry about without adding Thorn's welfare to the equation.

Cordelia sat in the back of the Range Rover with Tamsy on her lap and Finian strapped in a baby car seat on her left. Michael drove, with Arian sitting in the front passenger's seat beside him.

They traveled along the narrow Cornish lanes, the high banks on either side of the road blocking the moonlight. Michael kept up a stream of cheerful banter for Finian about everything from Winnie the Pooh to what dinosaurs ate. Despite this entertainment, Finian whimpered and whined, holding out his arms every time Michael glanced around.

When Cordelia tried to wipe Fin's nose, he batted her hand away and cried louder. In the end, she gave up, her chest aching to see the stream of tears running down his plump pink cheeks, wetting his blue sleeper. She stroked Tamsy, wondering if she lacked some vital maternal ability. Not that she would ever need to be maternal. She could never have an intimate relationship with a man. The nearest thing she'd have to a son was her ward, Thorn.

She leaned forward and peered out the windshield at the two spheres of light scooting through the darkness ahead of the car like sentient fireworks. "Are you sure they know where they're going?"

Arian gave her an indignant glare. In the dark, his pale blue eyes glowed eerily. "In our light form all gatekeepers are attuned to the Underworld. They can sense the illegal breach."

Illegal breach. Pompous oaf. Cordelia focused on her irritation, let the anger hold back her fear. She hung on to Tamsy, and braced herself against Fin's seat as the car swerved around a sharp bend in the road. Up ahead, the light orbs paused at a farm gate. Cordelia swallowed, her throat tight with anxiety as Michael swung the SUV onto a bumpy track. She peered out the windshield. "Can you sense if anything dangerous has escaped from the Underworld?"

Arian gave her a derisive glance. "Nothing leaves the Underworld without the king's permission."

The tension in Cordelia's shoulders eased a bit, even though her annoyance escalated. He could have told her that earlier. "Why are you so worried about this gate, then?"

His eyes flicked from her face to her cat, as if he thought the cat were the more intelligent. "A gate provides entry as well as exit, *wise woman*."

"You think someone might try to sneak *into* the Underworld? Are you mad?" she asked. Michael met her gaze in his rearview mirror and rolled his eyes in sympathy. She exhaled, releasing much of her anxiety.

The headlights illuminated a granite farmhouse tucked against a grassy hill.

"There're no lights in the windows," Michael observed, with a glance at Arian. "I can't sense any humans, so I'm thinking 'tis safe to stop here."

How could he sense humans? She'd never heard of such a thing. Fairies sensed each other's psychic signature, but humans didn't have a strong enough presence to detect.

"All out," Arian commanded.

"'Tis best Cordelia stays here with Finian. But I'll be coming with you," Michael said, walking around the car as she climbed out.

Relieved she could stay with Fin, she stretched her legs and surveyed the murky outline of the rolling hills and spiky trees.

"The child comes," Arian said in a tone that brooked no argument.

"I'm not agreeing. Not in a month of Sundays," Michael said.

Before Cordelia could climb back inside the car, Michael shut the door so Arian couldn't reach Fin. The two light orbs transformed into Dai and Olwyn, and all three gatekeepers advanced on Michael.

He maintained his relaxed pose. "The child will be staying in the car," Michael stated in a voice laced with so much compulsion, Cordelia momentarily lost all sense of where she was, concern for Fin's safety flooding her mind.

Although the Teg were now wise to Michael's silver tongue, even they paused and looked bewildered.

Arian recovered first. He stepped forward, but instead of going for Michael, he grabbed Cordelia's arm, catching her by surprise. Shock sparked along her nerves as he yanked her toward him, slamming her back to his chest, gripping her upper arms in a punishing hold. His hands pressed deathly cold against her skin. Goose bumps raced up and down her arms.

"Bring. The. Child." The chill of Arian's breath numbed the back of her head.

All traces of humor fell from Michael's face and he stilled. Even the breeze that had been flirting with his hair disappeared. "I'll not let you go putting the child in danger."

"He'll be safe," Arian ground out. "But if you defy me, the woman will not." His spiky silver fingertips slid around her throat. Points of pain pierced her neck, needled into her head. She clenched her teeth to stop from crying out.

Michael's stricken gaze darted from her face to Arian's grip on her neck, and his jaw tensed. "You have made enemies this night." He cut the gatekeeper a threatening sideways glance and then opened the car door.

Arian thrust Cordelia away. She huddled beside Michael against the car, her thoughts mired in shock.

"You all right, lass?" Michael stroked her cheek, then gently pushed her head to one side and examined her neck.

She rubbed her throat, and her fingers came away sticky with blood. Then she caught sight of Arian's impatient expression. With a stuttering breath, she straightened. "I'm fine. I love being assaulted at night in the middle of nowhere."

"She'll live. Stop making a fuss." Arian took a step toward the car and Fin.

Michael moved to cut him off. "Don't even think about touching him."

Despite her bravado, Cordelia trembled. A premonition of disaster drifted through her like a ghost while she watched Michael release Fin from his seat and gather the sleepy child into his arms.

They trudged across a wet, muddy field, water seeping into her shoes, dirt sticking to the hem of her dress. The Teg seemed to have no trouble seeing in the dark. Thank the Luna goddess the moon was waxing gibbous, nearly full. Every time the clouds broke for a few seconds, the moon gave just enough light to see where they were heading.

The clouds parted and Cordelia's pulse leaped at the sight of a monstrous creature crouched on the hilltop. With a shot of relief that almost buckled her knees, she realized the shape was an excavating machine abandoned beside the dark maw of a hole.

"We've arrived," Dai announced. But there was nothing to see. Cordelia had expected a dark swirling breach in the air, or at least something resembling a gate. They gathered along the muddy rim of the wide trench. Dai pointed to a toppled megalith half submerged in water lying in the bottom of the hole.

"Ruddy Badba. There are two humans near the stone." Michael pushed Fin into her arms and ran along the edge of the trench toward the rock.

"Humans," Olwyn said with distaste. "Probably dead. The gate must have drained the life from them when they uncovered it."

Fear slashed through Cordelia. She stepped back, clutching Fin as he twisted in her arms to watch Michael. "Keep away from the megalith, Michael," she shouted after him. "It can suck the life out of you."

She wasn't sure whether he heard her or not. But he didn't jump into the trench, just crouched on the lip, and peered at the two humans lying in the muddy water.

Olwyn and Dai jumped into the hole. Amazingly, they made no splash. They floated a little above the ground, keeping their black boots dry. Cordelia flexed her toes inside her sodden, dirty leather pumps with a touch of resentment.

Arian approached her, his eyes shining like an animal's in the dark.

She had to focus her will to stand her ground and not back away. "Please bring the two humans up here so we can check if they're alive," she asked.

He didn't even acknowledge her request. With a sneer, he narrowed his eyes to malevolent glowing slits. "I need some of the child's hair." He lifted a hand toward Fin. Cordelia stumbled back out of reach, nearly tripping on her dress's soggy hem.

She hugged Fin protectively, his chubby legs wrapped around her, his warm, tearstained cheek pressed into her neck. "Why?"

By now, she should have known better than to expect an answer. Arian lunged after her, grabbing at the little boy's head and yanking his hair.

Fin's scream rent the damp night air, sending crows flapping into the sky from the shadowy silhouette of an oak tree.

"You damn—"

Before she finished her sentence, Michael jumped in front of her. He shoved Arian in the chest, making him stagger back a step. "If you've hurt the baby, fella, I'll—"

"I've only taken some hair." Arian raised his fist, displaying the fluttering golden strands. "There's always a price to pay when a gate's opened unlawfully. Be thankful I did not demand blood of the pisky king's line."

As he turned away, Michael shouted, "I'm the king's brother, you oaf. If you were needing hair or blood, you should have taken mine."

When Arian reached the lip of the trench, he glanced back over his shoulder and shrugged. "You denied responsibility." Then he leaped down, soundlessly, and joined Olwyn and Dai.

Michael reeled around as though drunk and slammed the heel of his hand against his forehead in time with his words: "When. Will. I. Learn."

"Michael." Cordelia hitched Fin onto her hip and grabbed Michael's arm before he thumped his head again. "You couldn't have known he'd hurt the baby."

He stilled, his angry breaths filling the silence. She released his arm and it dropped to his side. Heaving a sigh, he wrested Fin from her arms, hugging the child desperately, eyes closed. "Sorry, lad. I'm sorry." Fin's whimpers faded as he snuggled closer to Michael.

Cordelia turned away, her heart pinching, unable to bear the anguish on Michael's face. He might have his faults but he certainly loved his nephew. She glanced behind her to where Tamsy had remained on the fence near the car. At the edge of her mind, she sensed the warm reassurance of her familiar's presence.

"Look," Michael said, still clutching Fin tightly.

The three gatekeepers had spread out across the trench. Arms stretched wide, they started to chant and glow.

"Damnation. They haven't moved the humans." Michael groaned. With soft words of reassurance, he detached the clinging child and pushed him into Cordelia's arms.

"Leave them, Michael." She tried to grab him but he was already striding toward the trench.

He paused on the lip of the hole. "Pass up the humans," he bellowed. The angry compulsion in his tone thumped into Cordelia's chest like a fist. She closed her eyes, struggled to drag air into her lungs. By the time she was aware of her surroundings again, a shining mantle of light extended from the gatekeepers' hands, shrouding the trench.

Michael had disappeared.

With an anguished cry, Cordelia ran forward and saw Michael wading through the water in the hole toward the humans. He caught hold of one, then grabbed the arm of the second, and started pulling them back to the edge of the trench.

The sheet of light spread farther, gaining speed as it dipped toward the ground on the opposite side of the megalith.

Michael would be trapped.

She screamed his name. Fin wailed, flailed his arms, and wriggled so much she struggled to keep hold of him.

Michael ran, the sloshing sucking sound of the mud marking his progress. He literally threw first one human, then the other out of the trench, then vaulted up the earthy bank and collapsed on his back beside her. The glowing mantle extending from the gatekeepers' hands blazed incandescent. Cordelia screwed her eyes closed and struggled to hold on to the squirming baby. Suddenly her arms were empty, clutching at thin air.

Her eyes sprang open. Temporarily blinded by the burst of light, she dropped to her knees, scrabbled around in the mud, feeling for the child. When she grabbed a warm body, she thought she had him, but she was grasping Michael's arm.

"Finian," she cried on a sob. "Where's Finian?"

The Teg had disappeared. Silent darkness pressed around them. Michael pulled away from her and sat up. "What do you mean where's Finian?"

She shook her head, a useless gesture in the dark but she couldn't seem to stop. "I had him; then my arms were empty."

Slowly her eyes recovered from the blinding flash. She started to pick out shapes in the dark: the ragged outline of trees and bushes on the hill, the excavator on the other side of the trench.

Michael rolled onto his hands and knees and crawled between clods of earth toward the lip of the hole. A strangled sob broke from his throat. A sound that clawed her heart, burned tears in her eyes.

She gathered her dress out of the way and shuffled on her knees through the mud to Michael's side. At the sight of Fin, her muscles locked, paralyzed with shock. He sat in the mud where the humans had been minutes before, deathly still, eyes open, mouth frozen in a silent cry, right beside the fallen megalith that led to the Underworld.

Chapter Three

Time paused. Cordelia's body ceased to feel, her heart silent, her breath still. Then fear oozed up as she imagined the poor little boy lost in endless darkness.

"Fin!" Michael's anguished cry kicked the air out of her lungs. It shuddered back in on a moan.

Michael launched himself at the trench and disappeared into the gloom. Was he, too, lost in the Underworld? Terror held her rigid until she saw movement on the far side of the hole. Her fingers clenched the gritty mud. Squinting, she made out Michael on the ground by the excavator.

Relief flashed, quickly chased away by confusion. How did he get over there? He scrambled to his feet and jumped toward the trench again. An instant later, he skidded to a halt beside her.

"I cannot get to him," he cried. "I can see him, but I cannot get to him."

She reached out in a blind need to comfort him. But he spun in the mud and launched himself wildly into the air, landing a moment later next to the excavator again.

He circled the area the gatekeepers had isolated. Each time he jumped toward Fin, he landed on the other side of the hole.

Finally, her numb brain stumbled back to life. She understood.

With her teary gaze fixed on Fin, she crawled to the lip of the trench. Biting down on her lip, she reached out. When her forearm passed through the Teg's shroud, her hand disappeared. With a yelp, she snatched back her arm and cradled it to her body, the burn of fear slowly fading. She stared unseeing into the night, her muscles trembling.

However many times Michael jumped, he wouldn't reach Fin. That part of the trench no longer existed in the physical world.

Michael trudged back to stand beside her, his hair and clothes soaked and filthy. His labored breaths echoed across the dark, silent field. He rubbed his face, spat out some mud.

She reached for him, brushed her fingers over the back of his hand, gritty with dirt. "I'm sorry, Michael."

He dropped to a crouch, elbows on his knees, and closed his eyes.

Her heart cracked, brittle as glass. He'd entrusted Fin to her and she'd let him down.

"'Tis not your fault, lass. Fin is my responsibility." He rubbed his eyes with his sleeve, looked up at her through his dirty, dripping hair. She ached to touch him, comfort him, heal his pain. If only the restrictive wards on her skin didn't prevent her from using her energies to heal, she could lay her hand on his heart center to ease his pain.

With a questioning mew, Tamsy rubbed against Cordelia's arm. "Oh, Tam." Cordelia gathered the beloved creature into her arms and hid her face in the warm fur.

"The gatekeepers have annexed the trench as part of the Underworld," she whispered.

Michael dragged a sigh up from the depths of his soul. "I'll bloody murder Arian." With Michael's clenched jaw and fierce eyes, she hardly recognized him.

"What are we going to do?" she whispered.

He sprang to his feet. "I know someone who has the answer to everything."

Tipping back his head, he bellowed at the top of his voice: "Troy." He peered around the field. When nobody appeared, his voice thundered into the darkness again.

How could anyone hear Michael from out here? Yet after his third shout, a light blazed off to their left. Cordelia jumped to her feet, energized by a flare of hope that the gatekeepers had returned to release Fin. But this pale golden light had a warmer quality than the cold brightness of the Teg.

A being appeared within the aura. Although he stood no taller than a normal male, everything else about him was extraordinary. Sparkles of rainbow color glinted off a jewel in the knot of golden hair at the back of his head. His jacket glowed cherry red, adorned with gleaming buttons. Creamy lace frothed at his wrists and throat. His eyes shone bluer than a summer sky, and the extraordinary radiance appeared to emanate from his skin.

"Troy." Michael brushed past her and ran into the man's embrace. She winced at the thought of Michael's dirty clothes against the man's finery. Yet when they broke apart, not a trace of dirt marred the velvet or lace.

"I gather you need my assistance, son?" the man said in a musical voice.

Son!

Cordelia gaped at him anew. Even as she stared in disbelief, she recognized the likeness. His eyes were the same blue as Michael's, and when he smiled, the similarity was obvious. But what manner of being was Troy?

Michael's words tumbled out in his haste to explain what had happened to Fin. Cordelia joined them, hugging Tamsy. When Michael finished speaking, she added a few details he'd missed.

Troy's curious gaze settled on her. She wanted to drag her tear-swollen eyes away, but his look held a subtle command she couldn't break. He spoke calmly, a pleasant half smile on his lips. "Do not fret over Finian. He will not be harmed."

The ache in her heart eased; the tearful tightness in her chest and throat relaxed. She now knew from whom Michael had inherited his silver tongue. She waited for the effect to fade, but the anger and distress fluttered out of reach.

"Who's your friend?" Troy asked Michael.

"This is the pisky wise woman, Cordelia."

Troy inclined his head to her.

"Cordelia, this here is me father from across the Irish Sea." Michael rushed through the niceties.

"Michael, lad, go and check if the humans live." Troy patted Michael's back and the tense set of his shoulders dropped, while the haunted look in his eyes faded.

Once Michael nodded and walked away, Troy extended a hand. After a moment of confusion, she realized he wanted them to shake hands like humans. She hesitated, wary. But surely, Michael's father meant her no harm?

When his fingers touched her skin, an enquiring tendril of thought slipped into her body. Subtle and smooth, he overwhelmed her psychic defenses. A woolly sense of well-being suffused her. Worries slid away. Vaguely, on the edge of consciousness, she heard Tamsy start to purr.

By strength of will, she held on to a shred of awareness. As he withdrew his senses, she crept after him, into his mind. Desolation, endless, bleak, the top of a mountain where clouds hung, never pierced by the sun, a woman with sleek dark hair and blazing violet eyes.

"Oomph." She grunted as he pushed her out, the sensation rather like a smack on the forehead. When she managed to focus her eyes, he was staring at her, the acute brilliance of his gaze dissecting her like a razor.

She pulled to withdraw her hand. His grip tightened, nearly to the point of pain. Her insides trembled as she sensed his limitless cold power. "I did not give you leave to pry, witch."

"Nor I you," she snapped, furious that he had one rule for her and another for himself.

After a long moment trapped in the scrutiny of his gaze, he released her hand. *"Touché."* He arched an eyebrow. "You hide the truth of your nature most effectively. From your appearance, I would not have guessed you are half water nymph."

A flash of panic speared her. "You won't tell Michael?"

Troy glanced at his son where he kneeled beside the humans. "He's a powerful earth elemental, strong enough to ground your allure so you could remain in control. You'd thrive together."

She shook her head, ignoring the tingle of longing for something that could never be. "I don't need him."

His lips twitched. "Denial fools only the denier."

"The humans are both dead," Michael said in a weary voice when he had tramped back to them. "I went and risked meself and lost Fin for nothing."

"Dead is a relative term." Troy walked to the edge of the hole. He didn't float above the ground like the Teg. Yet he made no sound, left no footprints, and his shoes remained clean.

If she hadn't touched his flesh, she would have thought him a shade who'd flown here in spirit form, leaving his body in Ireland. The Irish Tuatha Dé Danaan were of noble birth, often gifted with potent magic. But this man was something far more powerful.

Michael joined his father beside the trench and stared at Fin. Although Troy had drained Michael's anger, his guts ached as though they were twisted. He rubbed his eyes, too tired and wretched to shed tears.

"This is the first time I've seen Finian," Troy said softly. "Is Kea identical?"

"Aye."

Troy stared at the child, his face expressionless. With anyone else, Michael would be furious at the show of indifference. But Troy always observed life without becoming emotionally involved. How else could he remain the still, calm center of the hectic Irish fairy court?

Cordelia came up beside him, petting her purring cat. "I can't work out how I lost Finian," she said, her voice rough with tears. "One minute I was holding him, then . . ."

The simmering anger flared through Michael again. "That bloody gatekeeper Arian went and put him there on purpose. Arian must have taken his hair to bind him in the spell."

Cordelia shook her head. "I thought Fin might have moved himself."

"What!" Michael stared at her.

Troy raised a calming hand. "Does he walk unseen yet?"

Michael groaned and covered his eyes. "Aye," he said, reluctantly. "Both twins have just started disappearing from the nursery to follow Rose and Niall." He swallowed before he could utter the last few words. "Today Finian followed me."

"Bad timing," Troy offered, emotionlessly.

"You think?" Michael snapped.

Cordelia put her hand on his arm. Surprisingly, her touch soothed him.

"However Fin landed in trouble, we'll be needing to get him out pronto." Michael cast a questioning glance at Troy. His father would know how to rescue Fin. His father knew everything.

"Fin sits outside the gate," Troy stated. "Not in the Underworld per se, but still trapped within the demesne of Gwyn ap Nudd."

Cordelia glanced at the corpses. "How did the humans die?"

A few loose strands of Troy's golden hair danced in the breeze. He brushed them back as he spoke. "Their life force must have been sucked into the Underworld."

"Shite!" Michael paced away, kicked a clod of earth, wishing it were Arian's head. "I want the lad out now." He strode back to his father. "Can you free him?"

Troy released a protracted breath. He reached behind

him and drew his short black sword, Death's Kiss, from the scabbard on his back. He turned to Cordelia. "Take your cat to the safety of the car. Cats have a unique relationship with death that might complicate matters."

"I'll wait for you there." She blinked tearful gray eyes at Michael. He yearned to comfort her, reassure her she wasn't to blame, but now was not the time or place.

After she walked away, Troy jumped into the trench where the gatekeepers had stood when they sealed the gate. He tentatively swung his blade.

Light sparked with an electric sizzle as the metal met the gatekeepers' barrier. Troy slashed harder. The sword rent the fabric of the air. Swirling black smoke full of jagged shards of lightning filled the trench. An acrid metallic smell reached Michael's nose as he covered his ears to block the screeching noise. Troy danced back from the mayhem, an ironic smile on his lips. "Apparently, I have my limitations."

"I won't go leaving the lad alone in the wet like this," Michael said.

"I can't fracture the barrier long enough for you to jump through."

"Rip it again. Let me try."

"And have you stranded in the Underworld as well? No, lad. I can make sure he's comfortable and protected; then you must find another way to reach him."

Troy stepped forward again, both hands gripping the hilt of his sword. A streamer of light leaped from the end of his raised blade, arcing into the night sky. He slashed down. Michael threw an arm over his eyes at the blinding flash. When darkness returned, he stared back at Fin. The child was still trapped, but now he floated a few feet above the ground in a glowing cocoon, eyes closed, curled into a fetal position, breathing shallowly.

Troy leaped onto the bank beside Michael. "He sleeps in safety. Nothing dead can touch him while my light surrounds him."

"What about the Teg? They're still a threat to him."

"I know the Master of the Darkling Road that traverses the Underworld. I'll ask him to post a watch inside this gateway until you arrive."

Michael's heart nearly exploded out of his chest. "You'll go leaving the lad's safety to a damn shadow elemental?"

"Michael." Troy's voice rang with a steel edge of censure. "Do not make the mistake of thinking all shadow elementals are evil."

Michael groaned with frustration. "So what are you suggesting I do next?"

"You have five days to reach Fin before my light shield degrades. Make haste to Wales. Petition the Tylwyth Teg for Fin's safe return."

"You'll be coming with us?"

Troy shook his head. "I must return to Ireland. The Queen of Nightmares is plotting to murder King Esras and steal his lands. If I'm not there, she might succeed." He put a hand on Michael's shoulder. "You must take the pisky wise woman along. With her help, you're more than capable of rescuing Finian."

"Me?" All his life Troy had told him to stand aside whenever there was trouble. "You're getting me confused with Niall."

Troy met his eyes. "I think maybe I've done you a disservice, lad. I tried too hard to protect you from the truth of your nature."

Michael stared at him, uncomprehending.

Troy grimaced, dropped his gaze to his feet. The tension inside Michael twisted to near breaking point. When Troy raised his eyes, they were sad, apologetic. "You're like me, Michael. You're like me."

Michael continued to stare at Troy, baffled. "Everyone knows 'tis Niall who takes after you. Not me."

Troy looked at the blade in his hand as if he'd forgotten it. He reached over his shoulder and slid the sword into the scabbard on his back. "Niall takes after your leprechaun mother. He practices earth magic and has the leprechaun touch of luck. Those are his only gifts."

Michael shook his head violently, unwilling to discount so easily a belief that had shaped his whole life. "What about his skill with a blade? There's no denying he inherited that from you."

"Niall's skill with a blade is the result of practice and determination, not a gift." Troy laughed, but the sound held more incredulity than humor. "He chose to emulate me, though I'll never understand why."

Michael stared off into the darkness, suddenly adrift in a world where he no longer knew himself or his brother. Or the father who'd just tipped his world arse about face.

"Think of your gifts, lad: glamour, silver tongue, the ability to read people." He paused and waited for Michael's bemused gaze to find him. "These powers you inherited from me."

Michael stared at his feet half submerged in mud, his mind in free fall. "You were always so proud of Niall," he said, his voice sounding lost.

"Of course. Niall accomplished everything through strength of spirit. For you, life will be much easier and much harder."

Troy withdrew a jewel-handled dagger from his knotted hair, releasing the golden cascade of strands onto his shoulders. He palmed the blade and held out the ornate hilt to Michael. "When you reach Wales, you must go before the Ennead, the council of nine. Reveal this blade to Master Devin. He will tell you how to proceed."

Michael wrapped his hand around the intricately worked gold handle and stared at the huge rainbow-hued gem in the pommel. "Is the stone magic?"

With a small shake of his head, Troy pressed Michael's hand around the dagger and pushed it down to Michael's side. "This is the end of an era, lad." He pulled Michael into a fierce embrace, then drew back with a sigh. "Don't think badly of me, son."

"Why would I think badly of you?"

"When you understand my legacy, you will have every right to hate me."

Michael sat at the desk in Niall's office at Trevelion Manor. Although Troy had arranged for the Master of the Darkling Road to guard Fin, Michael and Cordelia had also organized a roster of pisky men to keep watch. The piskies might not be able to reach the lad, but at least he wasn't alone.

He stared at Troy's dagger, which rested in the middle of the oak desk. The metal blade glinted darkly beneath the lamp, while the multicolored jewel in the handle cast rainbows across the ceiling. During his childhood, he'd seen the decorative cross in Troy's hair on numerous occasions and thought it nothing more than an elaborate hair ornament.

Cordelia sat on the other side of the desk, hollow eyed and pale. Her hands absently stroked the cat on her lap. "Are we agreed, then?" she asked, her voice flat with fatigue. "We'll leave for Wales immediately and call Niall when we can?"

Michael gripped the back of his neck. Since the Teg gatekeepers had arrived, he'd done nothing but make mistakes. Niall would have died rather than let them take his son from Trevelion Manor. Yet Michael had carried the boy out to the ruddy car. Niall would have stepped up and offered his blood to appease Gwyn ap Nudd, not tried to talk his way out of responsibility. Michael hadn't even stopped to think. Now Finian had paid the price.

"Blood and fury." Michael slammed his fist on the desk, making the blade jump with a metallic clunk. Ye gods, he needed a cigarette. He'd glibly agreed to give up smoking when Rose was expecting the babies—a pledge proving harder to keep than he'd expected.

The door creaked open, and Thorn and Nightshade came

in. Thorn rushed to comfort Cordelia. Nightshade strode past the desk and threw his arm over Michael's shoulders. "What happened to Fin wasn't your fault," he said.

Michael lurched to his feet, shrugging away Nightshade's arm. He paced to the window and stared at the pale light of dusk creeping across the horizon. "I'm not wanting understanding." He seethed with frustration at his own stupidity.

The reflection of Nightshade's shocked face in the glass made him grip the windowsill until his fingernails bit into the wood. He didn't want to hurt his friend—but everything had changed this night. He'd never let Nightshade bite him again. The frivolous pleasure of dallying with death had lost its appeal. And for some reason, he hated the thought that Cordelia would disapprove.

He ran his hands back through his hair. "We'll have to decide what we're going to do. I can't speak to Niall yet to get his advice." After all that had happened, he could hardly believe Niall was still in midflight.

An idea struck him—a good one for once. He was amazed Cordelia hadn't suggested it. "Will you take a reading of the future for us, Cordelia? Tell us what's going to be happening."

She blinked at him tiredly. "Umm, yes. I can certainly try."

Try?

According to Niall, she was an expert at foretelling. "Why the uncertainty?"

"We'll discuss it in my room." She looked down to brush the creases from her clean dress as she rose.

She went to the door with her neat, precise steps, the cat trotting at her heels. Thorn moved to follow, and Michael shook his head. He passed the lad a note he'd made of some useful references he wanted to take with them. "You two find these and bring around the car. We'll not take long with this foretelling."

He caught up with her in the hall and followed her to the

medieval wing of the house. He'd assumed her bedroom was upstairs, but she ignored the stairs and took a side hall. "I have my own suite of rooms." She halted before a door and unlocked it with a key from her pocket.

Once inside, she showed him into a small, cozy room. The cat jumped on a sagging floral armchair in the corner, circled, and curled up on a hairy crocheted cushion. Streaks of morning sun penetrated the windows, painting strokes of light across the granite fireplace. A faded tapestry adorned the wall, and a multitude of shelves and tables filled every space. Each was crowded with ornaments: pearly shells, pinecones, china, and colorful knickknacks of all sorts.

She pulled out a leaf on a table by a pair of glass doors and then moved a straight-backed chair so he could sit there. With another key from her pocket, she unlocked the narrow double doors. A gentle breeze carried the fragrance of a summer's morning in from the garden: cool dew, the scent of sweet peas climbing a crumbling pillar, the tang of salt from the Atlantic. Michael sat, entranced, and looked up at dangling threads of pink and yellow shells jingling in time to the lazy hiss of the sea.

He'd never understood people who liked to be alone in quiet places. He loved crowds, noise, and music. But with his mind in turmoil, the peace was soothing.

Cordelia sat opposite him and folded her hands on the lacy tablecloth. "I can't read my own future, Michael. No one with the gift of foretelling can."

He nodded, linked his fingers, matched her pose. "Fair enough, lass. Read for meself."

A hint of pink crept into her cheeks. She looked down and twisted the silver ring on her little finger. "I doubt I can read for you either."

Michael pressed his fingers to his eyes. The deep empty well of loss inside him, which had eased for a few minutes, ached anew. "Just give it a try, lass. Anything we discover that helps us rescue Fin is good, for sure."

Her cheeks grew pinker. "I'm sorry, I don't think . . ." Her words trailed away and she bit her bottom lip.

He reached for the water-filled dish with the three white candles floating on the surface and dragged it in front of her. "Have a go," he said, a touch of irritation in his voice. He knew seers were not able to divine for themselves. But there was no reason why she shouldn't read for him. Unless she was scared of what she'd see, scared what his reaction might be. He tensed his shoulders, let them relax. He covered her slender hands with one of his. "'Tis all right, lass. I'm only asking you do your best."

She gazed at his hand silently, the tightly buttoned bodice of her dress rising and falling a little faster than usual. Then she looked up, but not at him, at her cat. The creature stared back with solemn gray eyes very similar to Cordelia's. The moment stretched. He had the sense she was drawing strength or inspiration from Tamsy. He wondered if the cat were more than a pet.

Finally, she looked at him. "I'll try if you promise you'll stay seated."

"Anything you say." He'd agree to stand on his head if she'd get on with the reading. His heart thundered as she struck a match and lit the three floating candles. The squat white stumps bobbed in the water while she repositioned the dish. When all three candles were producing thick ribbons of smoke, she sketched a symbol in the air and whispered some words. The smoke spread, then appeared to freeze in place, a golden glaze coating the surface. Michael slid his chair to the side, curious to watch, but she shook her head. "Stay opposite me or I won't continue."

With a sigh, he moved his chair back and angled his head to see her around the side of her strange scrying mirror. She had a cute little nose, which she wrinkled up when she concentrated.

As the minutes ticked by, his attention wandered to the window. Seagulls wheeled over the cliffs at the bottom of the garden, screeching to each other. A blackbird landed on the flagstones outside the door and peered at him.

"See anything?" he asked after what felt like an hour.

"Shh. I'm concentrating." She narrowed her eyes. Slowly, she tilted her head to the side. "Oh. Oh my goodness." Her hand flew to her throat. Her cheeks turned scarlet.

So she could see his future, after all. Michael was out of his chair and around the table in an instant. He leaned in beside her, searching the mirrored surface, desperate to know what would happen when they arrived in Wales.

What he saw stunned him. Naked, he lay tangled with an equally naked woman in a very imaginative position. Despite his somber mood, heat flared in his belly. The woman in the mirror threw back her head and moaned, the sound from the image filling Cordelia's small room. She dragged a hand through her hair, lifting the strands off her face. For a disbelieving moment Michael stared, then he whispered, "Sweet bejesus, Cordelia. That's you."

Cordelia nearly knocked the table flying when she shot to her feet. She had to put space between herself and Michael *now*. She tripped on her hem as she stumbled out the French window to the garden.

The warm swirling feeling in her belly spread, tingling in her thighs, across her ribs, into her breasts.

"No!"

She ran down the neatly manicured lawn to the lichen-covered wall dividing the garden from the sheer cliffs that dropped to the ocean. She stopped, fists crumpling her skirt, and let the cool wind whipping up off the water dull the sensations. Her allure churned so wildly, she feared it would break out of the containing wards painted on her body and drive Michael to madness.

"Cordelia?" The question in Michael's voice sent a chill through her that quelled the flow of sensation more effectively than the coldest wind. She dropped her face into her hands, wishing fervently that he would disappear, that this was all a nightmare. But she sensed him moving closer, the warm beat of his presence strong and fierce in her chest. A constant reminder of her vulnerability to him.

"Don't use your glamour on me," she snapped.

"I'm not, lass," he replied, sounding baffled.

"Oh rats' tails." If she felt like this when he wasn't using glamour, eventually her allure *would* grow too strong for the wards to control. Once they'd rescued Fin, she must keep away from Michael. Niall would probably banish her anyway after what had happened to his son. Tears welled in her eyes. She brushed them away with her knuckles, hoping Michael wouldn't notice.

"Is that image in your divination mirror what you're expecting to happen in Wales?" he asked.

"Gods save us, no," she said on a rush of breath. "Absolutely not."

She glanced over her shoulder to find his eyebrows raised. For the first time since they'd lost Fin, Michael's lips twitched, almost making it into a smile. "The timing is undoubtedly bad, but the foretelling did not look that terrible to me, lass."

Turning to face him, she scraped back the loose wisps of hair fluttering in her eyes. "There's no way anything like that can happen between us, Michael. Ever."

"I thought you foretold the future."

"Possible futures. Or in the case of that ridiculous image"—she jabbed a finger toward her room—"an impossible future."

He frowned. "So you're sure that's not likely to happen in Wales?"

She drew a shaky breath, released it slowly. "That image has nothing to do with Wales." She'd learned as a child that she must remain neutral during a reading or she could summon a false image. She feared the image of herself with Michael was nothing more than a representation of her desire.

Silently, she begged him not to ask any more questions. She'd rather jump off the cliff than admit she liked to watch him making love.

He rubbed the back of his neck and stared out to sea. "I'm thinking you'll not be able to give us any clues how to free Fin."

The wind ruffled the chestnut waves of hair around his blue eyes and dark, unshaven jaw. In the low morning sun, his gaze glittered with pain, bright as the jewel in Troy's dagger.

She was beyond selfish worrying about her own longings when all that mattered now was rescuing Fin. "Do you think Troy's knife is magic?"

Michael's eyes fixed on her again. He seemed to take a second to focus. "Don't know, lass. Troy said to take the blade to Wales and show it to someone called Master Devin."

"You'll just do as he bid?"

"Aye, lass. There'll be a good reason, to be sure."

"You trust your father? I thought Niall had issues with him?" And after her experience with Troy, she wasn't sure *she* trusted him.

Michael laughed, a hollow, lost sound that brought tears to her eyes anew. "I cannot deny you have a point. Me father's thrown me off kilter. What I do know is we must leave for Wales as soon as possible. 'Tis down to us to rescue Fin before the protective shield Troy spun around the lad disintegrates."

Chapter Four

Nightshade slouched sideways on the backseat of the Range Rover, his wings bent uncomfortably as the car shot along the motorway toward Wales. Michael slept beside him, head propped on a cushion against the door. Although Michael's face was serene in sleep, Nightshade kept remembering Michael's angry expression earlier when he'd rejected Nightshade's comforting touch.

I've lost him.

The thought circled in his brain, cutting and slicing and ripping until his heart stuttered with the pain.

His fangs ached in his gums at the musky fragrance of Michael's skin. Yet he would never taste him again unless he took him by force. The thought of Michael fighting him off cracked his heart.

Nightshade shifted to ease the ache in his shoulder from sitting sideways. Sometimes he hated his wings. They forever marked him out as a peculiarity, not only among humans, but also among The Good People.

The noisy silence in the vehicle oppressed him, the hum of the tires on the road maddening. Thorn drove, drumming his fingers on the steering wheel in time to the music from his headphones. Cordelia slept in the front passenger seat, her head lolling to the side. He hoped she woke with a stiff neck. Michael hadn't taken his eyes off her legs since she'd walked out to the car wearing fitted trousers.

The cat uncurled from its spot on Cordelia's lap,

stretched, and hopped between the front seats into the back. The creature paused and looked at him with enigmatic eyes. "Hello, cat." He did not want to like the creature because it belonged to Cordelia. The cat blinked at him, then stepped softly onto Michael's lap. After circling, it settled in a furry ball, a cheek pressed against his zipper.

Despite his mood, Nightshade laughed. The creature had waited until Cordelia slept, then swapped allegiance. Even the cat wanted a piece of Michael. For some reason, the thought made Nightshade feel better. He wouldn't give Michael up without a fight.

Cordelia woke to the emotionless voice of the satellite navigation system: *in one hundred yards, turn left; turn left.*

Michael was now driving. His hair shone lustrous as ever but his face was pale, with tiny lines of tension around his mouth instead of his usual smile. She hoped he'd caught some sleep before he took over the driving from Thorn.

"Where are we?" She massaged her tight neck muscles and admired the misty mountains in the distance.

"Would you believe Wales, the Neath Valley?" he asked dryly.

He glanced at her, his gaze flicking to her legs before moving back to the windshield. Nerves sparked beneath her skin. Was he remembering the image in her divining mirror of them making love? Maybe she shouldn't have worn trousers. With her legs on show, she felt vulnerable.

"Only a few more miles to Craig-y-Ddinas car park, then we'll hoof it," he added.

As Cordelia drank from her water bottle, she realized Tamsy wasn't on her lap. She glanced back, expecting her cat to be with Thorn. Her heart jolted when she saw the traitorous creature resting her chin on Nightshade's knee while he stroked her face.

Cordelia jerked her gaze away, stared out the window at the narrow road threading its way among stunted oak trees.

She pushed out her consciousness to meld with Tamsy and released shock and disapproval into the cat's mind. Tamsy gave a lazy mew, radiating pleasure. Why wasn't she frightened of Nightshade? Being confined in the car with him set Cordelia's nerves on edge. She had only been able to sleep because she was exhausted.

She could hardly reach back and grab her cat, so she sat stiffly, jaw clenched, while Michael maneuvered the car into the parking lot. He stopped in the middle, the engine idling. They all stared around at the numerous walkers in weatherproof jackets with backpacks. A little girl ran in front of their car wearing a pink My Little Pony anorak and matching cap.

Nightshade was the first to speak: "Shit!"

Cordelia wouldn't have vocalized her feelings in quite that way, but he summed up her sentiment exactly.

"This wasn't how I imagined the entry to the Underworld," Thorn said.

Michael laughed, short and sharp and very un-Michael-like. "We'll have to walk to the Sgwd yr Eira waterfall to find the way into Gwyn's demesne."

"Oh, that's all right then," Thorn said.

Michael pinched the bridge of his nose and Nightshade groaned.

"Thorn, sweetheart," Cordelia said, turning to look at him, "why do you think all these humans are here?"

"Don't call me sweetheart." A telltale hint of pink crept into his cheeks.

"They're all going to walk to the ruddy waterfall, you dunderhead." Nightshade punched Thorn playfully on the arm. Cordelia bit her tongue and turned away. Tamsy scooted onto her lap to escape the roughhousing. The two men wrestled on the backseat until Nightshade had Thorn in a headlock.

"What're we going to do?" She glanced at Michael.

He ran his fingers back through his hair. "Park and take a jaunt to the waterfall, with every tourist in Wales, by the looks of things. 'Tis bound to take us a while to find the door. Let's be hoping this lot have gone home by then."

He squeezed the Range Rover into a space and they all piled out. Nightshade wore a long coat and a hat, which looked like something from the 1940s and did nothing to make him blend in. Michael wore the same as usual, adding a leather jacket to his jeans and T-shirt. Cordelia slipped on her serviceable blue jacket over her roll-neck jumper and put on boots with nonslip soles. Some of the paths were bound to be steep and slippery. Thorn stood watching them prepare. "Coat, Thorn," Cordelia said as she hitched her tapestry cat-carrying bag over her shoulder and settled Tamsy inside.

"I haven't got one."

She glanced up and frowned.

"It's the middle of summer," he said defensively.

"We're in Wales. There are mountains." She pointed through the trees to the purple peaks in the distance. "The nights get cold."

He shrugged away her concern. "I'll be fine."

Then she looked at his feet. Michael and Nightshade both wore stout leather boots. Thorn was wearing blue plastic shoes that would have been ideal for the beach.

Before she could say any more, he scowled. "Stop treating me like a kid."

With a sigh, she went back to settling Tamsy, who'd got her claw caught in the bag's stitching. Thorn was right. She had to let him grow up. She was overprotective because he'd been an abandoned child. Letting go was difficult when he was all she had.

"Ready?" Michael asked, glancing between them. "Better be making a move. We seem to be attracting attention."

The family groups walking past were all staring at Nightshade, a few of them even detouring around the far side of the parked cars to keep their distance. Cordelia sympathized with them.

They started out, Michael setting a brisk pace up the steep path that rose between the rocks and the river Mellte. Cordelia was soon puffing, but she refused to be the one to ask him to slow down. She hugged her precious bundle of fur in the bag at her side, smiling every time Tamsy poked her head out to look around. They passed the entrance to some old silica mines, then tramped across an area of soggy moorland to a gate. Michael stopped and rested his elbows on the gate's top rung, waiting for Thorn and Nightshade to catch up.

He pulled out his cell phone and punched in a number. "Best I try Niall again now. 'Tis unlikely there'll be reception in the river valley." Cordelia twisted her hands together, dreading the call to the pisky king. Michael had already tried to reach him twice on the journey to Wales, but got no answer. After a few anxious moments, Michael snapped the phone shut. "Maybe 'tis best me brother doesn't know about his lad's plight when he can't do anything to help."

With a guilty flash of relief, Cordelia turned to gaze across acres of rough grassland dotted with ragged clumps of reeds. The falling sun hung low in the sky, painting a golden streak above the trees. "By the time we get to the waterfall, all the human tourists should be headed back. They need time to reach their cars before dusk."

Michael nodded and stepped aside as a man and woman came through the gate and took the path back to the car park. "'Tis a fair old clip to the falls. Farther than I expected," Michael said.

The sun gilded each wave of Michael's hair with gold. He leaned forward, gripped the top of the gate, his hands strong, capable. The muscles in his thighs and backside tensed beneath the soft denim of his jeans. Finian's fate had kept her mind occupied; now Michael's nearness swamped her senses.

His earth elemental nature gave her an anchor. The beat of his psychic presence close to her heart was warm, strong, and reassuringly solid.

Simmering behind his earthy nature, she sensed a hint of a power she couldn't categorize. That unusual part of him must come from his father. Frustration pricked every time she remembered her brush with Troy. What strange type of being was he?

Thorn stumbled up, folded his arms on top of the gate, and rested his head on them. "How much farther? My feet are killing me."

Cordelia and Michael exchanged a knowing look. For a second, mirth sparkled in his blue eyes, before it faded to be replaced by an ache of concern that echoed in her own heart. Instinctively, she reached to touch his hand, draw out his pain, heal in the way she'd been born to do.

Before she could touch him, Nightshade stepped between them. He slapped his own hand on top of the gate beside Michael's, making her step back. He angled his head toward her, long black hair whipping around his face in the breeze. The wicked white points of his fangs flashed beneath his top lip and his eyes narrowed to cruel silver slits.

Memories she'd hidden deep beneath layers of remorse and shame swarmed up: fangs, pain, the metallic stink of blood, so much blood, hot, sticky. A cry clawed at her throat but she clenched her teeth and bit the sound back. Cordelia lurched away. Vaguely aware of treading on Thorn's foot, she pushed past him to put some distance between herself and the vampire.

"What's the matter, lass?" Michael strode toward her, confusion creasing his forehead.

He was about to put his arms around her, comfort her; she read the intent on his face. If he embraced her while her defenses were weak, she'd melt into his arms. She stepped away, pressed her back to the fence, and held up a restraining palm. "No, don't. Just—" She glanced from Michael to

Nightshade, noted the stalker's tight lips, clenched jaw. "—just leave me alone." Her hand found the soft tapestry bag at her side, pushed inside to reach the comforting warmth of Tamsy's sleeping body.

Michael halted and turned, scanning the area, a puzzled look on his face. "There's nothing to be scared of yet." Cordelia shivered. If he'd met Nightshade's father, he'd understand her fear of nightstalkers.

After a few minutes, the tension eased from her shoulders sufficiently for her to move away from the fence. Her heart still raced, but she was in control again. Thorn watched her, squinting with concern while he rubbed his foot. "All right, Dee?"

She wished he hadn't talked her into letting him come. His only power, weak glamour, wouldn't protect him from harm.

"Let's get a move on," Nightshade said, giving his words a critical edge.

Michael touched his hand to his forehead in an exaggerated salute, then pointed along the path. "Onward and upward. Nightshade first, Thorn second, Cordelia third. I'll bring up the rear. I don't want to leave you two behind again."

"Huh!" Nightshade turned on his heel and stomped off through the gate. Thorn waited for Cordelia to reach him, then pulled her into a hug. She returned the embrace, proud of the young man he'd become, yet also sad he was no longer her little boy.

As they made their way along a path between the prickly pine-scented branches, they met five groups of walkers coming toward them. Finally, she heard the rushing of water. After the path descended to the river's edge, they walked beside the water for a short distance, then the white tumble of Sgwd yr Eira falls appeared through the trees.

* * *

Michael paused as they approached the cascading waterfall, a tremor of anticipation running through him. He'd only felt half alive since Fin was trapped. Now he was one hidden door away from entering Gwyn ap Nudd's realm and getting his nephew released.

"Sgwd yr Eira falls," he said under his breath, scanning the area for humans. "Now the work begins." He snapped his fingers at Thorn. "Give me the instructions you photocopied from *A Thief's Guide to Unlocking Magical Doors.*"

Cordelia's eyebrows shot up when Thorn dug in his back pocket and pulled out a folded sheet of paper. She stepped closer and peered over Michael's arm when he took the page and started reading. "The door should be behind the falls."

All four of them looked up together. A sheet of bubbly green water pelted down onto a stepped rocky ledge before thundering into the pool below.

"How the heck do we get behind it?" Thorn asked.

"There's a path behind the cascade. 'Tis obviously not visible from this angle." Michael took a step forward and paused for Cordelia to move aside so he could squeeze past on the slippery rocks. Her cat poked its head out of her bag, whiskers twitching, eyes wide with curiosity.

"Shame you're not a sniffer dog, fur ball." He rubbed a knuckle behind Tamsy's ear. "You could sniff out the door for us."

"She's not frightened of water like ordinary cats. I'll ask her to take a look." Cordelia crouched, scooped the cat out of the bag, and gently set the creature on its feet. After a delicate shake, the cat turned to lick the fur on its shoulder. Michael waited, curious to see how Cordelia would give the cat instructions. She crouched and rested her hand lightly on its back. Then she straightened and watched the cat pick its way along the path toward the falls.

In profile, Cordelia's small nose tilted up at the tip. Her lips glimmered temptingly with a trace of pearly lip gloss.

She watched her cat, her tongue pressed to the corner of her mouth in concentration.

Whenever he saw her at Trevelion Manor, she gave the impression of being self-contained, aloof. Yet when she let her guard down, she was warm, vulnerable, and strangely alluring. Something about the quality of her touch mystified him: soothing, yet arousing at the same time.

With a wave of certainty that stilled his breath, he wanted to kiss her. When Fin was safe and they returned to Cornwall, he'd take her away somewhere quiet. He'd kiss her for hours until she melted in his arms and begged him to live the image they'd seen in her divining mirror.

He cleared his throat, gave himself a shake. Best concentrate on what the cat was doing.

Tamsy stopped near the waterfall to lap at a puddle. Her little pink tongue curled at the edges like a rose petal. The cat glanced back at Cordelia, then disappeared behind the waterfall.

"Tread quietly so we don't startle her," Cordelia said as she moved forward.

Michael followed, his gaze sliding down to her neat, heart-shaped bottom. The instinctive stir of need low in his belly made him groan inwardly. He ran a hand over his face.

Behind the falling sheet of water, they discovered an uneven rocky path leading to the woods on the other side of the river. Cordelia crouched at the edge of the tumbling water, just clear of the misty spray, and watched Tamsy sniff along the moss-covered rock wall behind the falls.

When Michael stopped, Nightshade's hand landed on his shoulder. He had to make a conscious effort to relax and accept the touch. Now wasn't the time to break his bond with Nightshade and start the inevitable arguments and bad feeling.

For five minutes, the cat wandered back and forth, sniffing and scratching at the ground. Michael thought this had more to do with the smell of rats and voles than searching for the door to the Underworld. But he was proved wrong when she stood on her hind legs, scratched at the moss, and mewed.

"What have you found, poppet?" Cordelia stepped forward and traced her fingers over the wall by Tamsy's paws. Michael followed her through the cool cloud of spray onto the path behind the waterfall. He bent to examine the wet, mossy rock face, dotted with clumps of ferns. A whisper of breeze brushed his face. He was almost sure the draft came through the wall.

"There's a crack." Cordelia used a sharp stone to scrape the moss away, then ran her fingers up and down a fissure in the rock. "Look." She pointed to a symbol carved in the stone. "The sign of the maze represents the Underworld. That's promising."

Michael took the stone from her hand and cleared away the moss higher up where she couldn't reach. He felt beneath the shadowy overhang of a rocky outcrop. "There's a hole, but I can't get me finger in." Looking down, he tapped the base of the rock wall with his boot. "Can you hear an echo as though there's a space behind, lass?"

Cordelia put her ear to the rock while Michael kicked the wall. She screwed up her nose in frustration, giving a cute little huff. "Don't know." She grabbed the stone from his hand and cleared more moss from the base of the wall. Michael squatted beside her.

Their knees bumped. Her head jerked up. She opened her mouth, then snapped it shut and returned to her task, hugging her knees to her body with her free arm. He remembered her adamant denial that there could be intimacy between them. A plan of seduction had just started forming in his mind when a huge hunk of rock smashed onto the path a few feet away.

"Shit!" Nightshade and Thorn jumped back. Nightshade slapped at the dirty splatters on his black jeans.

"Where in the Furies did that come from?" Michael left

Cordelia scratching at the rock behind the falls and followed the other two men into the open. He shoved his hands on his hips and stared up at the rock face.

Movement caught his eye at the exact moment Thorn pointed and shouted: "Look. There's someone . . . something at the top of the cliff."

A lumbering brown form ducked behind a boulder. A moment later, another missile hurtled down toward them. They scattered, Michael retreating beneath the waterfall, the other men running back up the path.

More rocks followed in quick succession. Some rolled into the water; some smashed, scattering sharp shards in all directions. Michael turned his back, putting himself between the flying fragments and Cordelia.

She wrapped her arms around Tamsy and pressed her face against the cat's fur.

When the barrage ceased, Michael looked up. "What's your problem?" he shouted.

Silence met his enquiry.

"Right." He gritted his teeth and beckoned Nightshade. "Get up there and stop the idiot before one of us is hurt."

"Can I go with him?" Thorn asked, breathless with excitement.

"Not unless you've sprouted wings in the last few minutes, lad."

"Oh." Thorn looked crestfallen. Nightshade pulled off his coat and shoved it into the young man's arms. He popped his hat on Thorn's head, then stepped back where he had room to spread his wings. With a grunt, he thrust up from the ground with his powerful thighs, the draft from his flapping wings making them dip their heads.

Nightshade ducked and dived between the trees. Then he disappeared behind a rock, and a pitiful wailing filled the air. A few minutes later, the stalker reappeared with a hulking creature suspended by its collar. Their descent was more of a controlled fall than actual flight. From a few feet up,

Nightshade dropped the culprit in a heap before landing hard, knees bent, breathing heavily.

They all stared down at dirty brown hair, a wrinkled face covered with a tangled beard, and a thick dirt-encrusted coat tied at the waist with frayed, greasy string. The creature's feet were bare, the size of dinner plates, each trimmed with eight stubby toes.

The instant after Michael had taken in its appearance the stench hit him. He lurched back, a hand to his mouth. "Sweet bejesus." Bile stung the back of his throat and he swallowed. He drew in clean air to clear his nose.

Nightshade cursed and plunged his hands into the river, rubbing them vigorously. "If I've caught lice from that thing, someone's going to be sorry."

"Why were you throwing rocks at us?" Cordelia asked, stepping up beside Michael.

The creature's beady eyes glinted through the filthy mass of hair. "My job," it squeaked in a surprisingly high voice.

"What job?" Michael ground out. If any of those rock shards had hit Cordelia's face, she could have been scarred for life.

The creature huddled into a tighter ball, covering its head with two grubby hands.

"You're all right. He won't hurt you." Cordelia laid a hand on Michael's arm. As if by magic, the anger drained out of him.

"I won't hurt you," Michael repeated dutifully, infusing his voice with reassurance and compulsion. "Just tell us why you're here."

"Guard the gate." The beady eyes blinked behind the greasy knots of hair.

"The gate to the Underworld?" Cordelia crouched at Michael's side, taking herself down to the creature's level.

The shaggy head bobbed up and down.

Cordelia rose to her feet and leaned in to Michael, speaking softly. "I think it's a coblynau, one of the Welsh mine fairies. We passed mines earlier, so they'd be in this area. They're not really dangerous."

Michael slanted her a sideways glance. "If one of those rocks had landed on your head, lass, you wouldn't be saying that."

She frowned and gave one of her little huffs. "At least we know we're in the right place."

Michael nodded. She had a point. He turned his attention back to the coblynau. "You're going to open the gate into the Underworld for us."

"Oh no, no, no." The creature hugged its head tighter and wailed. "Them Teg ain't nice to coblys. They'll hurt me."

"Aye, well, join the club." Michael felt short on sympathy after the last two days.

Thorn prodded the creature with the toe of his shoe and the volume of the wailing went up a decibel.

"Good gracious, Thorn." Cordelia edged around the creature and grabbed Thorn's arm, pulling him back a couple of steps. "Don't you dare kick the poor thing. I hope I raised you with more respect for other beings than that."

"And if you get lice, you'll be walking home," Nightshade added.

Tamsy padded out from behind the waterfall and eyed the coblynau, the end of her tail flicking. With a screech, the filthy bundle scrabbled backward at a surprising speed, forcing Cordelia and Thorn to jump aside into the shallow water at the edge of the river.

"Keep it away." A dirty hand pointed at Tamsy.

Cordelia climbed back on the path and shook her feet, water leaking from her boots. "You don't like cats?" she snapped waspishly. Her charitable attitude had obviously not survived the dunking. Michael's lips twitched when she squelched past him and scooped Tamsy into her arms. "Unlock the gate to the Underworld, and I promise I won't let her attack you."

The coblynau whined and twitched, then heaved onto

two stubby legs. Still moaning to itself about the Teg, the creature waddled toward the waterfall. Michael covered his nose and stepped back when the thing passed him. It pulled a stick from a pocket and dragged the pointed end around the fissure in the rock they'd found earlier. The stick sank beneath the overhang until the rock door shifted with a clunk and hiss of air.

The coblynau looked at them, the only evidence of its face two eyes gleaming through the hair. "Get inside. Must shut t'door again."

The creature wedged a shoulder in the gap and pushed the door open just enough for Michael to squeeze through sideways. Cordelia dropped Tamsy into her bag and waited behind him. Thorn stood next in line, with Nightshade last.

Michael felt strange heading up the line, giving the orders, when all his life he'd been the follower, behind either Troy or Niall.

"Once we're through, we stick together," Michael said, "no matter what we find on the other side."

Chapter Five

Cordelia hugged her cat bag to her side as she slipped through the door in the rock after Michael. Cool, damp darkness pressed around her. When the coblynau closed the door behind them, the shaft of light filtering through the doorway would be cut off, leaving them blind.

Her heart thumped, and her mouth dried. She fumbled at the zipped pocket on the cat bag, her fingers clumsy in haste. With a spurt of relief, her hand closed around the tiny flashlight Michael had packed. She thumbed the switch and pulled the light from her bag.

Thorn's warm body pressed behind her in the narrow space, while the rocks resounded with the thud of the door. Her tiny light hardly penetrated the thick darkness. But the beam was enough to illuminate Michael's form, enough to see she wasn't back in the limbo of in-between.

"I'd better have the flashlight," Michael said, his fingers closing around her hand.

"No!" Panic gripped, her pulse skittering. She waited a moment for the dread to pass. "I'd rather hold the light."

His shoulders rose and fell. "Fair enough, lass. You'd better go up front then."

How considerate of him not to argue the point, or tease her about being afraid of the dark. She sidled past him, his warm hand on her back steadying her.

With the weak beam of light aimed at the ground, she walked forward, one small step at a time, watching for loose rocks or holes. The temperature plunged as the path angled down.

"There's magic at work in this tunnel. Feel the chill?" she asked over her shoulder.

"Better be keeping a watch out for traps, then," Michael answered.

The murmur of trickling water accompanied their progress. Cold drips plopped on her head every few yards. Goose bumps rose on her arms, even beneath the layers of her sweater and jacket. With just a T-shirt, Thorn must be freezing.

Cordelia stopped, felt inside her bag, and gently extracted Tamsy's crocheted blanket from underneath her. The poor cat mewed indignantly, but she wouldn't be cold, snuggled against the bag's fleece lining. She gave the blanket a shake, before reaching past Michael to press the woolen square into Thorn's hands. "Put this around you, and no arguments."

With mumbled thanks, he wrapped it over his shoulders. Proving, she supposed, that he must be cold.

In the faint beam of light, her breath formed a misty cloud as she moved forward again.

"How much farther?" Thorn asked, his words fractured by a shiver.

"Hang in there, lad," Michael said. Then his fingers brushed her shoulder. "You doing all right, sugarplum?"

She smiled at the name. A moment later, she realized he'd *intended* to raise her spirits. Intellectually, she already knew Michael was kind because he'd taken an interest in Thorn when her ward badly needed a man's example. But because Michael always joked and teased, she'd dismissed his kindness as an affectation designed to win friends and gain attention. Strange how she'd got him so wrong.

"There's a light at the end of the tunnel." Michael laughed, the rich deep sound of his voice echoing off the rocks. "Always wanted to say that."

Cordelia looked up, eyes wide with surprise. She'd been

so busy thinking about Michael, she hadn't noticed the light, or the last few minutes of tramping along in the dark. "I wonder what's out there."

"Get moving and we might find out," Nightshade snapped.

Cordelia picked up the pace, her eyes flicking between the path and the growing arch of light ahead.

"If you believe the tales, Gwyn lives in a glass castle on an island in the middle of an enchanted lake," Michael said.

"Enchanted how?" Thorn asked, his voice steadier, which made Cordelia realize the temperature had risen.

"The tales vary, but 'tis usually full of water nymphs or sirens who entice travelers to a watery grave. And so they reach the Underworld, but not the way they planned."

Cordelia jerked to a halt. Michael crashed into her back, knocking the wind from her lungs for a few seconds. "Water nymphs?" she squeaked.

"Aye, lass."

"You're sure?"

"'Tis just a tale. Don't go worrying yet. We'll probably find there's not even a lake."

Nausea burned in her stomach. She didn't want Thorn anywhere near a water nymph. She stepped away from the others and beckoned Michael. "Thorn might be traumatized. I don't think he's even slept with a female yet."

Michael laughed. "I doubt traumatized is the term he'd use. But don't worry, I'll keep him safe if need be."

Cordelia moved forward again, her sensible nonslip boots dragging through the pebbles on the floor. She wished she hadn't allowed Thorn to come. She wasn't keen on the thought of watching a water nymph rub her body over Michael, either. Watching him with a woman in her divination mirror was a very different matter from seeing a female with him in the flesh. As the arch of light grew larger, she squinted, trying to see the terrain outside. Branches hung over the exit. Grass and heather sprouted from the ground.

She trod in something squishy and looked down to find sheep's droppings.

With a mixture of trepidation and relief, she walked out into the light. Acres of purple heather-clad moorland extended to the base of snowcapped mountains. The jagged peaks surrounded a valley. At the lowest point sparkled a huge lake with a rocky island in the center. Perched on one side of the island was a gray castle, ribbons of smoke rising at intervals along the ramparts.

"Part of your story is accurate," Cordelia said in a flat voice.

"Does that mean there'll be water nymphs?" Thorn asked eagerly, bumping up beside her. He still had Tamsy's blanket around his shoulders. The blue crocheted square was even hairier than she'd expected. It was probably too much to hope the water nymphs would be frightened of cats.

Tamsy poked her head out of the bag and sniffed the air. She wriggled up, hooking her front paws on the side. Cordelia lowered the bag to the ground so she could jump out. "Are you hungry, Tamsy Tink?" She extracted a packet of cat treats from the bag's side pocket and sprinkled a few on her palm.

"I'm starving." Thorn delved into her bag. She slapped away his hand and gave him a chocolate bar from her pocket. Then she held one out to Michael, who grinned, and another to Nightshade, who scowled, but took the bar with mumbled thanks.

Wandering a few yards away, she chewed her snack and scanned the lake for any sign of movement. Laid out before her, the dark blue waters sparkled in the sun like a photo from a tourist brochure.

Thorn sat on a rock beside her and took a bite of chocolate. "I didn't think the Underworld would look like this."

"This can't be the Underworld." A few fluffy clouds hung in the azure sky as if for decoration. "It's too pretty."

Michael squeezed her elbow. The sensation zinged

through every cell in her body, yet no longer frightened her. "This is the land of the Tylwyth Teg," he said. "I'm thinking the entry to the Underworld will be on the island."

"It was getting dark when we came through the door." Cordelia raised her eyebrows and glanced at the sun.

Michael shrugged. "Maybe time stands still here. Your guess is as good as mine."

"Better make tracks," she said, gathering the chocolate wrappers. She turned back to retrieve her bag. Her step faltered. Nightshade held Tamsy in his arms, petting beneath her chin. Cordelia let her senses flow to Tamsy, sensed her pleasure, smelled the sweetness of the almond oil on Nightshade's skin. Gut instinct told her to snatch her cat from danger, yet Tamsy's sense of self-preservation was sharp, and all she radiated was contentment.

Jaw tight, Cordelia collected her bag and cast her cat a disbelieving look.

After a thirty-minute walk along narrow animal trails winding between the clumps of heather and lumps of rock, they reached the edge of the lake. Michael stared back the way they'd come and pointed to the rocky outcrop where they'd emerged. "Everyone take a good look and assign that view to memory. We'll probably be needing to leave that way."

Cordelia searched for landmarks: a bent tree, a rock formation in the shape of a horse. Planning their route out was optimistic when none of them knew if it would even be possible to leave. The tension in her shoulders made her back ache.

"I don't see any water nymphs, worse luck," Thorn announced, hands on hips as he examined the lake.

"No, looks like that part of the tale is wrong." Michael pulled a sheet of notes from his pocket. They all leaned in to read. Cordelia took a brief glance, but couldn't concentrate. The rippling body of water drew her like a magnet. She longed to strip off her clothes and dive under the surface, immerse herself in the element that sang in her soul. But she was always disappointed when she swam, because her wards cut her off from the revitalizing energy. Movement caught her eye. She stared at the lake, afraid to blink in case she missed something. She pressed her lips together, anxiety rising. About ten yards away, a female head bobbed into view, her flowing hair spread around her like a green silky cloak. Her eyes met Cordelia's.

The creature was beautiful, with large dark eyes, a small nose, and full lips. The lake wasn't home to a water nymph but something far more dangerous. *A Siren that would tempt the men to a watery grave.*

"You see anything, Dee?" Thorn asked, putting his arm around her shoulders as the Siren disappeared from view.

Cordelia sucked air through her mouth and shook her head. She wanted to tell Michael about the Siren before the others found out.

"Right." Michael walked to the waterline. "According to our notes, somewhere around the shore there should be a boat to allow visitors to cross."

Cordelia needed to find out if the Siren was alone. If her little group crossed in a boat, she could protect the men from one Siren, maybe even two, but if there were more, their attraction would overwhelm her ability to hold the men's attention.

She must keep the men off the lake until she was sure.

"I see the boat." Nightshade had climbed to the top of a massive hunk of rock protruding ten feet out of the ground. He pointed over the water. "There's a jetty by the castle."

Michael clambered onto the rock beside Nightshade and stared toward the island. "Aye. There's a boat all right. And 'tis coming this way."

"I don't believe they're coming for us. That would be too easy." Cordelia's stomach clenched and nausea burned in her chest at the thought of meeting more Teg, and worse, the King of the Underworld. She wanted to rescue Fin, but a big part of her just wanted to be back in Cornwall, in her sitting room overlooking the garden.

With a soft call, she attracted Tamsy's attention. She stroked her cat's head, let their minds meld. She relaxed into the warm glow of love, then silently instructed Tamsy to help her see into the water.

When Thorn leaped up the rocks to join Michael and Nightshade, Cordelia urged Tamsy to follow him.

"Are you wanting a hand up, Cordelia?" Michael shouted.

"No. I'm fine." She stroked the end of her plait while she waited for Tamsy to settle, then melded her mind with her familiar's and stared toward the lake through her cat's eyes.

Silver clouds of tiny fish swept through the water. In the deepest part of the lake, she caught sight of the Siren twisting and rolling in a solitary dance. She would call one of the men, probably the strongest spirit. *Michael.* Cordelia must ensure he didn't end up lured to a watery grave.

Fifteen minutes later, Michael jumped down from the rock beside her with his jacket slung over his shoulder; his biceps bunched beneath the sleeve of his T-shirt. Cordelia dragged her gaze away from his body and stared at the island.

"I'm sensing a presence in the water, lass."

She nodded. "It's a Siren. She poked her head out of the water earlier." She hadn't expected the men to sense the Siren before the creature was ready to reveal herself. She had only spotted it because her nature was so closely bound to the water. Michael's perceptiveness proved he was unusually sensitive to other life-forms. She should have figured out from his strong psychic presence that he was more powerful than anyone suspected.

Michael rested a shoulder against the rock at her side and leaned closer to speak softly. "Do you think she'll be causing us a problem on the crossing?"

They both stared toward the boat moving inexorably closer.

"Who will?" Nightshade descended from the air before them, wings outstretched. He landed elegantly on one foot like a ballet dancer. He shook back his hair and snapped his wings closed with a crack that echoed across the water.

With a smile, Nightshade tapped his ear. "I can hear your heart beating, bard, so whispering does you little good."

"There's a Siren here." Cordelia waved a hand toward the lake. "Odds are she'll try to entice one of you into the water."

Thorn appeared at Cordelia's side with Tamsy in his arms. "Will she want to . . . you know . . . have sex with us?"

"Thorn!" Cordelia gave him a quelling look. She turned the same look on Michael when he chuckled.

"You're thinking of water nymphs, lad." Michael walked around her and slapped the younger man on the shoulder. "All the Siren wants is to call you to your death. You'll have to find yourself a sexy little water nymph when we get home. Maybe I'll join you. I've yet to have that pleasure meself."

Cordelia wanted to melt into the rock at her back and disappear. If they ever found out her mother had been a water nymph, she'd die of embarrassment. Now she felt she had to defend the Siren. Although they were far more primitive than water nymphs, she identified only too closely with the creature's longings.

"She's lonely," Cordelia burst out.

Michael shot her an inquisitive look, and her cheeks flared with heat.

"She wants a mate," she explained. "She doesn't know you'll drown if she calls you into the depths with her."

"Aye, but that does not change the fact she's still a danger to us." His expression gentled. For a terrifying second, she thought he was so perceptive he'd guessed her secret. But he turned away, and the moment passed.

"Which of us will she tempt?" Thorn asked, his voice now subdued.

"Like any other female, she'll be attracted to power."

Nightshade tossed back his hair. Cordelia assumed he was intimating the Siren would call him; then he turned his silver gaze onto Michael. "She'll call the bard."

They all looked at Michael. He blinked in surprise and nodded toward Nightshade. "Why not you?"

Nightshade didn't answer, just gave Michael a long level look, the glittering water reflecting in his silver eyes.

"He's right," Cordelia whispered, a touch incredulous that she and Nightshade agreed on something.

Michael walked to the water's edge and stared silently toward the boat. The swish and splash of the oars intruded on the silence. After a long minute he turned back to face them. "So how do we play this?"

Cordelia swallowed, her throat tight with nerves and an edgy excitement that scared her. "I can help you resist her call."

Out of the corner of her eye, she saw Nightshade staring at her through narrowed eyes. He must be able to hear her racing heart.

"Aye then, lass. We'll trust you." Michael glanced over his shoulder at the water as the swishing of the oars came closer. "The boat's nearly here. Better get ready."

Thorn detached Tamsy's claws from his shirt and deposited her in the cat bag. Closing her eyes, Cordelia stroked Tamsy and relaxed. She could protect the men if she stayed alert.

She straightened her back. "Right, although we expect the Siren to go for Michael, we must prepare for her to switch her target if she fails." The boat scraped on the gravel at the water's edge, and the old Teg boatman beckoned them. Cordelia followed Michael and Nightshade, Thorn at her side. She could easily hold Thorn's focus and protect him, but Nightshade was a different matter. Her insides trembled at the thought of having to get close to him mentally or physically. Then she had an idea.

"Nightshade."

He paused and looked back at her warily. She unhooked her cat bag from her shoulder and, with a flash of trepidation, held her precious cat out to him. He frowned. "You take Tamsy. Keep your hand on her body during the crossing. Through her I'll feel if you're in trouble." His breath hissed out in what sounded like relief. With a nod, he grabbed the bag and hung the strap over his shoulder. Tamsy poked her head out and mewed at Cordelia. "It's all right, sweetheart. Be a good girl and stay safely inside."

"What time is it here?" Michael asked as he stepped into the boat. The elderly Teg boatman stared straight ahead without answering.

"The Tylwyth Teg could do with a course in manners," Cordelia whispered to Thorn as they approached the boat.

Nightshade sat beside Michael while Cordelia took the bench opposite them, with Thorn at her side. When they were all seated, the boatman braced an oar against the rocks and pushed the boat free of the gravel.

Cordelia gripped Thorn's hand. "You keep hold of me until we reach the other side. No matter what happens, don't let go." His chest rose and fell rapidly, his palm damp in her grip. She squeezed his hand, her heart pinching at the hint of panic in his eyes.

"What do you want me to do, lass?"

"Michael." Cordelia had to swallow before she could continue. "You need to focus on something to resist the Siren. Hold my other hand." Her insides quivered as his hand slid around hers, engulfing it. The allure undulated through her body, warm and slow, contained within her wards. She prayed her fear for their safety would damp down her response to him. "Look into my eyes. Whatever happens, don't look away. Concentrate completely on me, and I'll concentrate on you."

She steeled herself. Focused on the dark points of Michael's pupils, she tried to hold his attention yet still keep her distance. *Impossible.*

"I have a little idea how to help us hold our focus," Michael whispered, a smile in his voice. Before she could comment, the deep blue of his eyes drew her in, the tempting depths closing around her like the welcome embrace of warm water.

She found herself walking through the great hall beneath Trevelion Manor. She tensed, expecting the usual evening crowd, but the hall was deserted. A skitter of surprise raced through her. Before the sensation faded, she'd forgotten why she was surprised. A pale blue, silky dress flowed around her body as she walked. Her loose hair caressed her bare arms. Michael walked beside her, clasping her hand firmly in his. He stopped in the center of the hall, pulled her closer, and held the back of her hand against his chest so she could feel the beat of his heart. His lips curved in a wide seductive grin, his eyes twinkling. Warmth melted through her, pulsing hot in her veins. The warbling lilt of an Irish tin whistle drifted into her consciousness, its tune circling around her head. Michael placed his hand on the small of her back, warm and firm. "Dance with me, lass," he whispered against her ear.

There was a reason she shouldn't let him touch her, but her thoughts slipped from her grasp. His breath against her cheek sent shivers racing across her skin. She rested her hand on his shoulder, and his muscles flexed beneath her grip. The air whispered between her lips in a rush as he drew her closer, pressed his nose to her temple. "You smell of sweet peas."

"Michael." *Michael, Michael* . . . She repeated his name, again and again in her head. If she stopped, she might lose him.

He smiled, stroked the hair back from her face, his fingers gentle against her skin. "Move for me."

Her feet followed his small steps as he swayed around in a slow circle.

"I love the color of your eyes. Sometimes they're soft as a dove's wing, sometimes they rage like stormy seas." He eased her closer, cupped his hand behind her head, and pressed his cheek against her hair. "Ah, Cordelia. This feels good, does it not, lass?"

His lips brushed her temple. Heat swirled down to her toes, back up to bloom in her cheeks. He touched the side of his nose to hers, his breath on her lips. She tilted her face up, every cell in her body yearning for his kiss.

A bump on her knees shot pain up her legs. She jerked back from Michael, her pulse jumping.

"Dee! We're here, Dee." Thorn's strident tone pierced her stupor. He tugged on her hand.

She blinked at the sight of Thorn kneeling awkwardly in the bottom of the boat beside her, gripping the hand she was resting on Michael's shoulder.

"Let me go," Thorn ground out between clenched teeth.

Cordelia glanced around, confused. "Have we crossed the lake?"

Thorn snatched his hand from hers, then leaped out of the boat as if it were on fire. Cordelia's gaze followed his flight and met Nightshade's steely look. Only then did reality hit her: the firm warmth of Michael's arms around her, the herbal fragrance of his hair near her nose. She and Michael were kneeling in the boat, his arms holding her close to his body.

His fingers flexed against her back. "Looks like your strategy worked, lass." His lips brushed her temple, smooth as warm silk. Shame and shock tangled inside her. Cordelia pushed back, rocking the boat so violently Nightshade staggered and nearly dropped Tamsy's bag.

"It's easy to resist the Siren when she ignores us," she snapped.

"She didn't," Nightshade said in an accusing tone.

"Didn't what?"

His nostrils flared impatiently. "Ignore us, woman. The Siren followed us the whole way across. You two were so engrossed I don't think you even knew where you were."

* * *

Michael watched Cordelia clamber from the boat, heedless of the water soaking her boots. She ran about ten yards up the shingle beach toward the castle and hugged her arms around her body.

Nightshade gave Michael a narrow look of disapproval, then stepped out of the boat cautiously, avoiding the water, and went to give the cat back to Cordelia.

The old Teg boatman ignored them, staring up at a window in the castle tower from which faint strains of music floated into the still air.

Michael heaved himself off his knees back onto the wooden bench seat and sighed. The pleasurable sensations lingering from the vision he'd shared with Cordelia slipped away. He'd intended to share an innocent visualization with her. But something strange had happened.

He loved females, was attracted to all types of them: human and fairy. When needed, his control was absolute. But not with Cordelia, it seemed. Inside her prim exterior churned an elemental sensuality bursting for release. He'd thought to entrance her to keep her occupied. Yet he'd been the one entranced. Given another few seconds, he'd have kissed her.

He slapped his palms on his thighs and stood, furious with himself. This was neither the time nor place for such behavior. Could he not even restrain himself long enough to rescue Finian?

Thorn stood on his own, staring at the ground with his hands jammed in the pockets of his jeans. Nightshade glared at Michael while Cordelia had her arms wrapped around herself. Michael walked up the pebbles feeling like a prize jerk. He halted a few feet from Cordelia and rubbed a hand over his mouth.

"I owe you an apology, lass. Don't know what happened. I thought to distract us with a harmless visualization, but things got out of hand."

She sucked on her bottom lip, then looked up at him. "Thank you for being chivalrous, but the fault is mine."

He shook his head slowly. "Me lack of control is not your fault."

She looked away, a pretty pink coloring her cheeks. Instead of responding to him, she turned toward Thorn. "Sweetheart, come here."

The young man slouched closer, kicking the stones. She wrapped an arm around him and pressed her cheek to his. "I'm sorry I embarrassed you. Do you forgive me?"

Thorn hugged her while Cordelia stroked his hair.

"Correct me if I'm wrong, but I thought we'd come to speak to Gwyn ap Nudd." Nightshade wedged his hands on his hips, jaw clenched. When Michael smiled at him, trying to ease the tension between them, Nightshade turned away.

Michael pinched the tight muscles in the back of his neck. How in the Furies did Niall cope with leading a whole troop of piskies when he could barely cope with three people? He shook his head and turned to the Teg boatman, who was still staring at the castle. "We'll be needing to speak with Master Devin. Where do we go?" He expected the man to continue ignoring him, but the old Teg raised an arm and pointed to a door set into the wall on the side of the castle. That wasn't much help as the door was obviously the only way in.

While Cordelia whispered to Thorn, Michael went to Nightshade. The stalker glared at him as he approached. He wanted to tell his friend to just get over the incident and move on. But that would not ease the bad feelings between them. And he needed Nightshade on his side. "I'm sorry if what happened in the boat made you uncomfortable. Was not me intention."

Nightshade's silver eyes grazed over his face, tracked insolently down his body and back up. His nostrils flared and he hitched up his chin. "When I'm *uncomfortable*, you'll know it, bard."

Despite his apparent rejection of the apology, the tension

in his stance eased. It seemed that was the best Michael could hope for at the moment.

The crunch of stones behind him signaled that Cordelia and Thorn were ready to move on. Cordelia's expression appeared composed once more, and Thorn had lost his angry scowl.

"Time to do what we came for." After the temporary distraction of the experience in the boat, the reality of their situation crashed back on Michael. His gut churned as he made his way up the stone steps leading to the door into the castle.

The ancient wooden door was weather bleached, the hinges leaking rusty stains through the wood grain. Michael knocked, then tapped his fingers on his thigh while he waited for someone to answer.

"Try again." Cordelia's voice sounded tentative, as though she'd rather give up and go home.

He knocked twice more, getting no response. "Typical. We come all this way, and they won't answer the door." He'd expected to overcome perils before he gained access to the King of the Underworld's castle. He hadn't expected the biggest obstacle to be getting someone to open the blasted door.

A glance along the walls confirmed his first impression. On this side of the castle, the small curve of shingle beach provided the only solid ground. At each end, the lake lapped against rocks that rose sheer to the castle walls. If they could not enter through this door, they'd have to use the boat to reach the other side.

That would be a problem because the boat had now disappeared. He heaved a sigh and raised his fist to knock again.

"Just a moment." Cordelia stepped up beside him. "Probably a waste of time, but worth a try." She gripped the metal ring of the door latch and twisted. With a creak, the door swung inward.

Thorn laughed. Nightshade smiled reluctantly.

She glanced back, suppressing a triumphant grin.

"Hang on a minute." Michael went to the wall and banged his forehead against the granite a couple of times to knock some sense into his head. "Okay. That's done." He held out his hand, indicating she should precede him. "Brains before beauty."

"I can't win with that one, can I?"

"Nah, lass. Neither can I." He grinned. When she smiled back, heat flared in his groin as he remembered how her body had felt pressed against his in the boat. Prim on the outside, hot on the inside obviously hit his sweet spot.

As he followed her through the door, a dark-haired woman wearing a stained white apron over a brown dress walked around the corner in front of them. She would have been pretty without the puckered scar running through her eyebrow and across her cheekbone. She pulled up with a shriek and pressed a hand to her mouth. Her eyes flitted between Cordelia and Michael. "Are you human?"

The hope in her voice made him sorry to disappoint her. "No, lass."

She blinked, her curious gaze on Tamsy's bag. "You look human—or more human than the Teg."

"I'm a Cornish pisky," Cordelia said gently.

"Oh." The woman stared at them, then started to back away, her hand trailing along the wall.

"We're wanting to find Master Devin," Michael said, infusing his voice with reassurance.

Her shoulders dropped as some of the tension left her. "Master Devin isn't here. I'll fetch someone else."

"Not the Teg." The hint of panic in Cordelia's voice made Michael tense, but a flash of understanding crossed the human woman's face.

Michael flexed his fingers at his side. He'd considered what to do if Master Devin wasn't around. He could think of only one alternative. "Where would we find Gwyn ap Nudd?"

The woman's eyes flashed wide, and she stepped back. She stared at Michael for long seconds, then pointed an unsteady finger at the ceiling. "The king is to be found in the tower above us." She jerked her head to the side, indicating the direction from which she'd come. "The staircase is a short way back there."

Boots grated on the rough-hewn flagstone passage behind Michael. The woman screamed, a piercing sound so sudden and unexpected that Michael jumped. Wide-eyed, she turned and ran out of sight.

Michael glanced over his shoulder to see Nightshade standing behind him. "She obviously hasn't seen a nightstalker before."

Nightshade frowned and snapped his wings against his back. "I didn't even have my wings spread." He held his arms away from his body and looked down at himself with a frown. "What's so terrible about me?"

"Forget it," Michael said. All that mattered was persuading Gwyn ap Nudd to release Fin. Without Master Devin's advice, Michael would have to hope his silver tongue worked on the King of the Underworld.

Chapter Six

Damn Nightshade for spooking the human before she could be questioned. The woman must have sensed his predatory nature. Living among the Teg, her instinct for self-preservation would be sharp.

Cordelia followed Michael ten yards along the castle passage to an arched opening on the right where spiral stairs climbed steeply up a tower.

Michael paused at the foot of the staircase and looked back. He caught his bottom lip between his teeth and passed a questioning gaze over them all. "We ready for this?"

Cordelia dragged in a breath and heard Thorn do the same. She gripped his hand. He'd paled, making his green eyes seem huge and unnaturally bright. He'd talked her into bringing him and clearly he was regretting it now. So was she.

The small of her back tightened, jolting unease up her spine. In her experience, the attitude of a group's members reflected those of their leader. She wasn't looking forward to meeting the man who ruled the Tylwyth Teg.

"I'll go first. You bring up the rear, Nightshade," Michael said.

"Yes, bard. I know my place."

Michael pinched the bridge of his nose, then gave Nightshade a weary look. "Have we got a problem, you and me?"

Nightshade glanced away, lines of tension framing his

tight lips. Cordelia thought he wasn't going to answer, but finally he gave a single abrupt nod. "I have your back, bard."

Her neck prickled. She didn't want Nightshade at her back. She preferred to keep him where she could see him.

"Grand," Michael said, his tone laced with irony. "Let's be getting this over with."

As they climbed, Cordelia counted the stone steps to focus on something other than the nauseating storm roiling in her stomach. At a count of fifty, she paused to gaze out a tall narrow window overlooking the lake. The horse-shaped landmark she'd memorized stood out against the unnaturally blue sky. She prayed she'd soon pass beneath the rocky outcrop on her way home.

After another fifty steps, a second window gave a view of a quadrangle enclosed in the center of the castle. A few Tylwyth Teg made their way back and forth across the paved square where a fountain cascaded into a circular pool. Some of the Teg wore long white robes, others brown jerkins and trousers.

Thorn ducked his head into the opening beside her to take in the view. "D'you know what's strange?" He glanced up the dingy winding stairway, then back out the window. "If this guy's the king, why's he up at the top of this tower in what's got to be a pokey little room? Why isn't he in some grand hall on a throne or something?"

A trickle of unease ran down Cordelia's spine. She glanced at Michael.

"I was thinking the same thing meself, lad." Michael gave Thorn a slap on the back. Thorn grinned as though he'd won a prize.

"Do you think it's a trap?" Nightshade asked as the same thought formed in Cordelia's mind. She pinched her lips together. She hated the way she and Nightshade sometimes thought alike.

"'Tis a possibility I've been turning over in me head." Michael rested his hands on his hips, stared up the staircase, then looked at Nightshade. "Maybe we two should go ahead and check things out?"

Nightshade moved to pass her. She pushed out her elbow to block his way.

"No." Chills fluttered through her. She remembered the darkness that had invaded her divination mirror during her foretelling for Michael. She couldn't let him out of her sight in case something bad happened to him. "You two can go first, but Thorn and I will follow. We're not waiting here."

Michael gave her an appraising look. She fixed her mouth in an unrelenting line and met his gaze. He shrugged. "I'll not be arguing with you, lass, if it's determined you are." She was pleased he'd agreed, but surprised he had capitulated so easily.

While Nightshade sidled past her in the narrow stairwell, the scar on her neck from Dragon's bite tingled and her heart sprinted as though it wanted to run away. He paused and glanced back at her quizzically. She watched him from the corner of her eye but refused to meet his gaze in case she betrayed her fear. Dragon had thrived on exploiting weakness.

"You two hang back a couple of steps," Michael instructed with a nod toward her and Thorn. "If anything happens to me beautiful face, sugarplum, I'm counting on your brains to put matters right." He grinned at her, and her tension seeped away. Suddenly all she wanted to do was sit on the step, gaze out the window, and enjoy the glorious view.

Michael and Nightshade disappeared up the steps and around the corner. Gradually, the haze in her mind drifted away. With a jolt of annoyance, she realized she'd been fed a dose of silver tongue. No wonder Michael hadn't argued about her coming along.

She stood, shrugging away her lassitude and pulled on Thorn's arm. "Come on. Michael's gone," she snapped.

Thorn blinked and looked around. "Weren't we supposed to wait here?"

"That is *not* what I agreed to." Her sense of foreboding

blossomed like frost on glass. Her head pounded as she ran up the stairs, cursing Michael. The temperature plummeted and she halted.

"What?" Thorn whispered.

"Magic." She pressed her cheek to the outer wall, trying to peer up the spiral stairs.

"Let Tamsy go first. She'll know if there's danger."

"Gods and goddesses." Cordelia pressed her aching temples. She should have thought of that. She eased Tamsy out from her bag and set her gently on her feet. "*Go find Michael*," she whispered mentally, sending the feel of his psychic signature. Tamsy mewed and trotted up the steps. Cordelia sat on the worn stone and melded her consciousness with Tamsy, looked through her eyes.

The magical chill shivered along the connection, penetrated Cordelia's bones, made her teeth ache. Strong magic guarded the stairway, which didn't bode well.

Tamsy drew level with the underside of a boot and the leg of a felled man. Cordelia's heart jumped, fearing for Michael before she realized she could still feel his presence beating strongly in her chest.

Her cat trotted past the prone figure of Nightshade and rubbed around Michael's legs as he dragged the stalker up the stairs. What had happened? Cordelia drummed her fingers on her thigh in frustration.

She withdrew from the link with Tamsy and cupped her hands around her mouth. "Michael?" she bellowed at the top of her voice, hoping her call carried up the stairs.

"Aye," he shouted back.

"What's happened to Nightshade?"

There was a moment's silence. "He passed out."

Cordelia pressed her fingers over her eyes to think. What sort of magical trap had Michael and Nightshade walked into? Why had the charm affected Nightshade but not Michael?

"Um, Dee," Thorn said.

She snapped open her eyes, and he pointed out the window. "They've heard us."

"Oh, rats' tails." Cordelia peered outside to see a growing cluster of Tylwyth Teg men gathered in the courtyard, gesturing angrily up at the window.

She pulled her head back inside at the thunder of boots on the steps below.

Cordelia clutched her empty bag to her chest. She glanced up and down the stairs, gnawing her lip. She'd rather brave the magic than a group of angry Teg. "Michael, we're coming up."

Thorn blinked a startled gaze at her when she grabbed his hand. They mounted the winding stairs until the chill of magic seeped into her bones.

Thorn's footsteps faltered. His eyelids fluttered.

"Thorn!" She jerked on his hand, snaring his attention. "Stay with me."

The strength drained from her legs as she pushed up the next two steps, her muscles stiff and icy cold. When she paused to gather her energy, Thorn sagged against the wall. "Wake up!" She slapped his cheeks. When that didn't rouse him, she pulled his arm over her shoulders. She managed another two steps before stumbling to her knees beneath his weight.

The sound of booted feet ahead dragged up her weary gaze. Michael's strong denim-clad legs appeared before her. He heaved Thorn's body off her and pulled the younger man to his feet. "How you coping, sugarplum?"

Her head weighed so much she barely managed a nod.

"Another ten steps, lass, and you're there. Follow me."

Michael half carried, half dragged Thorn the next few steps. The sight of his strong body, unaffected by the magic, reassured her and gave her strength. She focused her energy into her thighs, pushed herself up a step by sheer force of will. "Good, lass. I knew you were strong." The sweet stroke of his praise infused her with purpose. The next few steps were easier.

"Nearly there." Michael grinned back at her, causing a warm fuzzy feeling near her heart. Then he ran on ahead with Thorn.

When her foot landed on the next step, the stone dipped beneath her weight. She grabbed the wall for balance and blinked incredulously at her feet. The granite sank like wet sand, swallowing her boots. She tried to wrest her feet free but the harder she pulled, the deeper she sank.

Darkness impinged on her vision, spinning circles of shadow around her gaze so that only pinpricks of light remained. She opened her mouth to call Michael, but no sound came out. With a creeping sense of dread, she realized this wasn't an illusion designed to frighten, but a powerful magical trap.

Her fingers clutched at her empty cat bag. How would she survive without Tamsy's reassuring presence? She lost her balance, slapped down her palms to steady herself. The stone oozed over her hands, up her forearms, sucked her in with frightening speed.

Tamsy? She extended her senses. But as the slick substance engulfed her, all she heard was a deafening hum of nothingness.

Michael? The thought trickled out with no force behind it. They weren't bonded in any way, so he wouldn't hear her. By the time he noticed she was gone, he would be too late to rescue her.

Michael hitched Thorn's limp body higher and pulled him up another step. Who would have thought the lad was so damn heavy? Two more steps and the chill in Michael's bones eased. Another step and a warm breeze fluttered his hair as he drew level with a window. He snatched in a breath and let the air hiss out between his clenched teeth as he reached the landing at the top of the tower. Strength flowed back into his muscles. Thorn groaned and opened his eyes.

"What's up?" he mumbled.

"A charm set on the steps, lad. Nasty one, as well."

He eased Thorn down, back against the wall beside Nightshade, who was blinking and rubbing his eyes.

"My body felt heavy; then everything went black," Thorn said around a yawn.

"I don't remember what happened." Nightshade wriggled forward to stretch his wings from their cramped position.

Michael frowned. He'd been weakened but never thought he'd lose consciousness. Why had the charm affected them differently?

Stretching the muscles in his back, he turned to give Cordelia a hand up the last few steps.

The stairs were empty.

Tamsy mewed, a tentative, confused call. Michael stared, blinked; his heart missed a beat, then raced in his suddenly hollow chest.

The cat yowled, a piercing, anguished cry, shooting distress through Michael.

"Cordelia!"

With Tamsy scampering beside his feet, he ran down the steps to the point where he'd last seen Cordelia. He stared around the corner. Had she fallen? Surely, he'd have heard her shout? Lethargy stole up his legs. His lungs tightened, each breath a struggle to draw enough air.

Tamsy sniffed and scratched at the rocky steps. Trusting the cat's instinct, Michael kneeled beside her, looking for a break that would indicate a hidden trap, but the rock was solid. Chills raced across his skin, and a barely contained panic sawed at his mind.

Tamsy nibbled and clawed at the stone.

He pushed the frantic creature away, ran his palms over the step. The sensitive pad of his finger found a soft bump.

Fear swelled and nearly swallowed him as he recognized a

corner of the cat bag. He plucked at the tip of fabric with big clumsy fingertips.

"Dee!" Thorn shouted and descended a step.

"Keep away." Michael gasped with the effort of speaking. He cast Thorn a fierce look, loaded with warning. The young man backed up, eyes wide, until his back hit the wall.

"What's the matter, Michael?" Out of the side of his eye, Michael saw Nightshade scramble to his feet. He ignored the stalker and concentrated on catching hold of the tiny tab of fabric.

Little by little, he teased and twisted the corner of the cat bag out of the stone. Hope pulsed, yet this could mean nothing. She might have dropped the bag. The noisy footsteps ascending the stairs below came to a halt. Whoever pursued them knew better than to chance passing through the magical booby trap.

When he had the whole bag exposed, his heart stalled as the end of the looped strap was about to be released.

"Hurry," Thorn shouted, his voice an anguished cry.

With a careful pull, Michael revealed the end of the loop—and a hand, gripping so tightly the knuckles were white.

Tears sprang into Michael's eyes at the sight of Cordelia's death grip. He'd thought she was mentally stronger than the others, that she'd overcome the worst effects of the charm. He shouldn't have left her to make her own way.

Thorn wailed and half tripped, half jumped down the steps to his side. "Get back." Michael clutched a handful of the young man's shirt and shoved him away before he bumped Cordelia's hand and hurt her.

Nightshade grabbed Thorn under his arms and dragged him back to the landing.

"Don't make Michael have to rescue you too, boy," Nightshade growled.

Gently, Michael pulled on the strap. He watched in an agony of impatience as the rock softened, allowing Corde-

lia's slender hand and delicate wrist to slide free. The silver
ring on her finger had cut her skin. Blood seeped from the
wound, trickled down her arm.

Breathing through his mouth to fight his emotion, he
stroked her fingers so she felt him, knew she wasn't alone.
Tamsy nuzzled her hand and Cordelia's fingers twitched.
Michael maintained a steady tension on the strap. He worried that if he raised her too fast, the friction of the rock
might scrape her skin. Tamsy paced restlessly, rubbing
against his knees, mewing nervously, and fluttering her
small pink tongue on Cordelia's arm.

Thorn and Nightshade stood silently on the landing,
watching.

Muffled voices and movement sounded from below. Michael hoped the Teg who'd laid the trap came up the stairs.
Michael wanted to grind him into the steps.

His breath jammed as her shoulder appeared, then the
bare skin of her neck, her ear. The rock peeled back smoothly,
leaving no mark on her clothes or skin. When her face
emerged, Thorn's frantic gasps reached a crescendo.

Her eyes were closed, her head lolled to the side. Thorn
sobbed.

"She's alive," Michael snapped. "Use your senses, lad."

Tamsy licked Cordelia's face, mewing incessantly. Michael lifted the cat's tense furry body aside. She must have
understood the need to keep clear, because she stayed out of
the way, but her eyes never left Cordelia's face.

Carefully, Michael pulled Cordelia from the rock. He
collapsed to his knees, hugging her limp body against him.
The magic trap had leeched away much of his energy; he
struggled to find the strength to stand. Nightshade ran
down the steps and grabbed him beneath the arms. "Hold
her tight." He pulled Michael upright and helped support
Cordelia as they stumbled back up to the landing.

Michael flopped against the wall and slid down. Cordelia's body settled on his lap. He hugged her close, cupped her

face to his chest. The gentle ripple of her psychic presence trickled around the edges of his mind.

Thorn squatted beside him, gripped Cordelia's hand, and pressed it to his cheek. "I'm sorry, Dee."

"'Twas not your fault, lad. 'Twas mine." He had nearly lost her just walking up the steps. What on earth would they face when they went before Gwyn ap Nudd?

Cordelia drifted. A warm trickle of pleasure leaked into her depths, loosening the ties that held her beneath the impenetrable dark waters. The beat in her chest grew stronger; her mind pulsed with images of a man's smile—Michael. With a surge of understanding, she struggled free, reached up through the murky layers to find light.

Tamsy's presence hummed warm and fuzzy inside her, encouraging her to come back. Cordelia concentrated on her breath, in, out, the cascade of her water elemental nature cleansing her fear.

Breath caught as she recognized the feel of her limbs. Muscles ached from the battle she'd fought with the sucking stone. She flexed her fingers, found warm flesh beneath her touch. She sighed, snuggled, clutched, seeking something to hang on to so she wouldn't lose herself again.

"Dee?" Thorn's anxious tone made her heart contract. She longed to comfort him, but she wasn't ready yet.

She turned into Michael's warm embrace, inhaled the fragrance of his shirt and skin, mountain air, herbs, the tang of male, the elemental smell of earth, solid and steady.

"Cordelia, sugarplum."

Warm breath tickled her hair. The pliant silk of lips touched her temple.

The water inside her soul stirred to life.

Her fingers tightened. Corded muscle flexed within her grip.

"She's awake. She just won't open her eyes." The gruff accusation in Nightshade's voice sent her growing consciousness scurrying away to hide.

"Shh." A warm hand covered her ear. Muffled voices floated around her but she ignored them, enjoyed the soothing beat of Michael's heart against her ear.

A furry body squeezed into the space between her tummy and her thighs. Tamsy's purr vibrated through her solar plexus, winding her up like a clockwork toy coming to life.

With a deep breath, she let her eyelids flutter up. Two large gray eyes stared back at her unblinkingly. *You found me.*

Ripples of love and reassurance flowed along the link from Tamsy.

She focused on her body: feet, legs, tummy—squashed beneath cat. Hands, one sore, arms, shoulders, neck. *Bottom?*

She concentrated on her rear, on the firm thighs beneath her. Michael's thighs. *And other parts of him.* The lapping swell of her allure surged like a freak wave on a calm sea. For a moment, she feared her restrictive wards had been scraped from her skin. But the sensual energy circled inside her, unable to escape.

Michael. His name drifted around her brain, didn't make it to her lips. She tried again. "Michael."

"Aye, sugarplum. You're safe."

Michael's lips brushed her forehead. She wanted so much to raise her mouth to his that she pressed her face harder into his chest.

"Are we going through the damn door today or not?" The gravelly sound of Nightshade's voice grated over raw nerves.

Cordelia opened her eyes, turned her head, met the simmering silver slits of his critical gaze. There had never been any love lost between them, but now he seemed to hate her as much as she hated him.

"Give her a moment or two to recover." Michael's voice rumbled through his chest beneath her ear.

Nightshade flashed his fangs, but the expected jab of fear failed to strike.

"Dee." Thorn kneeled in front of her, blocking her view of Nightshade. He gripped her uninjured hand.

"I'm all right, sweetheart."

Reluctantly, she eased herself from Michael's embrace and wrapped her arms around Thorn. "I'm glad you made it up those steps safely. I'd never forgive myself if anything happened to you."

When Nightshade moved to stretch his wings, she caught sight of the small wooden door in the wall behind him and she remembered why they were there. She pushed to her feet, and turned to Michael. His blue eyes caressed her with gentle concern.

"Thank you." She hadn't intended to whisper, but the words caught huskily in her throat. He raised a hand to touch her hair. The intimacy should have been uncomfortable, yet she felt as though she'd been waiting for him all her life.

His fingers brushed her ear, drawing a small needy hum from her throat. His eyes locked on hers, held her captive in their blue depths. "There's something between us, sugarplum. Something I want to investigate when we get home." A vision flashed through her mind, sweaty bodies, tangled sheets, groans of pleasure. She blinked and her knees wobbled. Michael's hand steadied her elbow while a smile tucked itself into the corners of his mouth.

Michael was everything she desired. That made him the most dangerous person in the world.

Chapter Seven

Michael reluctantly let his hand drop from Cordelia's elbow as she stepped away. The front of his body tingled where she'd been snuggled against him—and a certain part of him did more than tingle.

He pushed out a breath, expelling the lingering sense of her from his mind. When they arrived home, he must settle things with Nightshade before he became involved with Cordelia.

Nightshade stamped his feet and snapped his wings against his back, indicating he was annoyed. Best to distract him before he upset Cordelia again. "Hey, boyo." Michael slapped the nightstalker's shoulder. "You going to knock for us?"

Michael eyed the small wooden door set in the wall. In a few moments, they'd finally confront Gwyn ap Nudd and have a chance to negotiate Fin's release. His heart skipped a beat as Nightshade raised his fist to knock. When his hand met the door, it disappeared soundlessly through the wood.

Nightshade gave an unmanly yelp and yanked his hand back. "Shit!"

Michael suppressed a laugh. Thorn wasn't as diplomatic. He hooted and grinned at Cordelia, whose lips remained tight, even though her eyes sparkled with mirth.

Nightshade glared at them and ruffled his wings.

"'Tis an illusion, boyo," Michael said.

Cocking his head, the stalker gave him a narrow-eyed look. "You don't say, bard. I'd never have guessed."

Still grinning inside, Michael scanned the walls with his peripheral vision and spotted the real door, taller and wider than the illusion. Nightshade noticed it at the same time and knocked hard enough to rattle the hinges.

After the boom of the knock faded, silence fell. A strained tension hummed between them while they waited. The snap of a bolt from inside set Michael's pulse tripping as the door swung inward.

He'd expected a Tylwyth Teg to answer the door. The small creature framed in the doorway couldn't have been more different from the Welsh fairies. About two and a half feet tall, with pink hairy skin like a pig, the creature curled back its top lip, revealing jagged teeth in what could have been a grin or a snarl.

After staring dumbfounded for a few seconds, Michael recovered enough to speak. "We'd like an audience with Gwyn ap Nudd."

The creature's lip twitched, and he hitched up his coarse brown trousers. "Shove off."

He made to shut the door. Both Michael and Nightshade jumped forward to jam a foot in the gap.

"'Tis an important matter," Michael ground out, his patience dwindling.

"Don't be such a spoilsport, Brian. Let them in. Visitors are rare as hen's teeth and break the monotony." At the sound of the cultured voice from within the room, the creature shrugged its bony shoulders and stomped out of sight.

"What is that thing?" Michael mouthed to Cordelia.

She shook her head in bemusement.

"Ugly little beggar," Nightshade added.

Michael pressed a finger to his lips. Best not to insult the King of the Underworld's staff members before they were even through the door.

Unable to get a psychic vibe from Gwyn ap Nudd or the small creature, Michael led the group in warily. He stumbled to a halt. The others ranged around him, gaping. A dark-haired man sat in a huge gold throne in the center of the room. He wore evening dress, black suit, black tie, a top hat, with a gold-topped cane resting across a table at his side as if he were about to jump up and start dancing like Fred Astaire. The piggy creature sat on a cushion on the floor, polishing a shoe, while the man propped his bare feet on a red brocade footstool.

The only other furniture in the room was a wide-screen television mounted on the wall opposite the throne, muted, but showing an episode of *The Dukes of Hazard*.

Being raised in the Irish fairy court, Michael had learned to expect the unexpected. But even his credulity had limits. "Erm, Gwyn ap Nudd, King of the Underworld, I presume?"

Cordelia winced at his uncharacteristic lack of eloquence.

"The very same." Gwyn picked up a remote control, and the TV screen went blank. "Can't stand the Hazard boys, but I enjoy watching Daisy bounce around." One corner of his mouth lifted, and the piggy creature rolled its eyes.

With an elegant flourish of his hand, Gwyn indicated his companion. "May I introduce my servant, the epitome of sweetness and light, Brian, my bottle imp." The imp sniffed loudly without looking up.

Michael debated whether he should kneel before Gwyn. If he were visiting Queen Ciar in the Irish fairy court, she'd expect him to kneel and kiss her feet. He eyed Gwyn's bare toes and decided he'd give that a miss. He hoped he wasn't committing an unforgivable breach of protocol. To be on the safe side, he bowed and gave Cordelia a grateful glance when she followed suit.

"We come to ask a boon, great king," Cordelia chimed in.

"Don't tell me, someone's died, and you're sure it wasn't their time to go?"

"No one has died, I hope." Michael took a step closer and slapped a fist into his palm, determined to make Gwyn take him seriously. "Some humans opened a gateway to the Underworld in Cornwall. When you sent the gatekeepers to seal it, they trapped my nephew."

Gwyn stared at him intently. Brian's brush stilled on the shoe. He peered up at his master warily.

"Arian was among them?" Gwyn asked.

"Aye," Michael answered cautiously, trying to gauge the king's mood.

"Hmm." Gwyn rose from his chair, then strode to the window. For long minutes, he said nothing, but tapped his fingers against the wall. "I wish I knew what Arian was up to."

"But you're the king; surely you give the orders," Cordelia said, a hint of exasperation in her voice.

Gwyn turned smoothly, tall and powerfully built beneath his civilized attire. "I'm a figurehead, rather like the Queen of England—except without the crown jewels and embarrassing relatives."

Frustration blasted through Michael at Gwyn's casual attitude. For the first time he understood why Niall grew angry with him when he joked about problems. He followed Gwyn to the window. "We came to ask you to release Finian."

Gwyn shook his head. "At the moment, I've no power to help."

Cordelia came up beside Michael. "Can't you speak with Arian? For goodness' sake, we're talking about a child."

Gwyn's blue eyes flicked between them. Michael blinked, sure that for an instant Gwyn's eyes had flashed red.

"What race are you?" Gwyn asked, glancing at Nightshade.

"Cornish piskies," Cordelia answered.

"The nightstalker too?"

"All of us except Michael," she added.

"Michael?" Gwyn's probing gaze settled on him. "You look familiar."

Michael laughed, a short sharp burst of irritation. The last thing he wanted to do now was discuss his background. "Unless you've visited the Irish fairy court, we've never met."

"Ireland?"

"Aye, me father is the Irish fairy queen's bodyguard."

Gwyn's expression froze, while his body became preternaturally still. "You're Troy's son." The statement dropped like a stone into the pool of silence.

Unease slid through Michael. Troy hadn't mentioned he knew Gwyn.

"Do you take after Troy?"

The eagerness in Gwyn's voice flashed Michael's senses to high alert. But wariness did him no good. He had no idea whether answering yes or no would be more likely to persuade Gwyn to help.

Before Michael could decide what to say, Gwyn obviously came to his own conclusion. "Show me the Phoenix Dagger."

Gwyn must be referring to Troy's dagger. Troy had told him to show the weapon only to Master Devin. Should he deny knowledge of the dagger, and risk alienating Gwyn? His jaw tightened until his teeth hurt. He could normally talk his way out of anything, yet now that he needed his wits more than ever, they'd flown away.

With a jolt of frustration, Michael bent and yanked the knife from the webbing strapped around his lower leg. The scintillating oval stone scattered starbursts of color across the walls as he palmed the blade and presented the handle to Gwyn.

Gwyn's eyes lingered on the knife. He reached forward,

but instead of taking the hilt, he brushed a finger lightly across the egg-sized jewel. "The Phoenix Stone," he whispered, a hint of yearning in his voice. He glanced up at Michael, his gaze sharp, assessing. "You've inherited Troy's legacy or he would not have given you the dagger."

"How do you know?"

Gwyn laughed, a bitter parody of pleasure. "Oh, I know your father, Michael. We go back a *long* way."

"What type of being is Troy?" Cordelia asked.

A subtle tension ran through Michael. *He's Tuatha Dé Danaan* rolled to the tip of his tongue, but deep inside doubt wormed around, undermining his certainty.

Gwyn's gaze flicked from the Phoenix Stone to Cordelia. Then he looked at Michael. "You know that Troy manifests the Phoenix Charm?"

Michael held Gwyn's gaze silently, not wanting to reveal that he'd never heard of the term "Phoenix Charm."

"So why did he give us the blade?" Cordelia pressed. "Is the jewel magic? Will it help us rescue Finian from the Underworld?"

"In a manner of speaking." Gwyn gazed longingly at the stone.

"Do you have the power to use this dagger or the stone to help us?" Michael demanded, sure he was missing something important.

A smile settled on Gwyn's lips, but didn't touch the rest of his face. "Go before the Ennead, the council of nine. Ask to exchange yourself for the child. Let Arian see the dagger, but be crafty. Don't let him know you want him to use it."

"Use it for what?" Michael asked.

"Troy really didn't tell you?" Gwyn shook his head when Michael continued to stare at him. "How typical of his overarching arrogance. He believes he has the right to play with everyone's lives." Gwyn pointed at the darkly gleaming metal. "This is the ceremonial blade that was used to kill Troy the first time he died."

Cordelia's sharp intake of breath emphasized his final word.

Disbelief held Michael rigid. He shook his head in denial as little snippets of conversation he'd heard between Troy and the Irish fairy queen finally made sense.

"Troy cannot die. He can be killed, but his spirit always returns to his body, his powers multiplied," Gwyn said. "That is the Phoenix Charm."

"Nah." Michael turned away, shaking his head violently, denying Gwyn's claim.

You're like me, Michael. You're like me.

The memory of Troy's softly spoken words thundered in Michael's head. "I'm not like him."

"Troy obviously believes you've inherited his gift. If you can call such a curse a gift."

" 'Tis not true. I'm not—"

Michael swung around, desperate to get rid of the dagger. He thrust the hilt toward Cordelia. She stared at him wide-eyed in confusion, her gaze flicking to Gwyn then back.

"Take the cursed thing!" Michael shouted.

As soon as she gripped the handle, he turned and paced the room, holding the back of his neck. Everyone watched him. "Ruddy Badba!" He spun away, facing the bleak gray stone wall. Why had his father done this to him? The bloody Phoenix Charm should have passed to Niall. His brother would know how to handle death and resurrection.

Michael rested an arm on the wall and pressed his face against his sleeve. He fought to calm his raging mind and remember what his father had told him when he'd given him the blade.

When you understand my legacy, you will have every right to hate me.

A chill seeped up his legs, numbing his muscles with fear. At the same time, his head burned, his brain creating endless scenarios of bloody pain, the dark blade piercing his flesh.

Memories of Finian floated through his mind to taunt him: the golden-haired boy safe in his mother's arms, his tear-stained face in the car, sitting in the mud in the trench. Michael's fist clenched. With a yell, he thumped the wall.

Surely, there must be another way to save Finian? He didn't want to die to exchange himself for his nephew. Even if he could come back to life.

"No!" Nightshade half leaped, half flew across the room, his wings brushing the ceiling. He bounced and staggered to a halt in front of Michael. Cordelia jumped clear of his frantic flapping as Nightshade spun around to face Gwyn, guarding Michael.

"Approach on pain of death." Nightshade crouched, arms out, muscles knotted, ready to strike.

Gwyn took a few steps back. For a moment, Cordelia thought his outline wavered like a glamour. The hair pricked on her scalp, but when she blinked, he looked solid. "Michael has nothing to fear from me, nightstalker." He stared unblinking, blue eyes intense. "I've merely suggested the reason that Troy gave him the dagger."

"How's killing Michael going to help?" Veins stood out on Nightshade's arms as he repeatedly clenched and released his fists.

Michael stepped out from behind Nightshade, his skin pale, his eyes unnaturally bright with shock. He squeezed his eyes tight for a second. Then he pulled in a breath and held out a trembling hand to Cordelia. She hurried forward and placed the dagger in his palm.

He was going to die. She put a hand over her mouth, her

pulse weak and fluttery. Her knees wobbled, and she started to lower herself to sit on the floor.

"Behind you." Gwyn pointed. Cordelia turned and blinked at the armchair a few feet away. Ignoring the fact the chair had appeared out of thin air, she stumbled back and plopped onto the seat. Tamsy mewed pitifully, picking up Cordelia's distress, and jumped on her lap.

Michael held up the dagger and turned it over, sending scintillating flashes of light around the room. Two spots of color appeared on his cheeks, accentuated by the paleness of the rest of his face. "When Troy gave me this blade, that's what he intended?" he looked up at Gwyn. "That I should die?"

"I'll kill anyone who comes near you, Michael." Nostrils flared, jaw rock solid, Nightshade thumped a fist against his chest.

"I need to be sure this is the only way before . . ." Michael's words trailed away, his gaze fixed on Gwyn. The expression in his eyes was like that of a little boy who'd been abandoned by his daddy. Cordelia stretched her fingers, aching to slap Troy's perfect cold face.

The King of the Underworld shrugged, a negligent flex of his shoulders. "You could present your case for the child's release to the Ennead, the Tylwyth Teg council of nine. Seek a majority judgment. But Arian holds sway over most of the council members. I doubt you'll persuade them to vote against him."

"I'll persuade them." Nightshade's voice boomed through the room.

Tamsy's claws jabbed Cordelia's legs at the sudden noise. Cordelia snapped her head around to stare at Nightshade, her thigh stinging. "Could you take the volume down a decibel or two? We need to plan, not deafen each other."

"I'm protecting Michael, wise woman." Nightshade

stepped in front of Michael again, blocking him from Gwyn.

"Crikey O'Reilly." Michael shoved Nightshade in the arm. "Give me space to think, boyo."

Nightshade stared at Michael, hurt radiating from him like heat. He stomped to the window and stared out.

Cordelia gripped the arms of her chair, her emotions in turmoil. This was proving so much more complicated than she'd expected. She looked at Thorn, still by the door, his hands pushed deep in his pockets as if he wished he could hide his whole body there.

"May we have another chair, please?" she asked.

Gwyn extended his hand. Another wing chair blinked into being beside her.

"I thought you had no power?"

"Alas, I cannot take credit. It's the room, madam. Think about something and you'll make it appear." The room did have a strange feel. Her psychic senses had stopped working when they stepped through the door. She couldn't even feel Michael's normally strong presence in her chest.

She beckoned Thorn. He made his way hesitantly across the room and settled in the chair beside her.

"You all right, sweetheart?"

He nodded with a surreptitious glance at Gwyn. "Is someone really going to kill Michael?"

"He'll come back to life," Gwyn said.

"Can you be sure?" Michael asked.

"Have you never heard the epithet *Troy the Deathless*? If you take after your father, then . . ." He shrugged as if the answer was obvious.

Fear twisted and tangled inside Cordelia like eels. The more she discovered about Troy, the less she trusted him. And there was something about Gwyn that set her teeth on edge. She couldn't feel his psychic signature, and the way his gaze tracked Michael when he wasn't looking seemed shifty.

She found herself shaking her head. "Why didn't Troy tell Michael what he is?"

"Because he's an arrogant bastard who likes to manipulate people," Gwyn spat.

Cordelia stood, left Tamsy on the chair, and paced, twisting an escaped lock of hair between her fingers. "I don't like this." Michael shouldn't take advice from someone who obviously hated his father.

"Neither do I." Nightshade had turned his back to the window and stood facing the room, his expression guarded.

Cordelia halted and stared at him. Once again, they were in accord. She paced back to Michael and perched on the edge of her chair, facing him. "What evidence did Troy give you that you take after him?"

Michael reeled off a list of powers that they shared. Cordelia sucked her lip, unconvinced.

"What do you think?" he asked.

His eyes were so serious and troubled she could no longer imagine the teasing light that used to dance in the blue depths. Her heart ached for him. "I think we should try to persuade the Ennead to release Finian before we make any decision on the dagger thing."

"You'll waste your time." Gwyn snapped.

Michael met Cordelia's gaze. A silent accord passed between them like a touch. Michael gave a sharp nod. "We petition the Ennead."

Gwyn sighed. He walked back to his throne, which morphed into a comfortable armchair. "There are nine council members," he said as he slouched back. "Arian is the strongest and controls the gatekeepers and the huntsmen. Mawgan, our cunning man, leads the seers. He's easily swayed, unlike Arian, who is strong and single-minded. If Arian trapped the child, he will not change his mind."

Michael shifted restlessly. "How do we get out of this place? The steps caused us a problem on the way up."

Gwyn chuckled at Michael's comment, but Cordelia couldn't see the joke. "There is a certain irony . . ." His voice trailed away.

"Why don't the Teg fly over the trap on the steps in light form?" Cordelia asked, looking for inconsistencies to give her grounds for the suspicion she felt.

"Someone incredibly powerful laid that trap. Each of the four elemental types is affected differently. Cornish piskies are of the earth. So the stone will have stolen your energy. You should have been rendered unconscious within a few steps. One of you must be powerful to have withstood the effect." Gwyn glanced at Michael.

"A similar thing happens to the air elemental Tylwyth Teg. If they try to fly across the trap in light form they become corporeal and fall senseless to the ground."

"What about Cordelia?" Thorn piped up. Cordelia's breath stalled, knowing what he was about to say and powerless to stop him. "She sank into the stone."

Gwyn's blue eyes settled on her appraisingly, and heat jumped into her cheeks. "That's what happens to water elementals."

Everyone looked at her. She concentrated on stroking Tamsy.

"You're a water elemental, lass? That makes sense." The curiosity and satisfaction in Michael's voice made her worry he'd guessed the whole truth about her nature. "When I touched you in the boat, I thought your energy was"—he stared at her, eyes unfocused, remembering—"soothing and energizing at the same time."

She released a silent sigh of relief that her elemental nature had been accepted with little fuss. But she still didn't trust Gwyn. Why would the king exclude his own people from his tower?

"So how do we get out of this tower?" Nightshade demanded.

"We summon the cunning man to remove the charm."

Gwyn reached beneath his chair and pulled out a brown bottle with a corked top. He held it up to Brian. "Time to show them your party piece."

The imp scrunched his face into a snarl, but stood and straightened his jacket. "Get on with it then."

Gwyn uncorked the bottle with a flourish. For a moment, Brian stood unmoving, then the air around him started to swirl until a whirlwind whipped him up. With a whistle of wind, the mini tornado arrowed into the bottle, and the cork popped back into place.

Gwyn held up the bottle. "One bottle imp. Very useful when you want to throw him out the window to pass on a message." He walked to a large window overlooking the quadrangle and unfastened the catch. Taking aim, he lobbed the bottle out.

"Hah! I nearly missed the water and splattered imp everywhere."

Clutching Tamsy to her chest, Cordelia hurried to the window with the others. The bottle bobbed in the circular pool beneath the fountain. A passing Teg woman dressed in white robes fished the bottle from the water, and looked up at the window.

"Take him to Mawgan," Gwyn hollered down. The woman waved a hand in acknowledgment and hurried back the way she'd come.

"Now I suggest you plan what you're going to say." Gwyn glanced between them. "When Mawgan comes, he'll take you straight to the council chamber."

Cordelia went back to her seat, a trickle of unease exacerbating her fear. If Gwyn couldn't disable the charm on the steps, he was a prisoner in the tower. He claimed he had no power, but if a member of the Ennead came at his summons, he must still have some authority.

She beckoned Michael closer and whispered, "I don't trust Gwyn, and there's something strange about this room. I can't sense any of you. Do you think the tower's a prison?"

Michael gripped the back of her chair. "I don't understand Gwyn's role." He shook his head, staring into the distance. "I'm certain he's not what he seems. Troy told me to seek out Master Devin. I must find him before we face the Ennead."

Chapter Eight

The door to Gwyn's room opened. Brian slouched back in, dangling his bottle between his fingers. He sniffed and jerked his chin over his shoulder. "Mawgan's 'ere."

Holding Tamsy, Cordelia rose from her chair with a flash of expectation. Mawgan was the council member Gwyn thought would support them. A tall male Tylwyth Teg filled the doorway. He was the same height and slender build as Arian, but his long silver hair was tied back, and he wore white robes. His skin was pale with the same almost transparent blue eyes, but instead of the scorn that soured Arian's face, Mawgan wore an expression of patient inquiry.

His gaze flicked around the group, lingering a few seconds longer on Nightshade than the rest of them. He inclined his head in greeting. "You are welcome, piskies, even though your approach to the Ennead is unorthodox."

"We came to petition for release of a child you hold. We thought our best course was to appeal directly to the king." Michael said.

"We're told he can't help us because power lies with the Ennead," Cordelia added, wanting to gauge Mawgan's reaction.

The council member's gaze flicked from her to Gwyn, his expression guarded. "Gwyn ap Nudd is King of the Underworld," he said in a flat voice.

She would love to know what Gwyn's position really was. She'd never heard of a fairy king with no power.

Mawgan raised a hand to attract their attention. "When you go before the Ennead, there are a few restrictions. You may not carry weapons or use magic in the council chamber, or your claim will be disqualified. Please accompany me." He turned silently and made his way toward the steps with the stealth of a wraith.

Cordelia glanced at Michael's lower leg, where the Phoenix Dagger was hidden.

With a slight shake of his head, he whispered, "I'll not leave the blade with Gwyn. I have no option but to take it."

Flustered, Cordelia caught Thorn's arm when he moved to follow Michael out the door. She had her doubts about leaving Thorn with Gwyn, but compared to facing a potentially hostile council interrogation, the king seemed the lesser of two evils. "May my ward remain here while we present our case?" she asked Gwyn.

"I'd be delighted to have company." Gwyn extended a hand and a Monopoly board appeared on a table in front of him. "It'll make a change to play with someone who can count."

"I can count," Brian grumbled. "I just hate board games."

"I want to come with you." Thorn gave her a pleading look and she had an inspired idea.

"Sorry, sweetheart. I need you to keep Tamsy for me. I daren't take her into the council chamber in case they sense magic in her and disallow our case."

Thorn huffed and scowled, then accepted Tamsy into his arms. She hung the cat bag over his shoulder with an affectionate pat. She stroked Tamsy's chin and gave her a kiss. "Look after my baby for me, won't you?" Thorn nodded. He didn't realize she was talking to Tamsy.

Cordelia hurried after the others, proceeding cautiously when she reached the steps where she'd sunk into the stone, but the chill of the charm was gone. The group waited for her halfway down. Mawgan indicated they should proceed while he reinstated the magical trap.

When they reached the bottom of the tower, Michael paused and, with a smile, stroked his fingertips along her arm. "When you stayed behind, I thought you'd bailed on me."

She suppressed a little shiver of pleasure at his casual touch. "I've left Thorn and Tamsy with Gwyn."

"You comfortable with that?"

"Not especially."

Mawgan caught up and she dropped her voice. "Thorn's gullible. I don't want Arian manipulating him to get at us."

Michael nodded, and Nightshade grunted in agreement.

"Mawgan." Michael hurried after the tall seer. "I need to speak with Master Devin before we present our case."

The white-robed figure stopped. A flash of surprise crossed his face. "May I ask why?"

"I just need to talk to him."

"Hmm." Mawgan rubbed his chin. "Master Devin is absent, I'm afraid. Maybe you can see him after the hearing."

When Cordelia caught up with him, Michael cast her a frustrated glance. "Without Devin's advice, I'll just have to play it by ear and hope Mawgan supports us."

After a short walk along the corridor, Mawgan led them through a door to the enclosed quadrangle in the center of the castle, then took a flagstone path that cut diagonally across the grassy area. The few Teg they passed peered at them curiously. So far, Cordelia had seen no Teg wearing the same black leather as Arian, Olwyn, and Dai. Most were clothed in brown trousers and jerkins.

They followed Mawgan through a door into another bare stone corridor that looked like the one they'd recently left. He threaded his way along a maze of dingy passages leading deep into the castle. After a few minutes, he stood aside and indicated they should pass through a pair of huge metal-studded double doors. "The council chamber," he announced.

Cordelia entered and halted behind Michael. Just inside

the door stood a tall gold statue of an imposing Tylwyth Teg male, his fierce visage immortalized by the sculptor. The room was large, with a high domed ceiling decorated by points of light against the dark background.

"Like a planetarium," Michael whispered, head bent back to take in the design.

A circular gallery ran around the room with decoratively carved wooden chairs positioned every few yards along the perimeter. A quick count confirmed her guess there were nine. From the entrance where they stood, five steps led up to the gallery, and five steps led down to a lower level.

Mawgan pointed at the descending stairway. "You'll stand in the plaintiff's pit while you plead your case."

Michael descended a couple of steps and examined the shadowy wall of the lower level. His lips tightened. "I'm not comfortable with this."

A wry laugh broke from Cordelia's throat. "I passed *comfortable* a long time ago."

Michael ran back up the steps and laid his hand protectively on her back. "You stay here, lass. Nightshade and I will plead our case."

She was tempted to agree and annoyed she even considered letting Michael take all the responsibility. "I'm in this with you." Hesitantly, she reached in front of Michael and slid her fingers through his. "I'm the one Niall left in charge of the piskies. This mess is as much my responsibility as yours."

Michael looked down at their joined hands. Her heartbeat faltered at her own boldness. When the familiar seductive twinkle lit his eyes, and he tightened his grip on her hand, she sucked a breath into her suddenly empty lungs.

"The boys were my responsibility, lass. You stay up here out of harm's way." When he couldn't use his silver tongue to win her over, he had to resort to old-fashioned arguing.

The sound of footsteps echoing around the chamber signaled the council members were entering through a door on the upper floor. To forestall an unseemly disagreement, she released Michael's hand and made her way down to the lower level.

"Cordelia!" She ignored his urgent whisper and hoped he'd forgive her.

He ran down to join her, his brows pulled together. But he didn't say any more. Nightshade followed cautiously, snapping his wings as he scanned the gallery.

When she reached the lower level, she bent, examining the tiny blue mosaic tiles on the floor. A jolt of fear pinched her guts when she noticed manacles hanging from the walls. She clasped her hands together, made her way to the center of the pit, and looked up. The chamber was designed to make the plaintiff uncomfortable, surrounded on all sides by council members. No matter which way she turned, she couldn't keep them all in view.

Tiny high windows in the gallery provided just enough light to see the Tylwyth Teg who took seats. The hair on the back of Cordelia's neck stood up when Arian strode in, his boots drumming across the wooden floorboards. He dropped negligently into one of the chairs before Olwyn and Dai slid into the seats flanking him. Mawgan sat almost opposite Arian, a white-robed male Teg on either side of him. Mawgan and Arian eyed each other with ill-disguised contempt. The air prickled with tension. Two men wearing brown garb took two of the other chairs. All eyes focused on the last empty seat, an expectant hush falling over the room.

Whoever was going to fill the final chair must be important.

Someone entered through the same door they'd used and ran up the steps to the gallery. A young man wearing brown working clothes scrambled past the occupied chairs and panting, slithered into the vacant seat.

"I apologize for my tardiness." The late council member half rose and gave an awkward bow.

"No apology necessary, Avery," Mawgan said, the censure in his tone belying the words.

"Shall we get this hearing started?" Arian's voice rang with the same cold superiority Cordelia remembered. She had a horrible feeling this was a farce, the decision already made before they'd opened their mouths.

"Who is the council leader?" Michael asked, pointedly turning his back on Arian to face Mawgan. Arian puckered his mouth at Michael in disgust.

"There is no leader, plaintiff. We're an assembly of equals. Each of us has one vote to cast as he sees fit," Mawgan said. "Address us all."

Cordelia ran her gaze around the faces of the nine. The seers both looked to Mawgan. Olwyn and Dai watched Arian. The other three councilors appeared confused and uncomfortable. *An assembly of equals?* Whom did Mawgan think he was fooling?

Michael smoothed back his hair, and Cordelia tensed beneath the gaze of the nine inquisitors, not sure what to do with her hands.

The sound of urgent voices in the corridor outside broke the silence. A few indrawn breaths hissed from council members; then a man stepped into the open doorway. He paused for a few beats, silhouetted against the light. With a swish of his long coat, he paced forward and stopped at the top of the steps, staring down into the pit. "You were going to start without me, I see." He glanced at the young man who'd been last to arrive, now cowering in the chair. "Even gave my seat to a huntsman."

Cordelia stared, mesmerized, as the incomer tossed back his long dark hair to reveal pointed ears. His skin glowed dusky in color like moonlight through clouds. He managed to appear both dark and bright. Satin and velvet of purple, navy, and forest green shimmered in the low light, trimmed with muted gold. A strip of ermine edged the trailing sleeves of his floor-length coat. His face was perfect, exotic, eyes darkly outlined, and rubies glittered at his ears and fingers. With a flourish, he swirled the opulent folds of fabric away from his legs and ran up the steps to the gallery. Glamour shimmered around him, trailed in his wake. The man in his seat scurried off into the shadows.

The new councilor nodded to Mawgan and Arian, then returned his gaze to the pit. Cordelia's cheeks heated under his scrutiny, but his attention was focused on Michael. For long moments, he stared at Michael, his eyes intense; then a smile broke across his face. "Greetings." He inclined his head to them and took his chair.

"Master Devin." Mawgan stood and bowed. "We thought you were detained."

Master Devin? She gasped at the name, and heard Michael mutter something. If only he had arrived earlier, so they could speak to him alone.

Devin propped an elbow on the arm of his chair and glanced at Mawgan. "I was busy. You should have waited." Despite his relaxed pose, steel laced his voice.

To Cordelia's surprise, Arian stood and bowed stiffly. "Master Devin. Glad you found time to join us."

Devin leaned back, a sardonic smile on his lips. "I'm sure you are elated to see me, *worthy* council member Arian."

Hope fluttered inside Cordelia. Devin didn't like Arian. Maybe Michael had an ally.

Mawgan cleared his throat. "May I respectfully remind all present that magical powers are not permitted in the council chamber."

With a self-deprecating chuckle, Devin inclined his head to Mawgan and the shimmer around him disappeared. Yet his appearance remained unchanged. Either he could disguise his glamour, which only the most powerful fairies were capable of, or he really was incredibly beautiful.

Michael stared at Master Devin, sure he recognized him from somewhere. Yet he could not recall meeting him at the

Irish fairy court, and he certainly hadn't met him in Cornwall. Whatever manner of creature he was, he glowed like Troy.

Nightshade rumbled low in his throat, a drooling expression on his face as he stared up at the newcomer. Even Cordelia hadn't taken her eyes off Master Devin since he'd entered the chamber. Michael suppressed a twinge of something suspiciously like jealousy. Troy had told him Devin would explain how he should proceed. He hoped that meant Devin would support them.

Turning slowly, Michael scanned the members of the Ennead. He stopped when he was facing Mawgan. His best chance of success was to win over Mawgan and his cronies. Although Master Devin might be an ally, he held only one vote. The council members obviously respected him, but Michael had the sense they treated him as an outsider and would not follow his lead. That meant there were two factions, and Michael had already lost the votes of Arian's group.

"Yesterday . . ." Had the trouble really happened only yesterday? Michael started again. "A few days ago, some humans opened a gateway to the Underworld in Cornwall. I'm guessing they did this by accident as the gate caused their deaths. The Cornish piskies knew nothing of their activities until the gateway was open." He paused, licked his lips, and glanced around to gauge the expression of the council members. At least they appeared to be listening.

"Three of your number came and closed the gate by sealing it off." Michael ached to turn and point an accusing finger at the gatekeepers. But he flexed his shoulders and sought to state his case without laying blame. "When they annexed the area around the gate, an innocent child became trapped within the Underworld. We ask that the child be released."

Michael scanned the nine faces ranged above him. Devin smiled enigmatically, an unknown quantity. The two dressed like working men, whom Devin had called huntsmen, glanced around, checking the other councilors' reactions. They would follow the strongest faction. If only Michael could win Mawgan over . . . "I'm sure it was not your intention"—he cast Arian a sideways glance—"to trap a defenseless one-year-old boy in the gateway, for to do so is cruel and unjust. This child is the son of the pisky king. He is out of the country, so I'm here in his stead to request the immediate release of his son and heir."

Michael settled his gaze squarely on Mawgan, ignoring the ache of tension in his neck exacerbated by the awkward angle of his head.

"So which was it, plaintiff? Yesterday or a few days ago?" Arian cocked his head, a smirk on his face.

Trust the bastard to pick up on an irrelevant detail. Especially one Michael couldn't pin down. "Your time passes differently here. By my reckoning, should be a couple of days ago."

"Should be? How can you lodge a plea when you don't even know the dates of the occurrence?" Arian demanded.

"We'll assume two days past for the sake of the records." Mawgan's low authoritative voice filled the chamber.

"Let that be recorded," Devin confirmed with a flick of his fingers.

Lip curled with contempt, Arian stretched out his legs.

Devin glanced at Arian thoughtfully. He leaned forward, elbows on his knees. "Scribe, who traveled to Cornwall two days ago to close an unauthorized access point?"

Turning, Mawgan spoke over his shoulder. Someone recording the proceedings must have answered from the shadows. Mawgan turned back, eyebrows raised meaningfully. "Master Devin, I'm told Arian dealt with this breach."

Devin angled his head, the points of his ears peeping through his dark hair. The sight gave Michael a jolt of recognition, yet he couldn't pin down the memory.

"Perhaps you'd care to present your side of the incident?" Devin asked.

Arian stood. With a coldly calculating glance, he made eye contact with each of the council members. "As one of the nine, I am not obliged to give testament. My loyalty lies unquestioningly with the King of the Underworld." Dai and Olwyn nodded vigorously and frowned at the huntsmen, who appeared unimpressed. "In the interests of hastening this hearing, I agree to give an account of what happened two nights ago."

He paced back and forth between Dai and Olwyn, his boots clicking on the wooden gallery. Then he halted with a snap of his heels and spun to glare at Michael. "We responded to the illegal breach immediately on orders from the king."

Michael glanced at Cordelia, puzzled by the continual references to the king when he alleged he had no power. She raised her eyebrows with a shake of her head, obviously baffled.

Arian resumed pacing, the echo of his steps punctuating his words. "We gatekeepers received little help from the piskies, who claimed ignorance of what had happened in their domain." Arian flashed a skeptical look around the chamber.

Michael bit his lips before he said something he'd regret.

"The pisky king was absent," Arian continued. "In his stead, the woman who stands before us took responsibility, even though the plaintiff pleading their case is the king's sibling."

A ripple of confusion swept around the chamber, the council members exchanging frowns. One of the seers stood. "Let me clarify for the records. The plaintiff who stands before us was present when you closed the illegal access and he is brother to the pisky king?"

"Correct," Arian fired back.

"Is this right?" the council member demanded of Michael.

"Aye." Michael had a horrible feeling he was incriminating himself, but he had to answer truthfully.

"Then why were you not left in charge in your brother's absence?" The white-robed council member stared down at Michael, his brow wrinkled. His manner was not accusatory, merely puzzled, yet warning shot up Michael's spine. Arian had purposely taken the discussion in this direction to discredit Michael.

"I was responsible for the king's sons, not the—"

"Sons, plural?" Arian snapped.

"Aye," Michael said, meeting Arian's stare head-on. "Two boys. You saw only one."

"You were saying," Devin prompted Michael, with a quelling look at Arian.

"I was only responsible for the boys. I'm Irish, not of pisky blood. The pisky wise woman takes responsibility for the pisky troop in the king's absence."

"Very well." Mawgan nodded. The council member to his right took his seat, apparently satisfied.

Obviously not ready to let the subject drop, Arian remained standing. "I naturally assumed the king's brother would stand leader in his stead. His refusal to take the matter seriously led me to believe he was simple in the head."

Arian stared down at him, a vicious smile on his lips. Michael counted to ten, while Nightshade flashed his fangs at Arian and emitted a growl that reverberated around the walls of the lower floor.

Eyes narrowed, Arian flexed his fingers against his thigh as if wishing for his silver spikes. "The pisky wise woman proved herself incompetent. She seemed unable to grasp simple facts about the situation. I was forced to compel their attendance by taking the child."

"That's not true," Cordelia burst out. "We offered to accompany them. He made us take Finian."

"Dai, Olwyn?" Mawgan prompted. "How do you remember the situation?"

Dai stood, his expression neutral. "Arian speaks the truth."

Anger balled in Michael's chest, even though he'd half expected the hearing to play out like this. Cordelia had her teeth clenched; her eyes were flinty.

Arian appeared to relax now he'd riled them. He stopped pacing and leaned his shoulder against a pillar. "The plaintiffs claimed ignorance of the basic rules and procedures involved in their offence."

"What offence?" Cordelia shouted.

"Is this accusation of culpability grounded in fact?" Devin demanded, staring at Arian over their heads.

Michael massaged the tense muscles in the back of his neck, his head aching from lack of sleep and the awkward angle.

"What more do we need to know?" Arian made eye contact with each council member *except* Devin. "Cornwall is the piskies' domain. The illegal breach occurred a few miles from their ancestral home, yet they claimed no knowledge of the gate. They're either criminally negligent or liars."

His gaze slid down to Michael, a malevolent light of triumph in his eyes. "Either way, they owed a debt of blood to the King of the Underworld as reparation. The plaintiff denied responsibility on more than one occasion. I had no option but to demand blood payment from the king's son."

"You never asked for his blood." Cordelia stood tense and so angry Michael sensed the air vibrating around her.

"If you had asked for Fin's blood, I'd have said no," Michael added softly, knowing this sentiment would not help their cause.

"Arian!" Mawgan rose to his feet, his robes swishing around his legs as he stepped forward. "Am I to understand that you trapped this child intentionally?"

"Of course." Arian stepped forward, arms rigid at his sides. "The King of the Underworld demands blood price for such disrespect. *I* serve my king without question."

Dai and Olwyn nodded enthusiastically, like bobblehead dogs in the back of a car.

Arian glared, his gaze challenging. "If you sanction disrespect for our king, vote against me. I stand by my actions."

Mawgan dropped back into his seat, his shoulders heaving with his breath. A spurt of desperation shot through Michael. They'd lost. He could read the verdict in the council members' faces.

"We vote," Mawgan said wearily. "All who support the plaintiff's call for the boy to be released stand." With a glance around the chamber, Mawgan heaved himself to his feet. The other two seers joined him. Michael watched Devin, willing him up from his chair. If Devin supported them, there was an outside chance the two huntsmen might follow.

Devin stared at Michael, his face impassive. He didn't move.

Arian grinned. "Your plea is hereby rejected."

Chapter Nine

Master Devin rose to his feet and paced silently along the gallery. After running down the steps, he headed out the double doors without sparing the pisky group a glance. Cordelia stared after him, so drained and weary she could hardly think.

"I was sure he'd support us." She pushed her trembling hands in her jacket pockets.

Michael stared at the door, a look of bewilderment on his face. "From what Troy said, I thought Devin would be on our side, yet he voted against us."

"Maybe he didn't realize who we are." She rested a consoling hand on Michael's arm.

"What manner of creature is Master Devin?" Nightshade asked, a husky burr in his voice.

"A powerful one." Gripping the back of his neck, Michael winced, reminding her of the ache in her own neck.

As Cordelia rubbed her muscles, she pictured Master Devin's darkly exotic appearance. "He looks like a djinn with his golden skin and pointed ears. They're notoriously tricky and dangerous." Yet there was something compelling about him, too.

Nightshade's nostrils flared. "I've never tasted a shadow elemental."

"I'm guessing you won't be tasting Devin, either," Michael said with a sideways glance at the nightstalker.

When the last council members had left the chamber,

Mawgan descended the five steps and waited for them by the door. "I'm sorry about the child. Will you return to Cornwall?"

"No." Michael set his jaw, his face harsh shadows and angles.

Cordelia intervened, fearing Michael was about to lose his temper. "Cunning man, will you escort us back to the king, please? My ward is waiting with him."

Mawgan led them back the way they'd come.

"I should find Devin," Michael said when they started walking. "Despite the fact he didn't support us, he might still give me advice about the dagger."

"How can we trust him?" Cordelia placed a restraining hand on Michael's arm. "He didn't vote for us and he didn't even wait to talk to you." She realized she didn't trust anyone Troy had recommended. Her brain ached trying to work out what was going on. Was the charm placed on the steps meant to imprison Gwyn or to exclude intruders? How did Gwyn get food and drink? Where was his restroom? Goodness, she needed a restroom.

Mawgan showed her to a primitive toilet, then led them back up the spiral stairs to Gwyn's tower.

On the steps where the charm had been set, she hesitated. But she felt no chill or lethargy. When she entered Gwyn's room, Thorn grinned at her over his shoulder. "I'm winning, Dee." Tamsy mewed and rose from where she'd been lying on the cushion beside Brian. Cordelia winced inwardly at the thought of her cat touching the grubby, hairy creature.

She hurried across to Thorn, put her arm over his shoulders, and let him explain the state of play. Gwyn lolled back in his chair, one bare foot against the table leg. "Thorn's a master at Monopoly. He'd make a fortune as a property developer."

Gwyn smiled at her. Despite her uneasiness, she smiled back. While he was relaxed, she'd try to get more information out of him. "I've been wondering about your situation. If you don't mind my asking, why are you confined in this tower?"

He gave her a wary glance, then counted some Monopoly money and handed the notes to Thorn.

Michael came up beside her and folded his arms.

With a beleaguered sigh, Gwyn leaned back. "Very well, if you must know, a righteous fool took exception to something I did and cursed me to spend eternity within the walls of this tower. No food. No drink. No women." His gaze roamed over Cordelia. With a sudden flash of unease, she stepped back.

"Don't worry, pisky. I couldn't touch you even if I wanted to. I exist in a dimension between the mortal world and the Underworld. But one of these days I'll be free of this place."

His urbane expression fell away, leaving his face carved with bitter resentment. His gaze drilled into her. "Does that answer your question?"

"I'm sorry," she mumbled.

"The one who put me here will pay for his actions." Gwyn walked to the window and stared out across the lake.

Michael beckoned her to the far side of the room, to join Nightshade. "After what Gwyn's just told us, I've realized why we can't sense him." Michael pulled up the leather thong he wore around his neck and gripped the three linked stone rings hanging there: his fairy Magic Knot that held the essence of his mind, body, and spirit. "Someone has broken Gwyn's Magic Knot, separating the three parts of him. My guess is his mind and spirit are incarcerated in this room, while his body is trapped elsewhere," Michael whispered. "He's creating the appearance of a physical presence to fool us."

"Gwyn's body must be somewhere," Cordelia said.

"Aye. But 'tis not our business." Michael bent and tapped his shin where the Phoenix Dagger was hidden. "We must concentrate on rescuing Fin."

At the reminder of the dagger, Cordelia's fears for Michael flooded back. "You've decided to exchange your life for Finian's, then?"

As Michael opened his mouth to answer, Nightshade gripped his shoulder. "Find another way," he urged.

They all looked across the room when Thorn called Gwyn back to the game.

"Do you feel we're in the middle of a much larger game?" Michael glanced between her and Nightshade. "Everyone here seems to have their own agenda."

So does Troy, Cordelia thought, but kept quiet, because she didn't want to upset Michael.

"Arian and Mawgan were scoring points off each other using us. I'm sure Gwyn is manipulating us as well. And Devin . . ." Michael pulled a face. "He breezes in as though he owns the council chamber, has them all kowtowing, then backs Arian."

"It's called politics, Michael." Nightshade snapped his wings.

"I bet Arian thinks he's beaten us. He's probably congratulating himself for having Devin take his side. I'd like to see his face if I walk back into that council chamber and offer meself in exchange for Finian."

Fear swelled inside Cordelia when she imagined Arian's glee. "He'll be pleased. He hates you."

Michael grinned tightly. "He'll not be happy when I return from the dead."

Cordelia visualized the shock on Arian's face when Michael woke up after being "killed." She couldn't deny a spurt of satisfaction.

The momentary pleasure disappeared beneath the horror of reality. "You're really going to offer your life in exchange for Fin's?"

"Aye."

"No!" Nightshade elbowed Cordelia away and stepped before Michael. "I cannot lose you, bard."

The nightstalker's distress echoed darkly through her. She didn't want to lose Michael either. She'd only just started to understand him. He was kind and brave, not at all the shallow womanizer she'd imagined when she watched him in her divining mirror.

"Cordelia?" Michael took her hand. "Please say you're behind me on this, lass?"

Cordelia closed her eyes. The word *no* echoed inside her head, pulsed in her lungs, burned her tongue, but that was her selfish heart talking. Michael would do whatever was required to rescue Finian. He needed her support to give him strength and confidence.

She massaged her temples with shaking fingers. "Yes."

"No." Nightshade crowded her, trying to intimidate her into changing her mind. She wrapped her arms over her head and leaned into Michael's protective embrace.

"That's enough." Michael shoved him away. Nightshade stood, arms tense at his sides, nostrils flared like an angry bull.

"Kill yourself then, fool. But I'll have no part of it." Stalking away, he ruffled his wings against his back, and disappeared out the door.

Michael eased back against the wall, taking her with him. She kept her forehead pressed to his chest, wishing the moment could last forever. "Maybe it's best we let him go," Michael whispered. "There's no telling what he'll do if Arian agrees to my suggestion."

Hope flared. With every fiber of Cordelia's being, she prayed that Arian rejected Michael's sacrifice.

Nightshade ran down the steps from the tower room, his head throbbing with waves of anger. How could Michael be foolish enough to believe he would rise from the dead? Any idiot could sense Gwyn ap Nudd was not telling the truth about anything.

And that damn woman encouraged him.

Cordelia Tink obviously didn't care for Michael at all. All she cared about was saving Finian so Niall wouldn't roast her skinny hide. If only Niall would banish her from the pisky troop. The possibility brought a grim smile to Nightshade's lips.

At the bottom of the steps he turned right, choosing the route they'd taken earlier to reach the council chamber. Michael might be a fool, but Nightshade intended to do all he could to protect his friend.

With his excellent sense of direction, he had no trouble following the winding corridors back to the council chamber. The double doors groaned as he shoved them open and entered. The room was empty, the air heavy with silence as he made his way up the five steps to the gallery. He rested his hands on his hips and gazed down at the blue mosaic tiles decorating the pit floor. The pattern had caught his attention earlier, but was impossible to interpret at ground level. In the low light from the small gallery windows, the blues varied from that of a velvet night sky to a pale summer morn. Viewed from above, the design became clear: a maze. The same pattern they'd seen on the rocky doorway that led to the Teg's domain.

Nightshade descended the two flights of steps to the pit and crouched, running his fingers along the gaps between the tiles. A faint draft through the cracks confirmed his suspicion. The floor to the pit opened. Whatever was below, he didn't want to find out.

He tracked the circular wall, grasped one of the chains securing a set of manacles to the stone, and yanked. The fixing didn't shift. The restraints were strong, the metal clean. *Still in use.*

Although he heard nothing, a tingling sense of power stole through his body. He swung around, already sure whom he'd find. "Master Devin."

The djinn stood on the top step. He was still dressed elaborately, but the long coat had been replaced by a jacket of embroidered bloodred satin, the same color as the jewels glittering at his ears.

"You're suspicious." Devin descended a couple of steps. "A man after my own heart."

The djinn's exotic fragrance flavored the air, making Nightshade's fangs ache in his gums. A low growl of desire broke from his throat.

Devin laughed. The way his lips curved and his eyes sparkled reminded Nightshade of Michael. Was he forever doomed to compare all men to Michael?

Yet tasty as he looked, the djinn had not been on their side in the council hearing. Nightshade curled a lip to show the point of one fang. "I advise you to keep away from me, dark one. I have a yen to bite you."

Devin's grin widened. "Maybe sometime, Nightshade, but not here, not now. We have more pressing matters."

Having expected a categorical refusal, Nightshade was momentarily stunned by the djinn's response. He stared at the dark, enigmatic glint in Devin's eyes. Then everything he'd said sank in.

"You know my name."

"So I do." Devin reached the bottom of the steps and leaned a shoulder against the wall.

"How?"

Devin tapped the side of his nose with a slender finger tipped by a pointed nail. "That's for me to know and you to find out."

Ignoring Devin's simmering attraction, Nightshade focused on the danger. He could all too easily forget this creature was born of shadow.

"As you're checking the pit, I assume Michael's planning to come before the Ennead again?"

Nightshade stared at Devin, wondering at his questions, then resumed his perusal of the wall. He didn't dare completely turn his back on the djinn, so he kept him in sight from the corner of his eye. "Did Gwyn ap Nudd reveal our plans to you?" Seems he'd been right to distrust the King of the Underworld.

"Maybe I already knew." Devin pushed away from the wall and ambled closer. Nightshade tensed, extended his wings just enough to stabilize himself if he needed to move fast.

"I'm friend, not foe, stalker."

Nightshade swung to face the djinn, who stood glowing faintly like a candle in the night. "You voted against us."

"No, I abstained. A whole different bunch o'bananas."

"What do you want with me, dark one?" Nightshade asked.

"Isn't it rather ironic you should call me dark one?"

"I'm referring to your spirit, not your skin color."

Devin's eyebrows rose. His eyes still glittered, but the spark of humor hardened to a deadly sliver of warning.

In the blink of an eye, the djinn was in his face. He ran a nail across Nightshade's chest, the barest touch, yet it robbed him of coherent thought.

"Take care what you say to me," Devin whispered, his tone a dark promise of pain that drew a whimper from Nightshade's throat.

His mind screamed strike, yet his arms hung useless at his sides while he stared into Devin's midnight eyes.

"My spirit is no darker than yours, stalker. Do not goad me. You may be fast in shade form, but you have your feet grounded in the earth. I could destroy you with a thought."

Suddenly the djinn released him from his thrall. In a heartbeat, he stood at the top of the steps, staring down. Nightshade slumped against the wall, abrading his wings on the rough stones. He grimaced and stepped forward, his chest heaving with anger and humiliation.

"Don't ever do that to me again," he forced out between gritted teeth.

The djinn angled his head. His dark hair slid aside, revealing the pointed tip of one ear. "I came here to help you, stalker."

Nightshade snorted.

Devin's grin twitched the corners of his mouth. "Forget your pride, or you'll miss something important."

With a steadying breath, Nightshade pushed aside his seething anger and walked forward. "Speak then."

Extending a hand, Devin indicated the door. "I have something to show you."

Nightshade would pull out his fangs before he let the djinn walk behind him. "You go first."

Apparently unthreatened to have Nightshade behind *him*, Devin swung around and headed out of the council chamber.

A short distance along the corridor, Devin opened a door and passed through. When Nightshade followed, the beguiling fragrance of burning incense swamped his senses. He found himself in a large richly furnished room that seemed out of place in the austere castle. Bright tapestries decorated the walls, while oriental rugs covered the floor. Devin sat on the end of a massive four-poster bed surrounded by purple and gold curtains. He slipped off his black silk slippers, and stepped into leather ankle boots. "This is my bedchamber when I'm in the castle," he said with a glance up as he fastened the bootstraps.

A few minutes later, they left the room and made their way along corridors and down steps to a lower level. In the passage, they met a few human women in plain brown dresses and aprons who all stepped aside and eyed Nightshade warily.

Finally, the djinn led Nightshade into a narrow corridor ringing with the sound of women's chatter from a room at the end. Devin halted at the door, and Nightshade paused behind him. Five human women worked at sinks, scrubbing laundry and pushing clothing through a wringer.

"Ladies." Devin bowed with an elegant sweep of his hand. The women's giggles turned to gasps when they saw Nightshade. Two backed away and cowered against the far wall.

"You're safe with my friend," Devin said, his voice dark silky persuasion. The women visibly relaxed, but tension still hung in the room.

"What are we doing here?" Nightshade whispered. Devin raised his hand, requesting patience. Nightshade shook his head as he surveyed the laundry room. Hadn't the Teg heard of washing machines and dryers?

"Eloise—" Devin beckoned a slightly built woman with light brown hair spilling from beneath a grubby cap. She hesitated, then came two steps closer, maintaining what she must think was a safe distance. "Where's Rhys?" Devin asked.

Her eyes flared with fear. She clutched her wet apron in chapped red hands and shook her head. "Are you sure it's safe to talk, sir?"

Devin raised a calming hand. "Do not fear. Arian is busy elsewhere." Her eyes darted to the doorway, then settled on Nightshade while her teeth worried at her lip.

"This is Nightshade. He'd like to meet Rhys."

Nightshade raised his eyebrows. That was news to him.

The woman stared at him for a few seconds, then crouched and peered beneath the massive oak table heaped with piles of clean laundry. "Come out, my pet."

Nightshade expected a dog or cat, although why he would want to meet either baffled him.

A small black head peeped out. Nightshade's breath imploded, locking muscles, wiping thoughts. A little boy, no larger than Finian and Kea, crawled out from under the table. He wore nothing but a sagging diaper fastened with two huge safety pins. Chubby black fingers clutched at his mother's arm. He pushed himself up onto his legs and gave a coy smile.

"May I present your half brother Rhys," Devin said softly.

A lifetime of memories skated through Nightshade's head as he stared at the boy—a cuckoo in the nest, just as he'd been. His legs carried him forward without conscious thought. The woman jerked back, startled, as he dropped to his knees in front of her.

"Don't be frightened . . . Please." He raised a gentling hand, made sure he kept his wings folded tight to his back. Gradually, she relaxed her grip on her son. Nightshade pushed his hair back, and smiled at her, carefully, not too much, just enough to reassure.

"Hello, Rhys." The child angled his head, his silver eyes glinting between sooty lashes. His lips parted in a grin, revealing six teeth along with gaps. Slowly, Nightshade reached out and stroked the fluff of dark hair on his head. "How old is he?"

"Eleven months. He's just finding his feet."

"May I?" Nightshade held out his hand and, after a moment's hesitation, Eloise turned the child to face him.

Rhys blinked at him shyly. He touched Nightshade's hand, then turned away and pressed his face to his mother's skirt. "You're a cutie, aren't you?" Words Nightshade never dreamed would pass his lips slipped out as though he'd been saying them all his life.

The boy stretched out his hand again and grabbed one of Nightshade's fingers, then found his feet.

"Clever boy." He grinned like a fool and couldn't stop.

Rhys gave another toothy grin and stepped forward. Nightshade ached to hold him more than he'd ever imagined possible. Unknown emotions gripped his chest and throat, making it difficult to speak.

Eloise stroked the child's back, then glanced up nervously. "When will his wings grow?"

Gently, Nightshade turned Rhys sideways to see the two little bumps of flesh on his back. "The wing buds will develop a little over the next few years"—his heart clenched at the memory of pisky children chasing him around calling him hunchback. He couldn't bear to think of this innocent child going through the same torment—"then at puberty they'll grow much faster. That's when he'll get his fangs." He left unspoken the implication that he'd also develop his taste for blood.

What little color Eloise had in her face drained away. "I don't know what to do," she whispered.

Devin appeared at their side and hunkered down. He rubbed Rhys under the chin with his knuckle. "Nightshade is Rhys's half brother," he said.

"I heard you say that." Looking down, she sniffed. "What do you know of your father?" When she looked up, tears shimmered in her eyes.

"I've never met him. My mother was a Cornish pisky. He lived with the piskies for a while. By the time I was born, he'd gone."

She shook her head. "You were lucky."

Nightshade had never considered himself lucky. He'd longed for his father to come back and claim him. To finally meet one of his own kind . . .

"Dragon isn't a good father," Eloise whispered.

Devin laughed, an incredulous bark as if the sound had been knocked out of him. Rhys flinched. Nightshade curled a protective hand around the boy's tiny shoulders and scowled at the djinn.

"Eloise is being diplomatic." Devin nodded encouragement to the woman. "Tell Nightshade the truth about his father."

She gently encouraged Rhys into Nightshade's arms, then stood and paced to the sink.

With a burst of pleasure, Nightshade cuddled the child, stroking the soft tufts of dark hair back from inquisitive silver eyes. For the first time he understood why Michael was willing to sacrifice himself for Finian. Nightshade had only just discovered Rhys, yet he would defend his tiny brother with his life.

"Dragon doesn't really want Rhys, yet he is possessive about him. Whenever he returns, he demands to see Rhys and expects him to do things no child of his age can do. Then he punishes him when he fails."

Blood raced hot and fast to Nightshade's head. "Tell me."

Tears rolled down Eloise's face as she eased down the top of Rhys's diaper to reveal pink streaks of scar tissue.

Devin caught the woman's arm. She struggled to pull away. "Shh, woman. He needs to see." She sagged against the edge of the table, hanging her head, and stood mutely while Devin lifted the hem of her skirt to reveal similar scars on her legs.

"I wasn't here the last time Dragon visited." A hint of color crept along the djinn's cheekbones, and his eyes glittered with hate.

Nightshade stared at the vicious slash marks on Eloise's legs. He had believed his father to be selfish and irresponsible, but could he have done this? Could this monster Eloise was describing really be the creature whose blood ran through his veins?

"Arian is as bad," Eloise choked out, tears streaming down her cheeks. "He taunts my baby. I'm frightened of what Arian will do to him when Rhys is old enough to answer back."

Nightshade held Rhys tightly to his chest. His gaze lost focus and he played out exactly what would happen to Rhys in a few years. He had been there, done that. The pisky children who teased him were reprimanded, but there'd be no one to stop Arian taunting Rhys. No way could a small boy with wounded feelings and not enough maturity to keep his mouth shut defend himself against a full-grown male.

Eloise blinked and rubbed her eyes. She gazed at Devin, heartbreak on her face. "When you said you knew a way to keep Rhys safe, I didn't realize you meant someone would take him away." She pressed her hands to her mouth and sobbed.

Nightshade stared at her, at a loss to know what to say to give comfort.

"The decision is up to you, Eloise." Devin touched her arm gently.

She wiped her cheeks on her apron. "The choice is already made." She pulled Rhys from Nightshade's arms and rocked him. "The most important thing is to keep my baby safe." She turned swollen red eyes up to Nightshade. "I can already tell he likes you, and you're family. You must take him with you when you leave."

A whirlwind of emotion roared through Nightshade, hope, pleasure, a twinge of guilt at his joy. "I'll take you both. He needs his mother."

Devin's mouth set in a hard line. "The human slaves are magically shackled to the castle. There is a way she can escape, but we have to choose our time carefully." He rested a hand on the woman's shoulder. "Until I can help you escape, Rhys will be safe with Nightshade."

Footsteps sounded in the corridor outside the laundry room. Silence fell over the women, and everyone stared at the door. A huntsman halted in the doorway. "Master Devin, you've been summoned. The Ennead is reassembled."

Nightshade touched Rhys's cheek and smiled at Eloise. "You keep him safe for a little longer. I'll be back as soon as I can."

After pushing to his feet, Nightshade followed Devin out the door. He paused for one last sight of his brother before he hurried after the djinn.

As they neared the council chamber, a sick fear burned in Nightshade's stomach. What would happen to Michael? Could he really return from the dead? Nightshade stared at Devin's back and anger flooded him.

"I don't understand you," Nightshade snapped. He gripped Devin's shoulder and pulled him to a halt. "You went out of your way to help Rhys, yet all you had to do to save the pisky king's son was vote in our favor."

Devin shook away Nightshade's hand, his expression unreadable. "That was not the plan."

"Whose plan?" Nightshade growled.

The djinn's outline wavered; then he disappeared in a puff of smoke.

Chapter Ten

Michael rubbed his sweaty palms on his thighs and tried to calm his pounding heart as he stared down into the plaintiff's pit once more.

Most of the councilors had already taken their seats. Mawgan extended his arm, inviting him to descend the five steps to the lower floor. Cordelia's slender fingers slid into his hand, the simple touch giving him strength. She blinked up at him, tears glistening in her eyes. The prospect of his death must be almost as difficult for her to cope with as it was for him.

"I'm with you, Michael. Whatever happens, I won't leave you."

"Thank you, lass." His throat closed, trapping the words so they barely escaped his lips. He kissed her knuckles. "When I return, I want . . ." What did he want? To spend time with her, get to know her, make love to her. Yet to tell her now, when he might not survive, seemed insensitive. He must not make promises he wasn't sure he could keep just to make himself feel better.

He should concentrate on Finian, focus on what he would achieve, not what he might lose. An image filled his head of the boy in the mud at the bottom of the dark trench. Anger blazed through him, giving him strength. He squeezed Cordelia's fingers, then let go. Only he could cross into the Underworld. He had to do this alone.

He and Cordelia descended the steps side by side. She

held her cat bag across her chest like a shield. When they reached the bottom, he glanced back at the door. Where was Nightshade? Although he'd thought he didn't want the stalker here, he missed his friend.

"Back so soon?" Arian slouched in his chair, legs stretched before him, crossed at the ankles. "I thought you'd be half-way back to Cornwall by now with your tail between your legs."

Michael ignored his taunting voice and scanned the gallery. Two chairs were still empty. One of the robed seers was missing and so was the djinn. He wanted both of those council members present before he presented his plea. The seer had been sympathetic to his case earlier, and he still hoped Master Devin might support him if only because he knew Troy.

The missing seer entered from the gallery door and hurried to his seat. Mawgan gripped the arms of his chair and looked around. "Once again we await Master Devin," he said, his tone resigned.

"Start without him." Arian flicked his hand at the vacant chair contemptuously. "He has no right to keep the rest of us waiting."

As his words faded, a wisp of smoke appeared above the empty chair. A second later, the djinn materialized, seated with his legs crossed, eyebrows raised at Arian.

A beat of shocked silence filled the chamber, before Arian jumped to his feet. "No magic in the council chamber." He pointed at Devin. "You forfeit your right to hear this case."

An awkward silence fell while Arian glared at the other councilors, looking for support.

Devin rose to his feet. "I apologize for my unorthodox entry. I was busy elsewhere and thought to expedite my arrival."

"Apology accepted, Master Devin," Mawgan said. "The call was rather sudden, so your action is understandable."

Arian gave a dismissive gesture and flopped in his chair.

Nightshade strode through the door, then hesitated at the top of the descending steps. Instead of the air of wounded pride Michael had expected, his friend radiated a vital urgency.

Arian leaned forward, resting his hand on the intricately carved pillar beside his chair. "Nightstalker, forget them and join me in the gallery. The view is much better from up here."

With a grunt, Nightshade ran down the steps and strode to Michael's side. "He's determined to bait us."

Where had the stalker's new restraint come from?

Gripping Michael's shoulder, Nightshade leaned closer. "I was wrong, my friend. You do the right thing in offering your life for Finian."

Michael turned a questioning gaze on Nightshade, who answered with a quick, tight smile. What had happened to change the stalker's mind in the hour or so since they'd last spoken?

"We await your further plea, Michael O'Connor," Mawgan announced. "But be aware this is the last time we will gather at your call. Our decision on this appeal will be final."

"I do not appeal against your judgment." Michael scanned the council members, noting the surprised glances they shared. "I respect the opinion of the Ennead that a blood price was due in payment for the breach in our domain."

Being careful not to look at Arian directly, Michael watched the gatekeeper's reaction in his peripheral vision.

Arian leaned forward, elbows on his knees, hands clenched, and scrutinized Michael. "Why then do you take us from our duties once again?" Arian demanded, his tone wary.

"I have a proposition." Michael spoke carefully, kept his voice free of compulsion. He turned a full circle, making eye contact with each of the nine council members. "Do you agree a one-year-old child is an innocent who can have had no knowledge of the illegal gateway? That whatever his bloodline, he's not guilty of any crime?"

He circled again, noting the reaction of the councilors. The three seers nodded along with one of the huntsmen. The gatekeepers stared at him suspiciously. Master Devin smiled.

"Do you also agree that you wish the forfeit to be paid by one of the pisky king's blood?"

"Are you proposing you will pay?" Arian retorted, before Michael had time to make his point. "You had that option in Cornwall. As I've already borne witness, you refused to take responsibility."

Michael clenched his jaw as the councilors shuffled their feet, looking annoyed.

"That is my proposition, but if—"

Arian slashed his hand through the air. "It will take more than a drop of blood to appease the king now." He rose, his head angled arrogantly. "We're wasting our time here. This appeal is over."

The djinn surged to his feet and took a step forward. "You will regain your seat and hear the plaintiff make his case." His softly spoken words fell across the chamber like twilight shadows. Michael shivered and caught Cordelia's elbow when she whimpered and swayed. He couldn't determine if Master Devin had used glamour or something akin to silver tongue. He guessed the brush of horror they'd felt was only the fallout from what Devin had projected into Arian's mind.

Arian plopped back into his seat like a puppet whose strings had been cut. Glassy-eyed, he stared at Master Devin.

"Master Devin," Mawgan spoke softly, a plea in his voice. "Please take your seat."

The djinn held eye contact with Arian for a few seconds longer, then stepped back and sat.

"And may I remind you . . ." The seer's words trailed away when Devin turned his gaze on him.

"No magic or demonstration of power," Devin stated. "I know."

Nightshade chuckled. "Devin will back us this time."

Michael snatched a breath, his head light with nervousness.

"Continue," Mawgan said, looking at Michael.

"Me one goal in coming here is to win the release of the pisky king's son. To that end, I offer meself in exchange for the boy. Free Finian from the Underworld, and I will take his place."

One of the seers frowned. "How do you propose we place you in the Underworld, mortal? This is not possible."

"Oh yes it is," Devin said flatly.

Mawgan shook his head. "We can't accept a solution that requires we take a life. Who among us here could kill an innocent man in cold blood?"

Arian rose slowly, steadying himself against the pillar beside his seat. "I will."

Silence fell. Michael heard his own breath rushing in and out. Out of the corner of his eye, he saw tears running down Cordelia's cheeks. He locked his muscles and turned away.

"This upholds the blood price while releasing the child," Devin offered, his voice deep and penetrating. "I say we vote."

"No." Mawgan shook his head firmly. "This is not what we're here for."

"It's exactly what we're here for," Devin countered. "We resolve disputes. We free those taken in an untimely way, and we punish those who've shirked responsibility for their actions. On those grounds, the plaintiff has given us just cause to accept his plea. I say we vote."

"I second," Arian put it, his voice slicing through the air of indecision.

Mawgan rubbed his eyes and sighed. "Very well. We vote on the plaintiff's appeal. Do we accept him as blood price in exchange for the pisky child? All in favor stand."

A band of steel tightened around Michael's ribs, crushing his lungs. His heart shouted yes; vote yes. His mind shrank, ashamed, half hoping they'd vote no and not put him to the test.

Arian straightened where he stood. Dai and Olwyn rose to join him. Devin stood, slowly, his unwavering gaze fixed on Michael. The two huntsmen both looked at Devin and followed his lead. Mawgan shook his head and whispered to himself while he stared at his lap. One of the seers remained seated, but after a few seconds, the other rose to his feet. Mawgan cried out in distress and covered his eyes.

"The verdict is decided," Devin said. He placed a hand over his heart and spoke softly to himself. With a final glance at Michael, the djinn turned and left the chamber.

"When shall we do this thing?" asked the seer who'd risen in favor, looking at Arian.

"Now." Michael heard his own voice ring out, as if it belonged to someone else. "The child must be released immediately." Troy had said the light cocoon protecting Fin was good for five days, but Michael wanted the lad released as soon as possible.

Arian descended the steps from the gallery, then came down the final five to stand in the plaintiff's pit before Michael. "So you take responsibility for your brother's failings."

Was that what he was doing? Dying for his brother? When all along he'd thought he was striving to rescue a helpless child. Would Niall appreciate his sacrifice? Would Troy finally think him worthy?

The endeavor had felt urgent and secretly noble. A hollowness yawned inside him. He'd been tricked into giving up everything, because now the time to prove himself was here, he didn't believe he would rise from the dead.

Whatever Troy thought, Michael was sure he was not like his father.

"Leave the chamber while we prepare." Arian pointed at the door, surprisingly subdued and thoughtful in the face of what seemed like a victory for him.

The unreality of the situation danced in Nightshade's mind. Had he really met his baby brother a scant hour past? Was Michael really going to stand passively and let Arian deliver a fatal blow?

Michael stared at the wall as though he hadn't heard Arian speak. Tears trickled down Cordelia's cheeks, and she wiped them on her sleeve.

"Come." Nightshade gripped Michael's arm and led him toward the steps. Cordelia followed, her hand in her cat bag obviously seeking comfort from the creature.

When they reached the top of the steps, Devin strode back through the door and halted before them. He'd changed into a long black coat decorated with purple symbols.

"Come with me." Devin glanced at Michael, then looked to Nightshade for a response. The stalker nodded.

Michael pulled his arm from Nightshade's grip and rubbed his face. "Where would you be taking us, Master Devin?"

"To prepare." Devin made eye contact with Michael. They assessed each other for a few seconds; then Michael nodded.

Twenty yards along the corridor, Devin ushered them into his bedchamber. When they had all passed through the door, he turned the key in the lock, and indicated they should sit.

He supplied them with glasses of spicy honey wine, then turned to Michael. "Where's the dagger?"

"Did Gwyn tell you about the dagger?" Michael asked, frowning.

"Troy spoke to me, but we don't have time for an inquisition. Just be aware I'm on your side. What I tell you now is vital to your safety."

Michael hitched up one leg of his jeans and pulled Troy's dagger from its sheath.

When Devin took the blade, he cradled it lovingly like a long-lost treasure and stroked the huge egg-shaped gem. He tested the cutting edges and clucked his tongue. "You didn't think to hone the knife?"

"I'd no idea what it would be used for."

The djinn carried the blade to a table in the corner of his room and sharpened the knife on a whetstone. The grinding sound filled the chamber, stifling conversation, although none of them seemed inclined to talk.

Cordelia took Michael's hand. The sight did not hurt Nightshade as much as it would have a few days ago.

When he'd finished, Devin returned to them and placed the dagger on a table. "Listen carefully, Michael, *ya akhy, my brother*. You will die and enter the Underworld for good reason, which is as it should be. But you also need a good reason to return to life. Once you enter the Underworld, time passes differently. In a short time, the people you know here will seem like distant memories."

Cordelia's hand tightened on Michael's and he glanced at her. Nightshade squeezed Michael's shoulder, willing to share him if he must, but not to be forgotten.

"You need a strong tie to life." Devin paused, let his gaze travel over them all. "You need to bond with someone through your Magic Knot so you are joined in mind, body, and spirit with a living being."

Nightshade's hand clenched reflexively on Michael's shoulder, and Cordelia gasped.

"This is essential, Michael. You must choose either the wise woman or the nightstalker to be your mortal anchor."

Michael dropped his head into his hands. "I'm sorry," he said without looking up. "When we set out, I'd no idea of the commitment I was asking from you two."

"You don't have long to make your choice." Devin stood and knocked back his drink. Then he grabbed a long black sash from the back of a chair and draped it over his shoulder. "I'll leave you to decide. Be ready when I return."

He strode to the door and shut it quietly behind him.

"Ruddy Badba." Michael massaged his temples.

A few hours earlier, Nightshade would have fought for the chance to exchange Magic Knots with Michael and enhance their blood bond. Yet after meeting Rhys, his priorities had changed.

Before Michael had a chance to reject him in favor of Cordelia, as he obviously would, Nightshade crouched at Michael's side and gripped his arm. He ached to tell Michael about his baby brother, share the news that blazed inside him, burning away the loneliness he'd borne all his life. But he could not burden Michael with the knowledge of Rhys's plight when his friend was about to face the biggest challenge of his life.

Cordelia wandered to the bed and stroked her sleeping cat, giving Nightshade privacy to speak. "You are dear to me, Michael. I'm closer to you than I've ever been to anyone else. But I cannot exchange Knots with you."

Michael raised his head from his hands, scanning Nightshade's face.

"When I bond mind, body, and spirit," Nightshade continued, "it must be with a woman."

"Aye. 'Tis how I feel as well." Relief swam in Michael's eyes, softened his voice.

Nightshade smiled, sadness welling inside him for a love lost that he realized he'd only ever possessed in his imagination. "I want a babe." The words were little more than a whisper, his throat tight with memories of holding Rhys. "My own babe to hold in my arms. For that I need a female."

Michael smiled and shook his head. "Crikey O'Reilly, you're full o'surprises. I did not take you for a paternal sort of fella."

"Neither did I." Nightshade held Michael's face between his hands and before Michael could turn away, he kissed him hard on the lips.

Blinking, Michael rubbed the back of his hand across his mouth.

"Come back to us, bard." Nightshade swallowed, shocked at the tightness of tears in his throat. Jumping to his feet, he spun away and paced to the door. He held his wings rigid against his body and turned, hand clutching the door handle. "Good luck to you both." His gaze flicked to Cordelia, who was sitting on the edge of the bed, her glass of honey wine frozen halfway to her mouth.

Nightshade closed the door softly behind him and headed back to the laundry room for a few minutes with Rhys before he returned to the council chamber.

Cordelia sat rigidly beside Tamsy. The spicy gulp of honey wine she'd just taken scraped down her throat like a sharp stone. Nightshade closed the door behind him, leaving her alone with Michael in Devin's ornate room. She had expected Nightshade to argue for the right to exchange Magic Knots with Michael. Her plan had been to back down graciously. Giving up her chance of being with Michael would hurt, but there were too many reasons why she couldn't bond with him.

He stood slowly as if the movement pained him, stretching back his shoulders with a groan. "I'm sorry, lass. I never intended things to work out this way." He laughed sadly, a touch of his old humor on his face. "I never intended to give up me life so soon."

"You'll come back to life, Michael." She put down her cup and took a few steps toward him. The realization of how important she would be to his survival made her tremble. "I'll call you back."

He rubbed his face. "Much as I want to believe I've taken

after me father, I can't imagine how this will work. If me body is mortally wounded, how will I repair it?"

She wanted to reassure him, but she had no idea how anyone could die and return to life. "If you believe . . ." Her words trailed away at the skeptical glint in his eyes. How could she convince him of something she didn't believe herself?

"If you don't want to do this, I'll understand. 'Tis a lot to ask of you." He walked toward her.

She trembled as though her insides had been scooped out and replaced with jelly. She wanted him, yet the consequences of his discovering her water nymph nature terrified her.

"I never thought I'd bond with anyone. 'Twas not in me life plan." He gave a rueful laugh.

"Neither did I." Her grandmother had forbidden her to bond with a man and shame her father by revealing her true nature. Self-consciously, she pushed stray wisps of hair back from her face. Although Michael had dominated her senses since the day he walked into Trevelion Manor, until the last few days, he'd never given any indication that he found her attractive. Yet if he survived today, he would be intimately tied to her for the rest of his life. He could never undo the lover's bond forged when they exchanged Magic Knots, even if he fell in love with someone else.

He touched a finger beneath her chin and raised her face to look at him. "What are you thinking, lass?"

"How do you sense me, Michael?"

Little creases formed between his perfect eyebrows. "Here." He placed his hand over his solar plexus. "You're a swirly sensation. I suppose that's your water elemental nature."

His tone sounded only mildly curious. She tried to look away but he held her chin firmly between finger and thumb. "Why does me sense of you matter, lass?"

She couldn't admit she felt his psychic presence so strongly, he drowned out everyone else. She quickly changed the subject.

"There's something I need to tell you. I'm not sure how it might affect my ability to call you back." She pulled the silver chain out of her polo neck and let the single translucent stone ring fall against her chest.

His brows drew together. "Are your mind, body, and spirit combined in a single ring?"

"No. This is the body ring from my Magic Knot."

"Then where—"

Cordelia glanced over her shoulder at her precious cat curled asleep on Devin's bed, oblivious to her part in all this. "Tamsy holds my mind and spirit rings."

"You're bonded to a cat?" He stared at Tamsy, eyebrows raised. "Why?"

"She's my familiar. When I was twelve, my grandmother bonded me to her so Tamsy could help me with my work." And so Cordelia would never be tempted to bond with a man.

He stared over her head, eyes unfocused, and drew a slow breath. Then he lowered his gaze to her face and gave a sad smile. "If you're willing to accept my Magic Knot, maybe that will be enough to help me find my way back to you."

She closed her eyes, a maelstrom of mixed emotions churning inside. Part of her raged at her grandmother for taking her mind and spirit stones, thus hindering her ability to help Michael. Another part of her was terrified that when he discovered she was a water nymph, his attitude toward her would change. Nymphos were nothing more than a lascivious joke to most males. And how would she control her allure if he tried to kiss her and touch her?

Yet whatever the personal consequences, she must help him find his way back from the Underworld. She opened her eyes and met his troubled gaze. "I'll be your anchor in the mortal world to bring you back from death, but that's all, Michael. We can't be handfasted like man and wife."

"You mean no intimacy. Why?"

She looked away and chewed her lip. He'd find out soon enough. Why not just tell him?

"Cordelia, sugarplum." He curved gentle fingers around her cheek. "If you're worried I'll stray and embarrass you, lass, forget your fears. I'm sure we can keep each other happy."

"I'm not worried about you, it's *me*." She swallowed back tears, hating that she had given him another thing to worry about.

"We can talk over the relationship if I come back. If I don't, 'twill be the shortest bonding ever."

"You will come back." The possibility of losing him forever seared her heart, eclipsed all other worries. Wrapping her arms around him, she pressed her face against his neck.

He returned her hug, his lips brushing her forehead. His fingers stroked her jaw, lifted her chin. Gently, his lips slid over hers. Michael kissed her with a gentle intensity as though she was precious.

She hung in his embrace, her lips moving beneath the silky warmth of his mouth, her muscles limp with desire as he molded her to his hard body. After a few minutes, he drew back with a groan. "Ah, Cordelia, I want to carry you over to the bed and lose meself in you, but we have no time. Are you ready to exchange Knots?"

She nodded. He pulled out a leather thong bearing his three earthy-brown linked stone rings, drew it over his head and looped it around her neck. His Magic Knot settled against her chest, separated from her skin by her sweater.

Pulse racing, she unfastened the silver chain holding her single stone ring, hesitated, then lowered it into his hand. Her breath froze, waiting. Nothing happened.

"Put me Knot against your skin."

With trembling fingers, she dropped his Magic Knot inside her sweater to settle in the valley between her breasts.

He took her hand and stared into her eyes, his so blue and deep, the shimmer of expectation sending whispers of sensation up and down her spine.

The hot beat of his presence in her chest expanded, flooded her body with heat, flashed along her veins and nerves. He caught her against him. Pressed his lips to her cheek. Then the full force of his power hit her like a truck. Her head pounded, heart thumped, nerves screamed. Her legs folded, her body pumped so full of his energy she felt as though she'd burst.

Tamsy's distressed yowl cut through the quiet room.

"Cordelia?" His grip on her tightened to hold her up. "What's the matter?"

"You're . . . hurting . . . me." She gasped between each word, barely able to fill her lungs to speak.

"I'm not doing anything."

Suddenly the pressure inside her withdrew. She sucked in air, her skin prickling from the rush of energy. Tamsy's gentling influence shimmered on the edge of her awareness.

"Sorry, sugarplum." He stroked her face, kissed her hair. "I just let meself go."

She clung to him while the strength returned to her legs. She'd feared he'd be overwhelmed by her allure, but the swirling sensual energy inside her faded into insignificance compared with Michael's power. Troy's words about Michael came back to her.

He's a strong earth elemental. Strong enough to ground your allure. You'd thrive together.

"Let me feel you," Michael whispered against her ear. She relaxed, and although most of her energy remained trapped within her wards, she sent a subtle brush of awareness into his mind.

He groaned deep in his chest. His fingers flexed against

her back. "Sweet Anu." His breath puffed hot among the strands of her hair. "You're a water nymph."

She buried her face against his chest, trying to judge his attitude from his tone of voice.

"Sweet bejesus, Cordelia." His chest rose and fell beneath her cheek. His hand trailed up her spine, traveled down again to splay on the small of her back.

Her tension slowly leaked away when he seemed to accept her nature.

"Let me into your thoughts."

She raised her head and blinked. "Can't you read my thoughts?"

"You're shutting me out."

She must instinctively be protecting herself. The realization that she still had control over what he saw in her mind flooded her with relief. Maybe she could hide the fact that she'd watched him in the divination mirror.

She touched his face, relieved to see pleasure sparkling in his eyes. "When you come back, I'll show you my thoughts," she whispered.

He cupped her bottom in his hand and lifted her against the hardness of his erection. "When I come back, I want to see more than your thoughts, lass. When I come back, I want to make this joining between us physical."

A knock sounded. Before they had time to move apart, the door opened and Devin strode in. He nodded in greeting and grinned at Cordelia. "Michael made the right choice, I see."

"Is it time to go already?" Fear shot down Cordelia's spine, chilled her core.

"Don't worry." Devin's grin softened to an encouraging smile. "You'll get through this together." He slapped Michael on the back. "We need your shirt off."

Michael pulled the T-shirt over his head and dropped it on a chair. Devin's gaze flicked down to the front of Michael's jeans and the corners of his mouth crooked up. "You have enough incentive to hurry back to life now, do you, *ya rajol?*"

Michael grinned, and her heart wrenched to see him being so brave.

"Cordelia." Devin beckoned her closer and retrieved Troy's dagger from the table where he'd left it earlier. "When you call Michael back from the dead, you'll use the Phoenix Stone. The dagger was designed to both take life and restore it. Hold the stone in front of him. The diffracted colors will penetrate the nine energy centers of his body to heal him."

Michael rubbed his chest as though it was already sore. "I was wondering how I'd heal me body."

With trembling hands, she took the dagger from Devin and held it up so light streaked through the stone and sprayed colored rays on the djinn's body.

"You've got the idea. Just keep your head and all will be well."

Devin went and stood in front of Michael. "One final thing." He held up his left hand and flexed his fingers. The pointed nails glittered darkly; then the nail on his middle finger extended to a vicious inch-long point.

"Ruddy Badba." Michael stepped back, bumping into a table.

"Stand still, and don't be a wimp, boy."

Cordelia hurried forward, wanting to protect Michael, although she had no idea how. "Please don't hurt him, Master Devin."

"I'm only going to numb his chest."

"Oh." Cordelia stood helplessly with a hand pressed to her mouth while the djinn pushed the long nail into Michael's chest just over his heart. Michael hissed when the point pierced his skin.

Within a few seconds, the wound disappeared.

"How will that numb me chest?"

"I've poisoned you."

"You've *what*?" Cordelia shouted, making both men jolt with surprise.

The djinn gave Michael a wry grin. "You've got yourself one possessive woman looking out for you now, *ya akhy.*" He slapped Michael on the shoulder. "I only injected enough venom to dull the pain as the blade goes in."

"You have venom under your fingernails?" Cordelia stared at his hand, horrified. He might be beautiful, but with sharp poisonous fingernails, she couldn't imagine women were lining up to go out with him.

"Just one fingernail." Devin flipped up his middle finger, and Michael chuckled.

Michael tapped the area over his heart. "Me chest is less sensitive already."

"You can buy me a drink later," Devin said. "Now it's time to go to the council chamber."

The smile dropped from Devin's face and he stared at Michael. "I know you're scared, boy. But you'll be fine. I promise."

He turned his back to give them a moment of privacy. Cordelia rushed to Michael, pressing her palm over his heart center, willing her strength into him as he wrapped his arms around her. She inhaled the herbal, earthy tang of his skin. His lips met hers, and she kissed him with all the passion locked inside her, the allure swelling and surging like a storm within her wards, threatening to break free.

She framed his face in her hands and stared into his blue eyes, darkened now with fear. "I'll call you back, Michael."

"Aye, lass." He touched a finger to her lips. "I know you won't let me down."

Chapter Eleven

Michael gripped Cordelia's hand and pulled her against his side. He concentrated on the calm, flowing sense of her, soothing as the gentle lap of water.

As he followed Devin to the council chamber, he thought of Cordelia to keep his mind off his fate. The opposing images of the uptight wise woman in her long, high-necked dresses and the sensual water nymph still couldn't connect in his brain. Why had she hidden her nature from the piskies?

He'd be slapping himself on the back for getting hitched to a member of such a sensuous race if he wasn't about to be stabbed to death.

Sweet Anu. What was he doing? A tremor passed through his body into the earth and an answering surge of energy flowed up his legs from his element. He halted outside the council chamber and closed his eyes. His insides pinched and ached as though someone had pulled out his guts and stuffed them back in the wrong way. He couldn't do this. He'd never made any bones about the fact he was a coward. Pain was not his thing.

"Michael?" Cordelia's gentle enquiry barely penetrated the terrified darkness gathering around his mind.

Devin gripped Michael's arm and something like an electric shock jolted from his touch, firing every nerve ending in Michael's body and giving him strength. His eyes sprang open. "Stay with us, *ya akhy*. Be brave. Don't think about

what will happen. Concentrate on your bond with Cordelia."
For a flitting moment, raw emotion glittered in the djinn's
obsidian eyes. "I must leave you now. *Allah Maack*, God go
with you." Taking the Phoenix Dagger from Cordelia, he
preceded them into the council chamber.

Michael's head bobbed in assent automatically. How
could he ever be ready to die? Cordelia squeezed his hand
hard. He gathered her into his arms, and kissed her deeply
with all the passion he possessed in case it was their last kiss.
A sensual pull swirled around his mind, promising to drag
him down to a place where desire would sweep all worries
away. He loosened his hold on her with a groan of suppressed
longing.

Flushed and panting after the kiss, Cordelia trembled in
his arms. "Michael, I shouldn't let my allure run out of control like that in case—"

He pressed a finger to her lips.

"I need this to remind me what I'm coming back for, sugarplum. We'll work things out later."

He managed an ironic smile at the tightness of his groin.
"Looks like I'll be going to me death with a boner. Niall
would say 'tis fitting, I'm sure."

Before he surrendered himself to desire and kissed her
again, he released her from his arms.

After looping Cordelia's silver chain around his wrist, he
pushed the translucent stone ring onto his little finger. Head
high, he strode through the door into the council chamber
with her hand gripped tightly in his.

The windows were shuttered, leaving the room lit only
by oil lamps hanging on curly metal brackets at intervals
around the walls. The light flickered from all angles, casting
multiple shadows.

"Oh." Cordelia's exclamation brought his attention down
from the gallery. The blue-tiled floor of the pit had disappeared to reveal a lower level beneath the chamber.

The smell of wet dog reached his nose as he noticed the glowing red eyes in the darkness below.

"This is what I saw in my divination mirror before the Teg arrived." Cordelia's voice cracked as she grabbed his arm and tried to pull him back.

"Shh, lass. I can't just walk away now."

"You don't understand. The prediction didn't feel right, Michael." She gave a halfhearted tug, trying to drag him toward the door again. "You mustn't go down there."

"Let me look, lass." He eased from her grasp and descended the steps to the level of the plaintiff's pit. When his eyes adjusted to the darkness, he made out the shadowy forms of huge hounds below. Huntsmen walked among the animals, slapping at rumps with short leather-covered crops to keep them under control. A shiver stole through Michael. He had always liked dogs. He had a nasty suspicion, though, that these weren't ordinary animals, but hounds from the King of the Underworld's wild hunt, creatures capable of stealing souls.

He ascended the steps again. At the sight of Cordelia's crumpled, tearstained face, strength he'd never known he possessed rose up inside him. He must be brave for her, as well as himself. He gently took her shoulders and made her look at him. "I'm going to die here, this day, lass. What more is there to go wrong?"

Her eyes scanned his face urgently. "I don't know."

He kissed her once more, tasting salt from her tears.

"A kiss is the condemned man's last wish," Arian crowed as he entered the gallery door and strolled around the upper floor to the steps.

Michael looked up and released Cordelia, furious with Arian for besmirching something precious.

As the other council members filed in and took their seats, Nightshade hurried through the door. He walked up and gripped Michael's hand. "Hurry back, bard."

Michael gave a cocky grin full of a bravado he didn't feel.

He angled his head closer to Nightshade. "Take Cordelia and Thorn home," he whispered so she wouldn't hear.

Nightshade frowned and Michael repeated his instruction. "If I don't make it back, you will do this for me, won't you?"

"Of course."

He slapped Nightshade on the shoulder. A little of his tension filtered away now he knew Cordelia and Thorn would be protected.

Devin and Arian were talking a few yards away. Frowning, Arian held up Troy's dagger to the light and examined the gem. "What manner of stone is this?"

"I'm unfamiliar with the decoration, but the blade is suitable," Devin replied, his voice laced with subtle persuasion that most wouldn't notice.

Arian weighed the dagger in his palm, tested the cutting edge with his thumb. Michael tensed, waiting for Arian to reject the knife on principle. Instead, he shrugged. "Very well. I'll use the piskies' weapon." None of them spoke up to tell him the owner of the dagger was no pisky.

"Michael O'Connor." Mawgan's voice filled the chamber, not a summons, but a plea. "I beg you to reconsider this drastic action. There is still time to rescind your request."

Arian shot a dark look at the robed seer. "I disagree. The bargain is wrought. He knew what he was asking for."

Temptation to back down flashed through Michael. He inhaled deeply twice before he found enough air to answer in a steady voice. "I wish to go ahead."

"So be it." Mawgan sat and the other two seers took their seats beside him. Dai and Olwyn descended the steps, their translucent blue eyes fixed on Michael. His skin crawled as they came toward him.

When the two Teg pulled him forward, he glanced back at Cordelia and Nightshade. "Take her up to the gallery out of the way," he told Nightshade.

"No." She stood ashen faced, her fists clenched at her

sides. Her cat bag slid from her shoulder and Nightshade caught the strap and looped it over her head. Then he ushered her away.

Michael fought the tremor of his muscles as Olwyn and Dai led him down the steps. When they reached the bottom, the grizzled black hair of the hounds brushed against his legs. They sniffed him, but despite their red eyes and fearsome appearance, he sensed no aggression. The beasts were strangely silent, except for the snuffle of their breathing in the confined space.

"Keep the bloody hounds back," Arian growled at the huntsmen as he followed down the steps.

Pairs of red glowing eyes watched Michael from the darkest corners of the dungeon while the gatekeepers led him to a wall. They wrenched his arms to the sides and manacled his wrists. He pressed his head back against the damp stone and closed his eyes. Sweat prickled on his skin. Finally, here, in the shadows, his courage failed.

He panted, heart thundering as he floundered, grasping for the thread of Cordelia's presence to anchor him. Faintly, he sensed her as though she were a long way away. He let his mind flow along the tendril of connection, the strange newness of the sensation unsettling and unsatisfying. He needed to put his hands on her body, not make do with this wispy tenuous mental link.

Cordelia? He shouted her name in his head.

The sense of her surged through him, permeating every cell, leaving a gentle calm in her wake. He focused all his attention on the single ring of her Magic Knot around his finger. His breath steadied, his heart slowed.

"Open your eyes, pisky," Arian said. The gatekeeper stood so close that Michael could see the pale rings glowing around his pupils.

"I'm not a pisky," he ground out.

Arian's mouth tightened. "Oh, I know what you are," he whispered. Then louder: "You give your life for the pisky king's irresponsible leadership, for his dereliction of duty to protect those in his domain."

Michael blinked sweat from his eyes. The tone of Arian's accusation fired bolts of warning along his nerves. This should be a simple exchange of his life for Finian's. Not retribution for Niall's perceived failings.

Arian leaned in so close, his frigid breath chilled Michael's skin. "You give your life to pay for the overarching superiority of your father and your brothers." He whispered an incantation in ancient Celtic, *"As immortal blood damned him, so immortal blood will set him free. I take this life in the name of freedom for Gwyn ap Nudd, King of the Underworld."*

"As the Ennead has voted, so shall it be," Arian shouted.

Wait! The word formed in Michael's head. Then Arian struck his chest. Fiery pain exploded from Michael's heart. His breath leaked away. His head fell forward. Through tear-filled eyes he saw the dagger protruding from his chest. Sparkling waves of color pulsed in the Phoenix Stone. His energy drifted away like a memory of youth, his body growing heavy, weary of life.

Brothers, plural? The thought hung in his mind for a moment, then dispersed like mist in the wind.

Cordelia screwed her eyes closed, concentrating every shred of her mental energy on Michael. But however hard she tried to focus on him, he slipped from her like water through her fingers. She couldn't hold the connection with him, maybe because he had only her body stone.

She gritted her teeth, willing her mind to be stronger. At the sound of Arian's shout, her eyelids snapped up. Time stilled as Arian leaned closer to Michael. She thought they were talking, yet when the gatekeeper stepped back, the glittering hilt of the dagger protruded from Michael's chest.

With a cry, she clutched a wooden pillar. She focused on his psychic beat beside her heart until the pulse faded to nothing.

Tears flooded her eyes. "Michael." She thought she cried out his name, but the word slid breathless between her lips.

He hung suspended by the short chains anchoring his wrists to the wall, chin on his chest, blood seeping around the embedded blade, running down his belly, staining the soft, pale denim of his jeans.

The lamps blinked out one by one, and the chamber fell into darkness. Red eyes blazed. A single mournful wail rent the air. Then another hound took up the call, others joining until the pack was in full cry, sending a shard of pain through her head with each howl. She grasped her cat bag, hanging on to the panicked body of the struggling feline.

The scene she'd viewed in her divination mirror had been Michael's death. If only she'd known, she would never have let him come to Wales.

When the hounds' calls subsided, Nightshade's breath brushed her ear. "I can see in the dark. Arian has gone, and Master Devin has pulled the dagger from Michael's chest."

"Oh." She pressed her face against the top of Tamsy's head. Shock and pain warred with a sense of unreality. How could this be happening? A few days ago, she'd been safe and secure in Trevelion Manor while Michael sat on his stool and told stories in the great hall.

The lamps flared again, revealing Master Devin halfway up the steps from the pit, wiping the blade of Troy's dagger on a cloth. He balled the fabric and hurled it back into the darkness among the hounds. A few seconds later, he entered the gallery and walked toward them.

When she tried to let go of the pillar and stand, her legs trembled. Nightshade stepped closer and put a supporting arm around her waist. She sagged against his muscular arm gratefully. What nightmare had she entered where a night-stalker became her friend and protector?

Tight lipped, the djinn halted and presented the handle of the dagger. For long seconds, she stared at the hated thing, her breath stuttering in and out. This blade had killed Michael, probably still bore traces of his blood. But it was also the tool of his resurrection. She gathered her strength and gripped the handle of the dagger.

Devin dug a leather thong from his pocket and tied back his hair. "In fifteen minutes, the lamps will be extinguished and the shutters opened. As soon as you have sunlight, you must go to Michael before his body cools and revive him in the way I showed you."

Cordelia turned a tremulous gaze on the hounds still milling around below. "What about them?"

"As long as you wait until the shutters are opened before you go to Michael, they won't touch you. The hounds of the wild hunt guard the corpse for fifteen minutes to stop relatives from trying to resuscitate the condemned. After that period of time, the victim is assumed dead, and relatives may claim the body."

"What will the council members do when Michael returns to life?" She gestured toward the three seers who remained in their seats.

"Once the shutters are opened, the proceedings are complete. Michael can walk away a free man."

Devin shook out the strip of black fabric that had been hanging around his shoulders and wrapped his head, until only the dark glint of his eyes remained visible. After securing the cloth at his throat, he pulled on leather gloves. "Now I go into the Underworld to rescue the child," he said, muffled behind the headgear.

"You?" Cordelia asked.

He nodded and raised his arm to signal to the huntsmen.

From below, the cry went up, "Make way for the Master of the Darkling Road." Huntsmen jostled the hounds aside, slapping at their rumps to clear a path. Devin strode between the heaving canine bodies and paused when he reached Michael to glance up at her. He raised a hand in farewell, then turned and disappeared into the murky darkness.

* * *

Michael stood on a green hill surrounded by the purple glow of the Irish Wicklow Mountains and stared down into a sheltered vale.

Excited shouts heralded the arrival of two small boys who burst from a cave mouth into the sunny valley below. A short, dark-skinned leprechaun woman followed them out and plopped her plump behind on a hillock to watch them play.

The two boys were identical in not only their brown shorts and shirts, but also their dark springy waves of hair and cheeky faces.

The quieter one set an empty bottle on a rock and gathered a heap of pebbles for target practice. The other boy waited for his brother to prepare his game, then swooped in, arms wide like a bird, and knocked the bottle off its perch.

"Mick, 'tis not fair."

"Michael," the leprechaun woman shouted. "Stand Niall's target up for him again, you rascal."

With a grin, the naughty boy plucked up the bottle and scampered away. The other boy's face set with determination and he gave chase. They tumbled across the cropped grass, arms and legs tangled, cursing, and thumping each other.

"Oh, you lads have the devil in you." The leprechaun sprang up and pulled them apart, hanging on to their collars. Michael burst into noisy tears and buried his face in the woman's dress. Niall stood stoically rubbing his bruises.

A memory.

One from the depths of his mind, long forgotten?

"I'm surprised," a quiet voice said behind him. Michael turned to find Troy standing a short distance away, his flamboyant attire glowing and sparkling in the sunlight while he stared at the little drama in the vale below. "This is your fondest memory?"

"I don't think . . ." Michael turned back to the scene below, but no one was there.

What was he doing here? He struggled to backtrack. Odd thoughts and feelings jumbled together inside his head: Niall holding a baby, a woman with a cat, a nightstalker biting him.

"What's going on?" he asked.

"You're dead, son."

Michael's hand went to his chest. He remembered the glitter of a gem in the hilt of a dagger, the smell of dogs, the soft feel of a woman's body in his arms.

In a flash, he remembered the scenario that had recently played out in the council chamber. The strength drained from him. He clutched a nearby rock and sat down.

"I'm in the Underworld?" He blinked at his father.

"Not quite. Your mind has taken you back to the time you were happiest."

"So I'm in a dream?"

"In a manner of speaking."

"Then why are you here?"

Troy glanced down at the silent vale, a whisper of sadness crossing his face. "Not because I have a place in your fondest memory."

Michael rubbed his face. When he gathered his thoughts, anger blossomed in his chest. "Why didn't you tell me what the dagger was for?"

"The time wasn't right."

Michael surged to his feet, indignation feeding his strength. All his life he'd admired his father, yearned for his approval. For the first time, he questioned Troy's motives.

"You sent me to Wales to be killed?"

"I sent you to Wales to be reborn."

"Don't try to make this sound as though you were doing me a favor." Turning his back on Troy, Michael strode to a rocky outcrop overlooking the valley and filled his lungs with calming mountain air.

Michael glanced over his shoulder while Troy smoothed the lace at his wrists. "You manipulated me," Michael said.

Troy raised his eyes, his expression uncompromising, no hint of remorse.

"You're not even sorry?" Michael swung back to face his father, fists clenched in frustration. "You should have explained and let me make me own decision."

"Would you have come to Wales to rescue Finian if you knew you would face death?"

"Shit. Shit." Michael closed his eyes and banged a fist on his brow. How did his father always tie him up in knots? He wanted to say that of course he would choose to give his life for Finian, but deep in a shadowy private place, he doubted his courage.

Stepping forward, Troy reached a comforting hand toward Michael, but the touch passed through him as though he was a shadow.

Michael stared at his insubstantial arm, the reality of his death twisting hot and cold in his gut.

"Don't worry, lad. Your mind and spirit will soon return to your body," Troy said, his voice silky and soothing.

Hurt that his father would try to dispel his grievance with a dose of silver tongue, Michael flared with resentment as Troy continued talking in his irritatingly calm and patient tone.

"To achieve your full potential, you need to die and be reborn. The first time you must willingly sacrifice your life for a worthy cause. There is no worthier cause than giving your life to save another."

"So you saved someone the first time you died, did you?" Michael snapped back.

Troy dropped his head forward so fast, golden strands pulled loose from the diamond-studded spike securing his hair.

"Who did you save?" Michael pressed, sensing his father's hesitation. "A child like Fin, a brother?" He snapped his fingers. "I have it! You saved a beautiful damsel in distress. I bet there were damsels in distress around every bloody corner when you were young."

Silence stretched between them and for the first time in his life, Michael heard his father's breath catch as though he was struggling for control. Just as Michael started to feel uneasy, Troy raised his head, his eyes glacial and remote. "I didn't save anyone, Michael. But you will."

Thinking of damsels in distress brought a woman's sad gray eyes to mind. Cordelia was waiting for him. She would call him back to life.

He blinked, concentrated on how she'd felt, the warm swirl of comfort in his middle when she was near, but he couldn't sense her.

He huffed in frustration.

"Remember you're here for Finian," Troy said gently.

Michael's urgency to rescue his nephew returned. How had he become sidetracked? "Where is he?"

"Safe. Someone is watching him until we arrive. But we need to enter the Underworld. We won't have long before the wise woman calls you back." Troy circled his arm, stirring the air. The verdant valley faded to murky tones, shadows falling.

Michael glanced around. "We're still in the same place."

"We create our own Underworld, Michael, just as we create our own dreams."

A dark track opened before them, winding between the hills.

"If you have permission from the Master of the Darkling Road, you can use the safe routes," Troy said. "But always remember the Underworld is treacherous. Stray from the road, and you'll forget who you are and wander through the shadows for eternity."

Cordelia counted off the minutes in her head until the shutters in the council chamber were opened, and she could revive Michael. Nightshade stood like a silent sentry at her side. Unbelievably, his presence felt reassuring rather than threatening. The old adage, my enemy's enemy is my friend, was true.

Her fingers ached from clutching the Phoenix Dagger. She'd hoped the councilors would all leave the chamber so there would be no one to see her resurrect Michael, but Mawgan and the two seers were still there, along with the ten huntsmen below with the hounds. Despite Devin's assurances that no one would interfere when she went to Michael, she wanted Nightshade protecting her back.

After she'd counted off twelve minutes, she touched Nightshade's arm. "Let's start making our way down to Michael." They'd just reached the top of the gallery steps when the council chamber door crashed open. Silhouetted against the light in the doorway stood a tall man wearing a top hat.

Shock spilled through her. Gwyn?

How had he escaped from his tower? Would he interfere when she went to Michael? What had happened to Thorn? She hoped he hadn't come. She didn't want him to see Michael like this.

The hounds barked excitedly, surging against the restraint of the huntsmen until three broke loose and bounded up the steps to greet the man in the doorway.

After sitting somberly through the proceedings so far, Mawgan surged to his feet. "How did you get out?"

Gwyn stepped forward into the lamplight and alarm spurted through Cordelia. A hiss of surprise rose from the three seers. Gwyn's face was now pale and his eyes translucent blue.

Arian followed Gwyn into the chamber and kneeled at his feet, pressing his forehead to the floor. "My king."

Gwyn's hand hovered over Arian's head, and he smiled with satisfaction. "Don't look so shocked, Mawgan. Arian took Michael O'Connor's life in my name. You've grown careless, old man."

His pale blue gaze scanned the chamber. Cordelia and Nightshade stepped back into the shadows, but there was no hiding from him. He ascended the steps to the gallery, Arian on his heels, the three hounds following.

Cordelia hid the dagger behind her back when Gwyn halted at the top of the stairs, his black shoes mirror polished, reflecting the lamplight. "Well, well. The pisky wise woman and the nightstalker." He grinned darkly.

"What have you done with Thorn?"

"He's keeping Brian company. I like him. Maybe I'll keep him as a pet."

As Gwyn walked closer, Nightshade stepped in front of her, his wings slightly extended, his arms held ready to protect her.

She backed up toward the wall, hugging her cat bag across her chest with her free arm. Gwyn halted and scanned Nightshade from head to toe. "I'm afraid I don't have time to humor you at the moment."

With a sweep of Gwyn's arm, Nightshade flew through the air and crashed in a heap against the wall. Red flashed in Gwyn's translucent eyes. "Stay out of my way, stalker." The hounds drew back their lips and growled, drool hanging from their teeth. "Your father is a friend of mine, so I'd rather not kill you, but I will if you get in my way."

He approached Cordelia and she pressed back against the wall.

Gwyn nodded to Arian, who held out his hand. "Give him the Phoenix Dagger, witch."

She kept the blade out of sight, her mind racing in useless circles as she tried to think of a way to escape him and reach Michael.

Arian stared at her with an arrogant tilt of his head, nostrils flared derisively. "She's slow and foolish. Do not expect her to behave with any sense."

"You're a murdering, arrogant pig," she shouted at Arian. "And you're ugly as well," she added for good measure.

Gwyn laughed. "As curses go, that is not very imaginative. My loyal gatekeeper is right about you." He took another step closer and she huddled against the wall.

"Don't give him the dagger," Nightshade called, his voice cramped with pain.

"If you don't hand Arian the Phoenix Dagger now, he'll throw your cat to the hounds."

The air grew thick in her lungs; darkness flooded her vision. She had no doubt Arian would smile when he threw Tamsy to the dogs and laugh while she hissed and spat as the huge creatures ripped her to pieces.

If only Devin had stayed. He was the one person she could imagine standing up to Gwyn.

"No," she choked out, hating the tremble in her voice.

Gwyn's face hardened to a mask of loathing that froze her heart, and he signaled Arian forward. Summoning her courage, Cordelia clutched her cat bag tighter. She flexed her fingers on the handle of the Phoenix Dagger and held it ready. She had no training with a weapon, but she was armed, and by the gods, she would stand her ground and then get down the stairs to Michael.

Arian strode forward. She swung the blade at him. He dodged aside and caught hold of her wrist, squeezing and twisting until her bones and muscles burned with pain. Bending her arm back, he smashed her hand against the wall. With a cry of despair, her deadened fingers opened and the dagger clattered to the floorboards. The second his grip on her arm relaxed, she jerked away and scrambled around him, reaching for the shining hilt. He laughed and kicked her feet from under her, sending her sprawling while he snatched up the blade with a shout of triumph.

Cordelia lay defeated for a few seconds, hugging her wriggling cat, fighting back her tears. Losing the dagger could mean losing Michael, but she would not give up on him so easily.

"Open the shutters," Gwyn shouted as he and Arian ran

down the steps and stopped before the tall gold statue just inside the door. Olwyn and Dai's footsteps hurried across the wooden floor and the shutters snapped back, filling the chamber with daylight.

Massaging her sore hand and wrist, Cordelia pushed to her feet and shuffled forward to see what Gwyn would do with the dagger, ready for any chance to reclaim the blade.

"This blade has taken a life, now it owes a life," Gwyn crowed. He glanced up at Cordelia with a vindictive smile. "That life will be mine."

Fear shot through her as his words crushed her hope. Could the dagger only give back one life for each one taken?

Mawgan's cry of dissent echoed around the chamber as Arian raised the glittering hilt. Gwyn threw back his head and roared while rays of sun penetrated the Phoenix Stone and split into streaks of color, hitting the statue on the nine energy centers.

The figure of Gwyn lost substance and definition, leaving a shadowy silhouette; then he disappeared. The Phoenix Stone flared so brightly, Cordelia had to shield her eyes. When the light faded, she dropped her hand, fearful of what she'd see. In place of the statue now stood an imposing Tylwyth Teg man robed in black, white hair threaded with gold, translucent eyes glittering with red sparks.

He threw back his head and shouted in victory. Scanning the council chamber, he thumped his fist against his chest. "I, Gwyn ap Nudd, return to claim my domain and take my revenge on Troy the Deathless."

In the silence that followed, everyone in the room fell to his knees except Cordelia and Nightshade.

Gwyn's arrogant tone reverberated around the chamber, promising death and torment to anyone who crossed him, and especially to Troy and his descendents. The hatred in his voice terrified her. How could Troy have allowed Michael to put himself in such danger?

Cordelia crept back to Nightshade, who was leaning against the wall rubbing his head.

"Let's escape through the gallery door." He pointed to their left.

"We can't leave Michael's body in here alone with Gwyn." Cordelia's hand gripped desperately on the top of her cat bag.

Nightshade rubbed his face and cursed. "I can't fly down there and carry him out, because I've hurt my damn shoulder. All I'd do is attract Gwyn's attention. We need to get out of here and find another way into the lower level."

"All right," she agreed reluctantly, seeing no other option.

Arian had his back to them, while the three loose hounds sniffed around Gwyn's legs.

Cordelia and Nightshade sidled to the door and escaped onto the head of a descending flight of stairs. If she couldn't use the Phoenix Stone to heal Michael, she'd have to use her own healing energies. She ran down the stairs while she explained, urgency wiping away caution. "I'm a water nymph, a healer. The only chance we have is if I try to heal Michael, then call him back."

Nightshade blinked at her. "A water nymph?"

She nodded impatiently. "I need to go to Devin's chamber, and I need a woman's help."

Nightshade's mouth opened and closed like a fish.

"I have wards painted on my body to contain my allure so it doesn't run out of control. I need to wash them off."

"I could—"

"No!" She stopped at the bottom of the steps and yanked down the neck of her pullover, exposing the pale ridges of scar tissue on her throat and shoulder.

Nightshade's breath hissed between his teeth.

"Your father's marks."

All expression was wiped from his face, leaving his eyes hard and flat.

"That's the effect I have on males. If you touch me when the wards come off, you'll probably lose control as well."

Nightshade straightened, his nostrils flared, and he gave a single nod. "Go to Devin's chamber. I'll bring someone." When they entered the corridor, he sprinted away, leaving her to find her way back to the room where she and Michael had bonded. Tears tightened her throat and filled her eyes. She swallowed hard and gritted her teeth. She had not been trained to use her healing powers, but she must be strong and pray the skill came to her naturally. Otherwise, Michael would be lost to her forever.

Chapter Twelve

Nightshade burst into Devin's bedchamber with Rhys's mother at his heels. Because he was taking her child to safety, he was sure Eloise would help Cordelia.

Cordelia was kneeling in an alcove at the back of the room beside an old-fashioned faucet set into the wall above a stone bowl. When he entered, her head shot up. Fear flashed in her eyes, quickly replaced with relief. "Thank the gods, you're back."

Never in his wildest dreams had he imagined a time when she'd be pleased to see him.

"This is Eloise." He nodded to the woman at his side, who took a tentative step toward Cordelia.

"Good. Come and help me, please." She held out a cleaning cloth. "I need all the symbols on my skin scrubbed off." Her breath caught, and her chest heaved a few times before she continued. "We're running out of time."

Cordelia was naked except for her plain white underwear. He should have averted his eyes, but his gaze was drawn to the five intricate black Celtic symbols decorating her slender back. They must be the magical wards controlling her water nymph allure. She had a small round design on her nape, a large woven knot shape between her shoulder blades, the triangular symbol for inner strength straddling the delicate ridge of her spine at the level of her solar plexus, a triple spiral in the small of her back, and the top of a star peeping out over her panties.

Although she had her back toward him, he assumed from the way she rubbed at her chest with a wet cloth that she must have matching symbols painted on her front.

His throat closed and he swallowed painfully at the sight of the ragged edge of vicious scarring on her neck and shoulder. The cold weight in his belly that had settled there when she first showed him her injury solidified into lead, weighing down his spirit. No wonder the poor woman had always treated him with fear and loathing. How would he come to terms with this legacy of violence left by his father?

She glanced at him, and he finally turned his back, the pale scars on her skin burned into his retinas for eternity.

"I'm sorry," he said.

"This isn't your fault, Nightshade. Michael and I decided to come here. The consequences are on our heads."

"That's not what I mean. I'm sorry for what my father did to you."

The frantic scrubbing noise ceased. He glanced over his shoulder to find her staring at him with an aching vulnerability. "It wasn't totally your father's fault. I was partly to blame."

He stared at Tamsy pacing restlessly around Cordelia. How could a frail woman think she was at fault when a nightstalker savaged her?

"You can't have been to blame, wise woman," he said gently.

The wet rubbing noise started again, interspersed with her murmured instructions to Eloise. When the seconds lengthened to minutes, he thought she wasn't going to say any more.

Finally, she spoke, so softly he almost missed her words. "I'm half water nymph."

As if *that* explained everything.

He blinked at the blurred colors of a wall hanging. "How does your being part water nymph make my father's attack your fault?"

"It's not your fault if Dragon attacked you," Eloise said categorically. "He takes what he wants from human, Teg, or water nymph."

"He's here?" The stark terror in Cordelia's voice crushed Nightshade's soul.

"No," he said, trying to reassure her. Moving closer so they could talk, he sat sideways in a chair near the alcove.

"He visits occasionally," Eloise explained.

"Has he attacked anyone here?" Reluctant curiosity quivered in Cordelia's voice.

Eloise sat back on her heels, holding a dripping cloth. "Me," she whispered.

"Gods and goddesses, I'm sorry." Cordelia gripped the other woman's hand. "How badly did he hurt you?"

"She has a babe," Nightshade said, with a guilty flash of pleasure that he could finally tell someone. "My half brother."

Nightshade dragged his chair around to face them, practicality overcoming his observance of propriety. "I've agreed to bring Rhys home with us to protect him."

Cordelia put a hand over her mouth, stared wide-eyed from Eloise to Nightshade and back. "I can't think about this now. I must finish cleaning off my wards and get to Michael."

As the symbols disappeared from her body, Nightshade felt the pull of her sensual allure with disbelief. How could the cold, aloof wise woman have hidden this side of herself for so many years? The unbelievable discipline and self-denial left him speechless. And why would she want to hide her true nature? The restriction must be akin to his binding his wings. He couldn't tolerate that for a day, let alone a lifetime.

"I'm done." Cordelia stood and pulled on her trousers, sweater, and jacket without bothering to dry off. "Tamsy, you stay here." She touched her cat's head briefly.

"Can you show us a back way into the area beneath the council chamber?" Nightshade asked Eloise.

"That's the gateway to the Underworld," Eloise said.

"The wild hunt always starts from there. You should be able to enter through the huntsmen's door near the kennels."

After following Eloise through a maze of corridors, they descended to a lower level where the ground dropped away on the far side of the island. They emerged on a flat area to find slate-roofed stone kennels surrounding a paved yard.

Eloise stopped, her back pressed to the wall. The yard bustled with activity as huntsmen cleaned out the compounds and shouted instructions to each other.

"The place isn't usually busy at this time of day."

"I've lost track of what time of day it is." Nightshade stared up at the sky. The sun was at its zenith in an unbroken blue expanse.

Tears glistened in Cordelia's eyes. "We've taken too long. I *must* get to Michael."

"There's another rarely used door. The only problem is it'll be locked."

"Not for long." Nightshade flexed his fingers as they edged back.

They followed Eloise along the side of the castle and under an archway to a sun-bleached door in the wall. After Cordelia tried the handle unsuccessfully, Nightshade dug his fingernails around the lock, paring away the wood.

"Hurry, please." Cordelia rubbed the back of her hand over her eyes. Her allure teased his senses, and he understood how easily he could let the gentle ebb and flow of that attraction gather momentum and tempt him to do something he'd regret.

She must have seen his curious glance because she stepped away, her hands crossed defensively over her chest.

"You're in no danger from me, wise woman. Any male with integrity can resist the lure of a female, unless she sets out to seduce him."

He gave a final yank on the door handle and it came away from the wood, letting the door swing open. Inside, a dark corridor angled off under the castle.

"We have no light." Cordelia looked around frantically.

"I can see in the dark," Nightshade said in a soothing voice.

"Here"—Eloise untied her apron and pulled it free—"use this like a rope."

Cordelia looped one of the ties around her wrist and held out the other to him. "Quickly, Nightshade."

He turned to Eloise. "Fetch Rhys and wait for me in Devin's chamber. We'll probably need to leave fast."

They set off along the murky corridor, accompanied by the sound of water rushing through a gulley below. After a few minutes, muffled voices reached them.

Light glowed in the darkness ahead. "Quietly now," he whispered.

At the end of the tunnel, Nightshade pressed his shoulder to the wall and peered out into the dungeon beneath the council chamber. He counted four huntsmen and about twenty hounds. Gwyn wasn't visible, but Arian stood by the entrance to the chamber, issuing orders. Nightshade couldn't see the seers from this angle, but he didn't expect them to give him any trouble.

Cordelia moved to the other side of the opening. Her breath hitched. "Michael's just hanging there." She wrung her hands, her face a mask of misery. "We've taken too long. I'll never be able to heal him."

"Yes, you will." He waited until she met his gaze, then glared at her steadily until she pulled herself together. "I'll provide a diversion. You heal Michael."

He took out the short blade he kept in his boot for emergencies and handed it to her. "To protect yourself."

She accepted the knife, her eyes wide.

"You can heal Michael, wise woman. Bring him back."

Adrenaline seared away the slight ache in his shoulder. Nightshade leaped from the tunnel and snapped down his wings, clearing the hounds. He scanned the gallery as he soared to the high ceiling, confirming that Gwyn had gone, leaving only the three gatekeepers for him to tackle. Should be a cakewalk. He almost felt sorry for them.

Grinning at Arian's alarmed expression, Nightshade plunged down. Arian went for something at his belt, but he was too slow. Without touching down, Nightshade swept Arian up, and smashed him against the wall, knocking the breath from him with a whoosh. The sweet pain of his fangs descending brought saliva to his mouth. He angled his head and struck. Arian whimpered and went limp in his arms as disgusting cold blood flooded his mouth. Nightshade jerked away and spat.

When Arian recovered and opened his eyes, Nightshade gave him a wicked grin. "That was for me. This is for Michael." He drew back his fist and socked the gatekeeper on the jaw with a crunch, then released him to crumple to the ground.

Nightshade spun, ready for the attack by Dai and Olwyn, who had transformed themselves into light spheres. The two glowing orbs raced toward him. He considered changing into his shade form, but he could beat them easily as he was. He ducked aside and seized a table, using it as a shield. One brushed his arm, leaving an icy chill in its wake. When the other circled back, he judged the distance and speed and swung like a batsman, sending the orb spinning across the chamber to land among the hounds. The beasts growled and pounced like kittens on a ball of wool. With a muffled cry, Dai materialized beneath the legs of the excited pack.

Nightshade tracked the other orb while it circled, ignoring the rush of feet as the seers fled the chamber.

Swinging at the orb, Nightshade grinned as it careened off into the shadows. Pumped with adrenaline, he leaped from the gallery with a cry of victory and headed down to protect Cordelia while she healed Michael's body.

For Michael, time passed strangely, or maybe not at all. He walked beside his father for a long while, yet he felt as though they'd just left the vale. The Darkling Road wound through foggy hills, appearing in front of them, and disappearing once they'd passed.

"We're nearly there," Troy said.

"How can you tell? All looks the same to me."

"There are markers on the road if you know what to look for."

Ahead of them, a snort sounded in the murk. Troy halted and stared intently into the darkness. "Pig-faced trolls."

"Pig-faced what?" Michael strained his eyes to see through the fog. The snorts multiplied, and the ground began to vibrate.

"Damn, they've scented us," Troy said. With a whisper of metal on metal, he drew his short black sword from the scabbard across his back.

Michael still couldn't see anything.

Then they came into view, and he wished they hadn't. A group of about twenty short, thickset creatures with ugly flat faces and round snouts charged toward them brandishing swords.

"Better get behind me," Troy said, taking up a fighting stance.

Something inside Michael rebelled. All his life Troy had told him to stand aside whenever there was trouble. He'd just taken a dagger in the heart to save his nephew's life. He was damned if he'd let Troy order him to stand back this time.

The pig-faced creatures bore down on them, the snorting a frantic rattle as mucus trailed from their nostrils. Their stench nearly made him gag.

Michael was armed with a weapon that would inflict no damage, a weapon he'd used all his life. "Stop!" he roared, infusing every ounce of compulsion he possessed into his voice.

They slid to a halt, the last barreling into the first, resulting in a tumbled heap of squat, fat bodies.

Troy turned to him, an uncharacteristic look of wonder

on his face. "In all my days, I've never trusted my silver tongue to stop a charging assailant. Well done, lad." He touched his forehead in a gesture of respect and resheathed his sword.

Michael grinned at the unexpected praise.

Behind the creatures, a tall dark figure approached. He stopped when he reached the tangle of pig-faced trolls and reprimanded them. Then he strolled toward Troy and Michael, unwrapping a length of material from his head as he came.

Master Devin grinned at them, the subtle glow of his skin like moonlight through the tinted glass of Michael's Porsche. "Sorry about that. Took my eyes off them for a moment and . . . Well, you know what pig-faced trolls are like. Can smell a sausage from five miles away but have no brains."

"Are you implying I smell like sausages?" Troy asked, a rare smile twitching his lips.

"Would I dare?" Devin grinned wider. "I'm sure you smell like nothing less than caviar and truffles."

Troy laughed, a genuine burst of pleasure that Michael rarely heard. Although Troy had said he knew Devin, Michael hadn't expected them to be close. He felt slightly put out by their obvious affection.

Master Devin and Troy embraced, Troy clutching the back of Devin's head while he kissed his cheeks. He released him just enough to look into his face. "Well met, Devin, lad. Well met."

Devin stepped back and turned to Michael. "You allowed Arian his fifteen minutes of glory. Good show, *ya rajol*. I knew you had it in you."

Michael's eyes narrowed, irritation prickling while he tried to piece together the puzzle of what was going on. "Had I met you before I arrived in Wales?"

"I saw you a couple of times when you were a child. But you're one of us now, Michael."

"What do you mean?" Michael asked.

Troy rested a hand on Devin's shoulder. "Devin inherited my legacy as well. He's your older half brother."

Arian's words came back to Michael: *You give your life to pay for the overarching superiority of your father and your brothers.*

A shiver of unease passed through him, and he turned to Devin. "Why didn't you tell me you're me brother?"

"We didn't want anyone to know you're related to us," Troy answered.

"They do know."

Troy's hand clenched on his sword. "Are you sure, lad?"

Michael grimaced when he remembered discussing Troy with Gwyn and nodded.

"That probably explains a small problem we have," Devin said, concern darkening his face.

"Not a problem with rescuing Fin?" Michael asked.

"Possibly." Devin gave Troy an assessing glance. "I'm afraid Gwyn ap Nudd has escaped from the tower and he's wanting revenge."

Cordelia had waited for Nightshade to launch himself into the air and grab Arian. When all eyes in the chamber were on the nightstalker, she'd run toward Michael.

Now tears flooded her eyes and she dashed them away, her lips trembling. He looked . . . dead. He hung from the short chains attaching the manacles to the wall, his head dropped to his chest. Her heart stuttered at the cool, clammy feel of his skin. How could she heal a dead body? Devin had told her she must reach Michael before he grew cold.

Blood oozed from the wound in his chest. The injury was deceptively small and neat, a one-inch mark with only a little bruising around the area.

Gathering her strength, she hefted his body on her shoulder and struggled to pull out the pins on the manacles. She staggered as his dead weight fell against her. Breath heaving, she lowered him to the ground and dragged him farther into the gloom, out of sight. After pulling off her jacket, she pushed the bundle beneath his head.

She eased his arms straight at his sides and found her silver chain wrapped around his wrist, the single ring of her Magic Knot on his little finger. With a sob, she pressed his hand to her cheek.

She smoothed the hair back from his face, so perfect and innocent in death, and pressed her lips to his soft, cold mouth. Placing her palm over his heart, she closed her eyes and tapped into the energy circling inside her body. Even though she grieved for Michael, she was amazed at the sense of freedom she felt as her healing power expanded. For only the second time in her adult life, her aura was unrestrained. It was bliss.

Depending on intuition, she visualized green light flowing down her arm to her hand, bathing Michael's heart center, healing the trauma, sending love. Next, she laid her hand on his solar plexus and imagined golden yellow energy pouring into the swirling center of his body, giving him the will to heal himself. She paused for a moment to fill her lungs and focus, then moved lower and sent orange light into his belly. Then placing both hands over his groin, she visualized red light flowing from her to connect his body back to his element earth.

A scuffle behind her snapped her out of her healing trance. Glancing over her shoulder, she saw a huntsman wading toward her through the hounds. "No!" She raised a hand as if to fend him off. If he stopped her now, Michael would never recover.

Wings snapped through the air. Nightshade dropped down between her and the huntsman. "You're safe," Nightshade threw over his shoulder.

With a flash of incredulity, she noticed the wound on Michael's chest closing. A blast of confidence spurred her on. She closed her eyes and breathed deeply. When her heart slowed, she touched her fingers lightly to his throat and released blue light. Quickly, she moved on and pressed her palm between his eyes, sending indigo streaming into his spiritual third eye to bring his mind, body, and spirit back into alignment.

The hole over his heart had now closed, leaving only a silvery line marking the stab wound. Her healing power flashed around Michael's body, along nerves and veins, into every cell, repairing damage.

Cordelia focused the ebb and flow of her energy. Now she had healed Michael's body, she must face the hardest task of her life: calling him back from the Underworld.

As Devin moved forward, Troy held up a restraining hand. "Let's wait until the pisky wise woman summons Michael to return. I don't wish him to become involved in my disagreement with Gwyn."

Devin shot Michael a concerned glance. "Cordelia should have called you back by now."

Fear burned through Michael. "Gwyn won't hurt her, will he?"

"I imagine he'll consider her beneath his notice," Devin said. "Anyway, Gwyn is here in the Underworld now. I'm more worried about you."

Michael pressed his lips together and met his father's gaze. "Everything I've done these last couple of days has been to rescue Finian. I'm coming with you to make sure he's released."

"He's earned the right," Devin said softly. Then with a note of censure in his voice, he added, "Anyway, he's already well and truly mixed up in your disagreement with Gwyn."

Troy turned away. "So be it. I've sheltered you for too long." He opened his hand as if passing Michael responsibility for his life. "From now on, I'll not interfere in your decisions."

A short distance farther on, a golden glow penetrated the gloom.

"My light shield," Troy said, confirming Michael's suspicion that the glow must be from the cocoon surrounding Fin. He ached to hurry forward and check that the boy was safe. Instead, Devin and Troy slowed their pace, carefully scanning the area.

Troy withdrew his sword and Devin pulled a small implement from a hook on his belt.

"Watch out for shadows invading the Darkling Road. The dead become mindless wanderers, with no memory of who they were. The King of the Underworld can summon them to his defense. They can't harm you, Michael, as you're technically dead, but they'll suck the mortal life from Troy and me." Devin held up the implement in his hand. "A Taser's the best invention since condoms. Zaps the dead like it was made for the task."

The golden glow resolved into two shapes as they approached. One was the oval light barrier protecting Finian, the other was the radiance from a massive gold throne placed in the mud a short distance from the cocoon.

A black-robed Teg man lazed in the throne, threads of gold glinting in his white hair, his expression arrogant.

"Gwyn ap Nudd," Troy said, his voice glacial. "You have an annoying habit of escaping."

Michael's gaze skated from his nephew curled peacefully in his light shell to the intimidating figure seated on the throne. He'd known Gwyn was hiding his true appearance when they met him in the tower.

Gwyn pointed an accusing finger at Troy. "You've not explained our history to Michael, have you, Troy?"

"No excuses, no explanations," Troy said flatly.

"For crying out loud," Michael said under his breath. "Let's just get Finian out."

Gwyn rose to his feet and a long curved sword appeared in his hand. He pointed the blade at the golden cocoon around Finian. "Your doing, Troy?"

Troy remained stony-faced.

The king stalked around Fin. Michael tensed, waiting for him to slash at the light shell with his sword, but he stopped facing Troy, red sparks flashing in his eyes.

"You planned to cheat me of my blood price by rescuing the child and then resurrecting Michael. I won't allow that, Troy." Gwyn pulled the Phoenix Dagger from the folds of his robes and brandished the blade triumphantly.

Devin's breath hissed in. "*Ebn el kalb.* He's taken the dagger from the wise woman. She has no way of resurrecting Michael now."

Michael stepped forward, fists raised. "If you've hurt Cordelia, I'll . . ." He loaded his voice with threat that should have left Gwyn cowering, yet the King of the Underworld remained unmoved.

"You'll what, pup? You're mine now, son of Troy. You may walk the Darkling Road with your father, but once he leaves, you'll lose your way and wander for eternity through the mists. For a few weeks, you'll remember your name; then your mind will fade, leaving only your spirit to drift aimlessly, waiting to do my bidding."

Michael turned to Troy, expecting a response, yet his father remained silent.

Gwyn raised his sword and pointed it at Devin. "You, Master of the Darkling Road, are born of shadow. Your position gives you a seat on the Ennead. *You* owe fealty to *me*."

"Less than half the Darkling Roads run through the Underworld," Devin countered. "The majority exist in mortal realms. By that reckoning, I owe fealty to the king of the Scottish Seelie court, who oversees the mortal world."

Gwyn barked a laugh. "The Seelie court would not deign to acknowledge you. Your dark djinn heart is shrouded in shadows, even though you fight the call of your nature. You are mine and your father knows it. Go now, Devin. Do not stand against your king or you will make an enemy of me."

Devin shifted into a fighting stance.

Gwyn released a weary sigh before raising his sword toward Troy. "I want to make you suffer millennia of imprisonment and depravation, deathless one. But you would bear your punishment stoically and give me no satisfaction. So I will take one you love."

Gwyn glanced at Finian, and Michael leaped forward to protect the child, instinct wiping all caution from his mind. "The baby must be released." Michael stretched his arms out at his sides to shield the light cocoon from Gwyn.

Up close, a shadowy aura surrounded the King of the Underworld, while red sparked in the depths of his eyes like pinpricks of blood. "You gave your life for the child, expecting to be resurrected, son of Troy. Are you still willing to give me your life, knowing I will not release you?" Gwyn said.

"Don't agree to anything, Michael," Devin advised. "We'll find a way out of this."

Michael looked to his father for guidance, for some sign to indicate he was doing the right thing. Troy said nothing, his face unreadable.

What Troy thought of him didn't matter. The choice was his life or Finian's life, and at all cost he must protect his nephew. He remembered his father's comment: *no explanations, no excuses.* Troy should add *no emotion* to his motto as well.

"Release Finian," Michael said. "Troy will take him back to me brother."

"And you?" Gwyn asked.

A lifetime of weaving words made him pause and consider how to phrase his offer so that if, by some miracle, Cordelia found a way of resurrecting him, he would not break his word. "My death is your blood price." At least if he were doomed to wander in the mists, he would soon lose his memory and forget all he'd lost.

"Then we have a bargain." Gwyn extended his hand.

Michael clenched his jaw, but couldn't stop himself glancing once more at his father. Devin was frowning, but Troy appeared indifferent. Michael wanted to shout at him, break through his cold marble shell to discover if he cared.

Gwyn stepped back to the opposite side of his throne and indicated Troy should take Finian. Michael watched with a hollow sense of unreality as his father sheathed his sword and strode forward. With a wave of his hand, Troy dissolved the golden bubble surrounding Fin. He gathered the sleeping child into his arms, looked down, and smiled.

Troy glanced up at Michael, his smile dropping away. "This time I didn't interfere, lad." Michael's heart ached as though the blade was still in his chest when his father turned his back on him and disappeared.

Devin stared at his brother, looking as shocked as Michael felt.

"So what do I do? Just wander the paths until I get lost and forget who I am?" Michael asked, trying to make a joke of the situation. But his voice cracked, giving him away.

"No." Gwyn walked toward him and the golden throne blinked out of existence. "I have no intention of letting you off that lightly. Troy condemned me to an eternity of waiting, trapped, without the luxury of sleep. For every minute of the last thousand years, I've hoped for release. Now you will do the same."

"Not the tower?" Devin said under his breath.

Gwyn grinned, a malevolent stretch of his lips that chilled Michael's soul. At the same moment, the faintest tug on his senses caught his attention. On the edge of his perception, warmth and light called to him, a whisper of soft feminine energy tugging and cajoling him to return.

"Cordelia." His eyes glazed at the sweetness of her touch.

He felt himself drifting, slipping, a swishing sound in his ears.

Then a hand clamped around his wrist, tight as a manacle, anchoring him. Gwyn's voice boomed in his mind. "You still think to cheat me. For that, the pisky woman will be confined in the tower with you. An eternity trapped with a lover you can't touch will be a fitting torment."

Chapter Thirteen

Cordelia leaned over Michael, ran her fingertips around his face, and pressed her mouth to his ear. "Come back to me, Michael," she whispered.

She placed her palm on his hair and released violet healing light into the top of his head to summon his spirit back to his mortal body. She called his name in her mind, opening her awareness, longing to feel a hint of his presence.

His Magic Knot grew warm and vibrated against her chest.

She pushed out her senses, searching for the pulse of hot welcoming energy that was Michael.

With a potency that swamped her whole being, he filled her, wiping away her thoughts, stealing her physical control. She collapsed against his body, her skin tingling, limbs twitching. A jagged spike of fear cracked through the hum of power, carrying a frantic message. "Run, Cordelia, run."

Instinctively reacting to the urgent command, she tensed and jerked away from him. She had managed to sit back on her heels and started to rise when she stiffened and sank down again. Whatever the danger, she wouldn't leave Michael alone and vulnerable.

She gripped his Magic Knot, the sense of him growing stronger. Then his eyes sprang open, and he hauled in an agonized breath. Blissful relief swept away her energy for a second before renewed strength filled her. She held his hands and grinned down at him. For a moment, he blinked, disoriented; then his gaze focused on her. His lips parted, moved.

As she lowered her ear to Michael's mouth, a rumble of distant thunder filled the chamber. The building began to shake. The vibrations growing stronger, until dust and grit rained down. The hounds bayed, filling the air with an excited clamor.

Cordelia leaned over Michael, cradling his head in her arms, sheltering him from the falling dirt, and whatever new danger was about to descend on them. Darkness tinged with red and gold streaked out of the gloom, howling over her with the chill of a winter's wind.

Icy threads tangled around her being, stripping her of strength. The room skewed, distorted, fractured into a senseless mangle of shape and color. Her body dragged at her mind and spirit like an anchor, then the link snapped, and she spun, buffeted by a force so mighty, she couldn't hope to fight it. She tried to cling to Michael, but like a log on a rough sea, he was wrenched from her grasp.

Just when she thought she would be shattered mentally and physically, the turmoil ceased. Her consciousness swirled, taking a moment to settle; then all became still and dark.

Michael? He'd returned to his body, but now she couldn't feel him.

She couldn't feel Tamsy.

Dark fingers of terror crept through her. Her mind and spirit were lost in the endless void of nothingness between life and death. The same place she'd spent thirty terrible years when the evil druid trapped the whole pisky troop. Only last time she'd had Tamsy for company, and she'd been able to see out into the mortal world.

Michael's essence brushed her, light as a butterfly's wing. *Cordelia?* The psychic sense of Michael's mind and spirit grew stronger. With an electric shiver, he surrounded her, pulsed through her.

What happened? she asked.

Troy was the one who imprisoned Gwyn ap Nudd in the tower.

We're suffering the consequences. You should have left me. Run away when I told you to.

Despite the blissful shimmer of his presence around her, she yearned to touch him and feel his warm, live skin beneath her fingers.

He's ripped us out of our bodies and cast us in-between. We're in the tower where Gwyn was incarcerated, Michael added.

Panic swirled through her spirit, sucking away her control like a whirlpool. *Help me. I'm frightened, Michael.*

Cordelia, sugarplum, as long as we're together, we'll be all right. His thoughts smoothed over her worries like a gentle hand and she calmed.

How's he banished me here if Tamsy holds my mind and spirit? Do you think Tamsy's dead? Cordelia cast around for the psychic presence of her familiar, yet there was no sign of her.

I'm sorry for dragging you into this, he whispered in her mind.

The feel of him undulated through her, comforting her. Her thoughts drifted over her past, remembering her room at Trevelion Manor on a sunny morning, the murmur of the sea, Tamsy curled on her favorite chair, the cheeky blackbird that hopped on the patio outside her window each day looking for crumbs.

Cordelia? Michael's voice called her back from the distance and she realized how easily she could drift away and lose him in this dark, endless place.

We must hold on to each other somehow. Concentrate on me, sugarplum. Remember how our minds meshed on the boat trip. His presence surrounded her again, so strongly, she almost felt as though he touched her physically. As he drew her into his illusion, she felt the sensation of his hand wrapped around hers, his arms embracing her, his lips soft and smooth against her temple, his breath warm on her hair. Michael's fingers smoothed her back, guiding her into a dance. Her feet moved tentatively in dance steps she'd never learned.

Shiny fabric caressed her skin. Where Michael's hand rested against her back, the fabric clung hot and damp.

"I like you in blue." Michael looked down into her eyes, his gaze sparkling with mischief and a heat that set her blood humming.

She laughed coyly and turned her cheek to his chest. His heart beat slow and steady against her ear, the pulse of his presence echoing beside her own heart. "I feel you inside me, Michael."

He pressed his cheek to her hair, whispered silkily in her ear. "I like the sound of that."

"Oh." She felt like a girl, gauche and clueless.

His hand slid up her spine, leaving a tingling trail in its wake. His fingers touched her nape, stroked, featherlight, lifting the flowing strands of her hair loose around her shoulders.

"I love your hair," he whispered.

She lifted a hand and threaded her fingers through the chestnut waves that fell to his shoulders. "I've dreamed of touching your hair. Imagined how it would feel against my skin."

He eased her around in his arms and pulled her back against his chest. Her eyes closed as he smoothed his palms across her belly, while his lips brushed the top of her ear.

She reached up and he kissed her fingers. "You're a wonderful healer and beautiful as well," he whispered.

"I am?"

Images of her childhood flitted through her mind. She remembered her first attempts to heal injured creatures she'd rescued: a thrush that had flown into the window and broken its wing, the starving gray kitten she'd found abandoned in a hedge, which had instantly stolen her heart and been with her ever since.

I healed Tamsy. How had she forgotten?

Her grandmother must have taken that memory from her.

"Was your grandmother a healer like you?"

Cordelia shivered in Michael's arms at the thought of her grandmother's horrified reaction to that question. "No, she was the troop wise woman before me. But she was more powerful than I am, a true seer who needed no tools of divination to foretell the future. She was very proud of my father for being the king's advisor. She always feared I'd bring shame on the family name through my wild nature."

"You're not wild, sugarplum. You're the least wild person I know." His lips ran over her shoulder as he eased down the strap of her dress. "You should definitely become more wild. 'Tis me new life's purpose. To make Cordelia Tink wild."

Sweet shivers of longing fluttered through her as Michael's mouth did wicked things to her arm, kissing and nipping.

"I shouldn't let you do this. Grandmother would be turning in her grave."

"How do you think she gave birth to your father?"

"Oh." She'd never thought of that.

Michael lifted her hand to his mouth and feathered kisses across her palm, dislodging the confusing and rather disturbing notion of her grandmother with a man.

"We can do anything we want here, Cordelia."

His hand tightened on her ribs and his fingertips brushed the underside of her breast. She closed her eyes, held her breath until the sensation passed. She wanted more. She wanted Michael.

When she opened her eyes, they were standing in a bedroom. A large bed with champagne satin sheets stood close by, while the flickering glow of candles filled the room with warm light and secret shadows.

"We're bonded, love. This is the most natural thing in the world."

She let him lead her to the bed and sit beside her. His lips curled in a gentle smile, his eyelids lowered as if he were afraid to give her the full force of his grin in case he frightened her. "If you didn't want to do this, we wouldn't be here."

The words circled in her head while she tried to fathom the meaning behind them.

He caressed her throat and traced the thin strap of her dress to the top of her breast. The strap slid down her shoulder with a nudge from his finger. Then he repeated the move on the other side. The fabric sagged, exposing the tops of her breasts. She blinked, glanced up at Michael. He leaned in, pressed his lips to the corner of her mouth, then used a finger to turn her chin so he could fit his mouth over hers.

The movement of his lips set her floating on a warm swell of pleasure. Cool air touched her breasts as the dress fell to her waist. His hand brushed her nipple and she gasped in his mouth at the shock of sensation. He drew back his head far enough to look into her eyes. "You're mine, Cordelia. I'll keep you safe, wherever we are."

His hand closed over her breast, and his mouth became more demanding. She fell back on the satin sheets and kept tumbling through space while his fingers explored her, igniting sparks of pleasure.

She couldn't remember him removing her dress but suddenly they were both naked, writhing together. She reveled in the warm slide of his skin against hers.

"Have you done this before, sugarplum?"

Skin against her skin. Lips against her skin. Teeth against her skin.

Dragon.

The name exploded into her mind like a sudden storm, spreading dark clouds over her vision. The warmth of Michael's body faded. She clutched at him, afraid he'd left her; then his voice whispered, gentling her.

His arms surrounded her, pulled her onto his lap. "Stay with *me*. Forget the past."

She snuggled into him. But imagining Michael naked in her arms was difficult with no memory to draw on. Threads of darkness crept across her vision and a yawning emptiness stretched around her.

Cordelia, stay with me, love.

The beautiful fantasy Michael had woven for them unraveled. She struggled to recapture the feel of him. Instead, the memory of Dragon's dark gleaming body overwhelmed her mind. She started to quake.

No, she whimpered, trying to dislodge the fearsome image of sharp, bone-white fangs, as Dragon lowered his naked body over her. Then her father's furious face at the door, and the gurgling splutter of blood when Dragon turned on him and ripped out his throat. The vicious hunger in the nightstalker's eyes when he savaged her neck, her shoulder, her body rigid with terror. Naively, she'd thought she wanted Dragon, even flirted with him. She'd paid dearly for disobeying her grandmother.

She must put distance between herself and temptation before she did something terrible again. The last time she'd been with a man, her father died.

Nightshade pressed against the wall of the council chamber, his injured arm clutched to his chest. Moments earlier, he'd been guarding Cordelia while she healed Michael, and then a burst of energy had shot out from the entrance to the Underworld. The wind had picked him up and smashed him against the wall. Around him, huntsmen threw themselves flat on the ground, while the hounds leaped onto the wind, riding the swirling tornado of energy.

Finally the whirlwind had dropped, the hounds had found their feet and the huntsmen had risen to their knees. Gwyn ap Nudd had materialized, his robes flying around him. He'd scanned the chamber and his red gaze had settled on Michael and Cordelia.

A moment before the storm of Gwyn's arrival, Cordelia had been kneeling beside Michael and the bard's eyes were open. Now she lay insensate across Michael's chest, neither of them moving.

"What've you done to them?" Nightshade bellowed, taking a step forward.

Gwyn spared him a withering glance, then strode toward Cordelia and Michael, hounds and huntsmen scuttling out of his way. "The son of Troy has paid the price for his father's deceit. He is banished to the tower with his bond mate."

Nightshade tried to absorb this new disaster. His head throbbed and his shoulder ached, yet somehow he must help Michael and Cordelia. If their bodies were here, that meant only their minds and spirits had been captured. The strange environment inside the tower room suddenly made sense. The room must exist in between the mortal world and the Underworld. Only a powerful being like the King of the Underworld could manipulate the nothingness of in-between to create the illusion of his physical body and the objects in the room.

Arian appeared on the gallery above, his hand gripping the side of his neck.

"What's the matter with you?" Gwyn demanded.

The gatekeeper scowled at Nightshade and uncovered the bloody holes in his neck.

"Idiot. Do you not realize the nightstalker will have power over you now? Get out of my sight." Gwyn waved a dismissive arm. Arian stalked into the shadows. A moment later, the door above slammed.

Gwyn had yet to discover that Dai and Olwyn also carried Nightshade's bite. If necessary, he might bend their will, but after only one bite, his influence would be weak. He tested the mobility of his injured shoulder and winced as pain shot through his torso. He couldn't afford to be weak; he must protect Michael and Cordelia's bodies while he decided how to rescue their minds and spirits from the tower.

When he stumbled forward, a huntsman raised his hand and four hounds surrounded Nightshade, teeth exposed, growls rumbling in their throats.

With a grunt of pain, Nightshade leaned back against the wall. He was in no state to battle the wild hunt. He couldn't even fly, because the muscles in his back would pull on his injured shoulder.

Gwyn stooped over Cordelia, removed a leather thong from her neck, and held it up. A sick jolt shook Nightshade when he recognized Michael's Magic Knot. With dawning horror, he understood what Gwyn intended to do.

"No," he screamed. He tried to change into his shade form but nothing happened. "Shit." He lurched forward, but the snapping jaws of the hounds drove him back against the wall.

Tossing the thong bearing the stones on the ground, Gwyn held out a demanding hand to the closest huntsman. "Give me an axe."

The man fumbled at his belt and handed over a short-handled axe suitable for splitting logs or maybe bones.

Nightshade's breath stopped, his heart thundering. He shook his head and roared his fury again. Gwyn didn't even look up, just dropped to his knees, and in one practiced move smashed down the axe.

Nightshade closed his eyes reflexively, unable to bear the sight. Once Michael's Magic Knot was shattered, he'd be lost in-between forever.

Gwyn ap Nudd's howl of rage rent the air. Nightshade's eyelids shot up, his gaze drawn to the spot where Michael's three stone rings lay undamaged on one of the huge flag-stones. Gwyn flattened one hand on the ground to give himself purchase and smashed the axe down on Michael's Magic Knot repeatedly, grunting with the force of the blows. Eventually he ceased, his breath coming in ragged gasps.

He sat back on his heels, staring at the undamaged stones in disbelief. "Bloody Troy! No wonder he gave up his son without a word. He knew I wouldn't be able to incarcerate him. When the boy thinks to test the boundaries of his captivity and look for his body, he'll escape."

With a growl, he pushed to his feet and stalked back to Cordelia and Michael's bodies. "I will have my blood price. The female is no more than mortal. She'll bear a heavy price for the mistake of bonding herself to one of Troy's line."

Nightshade's sense of relief disappeared as Gwyn shoved Cordelia's body off Michael and her head hit the floor with a crack. Gwyn scanned Michael's prone form, dug in his jeans pockets, and then pulled something from his hand. Gwyn stood, holding up a silver chain bearing a single translucent stone ring. "He only holds one ring of her Knot. In the name of desolation and ruin, where are the other two?"

Face contorted with anger, he hurled the chain and its single ring at the wall. With a clink, the pale stone dropped to the ground, still in one piece. Nightshade closed his eyes in relief. When he opened them again, Gwyn stood in front of him, the corner of his lip twitching with contempt. "Where are the pisky female's other two stones?"

Nightshade stared unmoving, grateful he didn't know. Whatever Gwyn did to him, he could not betray Cordelia. With a blur of motion, Gwyn's hand shot out and gripped Nightshade's injured shoulder. Pain seared along his nerves like molten lava. Nausea rose in his throat and he roared in mindless agony. Gwyn snatched back his hand. "Tell me, stalker, or I'll send you to join the woman."

The pain faded slowly, and his labored breaths calmed. Gradually, conscious thought filtered back into his brain. "I don't know," he ground out, relieved he'd taken the precaution of leaving his own Magic Knot at home.

"I will not be denied." Gwyn swung away from him. "Has she left them in Cornwall? Is that it?" he raged, while he paced back and forth across the chamber. The hounds wandered into his path, getting in his way.

"Take the bloody animals back out." He stabbed his finger at a set of double doors, which must lead back to the kennels Eloise had shown them.

A sense of frustrated impotence burned through Nightshade at the thought that Eloise and Rhys were waiting for him in Devin's room. What would become of Rhys if something happened to Nightshade and he couldn't take the boy to safety?

When the hounds guarding him trotted out the door and the chamber emptied, Nightshade flexed his wings. Careful not to draw attention to himself, he stepped away from the wall. Could he pick up Cordelia's single stone on the silver chain without Gwyn noticing?

Suddenly Gwyn halted his manic pacing and his gaze lost focus. "I sense her. The pisky woman's mind and spirit stones are here." He swung around and strode back to Nightshade, brandishing the axe. "Tell me where they are, stalker, or you start losing limbs."

"The pisky witch has a familiar," Olwyn said from the top of the steps.

"Of course. The cat." Gwyn's gaze swept the council chamber, taking in all the levels. "Where's the cat?"

With a nasty grin, Gwyn gripped Nightshade's damaged shoulder again. Nightshade's teeth ground together as every muscle in his body tightened in screaming protest. "I-don't-know," he gasped out through the agony banding his chest. When Gwyn released him, he sagged at the king's feet, head bowed, swallowing tears of pain and humiliation.

Metal whispered against metal in the now silent chamber as Gwyn drew a long curved sword from the scabbard on his belt.

Nightshade had not imagined he would die like this, on his knees, close to tears.

His eyelids fell. Relief from the agony in his shoulder would almost be welcome, if not for the fact death meant deserting his friends.

Gut churning, he waited.

After what felt like an eternity, he raised his head. Gwyn no longer stood before him. He'd moved to stand over Michael's prone form, body tense, sword raised. "I cannot kill the son of Troy, but I can cleave his limbs from his body and make the healing so painful, he'll wish for death."

With a surge of strength from pure desperation, Nightshade pushed to his feet, using his wings to help him balance like a youth learning to fly. His mind careened through options. He must lead Gwyn away from Michael's body. He could take him to Tamsy, but Rhys and Eloise were also in Devin's chamber.

Shit. He didn't have time to think; he must get Gwyn away from Michael *now*.

"You want the cat?" he shouted.

With a determination he didn't know he possessed, he gritted his teeth and snapped down his wings. A cry ripped from his throat as the muscles in his back dragged at the damaged shoulder. He rose in the air, and halted by the main door, snatching a backward glance to check that Gwyn was following. His legs moved instinctively when his feet touched down, carrying him along the corridor toward the djinn's chamber. Heart pounding, he slammed open Devin's door and met Eloise's startled gaze as she jumped up from her chair with Rhys in her arms.

"Go." The word shuddered out; then he collapsed to his knees. Eloise didn't need to be told twice. Hugging her son, she ran past him and escaped, an instant before Gwyn strode up behind Nightshade and kicked him in the ribs.

He tumbled over, his head landing on a thick rug by the door. Through a haze of pain and guilt, he watched the poor cat stir from her comfy spot on the bed and lift her head curiously.

"Now I have you." Gwyn bore down on Tamsy, but when he reached to grab her, she pranced over his arm with an indignant yowl. He clutched at her and she evaded him again, her coat standing on end as though her tail had been jammed in an electric socket.

"Bloody cat. You will obey me in my domain. Keep still." Gwyn snatched at her and she scampered up the purple velvet hanging at the head of the bed and glared down with huge gray eyes from the gold-fringed pelmet on the wall.

Gwyn leaped onto Devin's bed and made another grab, but Tamsy was ready. As he extended his arms, she leaped onto the top of his head and clawed her way down his back, bounding once on the bed before leaping elegantly to the floor. Then she streaked across the carpet and disappeared through the open door.

"Stop that cat," Gwyn hollered at Dai, who had limped up to the doorway.

Dai blinked as Tamsy scooted between his legs. "Sorry, the creature—"

"Am I surrounded by idiots?" Gwyn shouldered Dai aside as he stormed out the door. "Sound the horn. I want the wild hunt in full cry after that cat immediately." Gwyn's voice faded as he walked away.

Dai wandered after him. "The whole hunt for one wretched cat," he grumbled.

Nightshade levered himself into a sitting position with his good arm. Somehow, he must fetch Michael and Cordelia's bodies from the council chamber. Then he'd have to think of a way to call their minds and spirits back. Nightshade gritted his teeth to counter the pain and pushed to his knees. Another five breaths and he regained his feet with the help of a chair for support. Then Eloise was at his side, pulling his good arm over her shoulders.

He pointed at the door. "I must . . ."

She shook her head and helped him to Devin's bed. Even as she eased him down onto his uninjured side, his mind battled to keep him on his feet so he could save Michael. Then pain blotted out his thoughts and feelings with a pulsing, mind-numbing insistence.

On the edge of consciousness, he thought he heard Master Devin's voice. He cracked open his eyes. In a hazy nightmare, he watched Devin hold up his hand while one of his pointed fingernails grew into a spike. He jabbed the nail into Nightshade's neck. Then everything went blissfully dark.

Chapter Fourteen

Cordelia's panic over her memory of Dragon ebbed away. Control returned, and she stopped her flight. She drifted alone, yet even in this limitless void, Michael's spiritual presence was so mighty, she could sense him radiating power like an invisible sun attracting her to his warmth.

She started moving back toward him, praying he understood her fears, hoping she hadn't hurt his feelings.

Out of habit, she searched for Tamsy's psychic presence. She shuddered with almost painful relief when she touched an inquiring tendril of feline awareness.

Michael, she reached for him, wondering if he'd hear her. He was there in an instant, surrounding her with pulsing power.

I thought I'd lost you, love, he said.

I sense Tamsy. She must be in the tower room. If I can enter her body, I can escape the tower and find Nightshade to help us.

Go, Michael said. *I'll follow.*

With familiarity born of much practice, Cordelia's mind and spirit skated along her psychic connection with Tamsy and slipped into the body of her beloved cat.

She stared out through Tamsy's mortal eyes. The tower room looked exactly as it had when they'd first met Gwyn. A few yards from her, Thorn and Brian still sat on either side of the Monopoly board, oblivious to the fact that she and Michael were trapped in the room with them.

Cordelia walked Tamsy toward Thorn and leaped onto

his lap. Somehow, she must ask him to fetch Nightshade. She tried to say Thorn's name but only a yowl came from Tamsy's mouth. Thorn scratched behind her ears. "Settle down, fur ball, before you poke your claws somewhere tender."

Communicating with him was impossible. If she wanted Nightshade's help, she'd have to go and find him herself. She jumped to the floor, then leaped onto the windowsill. Huntsmen and seers hurried back and forth across the quadrangle below. The stench of canine drifted in on the breeze, while the baying of excited hounds sounded on the far side of the building. The hair on Tamsy's back rose with a strange prickly sensation.

Tickling the edge of her perception, she sensed Michael's mind and spirit close by.

Urgent footsteps approached and she tensed, ready to flee. Master Devin appeared in the open doorway. "I'm looking for the cat."

Despite his help and advice earlier, she still wasn't sure whether she trusted him completely.

Thorn glanced at the djinn and his eyebrows rose. "Who're you?"

"Michael's brother."

"Huh!" Thorn scanned Devin up and down. "Where's Dee?"

"She needs her cat."

Thorn frowned for a few moments, then nodded at the window. "Over there."

Devin strode toward Tamsy and Cordelia held her ground, deciding to trust him. He picked her up and stared into her eyes. His were deep velvety brown, outlined with kohl, accentuating his exotic appearance. With Tamsy's superior sense of smell, his aromatic fragrance nearly made her swoon. "Pisky wise woman, are you in there?"

She stared back at him through Tamsy's eyes, momentarily stunned by his perception. Then she pulled herself together and yowled.

He grimaced. "Fish breath."

That was a fine thing coming from a man who smelled like an explosion in a perfumery. She tried to answer and another yowl issued from Tamsy's mouth.

"Tell Michael he's not trapped." Devin set Tamsy back on the windowsill, smoothing her ruffled fur. "Tell him to follow you."

She retreated into the depths of Tamsy's mind, loosed her consciousness so she could sense Michael more strongly, and reached for him.

He surrounded her in an instant, the zing of his energy making Tamsy's heart race.

"Michael?" Devin blinked and turned a circle, staring around the room. "I feel you, *ya akhy*."

From inside Tamsy, she couldn't hear Michael speak, but his hope surged through her.

Before she realized what he intended to do, Devin grabbed Tamsy beneath his arm, her bottom sticking out behind indecorously.

"You're with me," he commanded Thorn.

Thorn looked up from the Monopoly board. He opened his mouth to argue, but obviously changed his mind when he saw Devin's adamant expression. He rose with a farewell to Brian and followed Devin down the steps.

Cordelia grasped for the feel of Michael, trying to hold on to the wisps of his presence and drag him along.

At the base of the tower steps, Devin peered out, then hurried the short distance to the quadrangle. He sprinted across the open space, Thorn on his heels, and then made his way down a corridor.

When they reached Devin's room, he entered and slammed the door behind them. Cordelia stared through Tamsy's eyes at the astonishing sight there. Nightshade lay on the bed, one arm strapped up with white bandages, while Eloise sat next to him on the bed, watching over him, holding a cute baby nightstalker asleep in her arms. Laid out on the bed beside Nightshade were Michael's body and her body.

"Dee!" Thorn tried to rush to the bed, but Devin grabbed his arm and held him back.

"Wait a moment. Give her space."

Michael's presence seemed to expand to fill the room, then contracted rapidly. His body gasped in a breath. Relief surged through her and Tamsy to see that Michael was safe. But the sensation dissipated quickly when the fact sank in that she now had to make the jump to her own body.

After striding to the bed, Devin set Tamsy down beside Cordelia's body. She stared at herself through Tamsy's eyes, the experience surreal. Her skin was so deathly pale, she wondered if she could ever revive.

Blinking, Michael touched the new scar on his chest where Cordelia had healed his stab wound.

"Cordelia?" Michael pushed himself up on his elbow to look at her and winced.

"Nauseated?" Devin asked. When Michael nodded, he continued, "That's normal. Give yourself a few minutes and you'll be fine."

Michael lifted her hand and kissed her fingers. Sorrow shivered through her, chased by a burn of shame. While they were in spirit form, he'd seen her memories. He knew every intimate detail of what had happened between her and Dragon. He knew she'd led Dragon on. He knew she'd caused her father's death. When she returned to her physical form, how could she ever look him in the face again?

Michael's eyes lifted to meet Tamsy's. "Come back to your body, sugarplum. There's nothing to be scared of."

His psychic presence wrapped around her, gentling and soothing. Tamsy started to purr, the rolling vibration filling the chamber.

"Well, the cat likes you," Devin said to Michael with a wry grin.

Michael reached toward Tamsy, hesitated, then stroked

her face. Tamsy closed her eyes and angled her head to expose her throat for rubbing. "Please come back, Cordelia. We'll sort out whatever it is you're worried about."

"And we need to get you all out of here," Devin added. "We haven't long before Gwyn ap Nudd sets the wild hunt on Tamsy."

Michael sat in the chair staring at Nightshade, still prone and unconscious on Devin's bed. Despite the direction of his gaze, his awareness was focused behind him on Cordelia. She sat with Eloise and Rhys, softly explaining what they should expect when they reached Trevelion Manor.

With his encouragement, she'd finally left her cat and returned to her body. But she wouldn't look him in the face. Foolishly, he'd hoped for celebratory cuddles and kisses when they found their bodies. Instead, she'd given him a quick hug before falling into Thorn's embrace.

Michael had never felt more alone than he did now with his bond mate so close, yet so distant. He touched the small translucent ring of her Magic Knot. Was she still upset over her memories of Dragon?

His gaze refocused on Nightshade and anger crawled through him. He did not blame Nightshade for his father's behavior. Yet having lived through Cordelia's anguished memory of Dragon attacking her and slaughtering her father, Michael's fury burned for release. What other atrocities had Dragon committed?

Devin strode back into the room after checking on Gwyn's plans and locked the door behind him. "We need to get you all away from here. The huntsmen are ready to call out the hunt—Gwyn is going down to the kennels now." He paced over to Michael and placed a hand on his shoulder. "Feeling better?"

Michael rubbed a hand over his face. "Aye."

Hunkering down at his side, Devin said, "She'll come around, *ya akhy*. Be patient."

Michael glanced over his shoulder, and Cordelia's back stiffened when his gaze found her. "I hope so."

After standing, Devin moved to the side of the bed. "Pity we must wake the stalker. He needs more rest to allow his shoulder to heal. One of us had better give him a dose of the red stuff to boost his energy before we leave."

Michael pushed wearily to his feet. "I will if I must."

"You're weak after your ordeal. He can sink his fangs into me if he's quick." Devin gripped Nightshade's good shoulder and shook him. "Hey, sleeping beauty, time to rise and shine."

Nightshade grumbled drowsily.

Devin dragged a pointed fingernail across his wrist, before waving it beneath Nightshade's nose. When blood welled into the cut, the stalker's lips twitched, and his needle-sharp fangs slid into view. His nostrils flared while he blinked awake. His gaze slid from Michael to Devin. "I want to bite you," he croaked, his voice thick with sleep.

"No surprise there then." Devin grinned.

Glinting seductively, Nightshade's eyes fixed on the djinn. "Draw the curtains around the bed and lie with me, dark one."

"Not this time, my friend. The bloodletting must be purely medicinal, I'm afraid." Devin sat on the edge of the bed, rolled up his sleeve, and offered Nightshade his wrist.

Nightshade grunted derisively.

"Take it or leave it, stalker. Either way, you need to be on your feet and out of here in a few minutes. I suggest you chalk this one up to necessity and put your ego back in its cage."

"I'll make you swoon, Master of the Darkling Road," Nightshade said, his voice husky with promise.

"Doubt it," Devin retorted, his tone all business. "But give it your best shot."

Leaning back against the corner post of the bed, Michael crossed his arms, interested to witness what would happen.

Nightshade held Devin's left wrist to his mouth, tensed his jaws, then raised his silver eyes to Devin's face.

When Nightshade bit down, Devin's breath hissed in, then rushed out on a low moan. Michael grinned, despite his mood. The djinn's chest heaved, his breath coming faster. His right hand trembled against his thigh before his head fell back on a groan. After counting to ten, Michael gripped Nightshade's good shoulder to stop him from taking too much. "Feeding station is closed now, boyo."

In the blink of an eye, Nightshade surged to his knees, his lips drawn back on a snarl. With blood dripping from his fangs, he grabbed Michael's throat.

Michael held his position and raised an eyebrow, confident that his friend would never hurt him.

Nightshade blinked, his fangs retracted, and he sat back on his heels. "Err, sorry," he said, licking blood from his lips. "Instinct."

Cordelia and Eloise had jumped to their feet. Rhys was watching Nightshade, his inquisitive silver eyes taking in everything. "Oh crap," Nightshade said when he noticed them.

"That was cool," Thorn said from where he was playing with Tamsy on the floor.

"No. It wasn't." Cordelia's chest rose and fell a little too fast, her face bloodless.

"I'm sorry you had to see that." Nightshade cast a rueful glance over the women, his eyes settling on Rhys.

Shaking her head, Eloise said, "Don't apologize. I'm even more certain now that I've made the right choice in bringing Rhys to live with you."

Cordelia stared at Eloise in disbelief. "Why?"

"Because Nightshade is the master of his instincts. In that same situation, Dragon would have ripped out Michael's throat without a thought. Rhys needs to learn control. I think Nightshade is the right person to teach him."

"Oh." Cordelia nibbled her lip. Michael watched her mouth, the slow burn of desire flaring to life in his belly.

Devin held up his punctured wrist to Nightshade. "Finish the job, *ya sadeeky*, or I'll lay a wonderful trail for the hounds."

Nightshade ran his tongue over Devin's wrist, sealing the holes. He looked up from beneath his lashes. "I made you swoon."

"Nope." Devin shook his head. "I had full control of my faculties at all times."

"Didn't I make him swoon?" Nightshade demanded, turning to Michael.

Michael held up his palms. "I'm not getting involved." Although he suspected he could have nicked his brother's Taser and zapped him on the arse while Nightshade bit him, and the djinn wouldn't have noticed. Not that he blamed Devin for losing control. The pleasure from Nightshade's bite felt damn close to an orgasm.

Devin stood and swept back his hair, tying it with a black ribbon. He handed Michael a sword belt and a Taser. Then he donned a long coat and strapped a sword to his own belt. "I shall escort you to the entrance to the Darkling Road, and you can make your escape through the Underworld. As the Darkling Road is my domain, Eloise should be able to accompany you."

"But we're not dead." Cordelia had come closer and was hugging Tamsy. A twinge of jealousy hit Michael and he looked away, unable to believe he was envious of a cat.

"The Darkling Roads are not part of the Underworld," Devin explained. "They're neutral territory running through all dimensions. My aim is to keep them open for all to pass." He glanced at Eloise. "Even humans when the need arises."

"What's to stop the wild hunt from following us?" Michael asked.

"In theory, Gwyn doesn't have permission to hunt the

roads." Devin patted the hilt of his sword. "But we can't assume Gwyn will abide by the rules."

"I thought Eloise couldn't leave here," Nightshade said as he walked to her side to ruffle Rhys's hair.

"The slave charm confines her to the castle. The Darkling Road exists in another dimension." Devin flicked up his eyebrows. "The metaphorical hole in the fence."

"Why didn't you tell me?" Eloise clutched Rhys tightly, her cheeks flushed. "I could have taken Rhys to safety before Dragon—"

"If I'd known what Dragon would do, I'd have got you out of here sooner," Devin replied softly. "I never dreamed he'd . . . I'm sorry."

Michael's heart twisted to see the distress on Cordelia's face every time someone mentioned Dragon's name. Nightshade's father had better not show his face in Cornwall.

After pulling on his jacket, Michael stepped closer to Cordelia while she settled Tamsy in her bag. They'd only known each other properly for a few days, yet he needed to touch her in a way he'd never needed to touch a woman before. Not sexual touch, although he wanted that as well, but to shelter her and reassure her. He clenched his fists in his pockets to stem the urge to pull her into the protective circle of his arms. Seeing her hurting and being unable to ease her pain nearly killed him.

"Cordelia." She glanced up, and he smiled. "Penny for them," he said gently.

She squeezed her eyes closed. "I don't think now's the time or place."

He touched her arm, the barest brush of his fingertips. When she didn't pull away, some of the weight riding his shoulders eased.

Shadows fell across the room and he dragged his gaze from her to stare at the window. The brilliant blue sky dimmed to gray, then faded to solid black, unrelieved even by the normal scattered pinpricks of starlight.

Devin walked toward the door. "The wild hunt is on the move. Time to go."

"Tell me we don't have to go back to that damn council chamber," Nightshade said.

Devin nodded grimly. "That's why I've been waiting. We need the hounds out of the kennels and in the air before we risk entering the chamber. If we leave now, the timing should be about right."

Michael stayed at the back, herding the group into the hallway.

"Everyone normally keeps out of the way during the hunt, so we shouldn't meet anyone." Devin paused before he crossed the quadrangle. "All right bringing up the rear, Michael?"

"Aye."

"Let's go then."

While they ran across the open space, Michael scanned the sky, wondering what the hunt looked like in full cry. He hoped he wouldn't find out.

When they reached the door on the other side, Devin paused long enough for them to catch up. Once they moved on, Eloise couldn't keep up. Nightshade slowed with her, and glanced back at Michael. "Curse this injured shoulder. Will you carry Rhys for us?"

Michael trotted up beside her and lifted Rhys from her arms. "'Tis all right, lass," he said in response to her worried frown. "I'll not go letting anything happen to him."

The cute little lad stared up at him, blinking his silver eyes. Michael's chest tightened. So much had happened to him since his father had carried Finian to safety; he'd hardly given his nephew a thought. He longed to be back in the nursery at Trevelion Manor so he could cuddle the twins and make sure Fin hadn't suffered any ill effects from his time in the Underworld.

The group arrived at the council chamber panting. Devin raised a hand and everyone fell silent. "Wait here a moment."

When Devin beckoned him, he passed Rhys back to Eloise and followed his brother.

They halted at the top of the steps, peering down into the darkness where Michael had gone to die. The memory trembled through him, and he had to consciously steady his heart.

"Can you see in the dark?" he asked Devin.

With a nod, his brother glanced at him. "My night vision is one of the skills that improved when I died the first time. I wonder what powers you gained on resurrection? Have you sensed any changes?"

"No. I'll think about that when we're safely home."

"I only ask because you'll need every advantage possible if Gwyn sends the hunt after you. Troy says Gwyn doesn't play by the rules."

Michael gritted his teeth at mention of their father's name. "That's rich coming from him."

"Troy gives people enough rope to hang themselves, then stands back and watches the show. That's just his way. Don't judge what you don't understand, boy."

Throwing back his coat skirts, Devin drew his sword and unhooked his Taser from his belt, offering them to Michael.

Michael held the Taser in one hand and the sword in the other, remembering how Niall used to beat the crap out of him with the wooden swords they had as boys. "I think I'll stick with the Taser," he said, handing the sword back to Devin.

The idea of zapping Arian somewhere tender made him grin.

Hidden beneath Cordelia's hair was a lump the size of an egg. While she'd been away from her body, someone must have bumped her head darn hard. She leaned against Thorn, taking comfort from his strong arm around her shoulders.

"You all right, Dee?" he whispered.

She nodded even though her head had been throbbing since she'd returned to her body.

She couldn't tell Thorn as he'd only fuss over her, and she didn't want Michael to find out. He had enough on his mind without worrying about her as well.

Beside her, Rhys had his chin resting on Eloise's shoulder, his inquisitive silver eyes fixed on Cordelia, a tiny thumb wedged in his mouth. She couldn't remember Nightshade ever looking that sweet. The shameful truth was she'd held a grudge against Nightshade for his father's behavior, even when he was a child. The realization made her flush with guilt.

Nightshade tapped Rhys playfully on the nose and the baby grinned around his thumb. Cordelia's guilty conscience stung so much, she had to turn away. When Michael had touched her emotions, he'd fractured her carefully erected barriers to hold everyone at a distance so they didn't hurt her and she didn't hurt them.

Approaching footsteps echoed along the hallway.

Snapping back to reality, Cordelia pushed Eloise forward and grabbed Thorn's arm so he didn't lag behind. She shut the council chamber doors and hurried to the top of the steps where Michael and Devin were talking. "Someone's coming."

"Time for you to get going," Devin said.

"You're not coming with us?" Michael asked.

"I need to run interference here. Just follow the road markers I've explained and you'll cross the border into England. Gwyn can go anywhere in the Underworld, but in the mortal realm, he's tied to Wales. I won't allow anyone to enter the Darkling Road from here until you're safe. Remember Gwyn can call on the spirits of the dead, so watch your backs. And whatever you do, make sure none of your lot strays from the Darkling Road."

Michael called the group to him; then Devin embraced him. Now that Cordelia knew they were brothers, she could see the likeness. Despite the difference in coloring, they both resembled Troy.

"Walking the Darkling Road is like driving in the dark," Michael said, looking around at them all, his gaze stopping on her. "You can only see as far as the arc of your headlights." He attempted a smile, but his trademark grin looked forced. Would he ever regain his carefree sense of fun, or had this trip robbed him of that forever?

"I'll go last and keep an eye on everyone," Nightshade offered.

"Good." Michael made eye contact with Nightshade and the brief look held a pledge of trust on both sides, man to man. Cordelia suddenly felt left out. She was the pisky wise woman. Michael should be depending on her help, not Nightshade's. Yet she had chosen to keep her distance from him until she had her feelings straight. She rubbed her temples, then hugged her cat bag, her conflicting emotions nearly ripping her in half.

To ease her tension, she pushed her swirling allure out into her aura.

Nightshade made a strangled sound and swung around to stare at her. With a startled cry, she dragged her aura in tight to her body. She'd become so used to the freedom of being without her restrictive wards, she'd almost forgotten the danger. She must keep away from the males or risk enticing them.

"I need to walk at the back," she said.

"No, lass." When Michael came to her, she dropped her gaze, fearing she'd see disapproval on his face as she always had in her father's expression.

With a finger, he raised her chin so she had to look at him. "I never thanked you for bringing me back from the dead."

She blinked at him while she remembered those terrifying minutes when she'd thought she wouldn't be able to save him. His hand slid to her cheek and he leaned forward, brushing his lips over hers with a melting whisper of sensation that made her eyelids drift closed and her heart stumble.

"You'll walk in front of Nightshade, where you're safe."

"But I'm not warded."

His lips pressed together, and his blue eyes scanned her face. "Don't talk as though you've got some terrible disease."

She shook her head, accidentally on purpose dislodging his finger from her chin so she could look away.

But he wasn't ready to let her go. He caught her chin again and made her face him. "When we get out of Wales, we'll talk."

"There's nothing—"

"Cordelia Tink, I'll not be letting you go, lass." He pinned her with his uncompromising gaze. "So get used to the idea of being bonded to me."

A shivery burst of surprise ran through her at the authority lacing his words. His eyebrows rose, demanding her response.

"All right," she whispered.

He nodded and released her chin. She wasn't sure if he'd used his silver tongue, or if the effect she felt was because of the force of his will. With a glance full of promises, he pressed his lips to the tips of his fingers and blew the kiss her way. Then he strode to the front and led them into the murky obscurity of the Darkling Road, leaving her shaky with expectation.

Cordelia trailed behind Michael, Thorn, Eloise, and Rhys, with Nightshade's solid presence guarding her back. If she squinted, she could make out a faint route ahead. They seemed to be surrounded by marshland that, oddly, reminded her of the place on the Cornish coast where she thought her mother lived.

The interminable dingy road unrolled before them. Her feet ached. Her head throbbed and nausea crawled up her throat.

"You feeling all right, wise woman?" She was grateful Nightshade kept his voice pitched low.

"My head's aching. I'll be fine when we get out of here, and I get some rest." Each time she blinked, her eyelids stayed closed for longer, until she was almost sleepwalking.

Cordelia. A female called, softly, sweetly extending each syllable in a singsong voice. The fog to her right thinned to wispy streaks, revealing a reed bed dotted with rippling pools of water that sparkled beneath the moonlight. Thick, fluffy bulrushes grew in clusters. A bat fluttered past, angling around a clump of spiky reeds.

A glowing figure appeared in the middle of the marshland, her diaphanous gown floating in the gentle breeze.

I've waited a lifetime for you, my child.

"Mother?"

The water nymph drifted closer. Even as Cordelia watched her elegant approach, she knew this wasn't possible. Water nymphs could not float in the air. They swam or walked as she did. Yet in the enchantment of the moment, the truth didn't matter.

Come to me, my child. Let's spend some time together. Get to know each other. Defy your father.

Cordelia flexed her toes in her shoes, something holding her back even though she ached to step forward and go to the mother she had longed for but never known. During her teens, when she was struggling to come to terms with the restrictions her father and grandmother put on her, she'd spent weeks searching the network of tiny rivers where she thought her mother lived. She had so many questions to ask her.

Out of habit, Cordelia felt for Tamsy's bag. When it wasn't resting over her shoulder, she blinked and looked around.

Someone else will care for your cat. She can't stay with us. She has many more lives to live.

Cordelia shook her head, saying no to something important, she just couldn't think what. Without forethought, the question she'd kept secret in her heart all her life came to her lips. "Why did you give me up, Mother?"

The ethereal creature sighed with the mournful wail of wind whistling between reeds. *I didn't give you away, daughter. Your father stole you from me and hid your identity by warding your body.*

The wards were to conceal her? Her mind skipped back over her past, but that explanation didn't make sense.

When I came looking for you, your father killed me. Do not trust these men. They seek to control you, to deny your spirit and your true nature. Leave them and come to me. She held out her hand and a subtle compulsion pulled at Cordelia.

If she didn't go to her mother now, she would lose her forever. But her father would never have killed anyone. Confusion tangled her memories and thoughts.

Come, daughter. We will be together at last. The woman glowed more brightly. Like a beacon in the darkness, she offered answers to questions that had puzzled Cordelia all her life.

Cordelia stepped off the path into the water.

Shadows swarmed out of nowhere, snaking around her body, her face, sucking the spirit from her. Her knees folded, and she sank beneath the dark turmoil. She opened her mouth to call for Michael, but murky streamers streaked between her lips, swallowing the sound.

Chapter Fifteen

Michael strode along the Darkling Road, his concentration fixed on the shadowy path unfolding before him, watching for the pale markers that indicated distance and turnings.

He nudged Cordelia's Magic Knot ring against his chest absentmindedly. The stone was chilly and uncomfortable on his skin. Gradually, the discomfort penetrated his brain. He slowed, pulled the chain outside his T-shirt, and felt the ring.

Cold bit into his fingers. "Ruddy Badba," he whispered. He'd given up feeling for her after she'd shut him from her mind. He extended his senses and swung around to look for her. Behind him, Thorn had Rhys cradled in his arms. The child blinked sleepily, snuggled in one of Devin's jackets. Eloise came next, her face gray in the shadowy light. Then the path disappeared into the fog. He couldn't see Cordelia or feel her.

"Cordelia!" Despite the fact Devin had advised them to be quiet, her name burst from his lips. "Stay with Eloise and don't move," he instructed Thorn as he hurried past them.

He backtracked, the tense muscles in his neck tightening with each stride he took without seeing Cordelia or Nightshade. He should have kept a better watch on the group. After five minutes, a dark shape materialized out of the gloom on the road in front of him.

Nightshade kneeled on the ground, the top of Cordelia's cat bag held closed with the hand of his good arm, while the bag squirmed and heaved. "Nightshade!" Michael bellowed a few feet from him, yet his friend's gaze remained unfocused. Michael slapped his cheek.

The stalker blinked and ducked his head away from another blow. "Easy, bard. What's going on?"

"Where's Cordelia?"

Nightshade looked around, confused. "I don't know."

"You're holding Tamsy."

"Oh." Nightshade frowned and released the top of the bag. Tamsy sprang out like a jack-in-the-box and streaked into the fog at the side of the Darkling Road.

"Shit," Nightshade said. "I think that tells us where the wise woman's gone."

Michael's heart thudded as he tried to peer through the impenetrable swirling cloud. Tamsy must sense Cordelia even if he couldn't, but then the cat held her mind and body stones. Cold sweat prickled his skin. Fear scraped his thoughts when he remembered Devin's warning that the dead could suck the life from mortals.

"Stand up and hang on to me." Michael reached a hand toward Nightshade, impatiently snapping his fingers while the stalker rose stiffly to his feet.

Finally, Nightshade gripped him. "Whatever happens, don't let go." Michael stepped to the edge of the path and leaned into the fog, letting Nightshade take his weight. But the fog was too thick to see through. He pulled himself back and swore.

"I'll have to step off the path. Give me the bag handle." He wrapped the strap around his wrist, grabbed a breath as though he was about to dive under water, and stepped off the road. The temperature plummeted, but nothing sinister happened. He took two more steps, until the strap pulled taut.

A few yards in front of him, Tamsy stood among a writhing tangle of shadow snakes. Spitting and hissing, she swiped at them with her claws. Michael watched dumbfounded for a moment until the truth hit him. Cordelia must be beneath that heaving mass of shadows. He fumbled at his belt for the Taser Devin had given him. His chest burned from lack of oxygen, and he gasped, head pounding as the thin icy air seared his lungs.

Leaning forward, he stretched out his arm but couldn't reach her. "Damn." He wriggled his wrist, dropping the bag strap. Then he took two more steps and jabbed the Taser at the shadows. With a hiss and crackle, the wispy assailants shot off into the darkness. A few circled back toward him, but he zapped them again and they dissipated.

Cordelia lay frighteningly still and he wanted to lift her into his arms, but he didn't dare put away the Taser in case the shadows returned. For speed, he simply grabbed her ankles and, with Tamsy riding on her chest, dragged her the few yards across the soggy ground to the road. A hand grasped his belt and pulled him the last few feet.

As soon as he had her back on the Darkling Road, he dropped to his knees by her side and held his cheek over her mouth, feeling for her breath. Surely, he'd sense if she were dead.

The tense knots in his gut loosened when shallow puffs of air brushed his cheek. "Cordelia." He stroked her face, lifted her hand to his lips, and pressed his mouth to her chilled skin.

Nightshade kneeled at her other side and touched her hand.

"What happened?" Michael demanded.

The stalker closed his eyes in thought. "The last thing I remember is walking behind her. Then you slapped me."

"Something must have tempted her off the path." Michael heaved a sigh, light-headed from worry and lack of sleep. "I must get her out of here and warm her up."

Tamsy had settled on Cordelia's chest, her nose nuzzled against her chin. When Michael tried to lift her off, she hung on to Cordelia's jacket with her claws and spat at him. "Righty ho, cat. Have it your way."

Grasping Cordelia beneath her shoulders and knees, he heaved her into his arms, complete with feline passenger. The cat eyed him suspiciously. "You're going to have to cut me some slack, cat. She's mine as well now, so learn to share."

The walk back to find the others passed in a blur. Thorn had Rhys cuddled in one arm with Eloise tucked under the other, her head resting on his chest.

"The chick has found his wing feathers," Nightshade mumbled, pointing at Thorn.

During the trip, Michael had grown wing feathers as well. The trick wasn't learning to fly, but learning to stay in the air rather than crash and burn.

His arms ached, but he moved to the front of the group and paced on, glancing regularly over his shoulder to keep everyone in sight.

Relief swept through his weary body when he saw the small white runes on the edge of the path that indicated the exit he wanted. The others gathered behind him while he put a foot on the runes. The fog parted to reveal a dark wooden door.

With his hands full, he had to use his foot to push the door open. The temperature rose as he stepped through. They entered a small room lit only by slivers of light leaking around another door six feet ahead. The acrid smell of chemicals and dust filled the cramped, dark space.

"Eloise, can you get that?" He nodded toward the next door and stepped aside. Hinges creaked a moment before low light penetrated the small room, revealing shelves stacked with janitorial supplies. Nightshade closed the back of the store cupboard hiding the exit from the Darkling Road. Relief surged through Michael, bringing a wave of renewed energy. "We should have come out on the other side of the River Severn in England. I'm hoping this is Bristol."

Michael looked down at Cordelia in his arms, and the triumph of escaping Wales dwindled. She was in no fit state to drive back to Cornwall with the others. Once he'd sent them on their way, he must take her somewhere warm and safe to recuperate.

Michael watched Thorn accelerate away in the rental car, and headed back through the revolving hotel door. He dashed across the lobby to the elevator and returned to the room where he'd left Cordelia snuggled beneath the covers of a luxury king-sized bed.

He hung the DO NOT DISTURB sign on the hotel room door because they would probably both sleep through the night and the following day.

Kneeling on the bed, he touched Cordelia's neck to check her temperature. The thick quilt hadn't warmed her at all. When he was low, he drew energy from his element earth. He stared at the bathroom door. Cordelia should be able to draw energy from water, and the warmth would give her double benefit.

He went to run a bath and halted with a groan as he took in the ultramodern fittings, with a supersize shower but no bathtub. A hot shower would be better than nothing. He spread fluffy white towels over the ceramic floor, then turned on the water to heat.

She still hadn't stirred by the time he fetched her from the bed and carried her into the bathroom. Panic ticked in his chest as he laid her body on the towels, her skin pale and waxy. After unlacing her boots, he pulled them off with her socks. Then he sat behind her and raised her between his legs, taking her weight on his chest so he could ease her sweater off over her head. His fingers brushed the puckered skin on her neck where Dragon had savaged her and anger burst through him anew. He stopped, and wrapped her in his arms, just holding her, praying that after all they'd survived, she would be all right.

He lifted the cord holding his Magic Knot off over her head and hung it back around his own in case it was interfering with her recovery. She had only agreed to bond with him to save his life. He didn't fool himself that she'd have committed to him otherwise. Yet the link once wrought was unbreakable. He'd be forever bonded to a woman who had a closer spiritual connection with her cat than she did with him.

Even as his breath trailed out in frustration, his gaze slid lower to the ample cleavage visible above her white cotton bra. A little groan escaped him. He'd never been good at restraint. Wriggling back, he laid her down again and crawled forward to unfasten her trousers.

Once he'd stripped her to her underwear, he pulled off his clothes down to his shorts, then carried her into the shower. He sat back against the wall with her sitting between his legs. Using the detachable showerhead, he played the hot spray over her body. He pressed his face to her neck and kissed her scars, wishing he had the gift of healing. Even if he could remove the visible signs of Dragon's violence, nothing could erase her memories. Unless she let go of what had happened to her when she was a teenager, and trusted him, they could never be truly together. Sex was one of his favorite things, and he wanted to share that pleasure with her.

His lips moved on her shoulder, and his gaze roamed to her breasts. The white cotton bra clung wetly, her pale skin beneath the fabric darkening around her nipples. Desire balled hotly in his belly, raising his pulse, heating his blood.

He grew hard against her bottom so he tipped back his head, hoping the cool surface of the tiles would neutralize the effect. Instead, the lusty images from her divination mirror scrolled back through his memory in full Technicolor, making him ache for release.

"Sweet Anu." His breath shuddered out on a groan. His

weariness disappeared down the drain with the water as lust energized him. He wanted her so much he could hardly think.

He pressed his mouth to her ear. "Cordelia, sugarplum, come back to me." *Want me.* How ironic that females normally fell over each other to get in his bed, yet this woman who held his Magic Knot was afraid of intimacy.

He trailed his fingers along her arm, caressing the tender spot inside her elbow, hoping to draw her from her stupor. The sense of her psychic presence whispered around him and settled in his solar plexus where he'd always felt her. His burst of relief sharpened to longing when she wriggled her bottom tighter between his legs.

Tamsy yowled on the other side of the bathroom door, obviously sensing Cordelia's return to consciousness. Shoot him for being selfish. He was not going to let the cat in right now. He dropped the showerhead before turning Cordelia in his arms to see her face. With his fingertips, he smoothed strands of damp hair away from her eyes. "Wake up, love."

"Mother?" The single word whispered between her lips.

Mother? His charms were definitely slipping if she thought he was her mother.

"It's Michael." He pressed his lips against her cheek, tasting the water on her skin.

When her eyelids fluttered, he drew back. "Wake up, sugarplum. You're safe now."

She snatched in panicked breaths, then opened her eyes, blinking in the light like a newborn. "Where am I?"

"In a hotel in Bristol. You're safe."

A fine tremor passed through her body while she stared at him. He extended his senses toward her, enjoyed the tingling rush of her allure, silently willing her to relax. But she withdrew her energies until he could only feel the faint beat of her presence in his solar plexus.

She pulled away from him physically as well. Sitting up,

she stared through the misted glass shower cubicle at the bathroom. "Where's Tamsy?"

Her words chipped off a little piece of Michael's heart. Pasting on a grin, he pointed at the door. "She's waiting for you in the bedroom. Shall we go and find her?"

When she scrambled onto her knees, he tried to help her up but she shook her head. "I'm fine. Thank you for this." She glanced at the showerhead still gushing hot water over her legs.

Michael pulled up his knees to hide the state of his groin and swiped back his wet hair. "Well, I thought water for a water elemental kinda made sense," he said, amazed his voice sounded so chipper.

She crawled toward the far end of the shower enclosure, giving him an unforgettable view. He'd never realized cotton underwear became transparent when wet. There was now no chance he'd be decent to stand up in his shorts for the foreseeable future.

Once she crawled out of the cubicle, he snagged a towel from the floor and bound it tightly around his waist before she turned. Taking her elbow, he steadied her while she found her feet, then grabbed another towel and wrapped it over her shoulders.

"Oh my." She swayed and leaned against him. "What happened to me?"

"I was hoping you'd tell me that."

She closed her eyes, sucking her lip in thought. "All I remember is . . . No."

"What, Cordelia?"

She reached for the rim of the washbasin and grasped it for support, leaving him with his hands empty when they ached to help her.

"I thought I saw my mother. But I've never met her, so I don't even know what she looks like."

Maybe the woman was dead and Cordelia had seen her

after she'd left the Darkling Road. Michael didn't want to upset her with that suggestion, so he summoned what he hoped was a sympathetic yet interested expression and offered her his arm. "Let's get you snuggled up in bed with Tamsy."

When he opened the door, Tamsy trotted straight to Cordelia and wound around her legs, purring like a well-tuned sports car.

Michael picked up the cat and passed her into Cordelia's arms. She pressed her face against the creature's fur. He ignored the ache in his chest, gathered up wet towels, and hung them from the heated rail, pretending not to mind she'd rather hold her cat than him.

She dragged her feet wearily into the bedroom before flopping on the side of the bed. While she consumed the sandwich and coffee he'd ordered up, he fetched her a fluffy white bathrobe from the wardrobe. He stuffed his own sandwich in his mouth, then grabbed a robe for himself, and changed clothes in the bathroom.

A few minutes later when he returned to the room, she was snuggled beneath the covers, Tamsy curled against her body. She opened her eyes sleepily when he went to her side. "Thanks, Michael," she mumbled. "I can't talk now. I just . . ." Her eyelids fluttered down. "I just . . ."

Gradually, her breath slowed to the rhythm of sleep. He stroked strands of hair back from her forehead and trailed his fingertip across her pinkened cheeks. Although she was asleep again, she now looked normal and healthy. "I can wait," he whispered. He gathered her wet underwear from the floor and washed it out in the bathroom, then hung the wrinkled white cotton over the heated rail so she'd have something clean to wear in the morning.

When he returned to the bedroom, Tamsy propped her chin on Cordelia and watched him through slitted eyes. "Hey, moggie, all's fair in love and war." He sat on the edge of the bed and rubbed Tamsy behind the ear. She turned her head into his hand, purring.

Although he should probably sleep on the chair, he was too damn tired to worry about propriety. He slid into the bed beside Cordelia and closed his eyes. As he drifted off, a warm weight settled against his belly. He opened one eye to find Tamsy curled beside him. A strange feline presence brushed his senses. He chuckled, almost certain he was being checked out.

He hoped he earned her cat's seal of approval, because in the morning he must make Cordelia understand that he needed her. If she didn't let him make their bond physical, he was going to explode.

Cordelia woke when the early light of dawn filtered into the room. Unfamiliar striped curtains hung at the window. She frowned before memories from the previous evening trickled back. Michael had brought her to a hotel.

"Oh, goodness." Liquid heat flowed through her at the memory of waking to find herself snuggled against his near-naked body. She'd had to get away from him fast and ground herself through Tamsy before her allure spun out of control. She must get the wards painted back on her skin immediately.

Still wrapped in the soft robe she'd donned the previous night, she slid out of bed. A shock of surprise raced through her when she looked over her shoulder to see Michael asleep in the bed. Tamsy lay between them with her head on the pillow—their furry chaperone. Cordelia smiled and stroked her cat's silky belly.

Before she restored the symbols to her skin, she wanted to stand beneath the shower and soak up the vibrancy of the water. Searching for a pen with which to reapply her wards afterward, she checked all the drawers, making her way around the room to Michael's nightstand.

She glanced at him to check that he was still asleep and found herself drawn closer. Dark waves of hair fell across his forehead, nearly reaching his eyes, where the perfect dark crescents of his long eyelashes lay against his cheeks. He must have shaved while she slept, because his face was nearly smooth. A little quiver ran through her as she bent closer and her gaze fell to his mouth. The corners of his lips tipped up in a smile, even in sleep. She licked her lips before turning away. With him in her bed, she could so easily forget the lessons of her past and do something silly.

She pushed back her hair and looked for a pen on his nightstand. Her mouth dropped open. Next to the Taser lay a Gucci wallet stuffed with notes, and a gold credit card. He'd died, traveled to the Underworld, been resurrected, been banished in-between, and returned to his body, yet he'd managed to hang on to his gold card and a wallet full of cash. Must be the leprechaun in him.

Munching a candy bar from the mini fridge, she found a pen beside a selection of tourist leaflets extolling the virtues of Wales, just a short trip over the River Severn. She snorted. Beautiful as the place was, she wouldn't be setting foot over the border into Gwyn ap Nudd's domain again anytime soon.

Tamsy stirred, jumped off the bed, and followed Cordelia into the bathroom. After licking up water lying in the bottom of the shower, she sauntered around the room, sniffing everything.

Michael appeared to be sound asleep and, after what he'd been through in the last few days, unlikely to wake and walk in on her. So she left the bathroom door ajar for Tamsy to get out. After turning on the shower, she let the water run hot while she put the pen on the bathroom counter. Then she hung her bathrobe on the back of the door and stepped beneath the soothing stream.

Eyes closed, she turned her face into the spray. She opened her senses and let the vibrant energy swirl into her aura. Last evening, when she'd been unconscious, she must have picked up energy from the water passively. This time she consciously gathered the essence of her element, boosting herself until her muscles tingled and the blood raced in her veins.

She stilled at a sound from the bedroom. When silence returned, she shampooed her hair and turned her back to the water, enjoying the tickle of suds streaming down her skin. Clean again—what bliss.

With a blast of cooler air, the door to the bathroom opened. She froze at the sight of a blurred figure through the steamy glass. "You feeling better, sugarplum?"

Her heart thundered so loudly, she could hardly hear her voice when she answered. "I'm fine. Give me a few minutes, and I'll be out. Then you can use the bathroom." She stared through the glass, mesmerized by the white-robed figure, emotions twisting and tangling inside her. What would she do if he didn't leave?

His hand appeared around the end of the glass partition, holding a toothbrush and paste. "I got these sent up last night. Thought you might like to use the brush first."

A stab of guilty pain pierced her.

"I washed out your underwear. Your things were wet already after the shower, so I thought . . ." Once she grabbed the toothbrush, Michael turned away and his bleary image went to the heated towel rail. "They're dry now."

"Thank you."

Michael came back toward the shower. The feel of him beat in her chest, strong and dominating. She wanted so badly to touch him, let him touch her as he had in the fantasy he'd spun while they were in-between. But before she let him near her, she must reapply her wards. She knew Michael would never attack her as Dragon had, but her allure would drive them both wild with passion and they'd struggle to recover control.

"Cordelia, sugarplum, can I join you in the shower?"

"No!" Her throat contracted, hardly able to push out the word.

"Don't say no yet." His palm pressed against the glass. "Listen to me first."

She stared at his hand, remembered her silver chain wrapped around his wrist. He'd gone to his death with her Magic Knot ring on his finger.

She pressed her palm over her mouth.

"I know you didn't want to be bound to me, Cordelia. I've respected your wishes and kept out of your head. But we're joined forever." He paused, the drum of water beating in her ears. "You're mine now, love. And I'm yours."

Her breath rushed in and out, her chest tight with conflicting emotions. He thought she didn't want him. How could she tell him that the problem was she wanted him too much?

"Can I come in there with you?"

"In the shower?" she squeaked.

"I won't intrude on your mind, but I want to be with you, to touch you, to feel your hands on me."

Cordelia closed her eyes as little sparks of sensation rushed over her skin. Behind her eyelids, she imagined him walking toward her, a sinful grin on his face. Her allure expanded, reaching for him against her will. She had wanted him since the first moment she saw him, and he was hers. All she had to do was invite him to join her.

Her belly quivered. She gulped, the hot, wet air clogging her lungs. "I don't know, Michael. I'm—"

"I know you've got bad memories. But I'm *not* Dragon."

"Oh gods and goddesses, of course I don't think you're like him." She pressed her palm to the glass against his. "I've never been without my wards before, Michael. I'm frightened we'll lose control."

She screwed her eyes tight, an agony of indecision wrenching and tugging inside her. The slick hard glass beneath her palm softened. She thought she must be imagining the feel of his hand because she wanted to touch him so much. When his fingers laced through hers, the shock of realization jolted her eyes open.

The glass rippled away from his flesh like water. With a muffled yelp, she yanked her hand back.

"I put my hand through the . . . shite!" His voice filled the bathroom, gruff with surprise.

The glass looked solid. She couldn't believe what had happened. "Try again."

Once more, he flattened his palm against the transparent surface. After a moment, the glass stretched beneath the pressure of his hand like a sheet of plastic wrap.

Strange tingles ran over her skin. With barely a thought for her nakedness, she walked to the opening and gazed at him."

He stared at her, shock bright in his eyes. "Devin told me I'd discover new powers after my resurrection. This must be what he was talking about." He turned to the basin and, with a certainty that amazed her, poked a finger into the china as though it were custard. "I'm an earth elemental. As Troy manipulates air, I must be able to manipulate solids."

Chapter Sixteen

Michael withdrew his finger from the china basin, his mind stalling at the reality of his new power.

Standing naked in the center of the room, Cordelia stared at him like a deer caught in headlights. "What . . . what does it feel like?"

"Surprising. I don't have to push. My finger slides in easily."

He tried to focus on her face, but his eyes dropped to her breasts. Her nipples hardened beneath his gaze, peeping between the damp strands of hair trailing down her body. Heat and tension gathered in his lower back and groin. He could think of more interesting places to slide his finger than the basin.

He remembered her all uptight and starchy, wearing her long, high-necked dress. An illicit thrill raced through him to see her unclothed and vulnerable before him. "I imagined you like this, naked with your hair loose," he whispered.

A pretty pink blossomed in her cheeks.

Women had been nothing more than fun and games to him, but Cordelia had stuck with him when he needed her most, called him back from the Underworld. She'd lived under his nose for two years, but he hadn't been ready for her until now. He hadn't understood what he was missing.

Before he took things further, he needed her to accept his Magic Knot again and let him into her mind. Tension gripped his muscles as he retrieved the linked stones from his robe pocket. Last night, he'd transferred them onto her silver chain. He held them up, giving her time to back away if she didn't want them around her neck.

Two tiny creases formed between her brows, her gray eyes dark as storm clouds. Yet she bent her neck so he could place the chain over her head.

When his three stones settled in the damp valley between her breasts, he extended his awareness, gently brushed the edges of her mind. She looked down and gripped his stones in her hand. "I thought you'd taken them back, Michael."

"Only while you were weak, love. I'll be careful not to swamp you with me power."

She raised her eyes and nodded. His breath flowed out with almost painful relief, followed by a hot burst of excitement.

She was his.

"We need to dry you." After snagging a towel from the dwindling pile, he moved behind her, his gaze dropping to her bottom. *Sweet Anu.* He stifled a grunt of appreciation. Clenching his jaw, he flexed his fingers, imagining his palms stroking her firm, smooth arse.

While he toweled her hair, he watched her in the mirror over the basin, sensing little flutters of her emotions: curiosity, nervousness, arousal. She blinked slowly as though her eyelids were heavy, then spoke, her husky tone a caress. "I imagined you naked as well."

His hands stilled. All the blood rushed out of his brain, heading south, leaving his groin hot and heavy. "I need you, Cordelia. After the last few days, I really, really need you."

"I can't. I must reapply my wards," she said, with her palms pressed to her solar plexus.

"Afterward."

She breathed in and out five times, her breasts rising and falling in an enticing rhythm, her nipples playing peekaboo through her hair.

Then she opened her eyes and he met her reflected gaze. "All right," she whispered.

The fine tension running through his muscles eased as though someone had released his bindings. Only years of experience with women stopped him from grabbing her and pulling her against him. He prided himself on finesse and generosity in the bedroom. And she mattered a million times more than the women who'd warmed his bed in the past.

After releasing her hair down her back, he smoothed the strands, letting his fingers brush tantalizingly over her buttocks. Then he pressed his lips to her right shoulder, the opposite side from the show-stopping scars. Later he would kiss her scarred neck, when he'd given her enough pleasure to bury the memory of Dragon.

He glanced up at the mirror through his lashes. She blinked at him slowly, already languorous with arousal.

His fingers circled her waist. A gentle touch, undemanding, claiming the easy ground before he moved on to controversial territory.

Turning in his arms, she settled her hands on his shoulders. Her breasts pressed lightly against his chest, cradled in the fluffy toweling of his robe. When she touched a fingertip to his lips, the subtle caress of her essence flitted through him. His breath caught, rushed out on a needy sound that shocked him. He was used to having total control while he seduced women, yet one brush with her spirit had him floored.

A flowing burst of her allure shuddered through him, setting every nerve in his body on fire. He grabbed her bottom, lifted her against him with a groan.

Cordelia knew he was going to kiss her. The whisper of his intent caressed her mind a second before his firm lips claimed her mouth. Her eyelids drifted down, while the heat of his hands suffused her skin.

Her father's voice berated her inside her head. Futilely she fought her desire. Michael drew back and flashed the wicked sexy grin that lived in her dreams. "Cordelia, me love," he whispered, and the delicious tingle of his desires shivered through her mind, dislodging her father's voice.

She framed his face in her hands, tasting the smoothness of his lips, claiming him in the way she'd fantasized so many times. His tongue stroked hers, draining the strength from her legs so she sagged against him. She gave up trying to restrain her allure and let her energies surge around him, fueling his lust.

With a little grunt of desire, he deepened the kiss. The sensual sweep of his tongue drew her down to a place where nothing mattered except the hot wet intensity of mind-addling need.

She pushed her fingers into his luxuriant hair, while his palms molded her bottom, pulling her against the hard length of his erection. His hips moved in a slow sensual rhythm. She wanted to see him naked, needed to feel him skin to skin.

With a gasp, she pulled back from the kiss and stared at his flushed cheeks and glittering eyes, aware of his power inside her, around her. His huge dark pupils were ringed with a crystalline blue so clear and bright, he looked preternatural.

"You're temptation incarnate." She pushed apart the lapels of his robe, revealing a deep V of muscular chest before she pressed her lips to the tiny scar where she'd healed his fatal wound. Her heart stuttered at the thought she'd nearly lost him.

His hands worked through her hair, massaged her scalp. "Aye, sugarplum, take what you want of me."

Her tongue tasted, lips trailed over firm flesh, pressed the tiny bud of a nipple. His chest vibrated beneath her kiss on a groan. She inhaled the herbal tang of his skin like an addict.

His lips found hers again, hard, demanding. Her fingers

tugged the belt of his robe, plucked at the knot while he half carried her from the bathroom.

One of his hands gripped her bottom and pulled her close; the other caressed her breast. Sensation sprayed out from his touch, filling her body and aura with their blended desires. Her breath hissed out, followed a second later by his.

"Sweet Anu, your allure is mixing with me energy."

She should have warned him her allure could use a man's power against him. Dragon had known and yet still been overwhelmed.

A whirlpool swirled within her, drawing Michael into the turbulence. They fell on the bed together, arms and legs tangling. Michael shoved her on her back, rose over her, eyes blazing, jaw clenched. Fear quivered in her belly; then she relaxed. Michael would never hurt her. He stared at her, gasping air in and out of his mouth until the wildness in his eyes faded.

He swiped a hand over his face. "That's the energy you healed me with?"

She nodded, her tongue tied with desire and memories of fear.

"No wonder I came back." His lips slid into a sinful grin.

Rising to his knees, he shrugged off the robe before tossing it away. Her gaze trailed down his chest, admiring the sculpted ridges of muscle. Shivery tingles raced through her as she stared at his erection, her fingers trembling in anticipation.

"Touch me," he whispered.

She cupped the thick length of his arousal, stroked the silky skin. With a little murmur of pleasure, he pressed his mouth to her neck, trailed his lips onto her breast. When he moved down, he slid out of her hand. But her moan of displeasure caught in her throat as his mouth closed around her nipple. He gazed up at her beneath his lashes while he sucked, his fingertips teasing and tickling her belly.

A burst of pleasure shot through her when his hand

moved lower, worked magic between her legs. She fought to keep her eyes open to watch him, but her mind overflowed with the caress of his spirit and the sensation of his touch.

She writhed, clutching the sheet, body wild with the allure surging through her.

He pushed her legs wider, his hands and mouth working an elemental magic.

"Please . . ." she whimpered. Michael's energy blended with hers and pulsed through her so hard, she was going to burst out of her skin. Then she imploded, her whole being contracting to a point of light before expanding outward in a flash.

In the corridor outside came a crash of breaking china, jerking her from her pleasure-dazed stupor.

After a moment, Michael raised his head and grinned. "Crikey O'Reilly, lass, your allure almost took me with you, and I'm not nearly ready to finish. I want to make this last."

At the sound of a man cursing outside, they both looked toward the door. "I'm betting you did take that poor fella with you," Michael said. "He'll probably worry he's going to keep suffering from spontaneous ejaculation."

A twinge of discomfort tainted Cordelia's pleasure. If her allure had affected the man in the corridor, she needed to paint the symbols back on her body quickly.

She fidgeted, hoping Michael would take the hint and move. When he gave her room, she started to rise. He gripped her arm, not hard, but leaving her in no doubt he wouldn't allow her to retreat to the bathroom.

"We haven't finished, sugarplum," he said, glancing at his lap.

At the sight of his arousal, tension gathered in her belly again, sparking nerves beneath her skin she'd thought burned out by the recent rush of energy.

"In fact," he said, flicking up his eyebrows, "we've only just started."

A languorous heat drifted through her. He slid up the bed

and beckoned her to join him. "That was your appetizer. 'Tis time for the main course." He cupped his genitals and stroked himself. Her brain forgot how to work her lungs. Specks of light and dark floated across her vision.

There was no way she could reapply her wards, because her higher mental functions had given way to instinct. She crawled up the bed, pausing halfway to drop a kiss on his hip and revel in the hot musky scent of him. Muttering endearments, he pulled her up beside him, captured her mouth, and pressed her into the mattress in one smooth movement.

The morning drifted past while he kissed her and caressed her with expertise, rousing her until a tornado circled in a vortex at her energy center, until she forgot who she was. She claimed what she wanted of him, exploring his body using lips and fingers, watching him arch beneath her stroking hand in an agony of pleasure.

Finally, he lay panting, eyes screwed tight. "You're going to kill me with pleasure, and I want to die at your hands."

She rested her cheek against his chest, listening to the thump of his heart, his warm, comfortable presence surrounding her like a loving hand. This intimacy was more wonderful than any fantasy. In the future, maybe she could remove her wards when they were alone, so they could make love again.

He ran a fingertip lightly around her jaw, then touched the three stones of his Magic Knot against her skin. "Ahh, I have me second wind, love." With a wicked grin, he rolled her underneath him and nuzzled her neck.

Once more, his fingers found her tender places, making her body sing beneath his touch. She massaged the bulge of his biceps, stroked the firm length of his back, fingered the taut strength of muscle bunched in his buttocks. Michael's body was built to give pleasure.

He slid over her and settled between her legs, the hot weight of his erection pressing against the sensitive flesh he'd teased to readiness. Her breath stalled at the promise of dreams fulfilled.

"Cordelia."

She blinked, focused on the searing blue heat of his gaze.

With a slow brush of lips, he kissed her, then touched the side of his nose to hers. "Say me name, love."

"Michael." The word whispered over her lips.

"Again."

"Michael."

He licked his lips. "You want this, don't you?"

"Oh, gods and goddesses. I'm going to combust if you don't do it. Can't you sense how much I want you, Michael? I've always wanted you." She wriggled her hips beneath him, sucked in a catchy breath at the burst of sensation. "Please."

He grinned, slowly, a lazy satisfaction in his eyes. "Just checking."

"Stop teasing."

"That wasn't teasing." With a practiced tilt of his hips, he pressed a little way inside her.

He stopped. She whimpered, teetering on the edge of bliss.

"This is teasing," he whispered.

"Michael O'Connor." She slapped him on the backside, and he laughed.

"Oh, baby, spank me again." He flicked up his eyebrows. Although she thought he was joking, she slapped him again because she was through waiting. He jolted, the effect pushing him deeper.

"Oh yeah. Oh yeah." Michael breathed hot against her lips, pressed his hips down, filling her with heat and sensation. Cordelia's eyelids fell as his lips claimed her mouth in a deep drugging kiss. His hand glided beneath her hip, lifted her thigh, expertly moved her in time with his thrusts.

She clung to him, lost in the perfect rhythm of their bodies and minds, a warm sinful place where nothing mattered but pleasure. Hot flushes of desire swept through her, growing in intensity each time he moved. Her breath shuddered in and burst out every time he murmured naughty things in her ear.

Michael moved faster, while his hand stroked her breast, sending tingling shards of sensation across her skin. She grabbed at his back, hung on as though she might lose herself if she let go. He moaned, eyes closed tightly, teeth clamped over his bottom lip.

The waves of allure cascaded through her. With a cry, bone-melting pleasure flashed along her arms and legs, bursting out from the boundary of her body into her aura.

Dimly, on the edge of awareness, she heard shouting. Then the waves of energy swamped her. She floated on the warm swell of their pleasure.

Slowly, his power absorbed her allure and settled around her, held her in its embrace. The weight of his body pressed her into the mattress, but she didn't care. Nothing mattered for a while, but the feeling of being one with Michael. She'd desired him from afar, but now that she knew him, her feelings ran far deeper than lust.

She raised her hand, watching it curiously as though it didn't belong to her, then touched Michael's hair, let a chestnut wave slide over her finger. She'd washed off her wards, made love with Michael, and no harm had come to anyone. He could handle her allure, so maybe she could have a proper relationship with him as she had dreamed. The more she got to know him, the more she loved this sexy rascal with his kind heart.

After long minutes, he roused, and pushed himself up on his elbows, levering most of his weight off her. His blue eyes were hooded with satisfaction, his expression lazy and sated. "Sugarplum, you've wiped me out."

He dropped on his back beside her, with a long contented sigh. "Let's sleep; then we'll head home later."

Sirens outside intruded on the lazy atmosphere of the

room. He turned his head on the pillow to look at the window. "Sounds like something's going on out there."

A few minutes later, a knock sounded on the door. "Ahh." Michael rubbed his face. "What's the point of a DO NOT DISTURB sign if people ignore the damn thing?" He rolled over and pushed up to sit on the edge of the bed.

"You all right in there?" a man's voice shouted.

"Hang on a minute." Michael helped her beneath the duvet, then snagged the robe from the floor and pulled it on. Cinching the belt, he wandered to the door and unlocked it. "What's up?"

Cordelia half listened to Michael's conversation while sleep drifted over her, lazy and warm.

"The place has gone mad," the man at the door said. "Some men in a business workshop on the floor below went crazy and attacked the women. The police are down there now. I'm checking that everyone up here's okay."

Shock jolted Cordelia out of her sleepy daze. She sprang up and wrapped the duvet around her, then stumbled to the door to catch the man before he moved on. "When did this happen?"

He stared at her, pink suffusing his cheeks. Without warning, he grabbed at her.

"Hey!" Michael stepped in front of her and jostled the man away. "What's your problem, fella?"

The man staggered back, confusion on his face. Then he turned and dashed toward the elevator.

Dark and intense, horror thrummed her nerves. "It's not his fault, Michael. It's me."

"It can't be—"

"You saw his reaction. He was affected by my allure."

She spun back to the room, tears burning her eyes. "The pen. Where's the bloody pen?"

Michael stared at her. The warmth of his reassurance brushed her mind and, instinctively, she slammed down her defenses, pushed him away. Disbelief, then sadness, crossed his face. He strode to the bathroom and returned with the pen.

She didn't want to hurt his feelings, but she couldn't allow him to placate her. He didn't understand how serious this was. She dropped the duvet, sat on the edge of the bed, and, with a shaking hand, started drawing over her solar plexus to block the most powerful energy center first. Tears tightened her throat while her hand quickly formed the familiar symbols she'd applied to her skin a thousand times before. Next, she moved to her heart center, then her belly.

When she'd finished her front, she looked up to find Michael frozen, watching her intently, his mouth tight, eyes bright with pain. Her heart clenched, but her urgency overtook all other emotion.

"I'll need you to do my back for me." She grabbed a sheet of paper from the desk and sketched the symbols for him to copy.

He came closer and placed a hand on her busy arm, halting her drawing. "Is this really necessary, love?"

"You heard him." Fear and shame threaded steel through her voice. "I've caused innocent humans to do something terrible. My father was right. I should *never* remove my wards."

"I didn't lose control," Michael said.

"You're not human," she snapped. "You're not even an ordinary fairy. You're"—she waved an arm at him impatiently—"you're immortal. You're massively powerful. You can probably walk through walls for all we know."

She held out the drawing and waited for him to take it before she turned her back. "Please, just help me reapply my wards. The top one goes on my neck, then the rest mirror what I've drawn on my front." She stood up, the race of her panicked pulse so loud it filled her ears. After what felt like forever, the pen touched her back and she released a breath tight with anguish for her lost dreams.

"What does this mean for us?" Michael asked softly, while the pen moved over her skin.

She licked her dry lips. "It means I made a mistake. One I can never make again."

"What was the mistake, Cordelia?"

Her heart thumped so hard, her temples pounded.

"The mistake was leaving off my wards to make love with you."

Using his uninjured arm, Nightshade carried Rhys up the stairs at Trevelion Manor, Eloise on his heels. They had stopped at a motel for the night, but none of them had got much sleep, and they were all still exhausted after the last few days. Thorn had gone straight to bed when they arrived home, but Nightshade and Eloise needed to settle Rhys safely first. Nightshade had little doubt that Ana, Michael's leprechaun half sister, would welcome another baby with open arms.

When he reached the nursery, he halted in the doorway, taking in a sight he'd never expected to see. Troy sat cross-legged on the carpet. His golden hair was twisted up in an elaborate style and trimmed with peacock feathers that matched the color of his jacket. With a beautiful long-fingered hand, more at home wielding a sword, Troy pretended to pour from a small blue plastic teapot decorated with a teddy bear into a matching cup. Little Kea sat on his lap, his chubby fingers pulling at the gold-rimmed abalone buttons trimming the cuffs of Troy's jacket. The soft glow from Troy's skin blended with the early morning sunlight filtering in through the window.

As Troy watched the baby, his smile was so sad that Nightshade's heart hurt to think that Michael might end up as world-weary as his father.

Ana sat beside the babies' cot, knitting, keeping watch over Finian while he slept.

Nightshade continued into the nursery, Rhys stirring in his arms. "Ana, we need your help, please."

When Eloise entered the nursery, she gave a little gasp. Nightshade didn't blame her. The sight of Troy still took his breath away.

Troy angled his head with a studied casualness. "Is Michael well?"

"He is," Nightshade replied, Troy's feigned indifference not fooling him for a moment.

Looking down, Troy exhaled and ran a fingertip over Kea's plump cheek.

"He's not here," Nightshade added, although Troy would be able to sense that. "The wise woman lost consciousness on the Darkling Road. Michael took her to a hotel to recuperate."

"Michael will no doubt restore her spirits," Troy said. "He has a way with women." Kea grasped a button on the front of Troy's jacket, frowning in concentration while he tried to push it out of the buttonhole. Troy's poignant smile pulled at his lips again. "The little lad is desperate to undress me."

Nightshade couldn't suppress his wry smile, but forbore to add that he shared the boy's fascination.

Ana had set aside her knitting and jumped from the chair. The tiny leprechaun woman waddled closer with her funny bandy-legged walk and smiled. "You have a son, Nightshade?"

"A half brother."

"Oh, my." Ana's face crinkled in pleasure when he kneeled so she could see Rhys properly. "May I hold the wee one?" she asked, turning to Eloise.

Wide-eyed, Eloise blinked and nodded.

Nightshade passed his precious bundle to Ana, who oohed and ahhed while she cuddled the smiling child.

"He's a good boy," Nightshade said, pride filling his chest.

"No trouble while we escaped, and he slept most of the way home. I think he's ready for breakfast."

"And a clean diaper," Eloise added.

While Ana and Eloise took Rhys to the changing table, Nightshade wandered toward Troy, who stiffened and looked up sharply when he moved too close.

"I'm no threat to you."

Troy's gelid gaze grazed over him, but the subtle tension in his body eased.

Taking a risk, Nightshade hunkered down beside him and rubbed a knuckle along Kea's plump forearm. When Troy didn't flinch from his proximity, Nightshade slowly laid a consoling hand on his arm. After the last few days, he shouldn't have any energy left to feel compassion for another. But finding Rhys had woken an emotional side of him that sensed the anguish Troy hid behind his veneer of perfection.

"Michael will be back later," he said softly.

Not acknowledging the touch, Troy kept his eyes on Kea, cradled sleepily in his arms, and smoothed the boy's fine golden hair. "Then I'll be on my way."

Nightshade stood and stepped back when Ana shuffled across and placed a mug decorated with little green leprechauns down on the carpet. "Drink your tea, Troy. I'm thinking Michael will be pleased to see you."

She held out her arms, and Troy handed Kea over.

"Unlikely." Troy gave a wistful glance at Finian asleep in the cot. "Both Michael and Niall think I manipulate them."

"Nonsense," Ana said as she deposited Kea in a playpen in the corner of the room. "You do your best. 'Tis all anyone can ask."

He gave her a sardonic glance. "Damned by faint praise, Mistress Ana." He rose elegantly, his movements the agile stretch and flex of a highly toned physique. A flutter of desire caressed Nightshade as he imagined sinking his fangs into the pearly skin of Troy's neck.

Troy angled his head, eyebrows raised in question.

"Are my thoughts that obvious?" Nightshade grinned.

"Clear as diamonds of the first water."

After a quick check to ensure Eloise and Ana weren't watching, Nightshade decided his self-control was over and allowed the tips of his fangs to show.

Troy ignored his taunt. "I must away to Wales to deal with Gwyn ap Nudd."

"It would have been nice if you'd done that earlier." Nightshade favored his aching shoulder at memories of being smashed against the wall.

"Initially the situation served my purposes," Troy said. "Then Michael asked me not to interfere. As far as possible, I respected his wish."

"So now he's out of there, you're going to clear up his mess?"

"No, stalker." Troy turned glacial blue eyes on him and a shiver raced down Nightshade's spine. "Gwyn ap Nudd has always been *my mess*, as you so eloquently put it. I'll look to my responsibilities, you look to yours." He glanced across the room to where Eloise sat in one of the wing chairs with Rhys on her lap, nibbling a baby rusk. "I applaud your concern for your half brother and his mother, but be aware there are some who will consider you've stolen what is not yours."

Nightshade's grin faded, and he stared at Rhys, busy chewing as though nothing existed in the world except his food. "I considered the possibility of reprisals by the Tylwyth Teg, but I didn't think they'd bother to follow Eloise once she escaped from Wales, and Dragon rarely sees the boy."

"You'll be amazed how much interest Dragon can summon when he discovers you've taken the child."

After a final glance at his grandsons, Troy turned and

faded like mist in the sun. For a long time, Nightshade stared at the spot where Troy had stood, hoping he was wrong, fearing he was not. In his heart, he'd known there was a risk in bringing Rhys and Eloise to Cornwall. He hoped he hadn't brought more trouble down on the piskies.

Chapter Seventeen

Cordelia had thought she was falling in love; instead, she was falling apart.

Her carefully controlled existence had shattered because she'd disregarded the one thing her father and grandmother had impressed upon her—to keep her wards intact and her allure contained. She'd sought pleasure; as a result, innocent people had suffered. To make matters worse, she'd hurt Michael's feelings.

After they left the hotel, he drove the rental car in silence, an uncharacteristic grim tension around his eyes and mouth while he slammed through the gears. She stared out the side window as the Bristol suburbs thinned out to be replaced by fields. Wincing, she touched her sore tummy and chest where she'd pressed too hard with the pen. None of the symbols Michael had drawn on her back hurt. He'd been gentler with her than she'd been with herself.

Inexorably, her gaze slid to his strong hands gripping the steering wheel. The sinewy strength of his wrists and forearms made her allure simmer behind her wards. She tried to ignore his thighs and the other interesting parts of him hugged by faded denim. She swallowed and dragged her eyes away when her allure began to surge and roll, the pressure building inside her. Leaning her head back, she imagined diving into the cold Atlantic to calm herself.

Now she'd tasted the freedom of linking with him and loving him, the ache of need would torment her every moment she could feel his presence. She no longer trusted the wards to contain her desire for him.

"I'll have to leave Trevelion Manor—I'm not confident I can control my allure anymore," she said softly, pushing aside the awful pain she felt at the thought of leaving Michael and her home and Thorn and all the piskies.

His hands tightened on the steering wheel. Then he glanced at her. "Where will you go?"

A stab of disappointment brought tears to her eyes. What had she hoped? That he'd beg her to stay?

"I haven't decided yet."

"So what happens to our bond?" he asked, his voice tight with reproach.

She turned to the side window and surreptitiously wiped her eyes. "I can't remove my wards again." She glanced over her shoulder at his tense jaw and narrowed eyes. "I can never be the woman you want, Michael. Anyway, we're not even properly bonded because Tamsy holds my mind and spirit stones."

He slashed her a sideways glance that stung her skin. "Where does that leave me?"

"Umm." She sucked her bottom lip, trying to decide how to make this easier for him. "I'll go far enough away that you can't feel me. You can just go back to how you were before we left."

The car swerved dangerously down a side turning. She clung to the door as the tires squealed. Michael bumped onto the grassy edge of the road and skidded to a halt.

Before she could move, he released his seat belt and hers and pulled her into his arms. His kiss crushed her mouth while the overwhelming force of his mind cocooned her with him in a humming aura of power. Instinctively, her lips moved beneath his. The simmer of desire roared to life with the speed of a sea squall, crashing into the wall of her wards. When her lungs burned for air, he finally pulled back, his hands gripping her upper arms.

"Know what that means?" he demanded, his eyes fierce.

She blinked at him, her mind racing with surprise at this domineering side of Michael she'd never seen before.

"It means I'm not letting you leave me," he said adamantly.

Relief flooded her but stalled when her brain started to process again. "I can't stay with the piskies. You know what happened in Bristol."

"I'll come away with you," he said in a voice layered with subtle tones of reassurance.

"What about your pub? What about Niall?"

"Sod the pub. You're more important."

"Oh." Her breath trembled in wonder when he pulled her closer. She sank against the strong warmth of his chest. Leaving Thorn would be upsetting, but he was old enough to look after himself. Maybe she and Michael could find a cottage close enough to Trevelion Manor to visit, yet a safe distance from other men. Then she could remove her wards to make love to him.

Thoughts of making love shimmered heat through her until she could barely breathe from the power ready to burst out of her skin. Her hand found its way onto his thigh. Beneath the soft denim, his muscle clenched. His words whispered against her ear. "Cordelia Tink, I once thought you were straitlaced."

"I was an innocent, hardworking wise woman until you corrupted me," she whispered back, sliding her palm higher to rub the bulge growing underneath his zipper. She fumbled with the zip and button, thrilled by his little grunt of pleasure when her hand slid inside his jeans.

"Oh, yeah," he said between gasps. "I intend to corrupt you a whole lot more when we arrive home."

Michael stood beside the twins' cot in the nursery at Trevelion Manor, staring down at the two little boys snuggled together. Sadness tainted his sense of relief and satisfaction that Finian was safe and well and reunited with Kea.

When Rose and Niall returned from America, Michael would leave with Cordelia. He stroked the boys' soft hair, wishing he didn't have to be parted from them.

Even as Cordelia had announced she must leave, Michael knew he'd go with her. The decision came from his gut, or maybe his heart. But now the consequences of that decision had sunk in, his heart ached.

In the last two years, the pisky troop had become his people. Yet although the loss hurt, he would still make the choice of leaving with Cordelia if she asked him again now.

He just wished he didn't have to choose between her and his family.

Ana sat in the chair beside the cot. Her dark curls hung over her face while she dozed, watching over the wee ones. He dropped into the chair beside her and stretched his legs. His foot brushed something shiny on the carpet. After picking the wispy thing up, he placed it on his palm. Beneath the nightlight, the silky blue-green fibers of a peacock's feather glowed against his skin.

Only one person he knew wore peacock feathers. Troy must have dropped it when he brought Finian home. If only his father had waited around. He'd be able to advise Michael about Cordelia's allure.

Michael rested his head back on the chair and closed his eyes against a sudden stab of pain. Despite Troy's emotional distance, he'd always believed his father cared for him. Yet Troy had given him up to the King of the Underworld and walked away with hardly a backward glance.

"Penny for them." Ana's sleepy voice pulled him from his thoughts. He rolled his head on the chair back to see her. She blinked at him, her dark skin and hair making her little more than a shadow in the corner of the chair.

"I'm going to have to leave."

"You've only just arrived home, lad."

"I've bonded with Cordelia. She thinks she can't stay here."

Ana frowned. "I'm not sensing her in you, lad."

Michael sighed, his chest heavy with melancholy. "I don't hold her mind and spirit. Her cat does."

Nodding, Ana patted her stubby fingers on the chair arm. "'Tis not unusual for a witch to have a familiar, but I'm sad for you. I'm told 'tis the most wonderful experience being one with your mate."

Silence fell between them. The gentle rhythm of the babies breathing soothed Michael after the turmoil of the last few days.

"Why must the wise woman leave?" Ana asked, drawing him from his pleasant stupor.

Cordelia had asked him not to tell anyone she was a water nymph, but his sister deserved to know his reason for leaving. "She's a water nymph, she's worried that—"

"She's a healer?" Ana sat bolt upright, staring at him.

"Aye. She healed me in Wales when I was stabbed but she—"

"Why has she not shared her gift with the piskies?" Ana's kindly expression hardened into myriad lines. "An important power like that carries responsibilities, a duty to use the gift for the good of all."

"She has wards drawn on her body to contain her allure so she doesn't attract men."

Ana snorted. "She's a silly girl. Of course her allure runs out of control if she doesn't use the power for healing the way the gods intended."

Rhys snuffled and whimpered. After sliding down from her chair, Ana went to the cot and lifted him into her arms, whispering, and stroking his back.

Michael watched, waiting for her to say more, but she concentrated on quieting the child.

"Cordelia's expecting me to return once I've checked on

the boys." Michael stood and stretched, then headed to the door. He glanced back before he left.

Ana stared at him over Rhys's tuft of dark hair. "We don't want to go losing you, darling boy. Make the wise woman see sense for all our sakes."

Cordelia pulled her silky gown closed and cinched the cord before she wrapped a towel around her wet hair and headed for her small kitchenette. Tamsy stood on the counter, tail flicking as she eyed the tins of cat food on the shelf.

"Sorry, sweetheart. I should have fed you first."

Once she'd filled Tamsy's bowl, she checked the shepherd's pie in the oven and glanced over her shoulder at the door. Michael's presence beat insistently in her chest, each pulse sparking nerves beneath her skin. He had taken ages with the babies and she missed him.

When a knock sounded on her door, she wiped her hands and rushed to let Michael in. He grinned wearily and kissed her. Perversely, she felt more awkward with him now they were home. She wished she'd known him better before they went to Wales.

"I've made you some dinner." She showed him to the nook in the kitchen, where he sat. His troubled gaze jumped around her tiny kitchen, from the pine-fronted cupboards to her collection of cat ornaments haphazardly arranged on a shelf by the door.

He stared at the plate she set before him, gaze unfocused.

She sat opposite him, his obvious discomfort twisting her gut. Maybe now he was home with his nephews, he'd changed his mind about leaving.

"You don't have to come with me."

His gaze searched her face, the blue of his eyes darker than usual. "You don't have to go."

His words made her ache to stay in the home she loved, keep Thorn near her, and have Michael as well.

"Why don't you use your healing powers?" he asked.

Cordelia rubbed her temples. "I thought you understood that the healing power is part of the allure."

"Ana said if you use your energies to heal, then they wouldn't get out of control."

A flash of annoyance made her slam down her silverware. "I'm the one who's lived with this all my life."

"Have you ever tried to heal anyone?"

"Yes, you!" she shot back defensively.

They stared at each other, tension filling the air. His hand closed around hers on the tabletop. "I'd like to stay here, Cordelia. I'm sure you would too."

"Of course, I don't want to leave here, but I can't risk humiliating myself by letting my allure affect the piskies. They'd despise me." She imagined the male piskies losing control like the human men in the hotel, and bile rose in the back of her throat. "Oh, gods and goddesses." She pressed the heels of her hands to her eyes. "The last thing my father did before he died was call me a shameless hussy like my mother."

Michael stroked her arm, the sweet comforting touch of his fingers and his mind perversely making her tears flow. "Maybe we can stay in one of the cottages on the edge of the estate," Michael said. "Niall has three empty places awaiting renovation. There's one on the cliffs overlooking Merricombe Bay about a mile away."

Now she was home, she really didn't want to leave everyone. Michael's suggestion was worth a try. "Maybe I can try healing the female piskies to see if using my power helps control the allure."

Smiling, he cupped her cheek, his hand warm and strong. "I'll stay with you, lass. You'll be fine."

He rose and came around behind her. While his fingers worked the tense muscles in her shoulders, his lips brushed her ear. "I want you again, Cordelia," he whispered.

She closed her eyes. A dreamy trance fell on her at the

pleasure of his touch. He unwound the towel from her head, releasing her hair over her shoulders before gently rubbing the strands dry.

"Can you make love to me while you're wearing the wards?"

"I want to." Her head dropped back against him. "But there'd be no way for the buildup of allure to escape."

"Clean off the symbols," he whispered in her ear. "I'll draw them back for you immediately we've finished."

"Not here, Michael. Not after what happened in the hotel."

His fingers gripped her shoulders. "Then we move to Merricombe Cottage first thing tomorrow."

Nightshade had spent all morning helping Michael and Cordelia move furniture into Merricombe Cottage, even though his injured shoulder still ached. Now he wanted to spend time with his baby brother.

He strode out through the back door of the summer kitchen at Trevelion Manor toward the happy gathering on the lawn. Ana sat on a red and blue tartan rug under a sunshade beside Finian, who giggled while he whacked colored buttons on a toy, making little animals pop their heads up. Close by, Kea kneeled, digging a hole in the grass with a jumbo plastic screwdriver.

Rhys stood silently watching everyone, one thumb in his mouth, his other fist closed over the arm of the wooden bench where Eloise sat. Nightshade wished the boy would laugh or chatter. Compared to Niall's twins, he seemed unnaturally quiet.

Rhys's silver eyes followed Nightshade as he approached. Pausing, Nightshade spread his wings to catch the warmth of the sun. It was important Rhys get used to the idea that wings were normal. He didn't want the boy going through the agonies of self-doubt he'd suffered. Rhys sucked harder on his thumb; his little cheeks dimpled.

"Hello, little man." Nightshade crouched and smiled. He gently tugged Rhys's wet thumb from his mouth. "You going to say hello to me?"

Grinning shyly, Rhys turned and pressed his face into Eloise's skirt.

"Sorry," she said, flushing. "He's not used to anyone paying him attention."

With a silent pledge to make his father pay for hurting the child, Nightshade exhaled his anger.

Nightshade rubbed Rhys's fluffy black hair. "Come and see what toys the boys have over here."

Rhys peered up beneath his sooty lashes and raised his arms, allowing Nightshade to lift him. After carrying him to the blanket, Nightshade sat him on the corner farthest from the other boys. Kea ignored them and kept stabbing the ground as if his life depended on it. Finian stopped thumping his toy and looked up, grinning broadly. Grasping a yellow plastic duck, Fin held it out to them. Nightshade accepted the toy. "Thank you, Fin." He smiled at Rhys. "Look what Fin's given you." Rhys took the duck between his small pudgy hands, but he spared it only a glance before his gaze fixed on Finian.

Eloise came and sat beside them. "He's a bit overwhelmed because he's never seen other children or toys before. We lived a very simple life." She looked down and plucked some strands of grass. "I want you to know how much I appreciate your helping me. It's all right for us to stay here, isn't it?"

"Niall and Rose won't turn you away. You and Rhys will be safe. I'll make sure you are."

Gradually, Rhys settled and started picking up toys and examining them. A sea breeze relieved the heat as the afternoon wore on. Ana fetched lemonade and biscuits. Nightshade thought this might be the happiest afternoon of his life until a restless flutter of disquiet made him stare around the peaceful garden with a frown.

"You feel anything untoward, Ana?"

The small leprechaun woman crouched and pressed her palm to the earth. "There's something coming. *Someone* coming." She pursed her lips in concentration. "I sense an evil presence." She scrambled up from the ground. "We must get these wee ones away from here."

Nightshade tasted the evil now, a sickly metallic taint on the back of his tongue like bad blood. "Eloise, take Rhys." While Ana picked up Fin, Nightshade grabbed Kea beneath the arms and hugged the boy to his chest as he ran toward the house, leaving the toys and cups strewn across the lawn.

When Nightshade reached the kitchen, he paused by the key hooks and snagged the Land Rover keys. "Fetch Thorn," he shouted at the bemused pisky woman cutting vegetables at the table. "Tell him to meet us at the coach house."

Their footsteps pounded along the floorboards as they ran through the corridors to the far side of the house and exited into the coach house. Nightshade bypassed the motorcycles and cars, grabbed a third baby car seat from storage, and strapped the children in their seats in the back of the Land Rover. He started the engine and slapped an impatient hand on the top doorsill while he awaited Thorn.

When Thorn finally ran up, Nightshade gripped his arm hard enough to capture his complete attention. "You drive the Land Rover to Merricombe Cottage, and you stay there with Ana, Eloise, and the babies. Tell Michael to get his arse back here pronto. Tell him we have unwelcome visitors."

Chapter Eighteen

Michael smiled to himself. Cordelia pretended to be demure and conservative, yet the second they were alone, she had her hands all over him. Not that he was complaining. He loved the attention.

He sat on a decrepit wooden bench in the overgrown cottage garden overlooking Merricombe Bay with Cordelia on his lap. Her sweet rump pressed tantalizingly against his crotch while she nuzzled his neck. The sea hissed up and down the beach below. Seagulls wheeled lazily overhead, riding the wind currents. He inhaled the salty air, flavored with the fragrance of her skin. Pleasure and satisfaction drifted through him in languid waves.

Even though there were damp patches of peeling plaster inside Merricombe Cottage, he couldn't be happier. The cottage now contained a dining room set, a couple of lounge chairs and, most importantly, a bed sporting clean sheets, ready to be christened. He intended to give the new mattress a good workout, just as soon as he rid Cordelia of her wards.

"Michael," she breathed in his ear.

"Aye, sugarplum."

"Have you thought any more about your new powers?"

His head fell back against the wall behind the bench with a soft thud. Staring at the wispy clouds, he swallowed his discomfort. "I haven't told anyone yet."

"Not even Nightshade?"

"Nah." Why did he have to tell anyone? Sticking his fingers into things would make a cool party trick, but he'd rather forget what had happened in Wales, enjoy Cordelia, and go back to being the troop storyteller. He pondered for a few seconds, then let the thoughts drift away on a wave of desire, as his body responded to her wriggling bottom.

He caught her face between his hands, and nibbled her lips. She murmured seductively, setting a fire in his belly. He kissed her deeply, spinning silky threads of desire into her mind. "All I want to think about now is us. We'll wash the pen off your skin; then we're going upstairs."

From the guarded look that crept into her eyes, he knew she was about to disagree. He pressed a finger to her lips.

"We're half a mile from the nearest cottage, one mile from Trevelion Manor, and three miles from the village. Unless you're worried about the seagulls or any fish out there, you can relax."

As Ana had suggested, Michael planned to encourage Cordelia to use her healing powers regularly, so her allure never built to dangerous levels; then she could live without her wards. It infuriated him that her father had caused her so much heartache by making her ashamed of her greatest gift. But Michael didn't want to discuss her upbringing now. He wanted to make love.

After lifting her from his lap, he stood.

"Where are you going?" she asked.

Tapping the side of his nose, he said, "I'll be right back."

Earlier, he'd opened the window in the poky little bathroom on the back of the house to let in the fresh summer air, and scrubbed out the 1970s avocado-green tub. He returned and spread a fluffy towel on the floor to hide the stained cork tiles before running hot water for a bath.

Cordelia appeared at the doorway, her hair wispy around her face where he'd caressed the strands loose from her braid. Desire shivered through him at her ruffled appearance. There was something deliciously wicked about seeing the untouchable wise woman flushed and mussed.

"I don't know about this," she said, sounding vulnerable.

He beckoned her, and felt a little kick beside his heart when, despite her uncertainty, she came to him. Slipping an arm around her waist, he pulled her close and brushed his mind across hers. His lips traced a path over her face and hair, reveling in the silky feel of her skin. "I know we had a problem in Bristol, love. But we'll be careful now. Trust me." He loaded his voice with reassurance, and meant every word. *Him*—the master of empty sweet nothings whispered to paramours who were forgotten the moment they left his bed.

She had changed into one of her long, high-necked dresses when they arrived home. He grinned with perverse pleasure. "I've fantasized about unfastening the tiny buttons down the front of your dress."

"You're a naughty boy," she whispered in a breathy voice.

"Aye, sugarplum, and you're going to be a naughty girl." His fingers worked at the buttons, slowly revealing her throat and chest, rewarding each new piece of exposed skin with a kiss.

Her ribs rose and fell while he parted the fabric and dropped a flutter of kisses around his Magic Knot, hanging in the valley between her breasts. "Sweet Anu, I love your heaving bosom all prim and proper, hidden from view, waiting to be exposed and touched and teased."

A needy sound escaped her lips and arrowed straight to his groin. He unfastened the button on his jeans and pushed down the zipper to ease the tightness. Then he cupped her breasts, squashed them up, and kissed the cleavage raised high in the opening of her dress.

"Ye gods, Michael." She clutched at his sides, her fingers yanking his shirt from his jeans.

Her hands trembled as she caressed his back, while her tension thrummed his senses. He pulled away, breaking her grip. "Let's get those symbols off your skin before you explode." He was starting to hate the bloody wards that restricted her like manacles. How could her father have allowed his daughter to be tortured this way?

Quickly, he finished unbuttoning her dress and stripped it down, leaving her standing in her underwear.

As she unfastened her bra, he ripped his shirt over his head quickly so he didn't miss a second of watching her. Then he toed off his sneakers, yanked down his jeans and underwear, and pushed them off inside out on the floor, losing his socks in the process.

Flushed and dreamy eyed, she smoothed her hands over his chest. Despite his intention to wash the wards off first, he pulled her against him, pressing his lips to hers. He lost himself in their scorching kiss until her fingers brushed the side of his erection, making his stomach muscles clench.

He stepped back before his brain switched off completely and instinct took over. Dropping to his knees, he dragged down her panties with him. She squeaked in surprise when he pressed a quick kiss to her stomach, taking a second to inhale her enticing musky scent. Then he stood, and stepped into the tub, leading her with him.

When she was sitting between his legs, he lathered a washcloth and started rubbing the markings off her back, while she worked on her front. "If this takes too long, I'm going to spontaneously combust," he said.

"And I'll melt," she replied. "My allure's boiling under my skin."

They worked in silence for a few minutes. Michael tried to ignore the insistent throb of his arousal as his fingers slid over her skin. Maybe they wouldn't make their way to the bed until later.

When Cordelia's allure flooded free into her aura, Michael closed his eyes and bit down hard on his lip as the sensual pull set fire to his blood.

"Have you finished?" The husky tone of her voice almost undid him.

"Nearly." He rinsed out the cloth and wiped her back,

checking that the marks were completely gone. He kissed the skin he'd rubbed red, silently promising she wouldn't have to suffer this forever.

"I'm done." She dropped her cloth over the edge of the tub with a plop. His hands caressed her breasts, then slid down her belly. He pulled her against him, and found the sweet spot between her legs while he rubbed himself on her bottom.

She rested her head back on his shoulder.

"Kiss me," he whispered, drowning in ecstasy.

She angled her head. His lips found her mouth while he pleasured her. She wriggled beneath his caresses, making sexy little whimpers.

When her hand slid down between their bodies, fingers brushing him in teasing strokes, he couldn't wait any longer. "Turn around, sugarplum."

Water cascaded over the side of the tub as she rose and turned. He was ready for her, arms out, hands gripping her thighs, then hips, mindlessly guiding her to join with him.

Her knees pressed his flanks when he pulled her tightly to him. The hair between her legs brushed his stomach, drawing a groan from him while he positioned her, the tip of his shaft brushing the soft folds of her feminine flesh. He grabbed a breath, paused to look into her languid gray eyes. She caressed his face, ran her thumbs along his cheekbones. "I love you, Michael."

Before her words had a chance to penetrate his passionate haze, she lowered herself onto him, the sensual stroke of her around his erection matched by the sensuous roll of her allure through his mind.

Water sloshed around them, splashing on the floor as he gripped her hips, guiding her movements. His tongue found the silky wet skin of her breast, lips closing over the hard beads of her nipples, first one and then the other. He turned his cheek against her as the pressure inside him grew, wishing he held all of her Magic Knot so they could join completely in mind and spirit as well as physically.

With a cry, she gripped his shoulders as she came, her fingernails biting into his flesh in a pleasure pain that arrowed to his groin, sending him over the edge.

For a long time they didn't move. The water cooled around them, and his legs started to deaden. She raised her forehead from his shoulder. "When we make love, my allure is grounded through you."

"Aye. I'd sort of worked that one out." He grinned, and she smiled back.

"Maybe if we do this enough, it'll keep my allure under control."

"Does that mean you're willing to have a go at leaving your wards off?"

She stared over his shoulder, eyes losing focus. After a while, she heaved a sigh. "Being without them frightens me, Michael. I'll try for a few days to see how I get on."

He eased out of her, before turning her sideways on his lap for a hug. "I'll stay with you as much as I can. Until Rose and Niall get home, I'll need to spend time with the babies. But I'll be with you every night."

She nodded against his chest, summoning a smile of relief from him. They'd made progress. If the next few days passed without problems, she'd gain in confidence. If she tried healing some of the piskies, that would help too.

Through the open window, the crunch of car tires on the gravel parking area drew his attention.

Thorn's voice shouted his name. Michael clenched his teeth in annoyance. "I told Nightshade we didn't want any visitors today."

"Maybe Thorn's missing us." Cordelia rose, grabbed a towel, and started drying herself.

Michael stepped from the tub, rubbed water off his chest, and wrapped a towel around his waist. "I'll go and tell him to wait outside for a few minutes."

He closed the bathroom door behind him and strode along the hallway, ready to tell Thorn to be more considerate. When he wrenched open the door, the words died in his mouth. Thorn stood outside, his face tight with worry, baby Kea snuggled in his arms. Ana was behind him, holding Finian, while Eloise hovered nervously at the back cuddling Rhys. "Nightshade sent us over," Thorn said.

"Best dress quickly, lad." Ana rocked Fin, who'd started to whimper. "There's evil coming toward the manor."

Michael froze in disbelief at the sight of the visitors; then their words penetrated his pleasure-sated brain. He swiped wet hair back from his face. What in the Furies was coming after them now? "Come in. Make yourselves at home as best you can."

He ran back to the bathroom and burst in as Cordelia was buttoning her dress. "There's possible trouble at the manor. Ana, Thorn, and Eloise are here with the babies."

Cordelia looked through the crack in the door while he yanked the legs of his jeans the right way out and stepped into them. "What trouble?" she asked.

After pulling on his T-shirt, he gave her a quick kiss on the lips.

"Michael, tell me." She clutched his arm when he turned to leave.

"I don't know yet."

She hurried after him, her dress gaping open over her chest. "If the piskies are in trouble, I should come."

Turning, he gripped her shoulders. "I need to know you're safe, or I won't be able to concentrate."

"But Michael—"

"Stay here!" he commanded, loading his words with every scrap of compulsion he possessed. Her eyes rolled back, and her knees buckled. He caught her in his arms. "Damn." He'd forgotten that his existing powers had probably been enhanced by his resurrection. After carrying her into the sitting room, he settled her in a chair. Ana followed him inside the room, rocking Finian in her arms.

In an agony of indecision, he ran his fingers back through

his hair. He didn't want to leave Cordelia like this, but he must get away from Merricombe Cottage. If it were the Tylwyth Teg coming to seek retribution for being cheated of their blood price, they would search him out. Arian and the other gatekeepers must not be allowed anywhere near Cordelia or the children.

He stroked wet hair away from Cordelia's eyes, gently finished buttoning the front of her dress to preserve her modesty, and kissed her lips. With a reassuring pat on Ana's shoulder, he turned to leave. "When she comes to, tell her I'm sorry. I didn't mean to knock her out. I'm not used to me enhanced power yet."

Ana's brown eyes widened in her wrinkled face. "You've taken after Troy, have you not, Michael lad?" She gripped his hand, tears overflowing her lashes. "May the gods give you strength to face your enemies."

Nightshade stood in the center of the lawn behind Trevelion Manor, watching the sky. The dark, malevolent presence oppressed him, growing stronger by the second. The creature approaching must be powerful to exude such an overwhelming psychic force. He'd never felt his father, but he knew instinctively the evil tainting his senses came from Dragon.

Although Nightshade had sent for Michael, this was his fight.

He pulled the sling from his arm and tossed it away. He couldn't afford to wear an obvious badge of weakness. Flexing his injured shoulder, he flapped his wings and lifted a few inches from the ground before finding his feet again. His shoulder still ached but was healed well enough to fly.

A tiny black dot appeared in the distance, high among the feathery clouds. Most humans who chanced to glance up would mistake the dot for a bird, but not all.

His father's audacity was staggering. Apart from emergencies, Nightshade flew at night so he wouldn't be seen.

When Dragon descended, he came at such a rate, Nightshade half expected him to crash. But the strength in his father's wings pulled him up in time to land elegantly on his feet. Three glowing orbs accompanied him, scattering into shards of light before forming into Arian, Olwyn, and Dai.

Dragon scanned the garden and house before his gaze settled on Nightshade. Bleached, brassy-blond hair fluttered around his shoulders. He dwarfed Nightshade in bulk and height, standing at least a head taller. Nightshade gritted his teeth with frustration while his muscles quivered in anticipation of battle. Eager as he was for retribution for all the suffering his father had caused, he doubted he could defeat a creature of Dragon's size and strength by brute force.

Dragon's lips pulled back to reveal his teeth, in what could have been a smile or a snarl. "I've come for my son."

The words hit Nightshade like a punch in the gut. He'd fantasized so often that his father would stand before him and say this. Yet now the time came, the words were not for him.

"I'm standing right here, Father."

Dragon laughed, a thunderclap of sound, scattering the small birds from the shrubs. The gatekeepers remained still and silent while Dragon wandered forward nonchalantly. He halted just out of reach and cast a disparaging glance over Nightshade. "You were a lost cause from the moment of conception. The piskies are farmers who live uninspired lives. I could not call such a creature son." He hooked his thumbs in his belt and circled Nightshade.

Turning to keep Dragon in sight, Nightshade watched the leashed power of his father's movements. His anger escalated together with a demeaning sense of helplessness. All his life he'd prided himself on his strength and boldness. Yet the sheer size of his father drained his confidence.

"Now Rhys is a different matter," Dragon said, tossing back his hair.

Nightshade straightened his back, gathered his defiance.

"His mother's human. How does that make him better than me?"

"He was to be raised among the Teg. With their influence, he stood a chance of finding a backbone."

"If you think so little of the piskies, why did you bother to spend time here?"

"I found it amusing that they hated me, but were too cowardly to tell me to leave." Dragon snapped his wings against his back. "Anyway, there was a young female that interested me. A water nymph." He ran the tip of his tongue over his lips. "Is she still here?"

His father hadn't just come for Rhys; he'd come for Cordelia. Even as shock turned Nightshade's blood to ice water, years of practice kept his expression blank. "I know of no water nymph."

His father turned and wandered back to the three gatekeepers, flicking his hand at Arian.

Arian roused at Dragon's signal and stepped forward. "Where's the son of Troy?"

Nightshade exerted subtle compulsion to distract Arian. Although he'd only bitten him once, he should have some influence.

"Don't waste your time, pisky boy," Dragon said to him. "The gatekeepers are now my creatures."

Arian shot Dragon a furious glance, but his father either didn't notice or didn't care.

"I'm going to search for the deathless one." Beckoning Olwyn and Dai to follow him, Arian headed toward the back door of Trevelion Manor. Nightshade let them go with only a frustrated glance. He had to choose his battles, and the gatekeepers weren't going to find anyone to interest them inside the manor.

"So you face me alone." Dragon raised his eyebrows. "No piskies dare stand with you against me? Or do they not care about your fate?"

Dragon was on a fishing trip, but he wasn't getting any

information. Nightshade continued to stare at him, stony-faced.

"Bring me my boy, and I'll overlook the fact you stole from me."

"You don't deserve him," Nightshade snapped, remembering the vicious scar on Rhys's back.

"Arian gave the woman to me, and the child is of my blood."

"Rhys is my blood kin as well."

Dragon's casual stance hardened. He clenched his fists, his biceps bunching. Then he snapped his wings against his back with a crack. "I'll rip this place apart to find him and not you or any of your timid piskies will stand in my way." Pink tinged the silver of Dragon's eyes and his nostrils flared. "Last chance, pisky boy. Bring me my son and his mother."

As they stared at each other, the roar of a sports car cut through the silence. On the edge of his vision, Nightshade caught the red streak of Michael's Porsche approaching down the narrow road from Merricombe Cottage. With a screech of tires, the car halted in the yard before the coach house. Michael jumped out, brushing the hair back off his face, and looked their way.

Michael's arrival broke the tension. Dragon's stance relaxed when Michael approached with his jaunty walk and beguiling smile.

"The son of Troy the Deathless," Dragon said to himself. "I see the resemblance." He glanced at Nightshade. "Is he your creature?"

Nightshade laughed bitterly. A few days ago, he'd have said yes, but even then he would have been kidding himself.

Dragon watched Michael with a predatory gleam in his eye.

"We have a visitor, I see." Michael stopped and tossed his hair, glamour dripping from him like sugar in a flytrap. Dragon's nostrils flared, and the tips of his fangs appeared white against his lips.

"You are of the earth, son of Troy. I didn't expect that."

He took a few careful steps toward Michael, and Nightshade tensed, but Michael held his ground, his smile unfaltering. "'Tis the leprechaun half of me."

"Leprechaun!" Dragon guffawed. "The thought of Troy with a leprechaun is astonishing. But the result is . . . interesting." He circled Michael, who glanced over his shoulder, but made no move to keep Dragon in sight.

Nightshade's pulse sprinted. He had no idea what Michael or Dragon were planning, but he was sure both had tactics in mind.

"You bear no weapons," Dragon said. "I heard you were a storyteller, but I could not believe such a thing possible of Troy's progeny."

With a cheeky grin, Michael waggled his eyebrows. "Would you like me to tell you a story?"

Dragon laughed again, sounding genuinely amused. "You are either an innocent or a charming fool." He reached out and stroked Michael's hair.

Nightshade swallowed his cry of warning, but the effort nearly choked him.

"I'm not interested in a story, pretty boy, but I would like you to do something for me."

Michael grinned, the seductive glint in his eye sending hot pulsing bloodlust flashing through Nightshade.

Dragon took a step closer, his size dwarfing Michael. *Too close!* Nightshade's mind screamed the warning, his muscles locked in an agony of conflict. His instinct cried out for him to jump to Michael's defense; his mind told him to trust the bard.

"You can bring me my son Rhys and his mother." In a beat, Dragon's posture changed from languid seducer to predator. His hand shot out to grab Michael's throat, but the bard ducked away and danced back, light on his feet.

With a hard downbeat of his wings, Nightshade leaped forward. Dragon spun to face him, growling, fangs fully extended into lethal spikes twice the size of Nightshade's. A strip of red glistening scales appeared down his sternum, quickly spreading to cover his chest. Then he hissed, the sound eerily reptilian.

Nightshade fell back, his breath locked in shock.

"Didn't anyone tell you where I came by my name, pisky boy? I'm blood-bonded to a dragon."

Chapter Nineteen

While Nightshade squared up to Dragon, Michael surveyed the monstrous fangs and red scaly chest of the creature that had savaged Cordelia and killed her father. Dragon's face was darkly beautiful and his body finely honed muscle, but he reeked of evil. How had she ever been attracted to such a beast?

Dragon swung to face him. "I may not be able to kill you, son of Troy, but I'll have fun trying." The deep, gravelly voice grated on Michael's nerves.

When Dragon lunged forward, Michael darted aside, lighter on his feet than the bulky nightstalker. Nightshade circled around behind his father to split the attacker's focus.

"There he is." Arian's shout from behind drew Michael's attention, but not his gaze. Even as the three gatekeepers bore down on him, he dared not take his eyes off Dragon.

Holding perfectly still, Michael concentrated on the feel of Arian. Soundlessly, the gatekeeper closed on him. At the last minute, Michael dropped to a crouch. Arian's silver-tipped fingers rattled through the air where Michael's head had just been. Then Arian tripped over Michael to land in an undignified heap on the grass.

Dragon bellowed with laughter and caught Arian's arm when he tried to slash at Michael again. "Leave him," he commanded, effortlessly holding the seething gatekeeper.

"The King of the Underworld is owed retribution for this coward's deceit," Arian shouted.

"Gwyn's a fool," Dragon said. "Troy's trapped him before, yet he fell for the same trick again."

"I want the deathless one's son," Arian demanded, waving a silver-tipped finger toward Michael.

Dragon's patience obviously at an end, he yanked Arian around to face him. "Not until *I've* finished with him."

Wonderful, Michael thought. *They'll be drawing lots for me next.*

After releasing Arian, Dragon turned and swept back his hair, his nostrils flaring as he stared at Michael. "Tell me where my son is, and I'll spare the rest of the piskies." Images seared Michael's mind of the piskies battered and bleeding, the house trashed. The fury on Niall's face when he saw the devastation wrought on his domain.

Yet Michael refused to give a helpless woman and child up to Dragon. He wished he'd put some effort into testing his new powers. They might have helped him deal with this monster.

He needed to lead Dragon away from the children. He glanced at Nightshade's wild eyes, but couldn't signal to him in case Dragon saw. He'd just have to hope his friend was thinking clearly enough to recognize Michael's ploy. Hanging his head, Michael said, "I'll take you to Rhys."

"No!" Nightshade's shout burst across the garden. He faded to his shade form, the gray shadow shooting forward. The three gatekeepers dashed out of the way. Before Dragon had a chance to assume a fighting stance, his head snapped back with a smack of flesh on flesh. A spurt of blood and spittle flew from his mouth.

With a muttered oath, Michael jumped clear, expecting Dragon to fade to a shade as well. Instead, the scales down his chest spread over his ribs and shoulders.

Dragon jerked back with another grunt of impact, then punched the air, growling. He extended his wings and leaped skyward, ascending at an amazing rate.

The patch of shadow solidified into Nightshade and he stared at Michael for a beat. "What you said about taking him to Rhys was a ruse?"

Michael nodded.

"Crap." Nightshade smacked the side of his head. Then he snatched a breath and gazed up at his father. His forehead creased in puzzlement. "Damn it all, the bastard can't turn into a shade." With an incredulous laugh, he swept down his wings, and launched himself into the air.

"Nightshade, stay on the ground where you have the advantage of shade form," Michael shouted after him. But his friend was already too high to hear.

Michael watched while the two black shapes zoomed toward each other. He winced in pained anticipation of the impact. At the last moment, Nightshade veered aside and kicked out, his foot smacking against Dragon's ribs. The blow would have felled most opponents, but the larger nightstalker flipped sideways to follow Nightshade without even hesitating.

The children weren't safe only one mile away at Merricombe Cottage. The way Nightshade and Dragon were zooming around in the air, they'd fly that far in a minute. Michael hoped Cordelia had kept everyone inside out of sight. Keeping an eye on the gatekeepers, who were all staring upward, Michael retreated, taking silent steps back toward his car. He couldn't drive to the cottage and warn them of the danger because Dragon would see him. But if he reached the phone in his car, he could call Thorn's cell.

Arian's gaze jerked down from the fight and focused on Michael as he moved away. Michael thought of running, but there wasn't any point because the three gatekeepers would transform into light balls and catch him in an instant.

"Leaving us, son of Troy?"

This "son of Troy" moniker was really starting to tick him off. "The name's Michael O'Connor."

Arian strode toward him, his silent footsteps eating the ground. He stopped five feet away and his lip curled at the corner in distaste. "Your family owes the King of the Underworld a debt. I claim payment from you."

Michael wished he hadn't left the Taser in Cordelia's apartment. He would like nothing better than to wipe the supercilious look from Arian's face. "Didn't your minder tell you he had first dibs on me?"

Arian flexed his silver-tipped fingers. "He's otherwise engaged, fool."

He advanced on Michael, a cruel smile thinning his lips.

"Halt," Michael commanded, loading his voice with compulsion. Arian's outline shimmered with light as he protected himself from the silver tongue.

Even as Michael clenched his fists and held them up, he knew he was wasting his time. His best chance of felling Arian was with a quick kick to the happy sacs. He kicked out, caught the gatekeeper square between the legs. Arian's mouth dropped open, his eyes bulged, and he fell to his knees.

"You do have balls then," Michael said as he backed away. Dai and Olwyn turned to look at him, but instead of moving to detain him, they glanced nervously up at Dragon.

Michael raced toward his car. He yanked open the door and dialed Thorn. Arian looked up and glared when Michael pressed the phone to his ear.

" 'Ello," Thorn answered.

"Get the children out of the cottage and away."

"Michael?"

"Aye."

"Where do I take them?"

"Into the center of Truro."

Dragon was arrogant, but he wouldn't show himself in the middle of a city full of humans.

Michael cut the call and jammed the phone in his back pocket while Dai and Olwyn pulled Arian to his feet. The three of them dissolved into clouds of light before reforming as glowing orbs.

How in the Furies did he deal with light balls?

He could jump in his car and lead them away from the children and the piskies. He glanced up at the two night-stalkers, still diving around in the air, neither with the upper hand. The problem was that if Nightshade didn't stop him, Dragon would then be on the loose with no one to keep track of his movements.

In the distance, Michael heard the roar of the Land Rover engine leaving Merricombe Cottage, and some of the tension left his shoulders.

The three light orbs whizzed toward him like evil Yule baubles. If he couldn't hurt them, he must trap them somewhere. He needed to buy himself thinking time. He ducked into the coach house and rifled through the sports equipment store. "Ah-ha." He grabbed a tennis racquet and spun around, brandishing it as the light spheres circled and headed his way.

The orbs separated and approached from different directions. Michael narrowed his eyes, took a back swing, and let fly. The first light sphere hit his racquet dead center, passed through the strings, and missed him by a whisker. "Shite!"

He ducked behind a car as the other two orbs flashed over his head.

Time for plan B.

Dodging between the cars, he headed for the door to the house, went through, and banged it shut behind him.

The hall inside was silent and empty. The few piskies in the house must be hiding. He sprinted along the corridor, certain the door would pose no obstacle to the Teg. When he reached the main entrance hall, he looked back, suspicious that there was no sign of them.

Pressing his back against the wall, he glanced around. *Think, man.* How could he catch them? He pinched the bridge of his nose. In the fraction of a second his scrutiny relaxed, Arian materialized in front of him. Even before he'd fully solidified, he swung his silver-spiked fingers at Michael's throat. With the wall at Michael's back, he had nowhere to go. Instinctively, he raised a forearm to ward off the blow. Spikes raked his skin, leaving an icy burn that flashed to heat as blood welled in the four slashes.

"Ruddy Badba!" Michael dived to the side and sprinted toward Cordelia's rooms to get the Taser. Suddenly an idea struck him. He swung around and barreled into Arian, who was following, knocking the Teg back against the wall with the unexpected maneuver. "Want to see the nursery, boyo?" he shouted over his shoulder. "Follow me."

Michael took the stairs two at a time, his arm stinging like the Furies. At the top, he headed for the nursery, thanking the gods that the babies were safely away from here. Ana and Niall had used leprechaun earth magic to protect the children's room against evil. Michael had no idea how the magic worked, but if the spells kept evil out, he was guessing they would also trap evil inside. He just had to tempt the three gatekeepers into the room and shut the door on them. Piece of cake—he hoped.

He ran through the nursery door, leaving it open, hoping the gatekeepers would follow him. One of the windows stood open. He'd have to shut that before he left; otherwise the Teg would simply fly out.

Close on his heels, Arian prowled into the room without even pausing at the threshold. Praying his plan would work, Michael backed toward the babies' changing table in the corner by the window. He trod on a toy, making it squeak incongruously in the tense silence.

He'd spent hours in the nursery and knew the position of every piece of furniture, the contents of every cupboard. Rose had made sure there was nothing sharp or breakable in the room. But he could think of something that might come in handy.

Arian halted in the center of the space and glanced around, hands tense at his sides. The metal spikes clicked together like skeletal fingers.

Michael rubbed his palm on his thigh, his heartbeat fast but not manic. The fact that he was unkillable lent him confidence.

As if Arian read his thoughts, he sneered. "You may be deathless, but when I get hold of you again, I will make you wish for death, son of Troy."

"The name's Michael," he repeated. His back bumped into the changing unit and he made sure he knocked the table hard enough to wobble the toiletries on top. Feigning a move to stop the items from falling, he grabbed the talc. There was no way to conceal the tall plastic container in his hand, but he kept the label hidden.

Now all he needed was for Dai and Olwyn to grace him with their presence and he was ready for action. Or ready as he'd ever be.

Arian made no move to approach Michael. Instead, he drummed one set of silver spikes against his thigh. "Do you plan to throw that at me?" He glanced at the container in Michael's hand and laughed derisively. "Your father would be disappointed in you for putting up such a dismal defense."

Your father would be disappointed in you echoed through Michael's brain, resurrecting countless childhood memories.

"Me father's not here," Michael ground out. His father had left him in the Underworld. A choking pain rose in Michael's chest, tight and hot. He clenched his teeth until his jaw ached. He didn't care what his father would think. If he kept the babies safe and stopped the piskies from being hurt, he would be proud of himself.

Arian was obviously waiting for Dai and Olwyn to help him capture Michael, which gave him a frisson of satisfaction. When the other two gatekeepers appeared at the doorway, Arian beckoned them in and stepped forward. Michael held his position, thumbed open the lid on the talc, and visualized exactly how things would play out.

Arian moved cautiously, his hands spread, while Dai and Olwyn flanked him, obligingly forming a line in front of Michael.

Two more breaths, one . . . two . . . Michael raised his arm, angled the baby talc, and held his breath as he flung an arc of fine powder, hitting Dai, Arian, and Olwyn in the face. He didn't wait to observe his handiwork, but jumped to the side, yanked closed the window and latched it. While he sprinted for the door, the three Tylwyth Teg coughed and spluttered. Michael paused at the door and looked back in time to see Arian rip the silver spikes from his fingers so he could wipe his eyes.

He closed the door behind him, turned the key, and slipped it in his pocket. Then he relaxed against the wall and rubbed the back of his neck while he listened to the crashing inside the room.

Later he'd have to deal with the rats he'd caught in his trap. Now he wanted to check on what had happened to Cordelia, Ana, Thorn, Eloise, and the three babies. On the way downstairs, he saw a pisky woman peeping through a door. "Mari, there're three Tylwyth Teg trapped in the nursery. No one must open the door until I come back."

She nodded vigorously.

Michael reached the kitchen, took the phone from the wall, and glanced out the window while he dialed Thorn's cell phone. Nightshade and Dragon were no longer visible. Icy prickles of apprehension ran down his spine.

Thorn answered on the second ring.

"You all safe?" Michael asked.

"Yep. We're just parking. No sign of any trouble yet."

"Can I speak to Cordelia?"

A beat of silence. "She didn't come. She was fretting about you and stayed at the cottage in case you needed her."

The prickles down Michael's spine grew into claws of dread. He dropped the phone, stepped outside and stared at the empty blue sky and the lawn strewn with toys and the remnants of a picnic. Where were Nightshade and Dragon?

An unnatural silence hung over the garden as if nature held its breath. Even the hiss of the sea on the beach below the cliffs sounded muted as though he had cotton wool stuffed in his ears.

Spatters of blood dotted the flagstones of the patio and dried in sticky drips on blades of grass, while a metallic, sickly smell hung in the air. He swallowed around a tight lump in his throat. He ignored the knocking on the nursery window above and scanned the garden and sky for some sign of the nightstalkers.

Then he saw a dark shape lying beside the wall at the bottom of the garden. He sprinted down the lawn, skidded to a halt, and dropped to his knees.

"Nightshade."

The stalker groaned in response. Lifting an arm, he wiped blood from his oozing nose and lips.

The dark suffocating blanket of Dragon's presence still hung over the area, so he hadn't fled after the fight. Scanning the coastline, Michael found the point that protruded into the sea just before Merricombe Bay. *One minute's flight away.*

Dragon hadn't gone to Merricombe Cottage. Why would he? He'd follow his son to Truro.

Michael clutched Cordelia's body ring and concentrated, but with only one damn stone, he couldn't sense her well enough to be certain she was safe. Fear settled in his gut like a frigid rock.

"Nightshade," he said urgently, "where'd Dragon go?"

Nightshade's breath came in rattling gasps as he

moved. He spat blood, and his mouth opened, but no sound emerged.

"Where's your father?"

Nightshade gripped Michael's arm, his torn nails scratching the skin. His swollen eyes cracked open, revealing slivers of bloodstained silver. He licked his lips. "Water nymph," he whispered. "Gone for water nymph."

Chapter Twenty

Cordelia paced restlessly through Merricombe Cottage. Now Thorn and Ana had taken Eloise and the children to safety, Michael dominated her mind. On the edge of her perception, his psychic presence came and went like a shout on the wind. Initially, he'd been calm, but now she sensed his distress. She ached to go to him, check he was all right.

She halted in the small sitting room and pressed her forehead to the cool glass of the window. This wasn't fair. He'd asked her to stay at the cottage so he didn't have to worry about her, but waiting helplessly was eating her up. She slapped her hand against the wall. Niall had left her in charge of the piskies. If they were in danger, she should be at Trevelion Manor.

The tiny cottage suddenly seemed oppressive and claustrophobic. After hurrying to the back door, she went outside and filled her lungs with salty air. She walked to the bottom of the garden and gazed over the cliffs at the sea hissing up and down the shingle below.

She imagined water lapping around her body, feeding her energy. Without her wards, the sensation of freedom exhilarated her. She could never go back to having her nature locked down like an animal in a cage. Michael had liberated her.

Tamsy rubbed around her legs. Gathering her cat in her arms, she inhaled the warm furry smell of her coat. Even as she reveled in the sweetness of their affection, she wished Michael held all three rings of her Magic Knot. Her deepest bond should be with the man she loved.

A dark sense of malevolence drifted over her, dragging her from her thoughts. Tamsy tensed and scrabbled to jump down. The cat prowled back and forth, growling, the hair standing up along her spine. Cordelia walked to the side of the cottage and checked the path leading to the front. She couldn't see or hear anyone, yet an evil presence crawled across her skin with a subtle familiarity that set her heart racing.

The feeling pinched and tugged at her memory, dug deeply, dragged up the nightmare of the first time she'd dared go without her wards.

Dragon!

He could not be here. He must not.

Tamsy fuzzed up into a huge ball of spiky hair and sharp fear. She scampered up a pile of rocks and stared toward Trevelion Manor, spitting and hissing. Cordelia's gaze rose inexorably to the sky. Her stomach dropped away, her head light with fear at the sight of a black creature silhouetted against the cerulean blue.

"Nightshade. It must be Nightshade," she whispered, even though she knew it wasn't. Her hand went to her scarred throat, and she backed up. The black creature grew larger, then dropped at a frightening rate. She prayed he would crash, but at the last minute, he snapped out his wings and lowered himself to the ground elegantly. Her muscles locked with fear, she could do nothing but watch. His long black hair was now blond, his striking features swollen. Water dripped from his face and battered torso, suggesting he'd washed the blood from his injuries. He must have fought Nightshade. She'd have sensed Michael's pain if he'd been involved.

"You *are* still here," he said, his swollen lips pulling back in a parody of a smile.

Flaring his nostrils, he inhaled deeply. "You smell as sweet as I remember. I wonder if you still taste like plump, dark cherries?"

Cordelia's back hit the untrimmed hedge, hawthorn spikes jabbing her skin, halting her retreat. With a hiss, Tamsy leaped from the rocks toward Dragon. He braced an arm and knocked her aside. She twisted in the air before landing unharmed on her feet.

"Call off the moggie, witch. I have no more patience for fighting today."

Tamsy yowled and braced to leap at Dragon again. Cordelia pulled herself together and sent a sharp command to desist. She had no doubt Dragon would kill Tamsy with one blow.

"Go away," Cordelia snapped, the words tight with anger.

His eyebrows rose. "You were keen to see me once."

"Have you forgotten this?" Cordelia yanked down the top of her dress, tiny buttons popping off to land in the grass. She exposed her scarred neck and shoulder, her blood pounding in her ears.

His silver gaze scoured her bare flesh. For long seconds his chest heaved. He flexed his wings, clenched and released his fists. The metallic tang of his blood drifted on the air, mixed with his intensely masculine smell. A confusing haze filled her head, fogging her memory, eroding her resistance.

Once, long ago, she'd been enthralled with his size and power, the bulge of his muscles, his glistening ebony skin, his strong handsome features. He'd been gentle with her until the day he lost control. The flutter of softness in the memory terrified her.

She summoned Michael's face in her mind: the sparkle in his blue eyes, the wicked tilt of his grin. But the things about him that touched her heart were the tenderness on his face when he watched his nephews, his generosity when he made love to her. Michael would *never* hurt her.

Dragon stepped toward her carefully, his gaze fixed on her throat. "I didn't mean to damage you. I wanted you." The tips of his fangs slid into view against the darkness of his lower lip.

Deep inside her head, a warning voice shrieked. Dragon had bitten her in the past. Although she was bonded to Michael through the Magic Knot, he held only one of her stones. Dragon's blood bond still had influence over her.

"Go." The word slipped from her lips and her fingers released the neck of her dress. She wanted to close her eyes. Shut out the vision of this nightmare. But her gaze stayed fixed on the living memory of her shame.

"You still want me, water nymph. I feel you spinning your watery web around me."

She shook her head.

He grinned. "Deny it all you want. Your allure doesn't lie."

She pressed back against the spiky twigs when he stepped closer. Slowly he reached, gripped her arms, pulled her away from the hedge. He lowered his face to her hair and released a long satisfied sigh.

Cordelia's breath came in panicked gasps. Her mind screamed run, but her body was under his control. "You k-killed my f-father," she managed to stutter.

Dragon held her at arm's length and studied her, stroking his fangs with the tip of his tongue. "Any man who interferes with a nightstalker while he feeds must expect to be attacked." He flicked up his eyebrows. "Your father was selfish the way he hid your nature so nobody would know of his own indulgences. He deserved to die."

When he eased her into his embrace, she tried to tense her muscles, to push him away, but she flopped limply into his arms. A scream of frustration and anger was crushed in her throat. The world started to spin. Vaguely, she was aware that he pulled open her dress and eased the sleeves down her arms, exposing her bra.

He stroked her hair back. "You never wore your hair loose for me." He tilted her head aside, ran the wet tip of his tongue over her scars.

She whimpered, fighting the aching compulsion of his hold.

"I've often thought of you over the years," he whispered against her skin. "This time no one had better interfere. I will have you until I'm finished."

Michael. She concentrated on the memory of Michael's hands on her body, his lips against her face, the smell of him. Her link with Tamsy twanged with anger so hot and virulent it jerked Cordelia back to awareness.

She opened her eyes in time to see a pale streak as Tamsy leaped at Dragon before fastening her claws into his back and wings. He spun away from Cordelia, jabbed back with his elbow, ripped Tamsy away, and hurled her like a ball. Her body hit the cottage wall with a sickening thud and dropped limply to the ground.

Cordelia sobbed as the familiar sense of her cat's psychic presence blinked out. She launched herself toward Tamsy, but Dragon caught her around the waist and jerked her back, holding her fast against his front.

Her anger overpowered his influence. She battered her fists against his arms, kicked his legs, reached back to scratch whatever flesh she could get her nails in. "Let. Me. Go." If she acted immediately, she might be able to heal Tamsy.

His grip tightened around her ribs, squeezing the air from her lungs until darkness rimmed her vision. When her energy flagged, he turned her effortlessly, her resistance futile against his strength. His fangs lengthened as they had that terrible day he'd attacked her and killed her father. While his eyes shone a sickening pink, slick scales formed on his skin beneath her scrabbling fingers.

She froze in his grip, suddenly realizing that her defiance excited him.

"I told you that anyone who gets in my way must expect to pay." Jaw tight, and eyes flaring with desire, he yanked her dress down over her hips. The rest of the buttons popped off, and the fabric ripped. She crossed her arms over her bra, shivering, while the subtle hold of his blood bond once again penetrated her mind, holding her trapped.

She was stronger than this. Fighting his mental command, she managed one step toward Tamsy. He grabbed her wrist in a punishing grip. Leaning down, he pressed his nose against her breast and inhaled. "I smell your lover on you."

His eyes narrowed with determination. "Forget him, water nymph. You're mine. I'm taking you with me. I'll return for my son another time."

Michael rounded the final corner on the drive to Merricombe Cottage. The back of his Porsche swung out, sideswiping the earthy bank edging the narrow Cornish lane. Each second Cordelia was alone beat like a gong in his head, his heart drumming in concert. He swallowed repeatedly, mouth dry, throat tight.

He accelerated until the last moment, then stamped on the brakes. The sports car plowed through the dirt, skidding sideways. He jumped out, leaving the car door open, and raced in through the cottage's front door.

"Cordelia!"

Stopping, he held his breath, ears straining for any sound. She was here; he sensed her. So was Dragon. The taint of evil hung over the cottage, bringing unnatural silence.

Pausing at each open door, he scanned the sitting room, dining room, bathroom, and kitchen. His skin crawled while terrible images of Dragon hurting Cordelia raced through his mind.

He returned to the kitchen and looked out the window. His guts clenched and trembled. Dragon had Cordelia at the far side of the back garden, his massive dark form dwarfing her slender naked body. Michael grabbed a vegetable knife from the counter. He halted in the doorway, made himself take stock. From the kitchen, he'd thought Cordelia was naked; he now saw she still wore her underwear. The surge of relief gave him strength.

Cordelia stood motionless in Dragon's embrace, letting him kiss her neck—kiss the scars. Michael's breath ran out of control at the sight, his chest heaving, the air catching in his lungs as though they were full of hooks.

Why wasn't she fighting him?

If he didn't know their history, he'd assume she was willing. Dragon must have her under his thrall. A chill swept through Michael, and he tightened his grip on the handle of the knife.

Instinct told him to charge, drive the blade into the nightstalker, and pull Cordelia to safety. But he'd seen Cordelia's memory of Dragon ripping out her father's throat. The creature would slaughter him if he charged in unprepared; then Cordelia would have no one to protect her.

The most vulnerable part of a nightstalker was his wings, yet if he damaged the creature's wings, he wouldn't be able to fly away. That might make him desperate and more dangerous.

There was only one way Michael would have enough influence over Dragon to send him away without anyone else suffering. The tactic was a huge gamble, one that would stain his spirit with the nightstalker's dark presence forever, and might send Michael on an unplanned excursion to the Underworld.

He placed the blade on the wooden bench where he'd so recently cuddled with Cordelia and straightened his shoulders. He called for help from the earth, drawing energy from the ground until the power hummed through his veins and sparked along his nerves. Then he released the energy around his body in waves of glamour.

"Dragon." Michael imbued the word with compulsion, sliding the sound from his tongue, his voice tantalizing and husky.

The stalker's body tensed. His lips stilled against Cordelia's neck, and then he slowly raised his head. Turning, he released Cordelia so she sagged to the ground. Her panicked gaze found Michael's. He willed her to back away, but she remained kneeling in the grass, trembling, and blinking as though she'd just woken.

Dragon completed his turn and stood facing Michael, his silver gaze sharp. "You dare interrupt me, son of Troy?"

Michael wove his glamour into a mantle of disguise, applying layer upon layer of deception around his body, until his real appearance was masked and replaced by a likeness of Cordelia.

At the same time, Michael did something he'd never tried before. He projected his glamour over Cordelia and cloaked her with his image.

Dragon glanced down at Cordelia and blinked, confusion sweeping over his battered features. He stepped back, his breath hissing out. "What trickery is this?"

Michael had cloaked Cordelia in his glamour so she looked like him. Now he must draw Dragon's attention away from her onto himself.

Michael beckoned. "I've waited a long time for you, Dragon," he whispered seductively, imitating Cordelia's voice and loading the words with compulsion. "I've dreamed of you at night, imagined the prick of your fangs in my neck."

The nightstalker blinked, still confused and wary, but swaying. After licking his swollen lips, he pressed his tongue against his fangs. "I've dreamed of you, water nymph." He stepped toward Michael. As the distance between Dragon and Cordelia widened, the light of awareness in her eyes brightened. She stared at Michael, and he hoped she guessed what he was doing and didn't blow it for them. He just needed Dragon to come a little closer; then he'd have this tiger by the tail.

"Come to me," he whispered, the pitch of his voice huskily seductive.

Bile crawled up Michael's throat at the stink of blood and sweat coming from the stalker. If Dragon kissed him, he was going to puke. He swallowed the bitter taste and kept up a low murmur of encouragement. He walked his fingers playfully up Dragon's arm in the same way women often touched him.

He must move fast, before Dragon realized he didn't smell right. He skimmed his hand down the stalker's scratched and bleeding rib cage, onto his rock-hard abs, reluctant admiration flaring for the creature's magnificent physic. Then with a playful tilt of his head, he slipped his fingers into the front pocket of Dragon's jeans, offering up a silent prayer that he'd chosen the correct pocket.

It was empty.

With less finesse, Michael plunged his hand into Dragon's other front pocket while lines of suspicion creased the stalker's forehead. Michael ignored the shockingly large hard ridge he felt; he had enough problems without developing an inferiority complex. His fingers closed around the three linked stones of Dragon's Magic Knot. When he pulled, they came most of the way out of the pocket, then snagged.

A growl rumbled in Dragon's chest. Michael must have allowed his disguise to slip. He poured glamour around him, but the damage was done. Dragon yanked back, swinging a fist at Michael's face. Michael ducked and hung on to Dragon's Magic Knot as shocks of violent anger pulsed up his arm. He gritted his teeth, determined not to let go of the stones and lose his chance to control Dragon. Murky, tainted desires crawled along his new connection with the stalker.

Huge hands fastened around his neck, squeezed, the pressure incessant, unbreakable. Pain burned his throat, burst in his head, yet he tightened his grip on Dragon's stones. With his free hand, he clawed at the viselike fingers as he fought for breath. This monster would never hurt Cordelia again.

Chapter Twenty-one

"Michael!"

Cordelia watched Dragon roar in anger and fix his massive dark hands around Michael's neck. She struggled to stand, and fell back to her knees in the grass, her head fuzzy and spinning.

This couldn't be happening again. Dragon had killed her father. Now he was attacking Michael.

Michael can't die. She hung on to the thought, repeated the words in her mind. The worst that would happen was he'd have to return from the Underworld again.

After shaking her head to dislodge the last of Dragon's mind-numbing control, she hastily pulled up her dress, and poked her arms in the sleeves. Then she concentrated, and pushed to her feet, her legs still unstable, but steadier than before. Ten yards away, near the cottage, Michael was still on his knees, his face growing red, while he tugged ineffectually at Dragon's throttling fingers.

She ran toward the tussle, her legs getting stronger with each step. She kicked Dragon, aiming for his knees and ankles, balled her fists, and thumped his back and sides, pinched his arms, yanked on his wings. Yet he didn't even spare her a glance, his murderous gaze fixed on Michael.

Heart tripping with fear and exertion, Cordelia stared wildly around the garden, looking for something with which to hit Dragon, and noticed a small black-handled knife on the bench seat under the kitchen window.

She ran around the men and grabbed the weapon, before swinging back in range of the fight. Pausing, she adjusted her grip on the knife handle, then stabbed down into the nightstalker's biceps with all her strength. On a roar of outrage, he snatched a hand from Michael's neck to knock her away. His fist caught her shoulder, spinning her around so she fell sideways, her elbow and hip taking the impact. Still gripping the bloody knife, she gritted her teeth, and climbed to her feet. If she kept stabbing Dragon's arms, he'd have to release Michael.

Dragon's gaze jumped to her, before returning to Michael's face. "Come with me, water nymph, or I'll kill him."

She dragged in a breath and focused to steady her voice. "He can't die, you bloody idiot."

Dragon threw back his head and roared in anger. Blood seeped out of the stab wound in his biceps and dripped off his elbow, but it didn't stop him from gripping Michael's throat again. Cordelia circled, gathered her strength, and stabbed down, hitting the biceps of his other arm.

Before she had time to pull out the blade, Dragon leaped back, releasing Michael to topple forward to the ground. He spun to face Cordelia, eyes glazed pink, anger pulsing from him. "Come with me, witch, and I'll spare your lover's suffering. I'll leave the piskies untouched."

Ignoring Dragon, she ran forward and fell to her knees at Michael's side while he clutched his throat, gasping for air.

"Cordelia—" Dragon commanded her attention. He pulled the knife from his arm and tossed it away. Then he held his hands out to her. "Come with me."

She flung her arms around Michael, protectively. "After you killed my father, and after what you've just done to Michael? Are you mad?"

Then she remembered Tamsy. Her anger was transformed to hate, welling up hot and red, filling her head to the bursting point.

"You killed my cat," she spat.

"The bloody creature still lives, witch." He turned and stomped over to where Tamsy lay on the slate paving stones surrounding the house. "But I'll finish the job if you don't come with me."

"No!" Was Tamsy still alive? She tested her mental link with her cat. The overwhelming darkness of Dragon's presence and the vibrancy of Michael's blocked her senses.

Dragon raised his foot over Tamsy's body.

"Stop." Michael's voice came out a hoarse whisper, but filled her ears. "Or I'll crush the stones I took from your pocket."

Dragon hesitated, then withdrew his foot. With a look of horrified understanding, he stepped back. He dug in one of his front pockets, pulled out the torn lining. Fear shone sharp and bright in his silver eyes. "You cannot do this."

Michael had risen partway from the ground. He sat back on his heels, his neck bruised black and purple, blood and dirt streaking his arms. "'Tis already done, nightstalker. I own you."

"We'll see about that." Dragon strode forward, a muscle above his eye twitching.

Holding out a hand, Michael uncurled his fingers to reveal the three red-speckled linked stones of Dragon's Magic Knot lying on his palm.

Dragon froze, rooted to the spot, face tight, eyes wide. "Give me my Knot."

Cordelia's hand flew to her mouth on an exclamation of shock. "What have you done?" If Michael had touched Dragon's Magic Knot, he'd bonded himself to the nightstalker for life. He now had influence over Dragon. But at what cost?

Taking his time, Michael accepted her help while he got to his feet. He fingered his neck and grimaced before turning his gaze on Dragon. "I'm privy to the sickness of your spirit, and the perverted thoughts in your mind."

"Do not judge what you don't understand, pup."

A whisper of the darkness Michael sensed in Dragon brushed Cordelia's mind. She shut him out, a shiver of fear trembling through her. How could she ever join with Michael, mind and spirit, if he were forever tainted with Dragon's evil?

Michael gratefully felt Cordelia retreat from him. He did not want her stained with the horror of the nightstalker's essence.

Giving them a wide berth, Cordelia hurried to Tamsy and kneeled by her cat, her bottom lip clamped between her teeth, tears overflowing her lashes. Michael had half a mind to crush Dragon's stones and banish him to an eternity in the oblivion of in-between. But although reason said the world would be a better place with one less cruel predator, he could not condemn even Dragon to suffer that infinite emptiness forever.

Dragon's silver eyes bored into him, tension thrumming between them. They both stood silently in the garden, the sea rushing up and down below, the breeze gently ruffling their hair, yet a battle raged. The nightstalker psychically charged at him, testing Michael's strength.

The force of Dragon's attack was like being hit with a peashooter.

In a moment of revelation, Michael's world tipped onto a new axis. He finally understood what he was. The legacy he'd inherited from his father was not immortality or silver tongue or poking his hands through solids. The Phoenix Charm was simply a limitless psychic potential from which all other gifts and powers sprang. He would not die, because he was primarily a creature of mind and spirit. The physical world would bend to his will.

Michael did not crush Dragon's mind, although he could bring him to his knees with a thought. The magnitude of Michael's power brought with it unexpected pity. This depraved creature's egotistical belief that he could take whatever he wanted had brought him nothing but misery. With the barest effort, Michael defeated Dragon's mental assault. Snorting in frustration, Dragon again plunged aggressively along their newly formed mental link, trying to assert control. Michael smiled, pinned him down like a bug, and watched him struggle.

The nightstalker released a fraught breath and fear swarmed onto his face, vibrating along their connection. "Please give me my stones, Michael."

At Dragon's pleading tone, Cordelia glanced up from her ministrations, her hands spread on Tamsy's chest and stomach, the healing energy a tickle of silky ribbons across Michael's senses.

"Don't be frightened that I'll crush your Magic Knot and send you into oblivion," Michael said softly. "I don't plan on harming you. I just want you gone from here."

"With enough distance, you'll have no control over me," Dragon snapped back.

Michael flicked up his eyebrows. "Then go away. Leave Cordelia in peace, and forget about Rhys. Let Nightshade be a father to him. I have no wish to be subjected to your presence."

The nightstalker's lip curled. "Rhys is my son."

"Remember, I can see what you have planned for him." The brief glimpse of Dragon's thoughts concerning Rhys convinced Michael the child must never fall into the nightstalker's hands.

Dragon cast a longing glance over his shoulder at Cordelia, and swiped the back of his hand across his mouth. The red scales covering his skin faded, the pink tinge to his eyes disappeared. He seemed to shrink before Michael's eyes.

He looked back at Michael once more. "Give me my stones."

"I'll give them to Nightshade. He'll decide what to do with them."

His belligerent attitude returning, Dragon's nostrils

flared. "I'll not be controlled by you or any other. I'll find a way to rid myself of your hold; then I'll return for Rhys."

Michael gave a lazy grin, which was an effort because his neck had started to hurt like the Furies. "The luck of the leprechauns to you, boyo."

Sweeping down his wings, Dragon ascended slowly. Michael watched until the stalker was a tiny dot against the sky before going to kneel at Cordelia's side.

With her eyes closed, she held her hands over Tamsy's head. The cat's tail flicked, and her back legs peddled. An aura of energy enveloped them both, filling the air with sparkling points of light, tickling and teasing Michael's senses. After a deep breath, Cordelia opened her eyes.

"Is she fully healed?" he asked.

"Yes, thank the gods."

The cat's presence purred in his mind. Tamsy's gaze slid to Michael and held, a flash of almost human perception in her gray eyes. Then she looked at Cordelia and mewed.

"Oh, sweetheart, come to Mommy."

Cordelia gathered the cat into her arms and stood. Michael rose with her and embraced them both. Tears slid down her cheeks when Tamsy started purring. He led her to the bench, sat, and snuggled her beneath his arm.

Even as he held her, the darkness of Dragon's spirit drifted around the periphery of his mind, clearer to him than the sense of Cordelia. The fact that he was more intimately bonded to an evil predator than he was to the woman he loved made him bridle at the injustice.

"You can sense me, love, can't you?" he asked.

She raised her head and leaned forward to rub her lips over his. "Of course."

He closed his eyes and let the sun warm his face while he held her, wishing they could always be together like this. But finally, the truth he'd been avoiding sneaked into his mind. He was immortal. She was not.

* * *

Michael drove sedately back to Trevelion Manor with Cordelia in the passenger's seat hugging Tamsy. He'd called to tell Thorn to bring the babies home from Truro. Before they arrived, he wanted to check on Nightshade and send the three Teg away.

When he pulled up in front of the coach house, two pisky men came out to meet them and directed him to the room where they'd taken Nightshade. He made his way up to the bedroom and stopped in the doorway. Nightshade's eyes were so swollen, Michael was surprised he could see.

"Rhys?" the stalker choked out.

"Safe and well," Michael answered.

On a long sigh, Nightshade's body relaxed deeper into the bed.

"I nearly had that bastard of a father," he spluttered through puffy lips.

Michael sank wearily into the empty chair at the bedside. "Defiant as always." He rested an affectionate hand on Nightshade's arm.

Nightshade's breath hissed through his swollen, bent nose, his perfect profile no longer so perfect. "Is the wise woman all right?"

"She's with Thorn and the babies downstairs. Your father's gone."

Luckily, Nightshade didn't ask how Michael had persuaded Dragon to leave. Just now Michael didn't feel up to explaining the power he had over the nightstalker. He felt in his pocket for Dragon's Magic Knot, which he'd wrapped in kitchen paper and put in a plastic bag so he didn't have to handle the stones again. He withdrew the package and held it out to Nightshade, concealed in his fist. "I've something for you, boyo, a parting gift. Our blood bond can't continue now I have Cordelia."

Nightshade looked away, his injured fingers gripping the

sheet. Then he turned back and raised his hand. Michael dropped the package onto Nightshade's palm. The stalker frowned at the ball of scrunched paper wrapped in plastic.

"Your father's Magic Knot."

"His what?" Nightshade's slitted eyes opened as wide as the swelling would allow.

"'Twas the only way for me to master him."

With a glance at Michael as if he had spoken gibberish, Nightshade asked, "How on earth did *you* overpower him?"

Would this be the way of things from now on? With the exception of Troy, none of his family or friends would understand his nature. He still didn't fully understand it himself. "Before your father left, he threatened to return for Rhys sometime. You might need to use Dragon's stones as leverage to keep Rhys safe."

Nightshade's gaze dropped to the package and he blinked.

Michael stood and stretched carefully, his neck aching. "Cordelia will come heal you soon."

Nightshade continued to stare at his hand. With soft footsteps, Michael left and walked along the hall to the nursery. According to the piskies, the gatekeepers had banged on the door and windows for a while, then fallen quiet. He dreaded to think what sort of mess they had made of the room.

Strange to remember that a few hours ago he'd run from them. He paused outside the nursery door, drew energy up from the granite bedrock below the house until his body hummed. Before his death, he had accepted the trickle of power the earth gave him, but now he was master of his element, able to draw from an infinite well of energy when he desired. He let the power settle around him, remembered the insignificant spark that dwelt at Dragon's core, and opened the door.

Olwyn was asleep in a chair, while Dai and Arian sat near the shattered ruins of Fin and Kea's cot, stony-faced. The men jumped up and prowled toward him. Michael stood silently in the doorway, waiting for the moment they sensed his nature. For the first time, he understood why Troy was so often quiet and still. As his power drifted outward, Michael released a little of the darkness he'd found in Dragon's soul.

After three steps, Dai halted with a look of shock on his face, then retreated again. Arian came closer before he stopped. His mouth opened, yet no sound came out. He stared at Michael, his gaze flicking over him as though he didn't recognize him.

"What's happened? What is he?" Dai whispered.

Arian shook his head slowly, his eyes never leaving Michael.

Visualizing the broken cot whole, Michael sent the intention on a tendril of energy. Wood, plastic, and metal rose and fused themselves back together in a flurry of movement and sound. Dai backed up to Olwyn and shook her awake. The two of them dissolved into sparkling mist and coalesced into orbs, before shooting away over Michael's shoulder.

"Where's Dragon?" Arian asked.

"Gone."

"Not dead?"

Michael shook his head. "That decision's not mine to make."

"Is Troy here?"

"No."

Arian clenched and released his hands, rattling his metal fingers, his gaze speculative. Then he took a reluctant step back. "It's you I sense?"

"Aye."

"Stay out of Wales, deathless one." With those words, Arian dissolved, formed a light orb, and shot out the door.

The gatekeepers' retreat, strangely, gave Michael little satisfaction. He glanced around the trashed nursery and grimaced at the mess. He could have commanded the room to return to order in the same way he'd repaired the cot. Instead, he stood the changing table upright by hand, before kneeling to gather the toiletries strewn across the floor. He opened a window to let in fresh air, then returned to Nightshade's room.

Cordelia sat by the bed, her hands over the stalker's heart while he lay silent and still, eyes closed, face peaceful.

Michael wandered to the window, waiting for her to finish.

On a rocky outcrop protruding from the cliff to the south of the manor garden, a lone figure stood silhouetted against the streaks of orange and gold painting the horizon. Rainbow hues flashed from a jewel in his hair.

Troy, just the person with whom he wanted to speak.

The touch of Cordelia's fingers on his shoulder broke Michael's trance. "Nightshade will sleep now," she said softly. "When he wakes, he'll be much better."

"Thank you." He pulled her into his arms and kissed her hair. "I know you wanted to start by healing females, but—"

She put a finger on his lips. "I owe Nightshade all the care I can give him. I've not been fair to him in the past. Anyway, I think Eloise was right when she said he's the master of his instincts."

Running gentle fingers over his abused neck, she said, "Your turn for healing now, love."

Michael caught her hand, eased it away from his throat, and kissed her palm to distract her. "Later."

She turned her face up to him and he found her lips, the kiss gentle at first, becoming more demanding as passion flared.

His hand cradling her head, he eased away before he forgot what he needed to do. "How's Tamsy?" he asked.

"Settled in a favorite spot in the flowerbed outside my sitting room, catching the last rays of sun." She glanced down at Nightshade. "You gave him his father's Magic Knot?"

"Aye."

"But you touched it. You're bonded to Dragon."

Michael pulled her head against his chest and stroked her hair. He did not want to discuss Dragon's stain on his spirit.

"How does that affect *us*, Michael?"

"Not at all." He kissed her temple and released her before she asked more questions about their relationship. "There's something I need to do; then we can head back to Merricombe Cottage if you like."

"I want to stay here for the moment so I can keep an eye on Nightshade and make sure the piskies are all right. I don't want to leave Trevelion Manor anymore. I always thought my allure would run out of control without my wards, but whenever I touch you, my energy falls into equilibrium."

"Good." He smiled briefly, his mind moving on to the questions he had for his father. "I'll be back soon."

From the window in Nightshade's bedroom, Cordelia watched Michael stride across the lawn. He climbed over the wall to follow the precarious cliff-top path to the point where Troy stood. Although he hadn't said where he was going, she'd sensed his intention.

Since he'd touched Dragon's Magic Knot, he'd become distant and preoccupied. He claimed his bond with Dragon wouldn't affect his relationship with her. She didn't believe him. It already had.

Michael paused when he reached the narrow bridge of rock that led to the precarious outcrop where his father stood gazing at the sea. The gleaming burnt orange of Troy's silk jacket blended with the sunset as though he'd chosen it for that very purpose. The color match seemed too perfect to be coincidence. Michael glanced out of the corner of his eye to detect any deception. But there were no layers of glamour to peel away. With Troy, what you saw was what you got.

In Troy's hair, the Phoenix Stone flashed in the last rays of sun.

"You have your dagger back, I see," Michael said. "Arian told me you'd trapped the King of the Underworld again."

"Gwyn ap Nudd is unstable," Troy said. "Allowing him to remain at liberty sets a bad precedent. Devin and Mawgan manage the Ennead satisfactorily."

Michael joined his father on the rocky point, his toes hanging over the ledge. Below, waves crashed in and broke across the jagged rocks.

"I touched Dragon's Magic Knot."

"I know. I sense his darkness in you."

A gull wheeled in the air a few yards in front of their faces, riding the wind currents that bounced off the water and buffeted the cliff.

Michael pushed his hands in his pockets. "I was angry with you for choosing Finian and leaving me in the Underworld."

"And now you're not?"

Sucking in a breath, Michael released it on a sigh. He'd been childish. He'd gone to his death to rescue Finian, yet he'd still refused to accept what he was. "No. I didn't need you. Finian did."

Troy gave a single satisfied nod.

"You understand what you are?"

"Aye."

Troy stood unmoving as though he were part of the scenery. The uneven granite jabbed the soles of Michael's sneakers, making his feet ache. He shifted and wriggled his toes.

"Both Finian and Kea have inherited the Phoenix Charm," Troy said.

Michael forgot his feet and squinted at his father's profile.

Troy turned slowly and met his gaze. "If Finian were mortal, I'd have been more concerned about him being trapped in the Underworld."

Although Michael should be angry that Troy had kept him in the dark, all he felt was weary resignation. "You could have told me." Not that he'd have worried any less about the little lad.

Troy shrugged. "Finian still needed rescuing, and Devin couldn't do so, otherwise he'd have compromised his position on the Ennead."

"Did you set me up?" Michael asked.

"Do you really think me that cold-blooded?" Troy asked with a flash of disbelief in his eyes. "I would never wish my grandson to be trapped in Gwyn's domain. Yet once the situation occurred, it provided the ideal opportunity for you to embrace death for the first time and realize your power."

Definitely cold-blooded. But Michael would keep that opinion of Troy to himself.

"Why did the Phoenix Charm skip Niall?" Michael asked.

Troy shrugged. "Not all my lineage exhibit the trait. Some are long dead."

Michael gazed at a fishing boat chugging back to one of the tiny villages dotted along the coast and wished his life could be simple again. He'd secretly wanted to be more than a storyteller, to have a power others respected. *Be careful what you wish for . . .* "I don't know how to explain what I am to Cordelia. The concept is esoteric, not easily put into words."

"You don't need to explain. She'll sense your nature through your bond. She probably already has," Troy replied.

"But we're not fully bonded. Her cat holds her mind and spirit."

Troy frowned at him. "Haven't either of you asked the cat to return her stones?"

It's that simple?

"You sure the cat will understand?" Michael asked.

"Cats understand everything they choose to understand."

"Right. Of course they do." Michael dropped his gaze to

the churning water. He should be able to bond fully with Cordelia, share everything with her. The beauty of her mind and spirit would consign the dark memory of Dragon to the recesses of Michael's brain. Yet he could not rejoice.

The question he needed to ask circled in his head, hung on the tip of his tongue.

"Cordelia will probably die and leave you alone, Michael," Troy said softly.

Michael dropped to his haunches as though felled by a blow. He steadied himself with a bruised hand against the sharp rocks, welcoming the pain while he stared unseeing at the ground. Troy's words had struck him down before he'd even had a chance to ask the question.

Troy crouched beside him and gripped Michael's shoulder.

Thin wires of pain tightened around Michael's heart, until it hurt so much, everything in his chest went numb.

"How-how did you know what I wanted to ask?" Michael whispered.

"Because that's the question I asked when I was first in love."

Troy was so emotionally insular; Michael couldn't imagine him in love.

Below, waves crashed and splintered in a hail of droplets. Michael imagined falling, smashing his life away on the rocks, only to recover, whether he wanted to or not.

"Potentially, she can live forever if she's fully bonded to you," Troy said. "But she's mortal. She can still be mortally wounded or become sick."

"I'll look after her." He would make sure nothing bad happened to her. Watch her every minute. Protect her.

"Don't smother her." Troy patted his back, then rose and stared at the streaks of liquid gold marking the horizon. "My rule, 'no explanations, no excuses' does not apply to the one you love. Share everything with her." *While you can* hung unspoken in the air at the end of the sentence.

Images of the people who mattered to Michael flicked through his head. He wasn't bonded to all of them. Niall, Rose, and Nightshade would grow old and die. He might even outlive his own children.

"What happens to all the other people you love?"

"Don't love too many people, son. Walk away before that happens." Troy looked down at Michael, the falling sun gleaming on his skin, sparkling off his crystal buttons. He pulled the Phoenix Dagger from his hair, letting the golden strands tumble to catch the wind and flutter around his shoulders. He held out the hilt. "When the time comes, you'll pass this on to Finian and Kea."

"What do I tell Niall?"

Troy touched his forehead in a gesture of respect. "Whatever you deem right, my son." Then he melted into the air and disappeared, leaving Michael staring into space.

Chapter Twenty-two

Nightshade sat across from Eloise while she breast-fed Rhys before bed, fascinated, yet trying not to stare. The nursery had been set straight. Now the only evidence there'd been any disruption was the sweet smell of talc in the air.

He turned away as Eloise closed her blouse, before lifting Rhys to her shoulder.

"Nightshade, would you like to burp him?" Her softly spoken inquiry startled him.

He glanced at Michael, expecting a comment about baby vomit down his back. Oblivious to what was going on in the room, Michael stood staring out the window. Protecting Cordelia from Dragon had changed Michael. Nightshade felt guilty for attracting his father to Cornwall and putting the wise woman at risk. He'd have to find a way to make it up to his friends.

With a smile, he nodded at Eloise. "I'd like that."

When he started to rise, she waved him down. "Stay there. I'll come to you." She laid a small towel over his shoulder before passing the sleepy boy into his arms. "Let him rest his head on your shoulder. He'll be asleep in a few minutes."

Nightshade held his brother's diaper-padded bottom while he rubbed the child's back, his fingers drawn to the two bumps that would develop into wings at puberty.

A hand resting lightly on Nightshade's arm, Eloise bent closer. Her gaze flicked up to his face as her lips pressed against her son's head. She was so close that he smelled her skin and the tang of her blood. "We're comfortable with you," she said softly. "I can never thank you enough."

She was pretty in a pale, skinny way, which, unfortunately, held no appeal for him. Since they'd arrived in Cornwall, she'd been giving him signals, looks, casual touches. If he wanted her, she'd be willing. Yet humans had never attracted him. He desired strength, power, and attitude.

Clearing his throat, Nightshade looked down and adjusted his hold on Rhys so Eloise could withdraw gracefully. "I should be thanking you," he said. "Rhys is my blood relative, yet I didn't even know he existed."

With a sigh, Eloise stepped back. "Now you can be brother and father to him."

Father.

For his little brother, he would strive to behave like the sort of father he'd longed for when he was a child. His hand rubbed circles on Rhys's back while the child's breathing fell into the regular rhythm of sleep.

Nightshade replayed every dive and blow of his aerial battle with Dragon. He'd thought there was a certain masculine camaraderie between them, even while they pounded each other, a mutual admiration of each other's skill and fitness. Right up to the moment when Dragon grabbed Nightshade's wing, nearly tearing the appendage from his body, kicked him in the head, and smashed him against the wall. Then left him for dead.

What father would do that to his son? What father would scratch a helpless child and scar him for life? The blue band patterned with yellow ducks around the top of Rhys's diaper hid those scars, but somewhere in the boy's memory the pain would be remembered and mark him for life. He silently promised Rhys that Dragon would never harm him again.

His father's Magic Knot formed a bump in his pocket. Nightshade was tired and sore and wanted only to spend time with Rhys. But before he could feel certain his baby brother was safe, he must find Dragon and secure his blood vow to give up all rights to Rhys.

Cordelia opened her eyes to a shadowy view of her familiar bedroom at Trevelion Manor. Even before she turned to see if Michael had joined her in bed, she knew he wasn't there.

She pushed up on her elbow and looked around, opened her senses to locate him. His familiar psychic presence was absent. Unease trickled through her.

Ever since he'd touched Dragon's Magic Knot, he'd been distant. She'd hoped his chat with Troy would help. If anything, he'd retreated deeper into himself after his meeting with his father. She sat up and dropped her feet to the floor, rubbing her eyes.

Experiencing the darkness in the mind and spirit of the nightstalker must have been traumatic. Why wouldn't he talk to her? Her healing energies might help him if only he'd share what was troubling him.

After donning a dressing gown and slippers, she left her rooms. If he were anywhere in the house, she'd find him and make him talk to her.

Silently, she made her way up the stairs to the nursery, sure he must be with his nephews. When she peered through the door, the chairs were all empty. Only the gentle sound of three babies breathing filled the room.

Michael. She called him in her mind, hoping he might hear if he were awake. But because he only held her body stone, he'd never been able to sense her as she did him.

She checked the room he sometimes slept in when he stayed at the manor, her shoulders dropping with relief at the sight of his empty bed. If he'd chosen to sleep alone, she'd have been hurt.

When she'd searched the kitchen, Niall's office and the library without success, she gave up and wandered back to her apartment, a hollowness inside her full of unshed tears. After all they'd been through, they should be celebrating.

She went to her tiny sitting room to find Tamsy. Earlier, she'd shut the cat out of the bedroom expecting Michael to join her, but now she needed her familiar's company.

Pale light filtered in through the French windows, turning the darkness gray and drawing faint shadows. There, on the saggy, hairy chair Tamsy used as a bed, Michael sat, his head resting against the wing, eyes closed.

A preternatural glow radiated from his skin.

A fine tremor ran through her at the sight. Although she'd seen him stabbed and called him back from the Underworld, she hadn't truly appreciated how different he was from her until that moment.

He'd died and come back to life. He would probably do so again, many times. Would he end up distant and ethereal like Troy? She felt as though Michael was drifting away from her already.

In the low light, she made out a gray furry shape curled on Michael's lap. *Great.* Michael eschewed her bed in favor of her cat's company.

She should leave him to sleep. They could talk in the morning. That was the right thing to do. But she needed to touch him.

Cordelia kneeled beside the chair and stroked Tamsy. The cat lifted her head with a faint mew, blinked sleepily, then laid her chin back on Michael's leg.

She brushed her fingertips lightly over the back of Michael's hand, remembering the first day she'd sensed him two years ago. His psychic presence was so strong and dominating, he'd overpowered everyone in Trevelion Manor, even Niall. Although she had not admitted the truth to herself, she had fallen in love with him from that first look. Back then, he hadn't even noticed her. Yet now he was hers, and she wasn't going to lose him.

His fingers twitched and she smiled, traced a path up his arm, over the bulge of his biceps to the discolored bruising on his neck. Already the angry purple had faded to yellow.

By tomorrow evening, the marks would probably have gone. Every time she touched him, she gave him healing energy. But his body had healed itself.

She trailed her fingertips along his jaw, touched the silky waves of his hair, her heart aching with trepidation. She wanted to know what was troubling him. At the same time, she feared something had happened that might take him from her.

She memorized every curve and angle of his features. Her chest ached at his beauty. With a little sigh, she pressed her lips to his, kissing firmly to wake him in the best way she knew how.

His lips parted, and he drew in a breath. She retreated enough to give him some air and curved a palm around his cheek.

His eyes opened, and he blinked. "Cordelia." He looked toward the window. "What's the time?"

"Early hours."

When he made no move to continue the kiss, she dropped back to her knees and gripped his hand. "I wondered what had happened to you when you didn't join me in bed."

"Ahh," he rubbed the back of his neck. "Sorry about that."

Funny how whenever he was serious, she wished he'd call her sugarplum. "Don't be sorry, Michael. Just tell me what's wrong. You're shutting me out."

"You're right. There are things you need to understand." He stroked Tamsy and sighed. "I was hoping if I got your mind and spirit stones from Tamsy, you'd see me thoughts and feelings, and I wouldn't need to put stuff into words."

She reared back, a jab of surprise mixed with confusion. "You can't do that. My father said if I ever tried to take my stones from Tamsy, I'd kill her." She remembered the stern lecture she'd received on her responsibilities to her bonded familiar.

"Troy said all we have to do is ask Tamsy for them."

Cordelia shook her head slowly. "Why would Father tell me Tamsy would die if . . . ?" Her words trailed away when the truth hit her. Her father would have done or said anything to stop her from revealing her true nature.

"He lied to you, sugarplum. As long as you're careful, you're fine without your wards, aren't you?" She nodded, biting her lip. "Your father wasn't protecting you; he was protecting his own reputation. Your real nature is proof that the high-minded king's advisor dallied with a water nymph."

After lifting Tamsy to the floor, he helped Cordelia onto his lap. She pulled up her knees and curled against him. The feel of his arms around her banished the uneasiness from her mind. He tilted her chin up with a finger and smoothed his lips over hers. The heat built quickly between them until all she could think about was the demand of his mouth and the stroke of his tongue.

She didn't know for how long they kissed, but when early morning sun filtered in through the French window, Michael eased away and rested his forehead against hers. "Shall we try asking Tamsy for your stones?"

Cordelia turned to find Tamsy sitting beside the fireplace watching them.

"I thought she might wear them on a collar, but I couldn't find them." Michael glanced at Cordelia questioningly.

"They're inside her," she explained, her voice hardly more than a whisper. Although she wanted to pass the care of her mind and spirit into Michael's safekeeping, the thought of losing her connection with Tamsy after so many years clogged her throat with tears.

"I'm thinking she knows what we're saying," Michael whispered.

"Of course she does."

"Then I guess we ask her for them and see what happens." He lifted Cordelia off his lap before hunkering down beside Tamsy. "You've had a good long time bonded to Cordelia, and she's mighty fond of you, but 'tis time for her to bond with her mate. Would you let me have Cordelia's mind and spirit stones, please, Tamsy?"

Tamsy stood and stretched, then turned and licked the fur on her shoulder. Twitching her tail, she looked up at Cordelia, her pale eyes shining, the sweetness of her nature clear to see. Then she lowered her head and gagged.

Cordelia went to Michael's side and gripped his hand.

"She's not going to . . . heave them up, is she?" he asked, his nose wrinkled.

"I don't—" Tamsy retched again as though she had a fur ball stuck in her throat. "Goodness, I think she is."

The cat retched twice more before vomiting on the slate slab in front of the hearth.

"I'm not often speechless, but . . ." Michael blinked, horrified disbelief on his face.

Cordelia hurried to the kitchen and fetched a roll of paper towel, hoping Michael would accept her stones after what he'd just seen. This certainly wasn't the romantic moment she had hoped for.

After unfastening the French window, she collected Tamsy's "gift" in the kitchen paper, and set it down on the edge of the patio outside. Michael stood behind her and watched. His breath caught on an exclamation as she held up two small linked stones the color of quartz.

Joy and sadness mingled inside Cordelia, bringing tears to her eyes. She'd been twelve when her grandmother had asked one night to see her Magic Knot. The following morning she'd returned the single body stone to her. Although Cordelia had always loved Tamsy, seeing her mind and spirit stones again reminded her of her grandmother's deceit.

She glanced up at Michael's frown. "Don't worry. I'll sterilize them." His expression remained doubtful. When she gave them to him, she would have to make the occasion romantic so he'd forget where they'd come from. Even as she stared at him, a plan formed in her mind.

* * *

"It's time," Cordelia said.

"Where are we going?" Michael asked. All day, she'd been mysterious about her plans for their evening.

"Wait another few minutes and you'll find out." She lit two oil lamps and passed him one, then took his hand and led him out of her sitting room.

Trevelion Manor sat silently behind them in the twilight. She led him down the garden to the top of a narrow cliff path that gave access to the private beach. As they descended, the lamplight threw bright splashes against the rock face, deepening the shadows below.

The heat of the day had baked the rocks and, even now, they still radiated warmth.

She paused when they reached the beach and inhaled deeply. "Don't you just love the smell of the sea?"

He released her hand and wrapped his arm around her waist, pulling her against his side so he could lean down to sniff her. "I prefer the smell of your skin." He'd missed out on sharing her bed last night, so her plan for the evening had better include getting naked quickly.

She snuggled up to him with a sexy little murmur and scratched her fingernails over his T-shirt-covered abs, just above the waistband of his jeans. His breath hitched on a burst of desire. When he leaned down to kiss her, she ducked away and ran toward the sea, laughing.

"Hey, you tease." Holding the lamp out to the side, he trotted after her, feeling lighter and more carefree than he had since they'd arrived home from Wales.

She deposited her lamp on a rock, then ran to the tide line. His feet stumbled to a halt when she pulled her dress off over her head and tossed it on the sand. She stood naked in front of him, wearing only his Magic Knot around her neck, the water behind her like a millpond reflecting the silvery streak of the moon.

While he stared at her, she unraveled her plait and spread

her hair over her shoulders. Smiling at him, she backed into the sea, her footsteps sending moonlight-tinged ripples across the water's surface. She beckoned him seductively.

"Are you coming to make love with me, Michael, or are you just going to stand there and watch?"

Her words broke his trance. He dumped the lamp on the beach, and ripped his T-shirt over his head. He toed off the heels of his shoes, before kicking them away into the shadows, and made short work of his jeans. He was already aroused, but when her gaze dropped to his groin with a naughty little twitch of her lips, he hardened even more.

"You're a temptress," he said, his voice thick with yearning.

"I aim to please," she whispered through the sultry night air. "Tonight, I'm going to let my water nymph instincts take over."

Michael groaned when he stepped into the water and walked into the shimmering sensual aura of her allure. His belly quivered, the small of his back so tight with need he could hardly put one foot in front of the other. "Sweet Anu. What're you doing to me?"

"The water magnifies my allure." She crooked a beckoning finger and licked her lips. His legs moved faster toward her.

"You're in my power tonight, Michael."

In the back of his mind, he knew he could easily break her hold over him. But why resist every man's fantasy?

As he paced toward her, she backed away, keeping some distance between them. His breath strained in and out with lust while he waded through the deep water.

Finally, she halted when the water reached the bottom of her rib cage, her breasts bobbing temptingly over the ripples. Images flashed through his mind of him and her tangled together, their bodies joined in different positions, in various places. He shook his head, but the thoughts continued sliding through his mind, heating his blood until it burned beneath his skin. He rubbed his face. "I'm seeing—"

"My fantasies," she whispered.

"Cordelia." Her name broke from his lips on a moan. He reached for her and she stepped into his arms, her hands sliding over his wet body as though she were sculpting him. He kissed her hungrily, broke away and sucked salty water droplets from her neck and shoulders. One hand slid underneath her bottom, holding her tight to his aching erection, the other caressed her breast.

Then suddenly she was gone, dropping from his grip beneath the water's surface, leaving barely a ripple. He stared, half crazed with lust, unable to comprehend how she'd slipped from his arms. Before he had a chance to move, fingers glided up his legs, stroked the sensitive skin on his inner thighs, then moved higher.

His eyes rolled back and his eyelids fell as, first her fingers, then the warm suction of her mouth closed over his erection in the cool water. He spread his arms, let the sea take his weight while she stroked and licked him, driving him half mad.

A moment before he came undone, she released him and rose, water streaming from her head and shoulders. Her eyes glowed like moonlight on the sea. When he recovered the ability to think, he realized she had been under the water far longer than one breath would last.

"Cordelia—"

Her wet lips covered his, wiping out his thoughts. The seduction of her allure curled around him and through him like teasing fingers.

She broke the kiss and stroked his face. "Oh, Michael, I love you so much. You're so powerful, yet at heart you're still just a naughty boy." With a tug on his hand, she said, "Come back to the beach now."

He followed her out of the water, keen to see what she had

planned for him next. She led him to a rocky nook at the back of the beach, glowing with warm light. The sheltered spot was the size of two king-size beds, covered with towels and blankets.

He threw himself down, pulling her with him, then rolled over her, trapping her beneath him. "Now I know what you've been up to today."

Grinning, she whispered, "I wanted everything to be perfect."

"Anywhere is perfect, providing I'm with you."

"Sweet-talker."

"Guilty as charged. But this time 'tis true. I love you, Cordelia."

They fell silent, staring into each other's eyes. His chest filled so tight with emotion, his breath caught and his stomach fell away. He stroked the wet hair off her face and ran a fingertip over her lips. "I really need an orgasm after what you did to me in the water."

She batted him on the shoulder. "You're incorrigible."

"I'm burning up with wanting you." He feathered his lips over hers and cupped her breast, stroking the nipple with his fingertip.

When she wriggled to get free, he eased off her, so she could reach to the side and grab something. She held out a silver box engraved with the Celtic symbol for the sea.

He propped himself on an elbow and opened the box with a flutter of apprehension. He knew she was giving him her mind and spirit stones, and he wanted them. But he wasn't sure he'd ever get rid of the mental image of Tamsy regurgitating them.

He lifted the box lid, stared at the contents for a beat and burst out laughing. Inside was a red cat collar with Cordelia's mind and spirit rings attached beside the tiny bell.

"Tamsy wanted you to have them," Cordelia said, trying to keep a smile off her face and failing. "What you saw this morning was a figment of your imagination. They've been on her collar all along."

"If you're wanting me to forget, sugarplum, you're going to have to do a lot better than that." He leaned over and nipped her breast. With a squeak, she dissolved into giggles as he nibbled her.

While he stroked his tongue across her nipple, desire rolled over him again in a hot wave. He dropped the cat collar back in the box and moved to lie on top of her.

"Not yet." She pushed him away. He flopped on his back with a disgruntled huff as she plucked the collar out of the silver box. "When we make love, I want us to be completely bonded."

She quickly released her two rings from the collar, then borrowed Michael's leather thong to thread the other rings on beside her body stone. Then she knelt up, facing him and he joined her.

The humor fell from her face as she held up the leather loop bearing her three translucent stones. "After you put this on, Michael, you'll know all my secrets."

"Only if you invite me to." He stroked his fingertips over the back of her hand soothingly. "I'm not going to barge in on your thoughts and pry."

She blinked rapidly, and her cheeks flushed. "I used to watch you in my divination mirror . . . watch you with other women."

A little burst of shock blossomed inside him, growing hot and arousing, spreading to fill his body. His erection throbbed in time with the beat of blood in his ears while he imagined her watching him, getting all hot and bothered in her prim buttoned-up dress. Maybe he should be annoyed, but sweet bejesus, the thought aroused him so much he could hardly think. His fingers reached for her knee, slid up her thigh. "Gods, love. You're going to sizzle me brain." He ducked his head. "Put that thing over me head, quickly."

Once the leather strip dropped against his nape, he looked up, catching her wide-eyed expression of uncertainty.

"Are you angry?" she asked.

He growled in his chest, the primeval need for his mate stealing his power of speech. Wrapping an arm around her, he threw her down on her back before stretching out on top of her.

"Just horny," he whispered and sealed his mouth over hers.

Her arms and legs enfolded him, pulling him close. As he slid into her welcoming heat, the crystalline wave of her spirit showered over him, banishing the last traces of Dragon's darkness. Her allure danced through him, sparking every nerve, while her spirit softened the effect, smoothing the surges of almost unbearable pleasure. He rode the swell of bliss for as long as he could before crashing with her over the edge of ecstasy.

"Michael," she whispered against his ear.

He had no idea how long he lay insensate on her before he roused at the sound of her voice. Her presence surrounded him, bringing his world into focus. The earth breathed beneath him. Tiny sparks of life penetrated his consciousness all around, from the tiniest worm in the sand to the piskies in the manor up on the cliffs. Through the lens of her spirit, he sensed the mighty power of the sea feeding the earth and drawing energy in return.

Taking his weight on his elbows, he raised his head and stared into her eyes. Then he noticed her shoulder and throat. Her previously scarred skin was smooth and unblemished. "Did you heal yourself?"

"No." Her fingers skimmed her neck, and she gasped with surprise.

"I must have healed you." With a flash of soul-deep relief, he knew he wouldn't lose her, no matter what Troy had said.

He had the ability to repair anything wrought of the earth, including her body.

Her fingers stroked his hair. "I thought you'd swamp me with your power, Michael, but I feel as though . . . as though you're focusing your energy through me."

Seeing himself through her eyes, his path suddenly became clear. Although in the last few days, he'd changed forever, his life did not have to alter. He could live the life he'd always enjoyed, while using his power to help those he loved.

His father might cope by walking away from those he started to care about, but that would never be Michael's way. The people he loved *were* his life.

The jaunty beat of Irish music lifted Cordelia's heart as she peered through the excited crowd of piskies. In the far corner of the great hall, Michael slid from his storytelling stool, accepting the applause for his tall tale.

Michael's presence simmered tantalizingly in her mind, his thoughts never more than a whisker away from sex. She eased between members of the crowd, who stepped aside respectfully when they saw her. A wicked grin spread across Michael's lips and sparkled in his blue eyes as he came to meet her. He wove between the tables and chairs, holding out his hands when she drew near.

She blushed beneath the curious stares. The piskies must be wondering at her sudden wardrobe change. She'd searched everywhere to find a dress exactly like the one Michael had imagined in his fantasy of them dancing. The silky blue fabric slid around her legs like water, and the spaghetti straps revealed her smoothly healed neck and shoulders. When Michael's appreciative gaze skimmed down her body and back to her face, she didn't care what anyone else thought.

With one hand behind her back, hiding her gift for him, she took his outstretched hand, and he pulled her close for a kiss. She twisted aside when he tried to peek over her shoulder.

"You keeping secrets from me, sugarplum?"

"Would I dare?" She threw up her arm and flourished the green trilby. "Ta da!"

"Me St. Paddy's Day hat." He gripped the brim and, with a grin, set the hat at a rakish angle on his dark wavy hair. "Where did you find it?"

"This is a new one. Thorn helped me buy it on eBay."

"You're too good to me, love, so you are." As the music changed to a haunting ballad, Michael wrapped his arm around her waist and led her to the small dance floor. She hooked her arms over his neck and stared up at the mischievous look sparkling in his blue eyes.

"Bet you never thought the fantasy we shared in Wales would come true, did you?" he whispered in her ear.

"No." But she was thinking about far more than the dance.

Loving Michael O'Connor was her ultimate fantasy.

So you like vampires? You're not alone.

Don't miss the part steampunk Victorian historical, part futuristic thriller

Crimson & Steam

by

Liz Maverick

Coming January 2010

. . . He found her on a stretch of Santa Monica Boulevard, just inside an alcove. She stood frozen, silent, her face obscured by shadow. He grabbed her by the shoulders and spun her toward some dull light oozing from a nearby store's half-broken bulb.

"Coward," she spat. "Do I have to make it really easy for you, so you can't refuse? Should I just rip my clothes off and beg?" She pulled the tie holding together her wrap blouse, and the fabric cascaded away. "Do it. Here in this alley, Marius. Please."

"Jillian, don't!" Marius's blood raced. Exposed neck, pale shoulders, pink-tipped breasts—all delicate flesh and the black lace of her transparent bra. He'd never seen Jill this way. He'd only dreamed of it.

"I will. I'll beg," she continued. "I'll do whatever you need to make this okay. I'm not afraid of what we have. Why the hell are you?"

She pulled the hem of her skirt up and leaned back against the brick wall. Marius tried to wrench her skirt down, but she was pulling out all the stops and rudely pressed her palm against his groin. "Don't try to tell me no," she murmured. "I know what you want. I know what I feel."

"Stop, Jillian. Stop!" Marius begged. He forced himself to ignore the pulsing of his erection in her hand and grabbed the ends of her shirt, tying them together as best he could. Without thought, he closed his eyes and pressed his mouth to the crown of her head. "Please," he whispered. "I never meant to hurt you, and—"

"'Hurt me . . . ,'" Jillian echoed.

She reached into her pocket and pulled out a switchblade. Flicking it expertly open she said, "Hayden gave this to me. Hayden, your worst enemy. At the time I thought it was a really shitty birthday present, but it always seems to come in handy." Transfixing Marius with her stare, she held the knife to her neck. "Could you resist me if I made myself bleed for you? I know what it's like when you smell blood. That means my blood will make you insane, if you feel half of what I think you do for me. You won't be able to stop yourself, and it won't be your fault." She swallowed hard. "I'm not afraid."

"Enough!" Marius roared, baring his fangs. The switchblade clattered to the pavement. "Enough." He took her face in his hands. "This isn't you. This is not who you are."

Jillian slowly pulled free and backed up, collecting her weapon.

"Do you think this helps?" Marius continued, unable to contain himself any longer. "Do you think I feel no pain? I watch you run around with Hayden Wilks, and you think it doesn't kill me? He gets to have you in every way that I cannot. It makes no difference that I understand why you're with him, that I know you don't love him. It doesn't matter, because . . . yes." His hands dug into Jill's shoulders as he struggled to stay in control. "I can feel you. Do you understand? I can sense you. I know

when he's with you, when he's touching you, when . . ."
He had to look away. "Knowing I could make you feel so
much more, that my feelings for you go so much deeper,
that you've given yourself to someone who doesn't deserve you because I'm not allowed to have the life I want
to live . . . It makes me feel like dying sometimes. You
must understand how much I care about you. But—"

"But not enough," she interrupted. Then, with a hitch
in her voice she added, "Soul mates aren't supposed to
end like this."

Marius dropped his hands. "I'm sorry."

CRIMSON & STEAM
by
LIZ MAVERICK

THE
ℬATTLE
SYLPH

Welcome to his world.

(CHECK OUT A SAMPLE:
www.ljmcdonald.ca/Battle_preview.html.com)

New York Times Bestselling Author

C. L. WILSON

Once he had scorched the world. Once he had driven back
overwhelming darkness. Once he had loved with such passion,
his name was legend…

Lord of the Fading Lands

Now a thousand years later, a new threat calls him from the
Fading Lands, back into the world that had cost him so dearly.
Now an ancient, familiar evil is regaining its strength, and a
new voice beckons him—more compelling, more seductive,
more maddening than any before.

Lady of Light and Shadows

He had stepped from the sky to claim her like an enchanted
prince from the pages of a fairy tale, but behind his violet
eyes she saw an endless sorrow and the driving hunger of
his beast. Only for him would she embrace her frightening
magic and find the courage to confront the shadows that
haunted her soul.

King of Sword and Sky

The magical tairen were dying, and none but the Fey King's
bride could save them. Rain had defied the nobles of Celieria
to claim her, battled demons and Elden mages to wed her.
Now, he would risk everything to help his truemate embrace
her magic and forge the unbreakable bond that could save
her soul.

Queen of Song and Souls

As war rages all around them, and the evil mages of Eld stand
on the brink of triumph, Rain and Ellysetta must learn to
trust in their love and in themselves, and embrace a forbidden
power that will either destroy their world or save it.

To order a book or to request a catalog call: **1-800-481-9191**
or you can check our Web site **www.dorchesterpub.com**.

New York Times Bestselling Authors
Katie MacAlister
Angie Fox
Lisa Cach
Marianne Mancusi

My Zombie Valentine

FOUR WOMEN ARE ABOUT TO DIG UP THE TRUTH

Tired of boyfriends who drain you dry? Sick of guys who stay out all night howling at the moon? You can do better. Some men want you not only for your body, but your brains. Especially your brains.

It's true! There are men out there who care—early-rising, down-to-earth, indefatigable men who'll follow you for miles. They'll take the time to surprise you, over and over. One sniff of that perfume, and you'll have to use a shotgun to fight them off. And then, once you get together, all they want is to share a nice meal. And another. And another.

Romeo and Juliet, eat your hearts out.

ISBN 13: 978-0-8439-6360-1

☐ **YES!**

Sign me up for the Love Spell Book Club and send my
FREE BOOKS! If I choose to stay in the club, I will pay
only $8.50* each month, a savings of $6.48!

NAME: _____

ADDRESS: _____

TELEPHONE: _____

EMAIL: _____

☐ I want to pay by credit card.

☐ **VISA**   ☐ **MasterCard**   ☐ **DISCOVER**

ACCOUNT #: _____

EXPIRATION DATE: _____

SIGNATURE: _____

Mail this page along with $2.00 shipping and handling to:
Love Spell Book Club
PO Box 6640
Wayne, PA 19087
Or fax (must include credit card information) to:
610-995-9274
You can also sign up online at **www.dorchesterpub.com**.
*Plus $2.00 for shipping. Offer open to residents of the U.S. and Canada only.
Canadian residents please call 1-800-481-9191 for pricing information.
If under 18, a parent or guardian must sign. Terms, prices and conditions subject to
change. Subscription subject to acceptance. Dorchester Publishing reserves the right
to reject any order or cancel any subscription.